THE
SUN
AT
TWILIGHT

AN EMPIRE AT TWILIGHT NOVEL

N . L . HOLMES

WayBack Press
P.O.Box 16066
Tampa, FL
⚱

The Sun at Twilight
Copyright © 2021 by N. L. Holmes

Empire at Sunset™ 2020

Cover art and map by Streetlight Graphics. Author photo by Kipp Baker.

Quotes from Royal Hittite Instructions and Related Administrative Texts by Jared Miller, Society of Biblical Literature, 2013, and Hittite Priesthood by Ada Taggar-Cohen, University of Heidelberg Press, 2006.

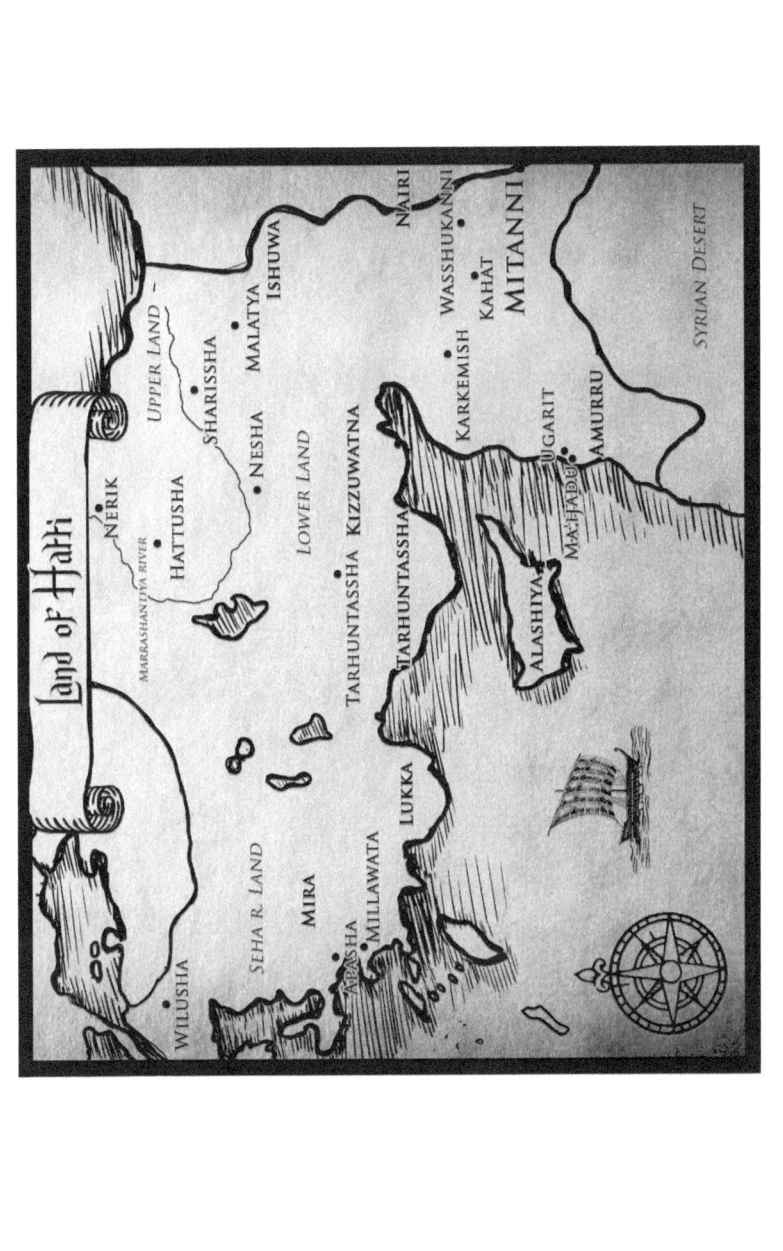

Dedicated to my husband Ippokratis

HISTORICAL NOTES AND GLOSSARY

The Late Bronze Age in Anatolia (modern Turkey) is still relatively mysterious, even after more than a hundred years of Hittite studies. We cannot know how they actually behaved, but one is struck by the humanity of their principles, especially in the brutal context of their neighbors. Torture and the death penalty were exceedingly rare. Women seem to have enjoyed substantial rights.

Of the historical figure of Tudhaliya IV, Great King (emperor) of Hatti, we know nothing of his personality, appearance, or relationships with others, except for the well documented friendship with Kurunta. His piety and his paranoia seem to emerge from his actions as king, but their motivation is up to the novelist to explain. Even the most basic events of his reign are debated—for example, did Kurunta really attack Hattusha in order to declare himself Great King, or was the splitting of the empire peaceable from the start? Was the *tawananna* Puduhepa really deposed at some point? Was Tudhaliya seriously ill? Historians are divided, and so I have made the choices that best serve my story. Likewise, I have adopted I. Singer's theory about the parentage of Kurunta, although many historians believe that Tanuhepa was his step-grandmother.

The first loyalty oath of Tudhaliya's reign—as far as we know—was probably sworn elsewhere and certainly not at his father's funeral, but I have compacted these events. The words given are really extracted from the oath. In short, anything that is considered firmly historical I have respected; whatever is debated or frankly unknown, I have felt free to elaborate—and this includes dates. Since the Hittites did not date their documents—even internally, by regnal year—the chronology of their history is vague. Our story begins some time around 1237 BCE, when Tudhaliya IV is thought (by some) to have acceded to the throne. Other events are not even so firmly dated. For example, the defeat by Assyria in Nairi is believed to have transpired near the beginning of his reign, but the exact year is unknown; thus, I have taken the liberty of placing several such events, whose actual dates are nebulous, within a period of five years. All the characters are real, except for those whose name I have supplied because we do not know it.

The religious rituals of Hatti Land are complex; one wonders how the king had time to do anything else. I have simplified them considerably. There was some kind of oracle read in oil, but I have invented the precise form of scrying with oil in the story. The Hittites took oracles in many ways and for many reasons, and the general form of questioning is accurate.

The office of *tawananna* was a surprisingly powerful female role in government. The wife of the king *(labarna)* held her office as *tawananna* until death, even after her husband had died. Thus, her son's wife might never become *tawananna* as long as her mother-in-law lived. Puduhepa, one of the best documented and strongest women of antiquity, lived for ninety years, serving as the *tawananna* of three generations of kings.

THE CHARACTERS

(Those marked with an * are fictional or the names
are supplied for a real but unnamed personage)

Alalimmi: a field marshal of the Upper Land.

Alantalli: Luwian king of Mira and father-in-law of
Kurunta.

Amatalla: cousin of Queen Ellat-gula.

Ammish-tamru II: vassal king of Ugarit.

Anitti: wife of Kurunta, daughter of Alantalli.

Arnuwanda: eldest son and successor of Tudhaliya IV.

Benteshina: king of Amurru in Syria; husband of Tudhaliya's
eldest sister **Gasshulawiya,** known as the Great Lady.

Ehli-nikkal: the eldest daughter of Tudhaliya (Great Lady), later married to the king of Ugarit.

Ehli-sharrumma: Tudhaliya's cousin and king of Ishuwa.

Ellat-gula*: the fictional name of Tudhaliya's Babylonian queen and sometime *tawananna*.

Halpa-ziti: Tudhaliya's cousin and viceroy of Aleppo (Halep).

Hannutti*: younger full brother of Tudhaliya.

Hattushili III: Tudhaliya's father, who took the throne from his nephew.

Hishni: older half brother of Tudhaliya.

Huzziya*: younger full brother of Tudhaliya.

Ini-tesshub: cousin of Tudhaliya and viceroy of Karkemish.

Kudur-enlil: previous king of Karduniash; Ellat-gula's father.

Kurunta (Ulmi-tesshub): the throne name of Tudhaliya's cousin Ulmi-tesshub, viceroy of Tarhuntassha.

Lurma-ziti*: Tudhaliya's older half brother.

Mahhuzzi: secretary of Puduhepa and later vizier.

Mashamuwa: ambassador to Assyria and Babylonia.

Mashturi: Tudhaliya's uncle by marriage (his wife is Hattushili's sister **Mashanauzzi**) and vassal king of Sheha River Land.

Murshili III (Urhi-tesshub): throne name of Tudhaliya's cousin Urhi-tesshub, displaced as king by Hattushili III.

Muwatalli: brother of Hattushili, king, and father of Ulmi- and Urhi-tesshub.

Nerikkaili: eldest half brother of Tudhaliya and briefly his heir.

Nuwanza: a relative (here a lower-rank half brother) of Hattushili, field marshal under three kings.

Patiya: mother of Queen Ellat-gula.

Pirwannu*: Tudhaliya's valet.

Puduhepa: *tawananna* of Hattushili, Tudhaliya, Arnuwanda and Shuppiluliuma. She lives to a ripe age and is actively engaged in foreign policy. Texts describe her as a midwife (if that is the correct interpretation).

Shagarakti-shuriash: king of Karduniash and brother of Ellat-gula.

Shanda-kurunta*: younger full brother of Tudhaliya.

Shattuara: the vassal king of Hanigalbat who rebels against his Assyrian masters, resulting in the destruction of his country.

Shaushga-muwa: son of Benteshina and Gasshulawiya; king of Amurru.

Shulmanu-asharedu: Shalmaneser, king of Assyria.

Shuppiluliuma: younger son of Tudhaliya, who eventually succeeds his brother and rules as Shuppiluliuma II, last king of the Hittite empire.

Tarhun-miya: Tudhaliya's secretary.

Tashmi-sharrumma: thought to be Tudhaliya IV's birth name.

Tattamaru: Puduhepa's nephew by marriage, priest of Wurushemu, and military commander.

Tiwatipara: Tudhaliya's charioteer.

Tukulti-ninurta: king of Assyria, successor of Shulmanu-asharedu.

Walwa-ziti: vizier under Hattushili and Tudhaliya.

Zuzu: Tudhaliya's eunuch chamberlain.

GLOSSARY OF
TERMS AND GODS

Ahhiyawa: one or more of the Mycenaean Greek kingdoms. They have an interest in expanding into the Luwian territories across the Aegean.

Akkadian: the language, in different dialects, of Assyria and Babylonia. Its cuneiform writing system is also used in Hatti.

Alashiya: the island kingdom of Cyprus.

Anzili and Zukki: two of the goddesses of childbirth.

Arinna: holy city of the sun goddess.

Arinnitti, "she of Arinna": another name of Wurushemu, goddess of the sun.

Fears and Terrors (Nahshariattes and Weretemas): divine personifications of those phenomena, like Deimos and Phobos among the Greeks.

Gulshesh: the Ladies of Destiny, Ishtushtaya and Papaya, who spin out the thread of men's lives and sever it when their time on earth is up.

Hanigalbat: the remains of the old Mitannian empire or *Hurri* to the Hitittes.

Hattusha: capital of the Hittite empire. Formerly belonged to the indigenous Hattic people.

Hutellura: a group of goddesses of childbirth

iku: a unit of measurement about 10-15 meters in length.

Illuyanka-serpent: in Hittite and Hurrian mythology, a dragon defeated by the god Tarhunta/Tesshub.

Ishtanu: a sun god and god of justice.

Karduniash: the name of the Kassite kingdom of Babylonia.

Karkemish: a major city in inland Syria on the Euphrates River.

Kashka: tribes that inhabit the south shore of the Black Sea, just north of Hattusha.

Kizzuwatna: an originally independent kingdom in mountainous eastern Anatolia (later Cilicia), eventually absorbed by the Hittites. The homeland of Puduhepa.

Lalanda: a town in southwestern Anatolia, whose exact location is unknown.

Lawazantiya: Puduhepa's hometown.

Lelwani: goddess of the underworld, the "night sun."

Lukka Land: a coastal region in southwestern Anatolia (later Lycia) known for its lawless and disorganized population— pirates, moonrakers, and brigands.

Luwian: the language and ethnic identity of the Indo-European people of Anatolia displaced by the Hittites. They continue to live in the southern and western parts of the empire.

Malitiya: a town in eastern Anatolia, later known as Malatya.

Marrashantiya: the River Kizilirmak in Turkey.

Marwainzi Gods: violent gods of the Luwian underworld.

meshedi: guards of the Hittite king, along with the Golden Spearmen.

Mira: a Luwian vassal kingdom on the Aegean coast of Anatolia.

Mizri: the name given to Egypt by other countries, including Hatti.

Neshite: the language spoken by the Hittites, deriving from their earlier capital Nesha.

Old Women: priestesses of Lelwani. They preside over deaths and births, among other things.

panku: the plenary council of palace functionaries that once exercised moderating power over the king's policy making.

parishu: a unit of weight or volume. 250 *parishu* equal 15 tons.

Pirinkir: the god and/or goddess of the morning and evening star, Venus.

Puruna: the Euphrates River, boundary between Hatti and Assyria.

Runda: the god of the hunt or luck. "Kurunta" is a variant form.

Sharrumma: a Hurrian storm god, adopted into the Hittite pantheon as the Storm God of Nerik, son of Tarhunta.

Shaushga: the Hurrian goddess of love, beauty, and war, similar to Assyrian Ishtar.

Sheha River Land: a Luwian vassal kingdom in western Anatolia, north of Mira.

Stone House (*hekur*): a peak sanctuary that seems to be the place where the ashes of a king are buried and where he is subsequently worshiped.

Taite: the final capital of Hanigalbat after the fall of Wasshukanni.

Tarhunta: the Hittite and Luwian god of storms, their main divinity. Worshiped under several regional variations, including the Storm God of Hatti, he is equated with Tesshub, the Hurrian storm god, father of Sharrumma.

Tarhuntassha: the capital of the vassal kingdom of Tarhuntassha, founded by Muwatalli.

tawananna: the office of queen or queen mother in her formal diplomatic, religious, and political dimensions.

tuhkanti: the crown prince of Hatti.

Ugarit: a maritime vassal kingdom on the northern coast of Syria.

Upelluri: the god of dreams.

Ura: a port in coastal Tarhuntassha near Kizzuwatna.

wakshur: a unit of length.

walhi: a sweet, highly alcoholic beverage, perhaps mead.

Wurukatte: the god of war.

Wurushemu: the sun goddess of Arinna.

CHAPTER 1

I T WAS DAWN. TASHMI-SHARRUMMA STOOD with his back to the rocks in the vain hope of blocking the wind and snow from his eyes, which were watering, more from sleeplessness than from cold. Before him, the court cut into the bedrock was full of ash, hissing and steaming as the snowflakes danced their way to death in the cooling remnants of the bone fire that had burned all night. The Old Women had not yet come with their tongs to pick out the calcined bones of his father, wash them with wine, and soak them in oil.

Tashmi-sharrumma was alone. No one had dared to stay with him, watching all night as the pyre blazed against the winter darkness. They knew him well enough to know he wanted to keep vigil by himself—even his mother had discreetly left him to his solitude. His cousin Kurunta would have stayed, but Tashmi-sharrumma had sent him away.

He needed to cry out to the gods, yet he couldn't find any words.

He was now the emperor of all the lands that called

Hatti their master. He feared he no longer knew who he was or who he should be. Until two days ago, he had been Prince Tashmi-sharrumma—an imperfect, uncomfortable identity he had inhabited for thirty-five years. But since the day before yesterday, things had changed. The old king had become a god, and Tashmi-sharrumma had been consecrated in his place. He was now Tudhaliya, Great King, the fourth of that name. Now he alone shepherded the people of the Storm God; he alone bore responsibility for injustices and wrongdoing. From within his fur-lined cloak, he drew a deep breath. His new name and his new responsibility perched upon him awkwardly, a little too big, a little too heavy.

And within in the young king's chest, fear hunkered like an unquiet animal. His father had been a great king, but Hattushili's sins had been many. And now they were Tashmi-sharrumma's own. Suddenly "alone" was a frightening word, even for a man who valued solitude.

"Storm God of Hatti, forgive my father's wrongs. Don't bring his guilt down upon my head and the heads of your people," Tashmi-sharrumma murmured, his breath hanging in a cloud before his face, until cloud and words dispersed into the air. He watched the snowflakes' manic descent. The ash was still too hot for the snow to begin piling up, but the air was thick with it, veiling the brutal gray wall of rock that rose at his back, softening the gray rock of the buildings across the court. Rock was alive, divine… but not kindly. Tashmi-sharrumma shivered.

He stared up into the falling snow. The very air was seething with it; flakes struck him in the eyes and melted upon his face. The funeral party would be lucky not to be trapped up here in the mountain Stone House, mortuary temple of the late king Hattushili son of Murshili. The rites would go on for a fortnight, and then everyone would return to the capital—if the roads were not impassable, near though the site was to the city walls. Tashmi-sharrumma almost hoped the return would be delayed.

He wasn't a coward, he told himself. He had fought on the field of battle since he was twelve years old and had served as the chief of his father's bodyguard from his eighteenth year. He had been a priest of the Storm God of Nerik almost since he'd been old enough to read, facing the hostile onslaughts of darkness armored only in the power of ritual words. He had learned to set aside his own preferences and pleasures for the needs of the kingdom, a campaign that took perhaps even more courage. But he couldn't repress the sense of dread that sat like a suffocating weight upon his chest.

He was the son of a usurper. He would be punished.

Now the black-wrapped Old Women—the priestesses of Lelwani, Queen of the Underworld—were approaching, their tongs in hand. Tashmi-sharrumma watched them as they began their duties, scattering the ash, quenching the coals with wine, completing the work the Storm God himself had begun. Steam rose in angry clouds from the extinguished ashes so that the priestesses seemed to be pouring out smoke from their beakers. Their mantles whipped in the wind; only the rock at his back shielded the young king, but far from keeping him warmer, its presence behind him radiated cold like a piece of bronze left out in the winter. He turned away from the priestesses. Although they were the sole human figures in a world of stone and ice, the women's proximity didn't comfort him. They were like the black ravens that violated the bodies of the dead on the battlefield.

Tashmi-sharrumma suspected he was almost invisible where he stood, his gray wolf-fur cloak one with the gray of the stone. The women didn't seem to see him. Their voices, half blown away on the wind, rose in broken pieces of melody as they chanted. They stooped from time to time, lifting an unburnt fragment of bone with their tongs and dropping it into a bag. This very night, the late king's mortal remains would be cushioned in purple wool and laid upon his chair, and he would preside for one last time at the banquet his family shared with him.

That's all that is left of the body that used to be my father's, thought Tashmi-sharrumma, an unexpected wave of quiet sorrow filling him. He accepted this. Death was something he had seen plenty of in his not-so-long life—men dead on the battlefield, struck down because they had dared to oppose their rightful lords. The young king's own firstborn son, dead within weeks of birth, was harder to explain. One minute, the living were here—warm and solid and heavy— and then they were gone, and nothing was ever the same again. Tashmi-sharrumma thought of his father's laugh and his hand upon his small son's head, back when the late king had just been the brother of a king, the uncle of a king.

My father's soul has become a god. Tashmi-sharrumma looked up into the snow again as if he might catch a glimpse of the late king's spirit rising through the white air. This was more difficult to understand. He wondered if Hattushili now saw all the events of his long life with the pitiless clarity of godsight. Did the light of divine justice make him regret his black deeds? Did his father acknowledge that he should never have seized the kingship and that it should have been his nephew Urhi-tesshub, and not Tashmi-sharrumma, upon the throne?

⁂

The wan light of the winter sun, invisible behind the clouds, had given up, and the funeral banquet had begun. The bones of Hattushili, wrapped in purple wool—dyed with the priceless blood of the murex shell, tribute of coastal vassals—rested in his accustomed chair at the head of the table. At his side sat the *tawananna*, Puduhepa, the old king's wife of thirty-seven years, still beautiful in her fifties. She was grave but smiling, gracious as ever, with a fortifying word for every relative present. Her words could slaughter, but tonight, she was all comfort and condolence.

The guests, for the most part, were the sons and cousins and nephews of the late king. Hattushili's family was fecund, Tashmi-sharrumma realized—a mixed blessing. The brothers of the deceased were all dead, except for old Nuwanza, but their sons were here. Many others were viceroys or minor kings elsewhere in the empire and couldn't get back through the snows of winter to their ancestral city. Tashmi-sharrumma's married sisters weren't here, of course; their husbands or ambassadors would make calls of condolence in the summer, after the weather became milder and the roads more reliable. But his brothers and half brothers were present in force. Hattushili had taken seriously his duty to populate the diplomatic corps with royal princes.

Through lowered lids, Tashmi-sharrumma eyed his eldest half brother, Nerikkaili, as he made his way to his seat. The son of a second-rank wife, Nerikkaili had been their father's heir, the *tuhkanti*, before Tashmi-sharrumma had turned twenty-five. He was again the designated heir until the new king should produce one of his own. Nerikkaili had substance. The room seemed smaller in his presence; he was big and good-looking, rich of voice and expansive of gesture. People scooted their chairs aside to make room for him to take his seat. He had the smooth, cynical affability of a diplomat and the self-assurance of a military commander, in which capacities he had served for nearly forty years, longer than the new king had lived. Had Tashmi-sharrumma not been a first-rank son, the offspring of a queen, it would have been Nerikkaili sitting on the throne that night. Nerikkaili leaned forward and raised his cup to the king. There was always something a little ambiguous about that smile, a wry twitch of the corners that might or might not be mockery. Years of diplomacy had made the older man's expression hard to read, but Tashmi-sharrumma realized that he'd better learn how. His brother would be a formidable rival.

The face he longed to see, though, was that of his cousin Kurunta, beloved companion of his childhood. The king strained his eyes through the dim, flickering light of too few oil lamps to find him, and Kurunta looked up from the table. Even from here, Tashmi-sharrumma could see the broad smile that lit the man's face. Dearest Kurunta, always laughing, mischievous, daring. The king's cousin rose and slipped behind the diners, and a moment later, Tashmi-sharrumma felt him lean beside his ear, long black hair hanging alongside his own. Kurunta rested his forearms on the new king's shoulders and whispered, "How're you doing, Tash? Feeling all royal?"

"Not very." The king managed a strained smile, not looking back at his cousin. To Kurunta, Tashmi-sharrumma was still "Tash." No one but Kurunta had ever called him that, and the king realized that the days of happy familiarity with his cousin might be coming to an end with his new responsibilities. "I haven't slept all night."

"Oh, you haven't, eh? Regret that you didn't let me keep watch with you last night, don't you? We could have had some fun up there in uncle's Stone House alone together."

"My father has just died, you know." Tashmi-sharrumma's voice trembled a little despite his best efforts to keep it steady, and tears burned inside his lids. He fought them back. The king of Hatti Land didn't cry in public, and the gods knew he wasn't the tearful sort—people accused him of having no emotions. Kurunta laid his cheek on his cousin's head, right upon the crimson cap that was the crown of the Great King, and Tashmi-sharrumma leaned back against him as if he could draw strength from the very touch of Kurunta's body.

"Your father is a god now, Tash. The banquet is for rejoicing that we're all alive. So rejoice, will you? You're always too serious."

"Thank you for your advice." The king forced a grin. His cousin clapped him affectionately on the shoulder and slid back to his seat.

As the consumption of wine and beer and *walhi* beverage rose, the tenor of the meal became more hilarious. Tashmi-sharrumma tried to keep a pleasant expression on his face, but he knew people had seen and judged his red eyes. The words with which his father's funeral ceremony began were still echoing in his mind: *When a great catastrophe befalls Hattusha, and the king becomes a god...* He was exhausted, besides; his chin kept sinking to his collarbone. The conversation around him drifted into a meaningless buzz. He picked at his food, but it didn't interest him. He forced himself to sip at the cup of beer someone had just replenished. He knew people would be watching him from now on.

Tashmi-sharrumma wondered what people saw when they looked at their new king. He was tall, like all of his family, and his brown hair was brushed into a fluffy mane. His garments were rich, and heavy silver jewelry adorned his ears and wrists, a broad collar of gold around his neck. His personal adornments were worth a small kingdom. But he was ill favored, with a long, bony, equine face and hooded eyes. His teeth were sharp and so crooked that he couldn't fully close his lips over them, and they forced his jaw sideways when he chewed. They gave his most innocent smile a carnivorous edge.

He had been self-conscious about this unfortunate face in his childhood, but now he had mostly made his peace with it. It was simply a fact—and no doubt it was a good thing when a prince resembled his royal father. He tried to keep his expression calm and benevolent and to look people in the eye when they were speaking, to seem like he heard and cared. He did hear and care, but he was short of sight and didn't see their faces all that clearly—he concentrated better staring into space. This was only one of the many ways in which he had learned to do violence to his own preferences.

Suddenly, he jerked upright—someone had poked him in the side.

His wife laughed at him. "You were asleep." Her face was pink cheeked and glowing as if warmed with wine, although she had drunk little. Ellat-gula was the sister of the king of Karduniash, far away on the mighty River Puruna. Their marriage, when Tashmi-sharrumma had been twenty and she had been fourteen, had cemented an important treaty between Hatti and that land on the other side of Assyria. But the Babylonian bride had also been beautiful and intelligent. She was still considered extremely attractive as she approached thirty, yet her intelligence, left with nothing important to sink its teeth into, had taken on a tinge of wiliness. Her ambition had started to be a problem. She wanted very badly to become the *tawananna*, Tashmi-sharrumma perceived, but that couldn't happen until his own mother's death, and Puduhepa was thirty years younger than her husband. A long life almost surely stretched out before her.

That present *tawananna* leaned over to him now, across the bones of the late king. She laid her hand upon Tashmi-sharrumma's forearm and squeezed gently, an intimate gesture that was both knowing and comforting. "Are you ready to receive the oath of loyalty, My Sun? Shall I instruct the vizier to bring the tablets?"

The young king nodded almost invisibly. These brief signs were a part of their private communication, a kind of silent code that they had shared since his childhood. She had always been at his side, training him, engineering his

27

ascendance over his brothers. He knew that for thirty-five years she had dreamed of the moment when Nerikkaili and the other second-rank sons of the late king would swear to serve her eldest boy.

She signaled her secretary, Mahhuzzi, who hovered at her elbow as always. He scurried like a weasel into the darkness. A moment later, Walwa-ziti, the elderly vizier, approached his new king and lowered his rotund little body to the floor. The old man had a kindly and innocent appearance, with his thinning white curls and smoothly shaven double chin, but Tashmi-sharrumma realized that he would be foolish to underestimate the fellow. The vizier was faithful to Puduhepa, yet that fidelity might not transfer to her son. The king would have to trust him—but only for a while. At some point, he would choose his own advisors.

Walwa-ziti rose laboriously to his feet and extended a set of tablets to the king for his approval. "Is My Sun ready to administer the oath of loyalty?"

The young king nodded and watched his vizier toddle to the center of the banquet hall. Already diners were falling silent; they knew what was to come. The older of them had lived through the death of other kings. The vizier's scribe was unfolding his wooden writing tablet, prepared to note down the names of those who swore. Everyone else would be required to do so as soon as they could reach Hattusha in the spring. The new king and his mother had helped to draw up the text, and not all those present here would be happy about it.

"Thus speaks Tudhaliya the Great King," began Walwa-ziti in his rich, rolling baritone. "I have become king, and you courtiers must swear an oath upon the person of My Sun as follows. 'We will protect Our Sun with regard to the kingship, and thereafter we will protect the sons of Our Sun and their sons and grandsons with regard to the kingship.'"

Tashmi-sharrumma couldn't make out the faces of his brothers, uncles, and cousins in the flickering semidarkness, but he knew they were as aware as he of the troubled succession within their family. He wondered what Nerikkaili was thinking. As yet, there was no heir of Tashmi-sharrumma's body. Would the *tuhkanti* be humble enough to step aside yet again for that hypothetical nephew, as he had done already for his half brother?

Walwa-ziti's velvety voice rolled on, laying out all the permutations of treachery, indiscretion, and lukewarmness toward a sovereign that might occur to an ambitious prince. And then, at last, the tablet was read, and each man had to approach his king and swear under pain of a grim death to forget how Hattushili had taken the kingship and the illegitimacy of his son's seat in the lap of Halmashuit, the divine throne.

Nerikkaili was the first to be called. He strode forward firmly, as if he had not drunk beer and *walhi* all night long, knelt on the step of the new king's dais, and repeated in his booming voice the ancient words of homage to the shepherd the gods of Hatti had chosen to rule over their people.

"I, Nerikkaili, second-rank son of Hattushili, so swear by the thousand gods of Hatti."

Tashmi-sharrumma couldn't make out his features clearly at that distance, but nothing in Nerikkaili's mannerisms contradicted the frankness of his face, the assurance of his voice.

Next came Lurma-ziti, the second half brother with his twisted back, and Hishni, an affable middle-aged man and seasoned veteran. Tashmi-sharrumma intended to make the latter the chief of his bodyguards, a role he himself had filled under the old king. Walwa-ziti called upon Tashmi-sharrumma's younger full brothers, then came his cousins, the viceroys of Karkemish and Halep, at the eastern borders of the empire. The diplomatic corps. The palace officials. The scribes and men of the chancery; the military men. Nearly everyone who swore loyalty had royal blood. Nearly any of them could have fancied himself upon the throne in the place of this younger son of a usurper.

Tashmi-sharrumma glanced sideways under his eyelids at his mother. The specific additions, designed to say, "I know what you're up to," had been her suggestion. She was a woman who left nothing to chance. She was satisfied by the oath sworn by these sons of the kings of Hatti. There was something smug about her smile, her high color, her proudly lifted chin. This was the hour of her triumph. Ellat-gula, too, was beaming her satisfaction, because her position was only as strong as that of her husband. There was no love lost between the Babylonian and these abundant and mostly pure-blooded Hittite princes.

Tashmi-sharrumma realized with immense relief that the evening was winding down. Tomorrow he would place the bones of his father in their niche in the Stone House, and Hattushili would take his place as a god in the pantheon of Hatti. For the moment, the young king was ready to go to bed. He rose, and the court rose with him. He turned and made his way from the banquet hall and heard the scrape of chairs and clatter of knives and cups as the others followed suit. The ordeal of the funeral banquet was over.

Much as he longed for sleep, the king dawdled en route to his apartments. He took off his red cap. The biting cold of the winter night invigorated him. He stopped, and the other guests of the banquet hustled past, scarcely noticing his solitary, fur-wrapped figure. Tashmi-sharrumma drew a long, icy draft of air into his lungs and let it sink into him. The stillness of the hour settled him. Sounds were far away. Silent in the silent darkness, he was alone at last. After savoring the peace of the gods' night, he moved on.

The guard at the door of the royal chambers stood at attention, a carven figure. At the king's approach, he came to life and opened the heavy panels, and heat and light poured out, breaking the spell of soundless cold. The moment Tashmi-sharrumma stepped inside the vestibule to his bedchamber, his eunuch chamberlain came bustling up to him, face crumpled with uncertainty. Zuzu was a tall, thin, willowy personage who appeared to sway in unseen breezes. He seemed to have grown anxious overnight as if he expected his master would discharge him for the slightest imperfection now that Tashmi-sharrumma was Tudhaliya the Great King.

"My Sun, my lady the queen is waiting for you in your chamber. Do you want me to tell her to leave?"

Tashmi-sharrumma drifted past him, suppressing a sigh. His first thought was that he would have preferred to be by himself. His sole desire was to sleep. But this was only the first of many times he would have to set aside his own wishes as ruler of this bleak land. He said, over his shoulder, "No, that's fine. I'll receive her."

"Will you want your valet, My Sun, or…?" Zuzu coughed discreetly. *Or will she undress you* was what he left unsaid.

"No, I'm fine."

Two of his wife's ladies-in-waiting were fluttering by the inner door, fat butterflies in bright woolen gowns. From closer up, he realized that they were her mother, Patiya, and her cousin Amatalla. As he approached, they dropped into an obeisance and rose, all smiles and squeals of excitement.

Patiya beamed. "Congratulations, My Sun," she said in her broken Neshite. "May gods prosper your reign for long time!"

"Yes," he replied vaguely. "Long time. Thank you." She hovered around him, oblivious to his mild sarcasm, with Amatalla close behind. They wanted to pet him and flatter him, remind the newly powerful man that they loved him. He wanted only to find a bed. He pushed past them, smiling, nodding, and making courteous noises. The guard opened the door of his inner room for him and closed it in the faces of the hovering Babylonians with a clang.

The winter's night had settled upon the mountains, and several braziers were lit against the cold, although the lamps couldn't scrub out all the shadows. With longing, he eyed his bed, where fox skins had been thrown across the covers, but his wife intercepted him. She was already undressed. Her body—rosy with cold, her nipples stiff as apple buds—was enveloped in a fur-edged cloak.

"Hail, My Sun! Come here and let me to bask in your light." Ellat-gula grinned, her eyes bright with a desire that blunted the mockery of her words. Tashmi-sharrumma smiled back wearily and reached out to draw her cloak tighter across her. She was small and plump, full of pleasant roundnesses, but he knew better than to think she was soft. Her mind was like a sharp-toothed little fox prowling inside her. He took her hand, kissed her knuckles, and dragged himself to a chair, where he sat heavily and stretched out his legs. He threw the red crown on the bed. She followed him and settled herself on the floor at his feet, leaning on his knees.

"I don't feel any more majestic than I did two days ago," he said, returning her grin. "Rather less so. I'm too old to spend whole nights awake anymore." But he knew there would be many of them ahead—long nights spent restless and unable to flee the responsibilities that were his alone now. The smile slid from his face, and he stared unseeing into his lap. His eyes wanted to fall shut.

Ellat-gula took his hand, which was dangling over the arm of the chair, and caressed his fingers. "But you will not be alone, my husband. Think of all the things we can accomplish together for our people."

We. Our people. They had been married fifteen years, and everyone still thought of her as the Babylonian.

"You're not the *tawananna*, my dear," he reminded her dryly.

Her smile disappeared with a soundless tinkle of breaking ice. "No," she snapped, turning away and letting his hand fall.

He lifted that hand and stared at the callused palm, the long fingers. *This is the king's hand now, touched by the sacred oils. This is the hand the thousand gods of Hatti have chosen to guard their people.* Tashmi-sharrumma's body was no longer the body of a mere man, but something already filling up with divinity, like a sponge in a dish of wine... He heard Ellat-gula speaking as if from a distance, and realized his reverie had slid off into sleep.

"... good news."

"Forgive me. What's that, my dear?"

"I say, I have some good news. Some more good news. On this day of good newses—can you say that?" She dimpled up at him, playing simple. She wore her hair Hittite fashion—long down her back, parted in the middle. It was thick and dark and lustrous, as undulating as the waves of the Interior Sea. It reminded him of Kurunta's hair but darker still, blue-black like the feathers of a raven. *There's still something very foreign about Ellat-gula,* he thought, running his gaze over her olive skin, her small bowed mouth, her cheeks like apples. It occurred to him his own daughter was thirteen, nearly old enough to be married away to some court where she would be a foreigner. He needed to think carefully about who got her.

Tashmi-sharrumma realized his thoughts were drifting. "I don't believe you can say that, though I couldn't say why. What's your good news? Forgive me; I'm so tired I can't concentrate."

Ellat-gula folded her plump arms across his knees and gazed up into his face. His eyes skittered across the chasm between her round breasts, unmoved, then back to her eyes. They were big and black as olives, the lids darker still with kohl. He tried to imagine his sisters adorning their eyes like that, the ones who were married to the south. Two of them lived in Mizri, where even the men painted their eyes. He forced his drifting attention back to his wife.

"I am expecting, my husband." She waited, watching, and then laughed as her "newses" sank in. A wave of delight washed over him. The gods had blessed his anointing after all! It was the best of omens. Exhaustion dropped away from the king, and he rose, lifting his wife to her feet. He was as giddy as a child. He took her gently by the shoulders and kissed the white part in her dark hair. She caressed her plump belly, with its crescent navel, like a sacred object, and he averted his eyes.

"My dear! How wonderful! How, how... wonderful!" He laughed at his own lack of words. "May the Hutellurra guard you. When are...?"

"Midsummer." She was as beautiful as he had ever seen her, glowing triumphantly. And her triumph was this, he knew: if she could bear him an heir, her place in Hatti was assured. She would be "the Babylonian" no longer. He would have to take a secondary wife and no doubt concubines, now that he was king, and he wondered how she would react. Perhaps if she had a son it wouldn't matter to her. He had no illusions about the genuineness of her love for him, any more than of his own for her—what she really wanted was to become the *tawananna*.

As if she had read his thoughts, Ellat-gula began to stroke his back, and she whispered in a coaxing voice of sweetness, "You must keep your mother away from me, My Sun. I will feel afraid as long as she's around."

He stood stiff and uncomfortable, pretending not to catch her drift. "But she's an experienced midwife. She's helped to bring to light almost all the sons and grandsons of my father, raised them as her own…"

"I don't trust her. She is jealous of your love for me." Her voice had grown suddenly brittle, her soft little mouth as hard as a beak. "Have you never wondered why our firstborn died, Tashmi-sharrumma?"

The king drew away from her, chilled. "What are you saying—that the *tawananna* killed my son?"

It seemed she dared not go that far. She shrugged vaguely, leaving him to draw conclusions. "Who had more of opportunity? All I know is she is no friend to me. You must protect me, My Sun. You must not let her put a curse on me or make me lose this child, your child."

The thought that his own mother might put a curse on his pregnant wife was almost beyond the realm of belief. Almost, but not quite. Puduhepa was not a monster, but she was ambitious. *Still, her own grandson?*

"Cursing is serious business." He remembered what happened to Uncle Arma-tarhunta when his father thought the old man had put a curse on him. Witchcraft was one of the few acts punishable by death. "She would never risk it, even if she wished you harm."

"Don't be naive, my husband. She has enough supporters at court to do whatever she wants. And she hates me. She hates me enough to harm Hatti to get back at me."

Tashmi-sharrumma could hardly believe what he was hearing. He drew Ellat-gula to the bed and sat down with her beside him. His fingers around her arm must have been tight enough to hurt, and she shifted uncomfortably.

"What do you mean?" He remembered the two Babylonian women at the door. Were they there still, their ears pressed to the crack? His voice was hard and urgent, but he was careful to speak low. "Has my mother tried to harm you? Why do you say this?"

"She accuses me of plotting for Karduniash. She wants to break our treaty and throw my brother's country to the Assyrians. Of course, I do not want that. Surely no one is surprised if I oppose that. But it is not just for my brother's sake. Both our countries need each other to keep the Assyrians from overrunning everything. Look at what they did to Hurri—there's nothing left but that little bit called Hanigalbat, and who knows how long that will last. We have no more buf... buffers—is that the word? If they ever think their neighbors to north and south are not united against them, they will feel they can get away with anything."

"But has she tried to harm you?"

"She undercuts me all the time in the court and before all your relatives. She claims my actions as priestess are not worth anything because I haven't done them right, and she says that Amatalla has stoled from the gods. She wants to isolate me. She says my mother is a spy. She has said in public that Karduniash should be thrown to wolves to keep the Assyrians busy. If our son had lived, he would have been half Babylonian. He would've been a living reminder of the policy of alliance she has turned away from."

Tashmi-sharrumma sat back for a moment, trying to digest this possibility. His mother had been running the government for years—all the time his father was bedridden and probably well before that. The royal advisors were devoted to her, he was sure. Otherwise, they would not have been there. His father's brothers hadn't loved her, but they were all gone. She could count on the support of a whole generation of young princes she had raised as her own. Mahhuzzi, her secretary, was like a ferret slinking through the halls, pouring like a shadow into locked rooms, whispering into the ears of the courtiers and cousins whatever his mistress wanted them to believe.

Suddenly, the delight Tashmi-sharrumma had felt at the announcement of Ellat-gula's pregnancy grew a crust of rime. His unease was back. His mother had been the one sure supporter, apart from Kurunta, throughout Tashmi-sharrumma's life. She had steered a younger son—her son—to power over all his brothers, men more distinguished than he in every way. Why would she have wished him harm now? It was she, after all, who had made the match with Karduniash fifteen years ago.

Is this inability to trust anyone part of the Oath Gods' punishment? He sighed, glum. "Stay away from her, then. I'll see to it she leaves you alone."

"You are not mad at me, are you?" Ellat-gula looked up at him coyly from under her lashes and ran her forefinger down the bridge of his nose.

"No," he said a little sharply. He drew away in discomfort from the warmth of her body. Exhaustion had descended upon him again. "Why should I be?"

He realized that his wife was a stranger to him, even more than women in general. The time he had spent at her side was scant compared to his years in the field, or on diplomatic journeys, or with the *meshedi*, the king's guard. He knew the men of his father's army better than his own queen. He didn't have any idea if her complaints were valid or exaggerated. *Maybe all this is just the rivalry of beautiful women.*

His shoulders ached, and he fell back on the bed, his legs hanging off. Before he even heard Ellat-gula's reply, Upelluri, the god of dreams, had claimed him.

CHAPTER 2

THE STORM GOD HAD RELENTED. Snow lay ten *wakshurs* deep upon the mountains and the flat roofs of the city. It mantled with ermine the battlements of the citadel but was no longer falling. The steep, undulating plains stretched out around the walls under an immaculate blanket. The sky itself was white. Only the dun of the city walls and the black, vertical ribs of stone to which the snow couldn't adhere stood out against the whiteness.

From the roof of the royal palace, the new king had a view that rivaled the gods'. He stared across the capital, the wind whipping his face and making his nose run, bringing tears of cold to his eyes. Below him, down a long, log-paved causeway borne by a towering bridge wall, stretched the city of his ancestors. Indeed, it had existed even before his own people. The Hattic kings had raised it and then burned it as they had fled before their conquerors, cursing anyone who would rebuild Hattusha. The Kashkans had burned it down time and again. So much for the "impregnable" walls reared across rocky outcrops and plunging ravines.

An eagle's aerie dug into the living rock, a fever dream of mountain giants, the city was more vulnerable than it looked. Tashmi-sharrumma's father was the most recent of the rebuilders. He had added interior walls and beautified the palace as if to reinforce that Hattusha was, as its name implied, the City of the Hittites... and he, Hattushili, the man of Hattusha.

Tashmi-sharrumma visored his eyes against the glare with a hand and turned to take in the panorama of this city of his birth. His heart swelled with affection at the sight, yet there was a flutter of unease as well. The city was like the legitimacy of Hattushili's claim to the throne—not as strong as it appeared.

Nearly forty years ago, in preparation for war in the East, his uncle Muwatalli had divided the kingdom and moved the capital south to the region of Tarhuntassha, where he had built a city of the same name: City of Tarhunta, the Storm God of Lightning. Muwatalli had appointed his youngest brother, Hattushili, as a kind of viceroy in the north, ruling from Hakpish, and he himself had transferred all the archives, all the statues of the gods— the entire government—to the south. Hattusha, he had said, was too vulnerable to the Kashkans, who would take advantage of his absence in the East to attack the ancient capital, as they always had. There were many who felt that that abandonment of the city that was the heart of Hatti Land was foolish and would anger the gods, although the king claimed that he was obeying a divine command.

What did my father think of this division? The young king tried to imagine what it must have been like to watch the ancient capital empty out and yield its dignity to brash new settlements. But Hattushili had kept his opinion to himself.

Then Muwatalli had became a god, and his adolescent son Urhi-tesshub came to the throne. Urhi-tesshub returned the capital to Hattusha, and no one complained, least of all Hattushili. But little by little, the new king began to reabsorb the "northern kingdom" back into Hatti, and with it, he took all the privileges of his uncle, the king of Hakpish.

For the first time in his life Tashmi-sharrumma wondered if his father had in fact engineered the division of the country. It had benefited Hattushili alone. Its ending had signaled the opening of the civil war that resulted in Tashmi-sharrumma's own seat in the arms of Halmashuit, the divine throne.

He was to meet with his mother and the Lords of Hatti soon to consider the decisions that faced him and devise a plan of action for the empire. The thought that personal gain might have guided such decisions in his father's career was sobering. Coupled with Ellat-gula's revelations about his mother, it was more than sobering. Tashmi-sharrumma realized with a leaden heart that he could trust no one to be disinterested—his own parents were no better than his uncles, his cousins, and his scheming vassals. They just had had the good taste to scheme on his behalf. He had never thought of himself as particularly innocent, but some last shred of idealism had in fact been scraped from him since last night.

And yet the gods had chosen him as their vicar. He couldn't abandon the values they held dear—justice, clemency, fidelity. He was already under their displeasure for the sins of his father. He dared add no iniquity of his own.

Tashmi-sharrumma stared down into the public court of the palace. Two servants crossed below him, arms wrapped around themselves, leaving footprints in the snow. No one looked up to see the king standing alone at the edge of the roof. Here he could be by himself for a few precious moments and find time to think in the silence and fresh air. The air was more than fresh, to be sure; the cold gnawed like a fox, burned like a fire, cut his exposed face like a knife. The atmosphere was still white with the memory of falling snow.

Tashmi-sharrumma loved the bite of the rocky highlands that surrounded this city where he was born. It was a hard land, and it bred hard men. His brothers were rough, cruel, and—except for the lower-rank half brothers who filled the chancery—only marginally lettered. They were suited best to leading armies and giving councils of war. Although he couldn't easily have said why, Tashmi-sharrumma had never felt that he fit into this family of men of stone. His love for music? His fascination with the scribal arts? His propensity for thinking? Yet it was he the gods had chosen. He was as mystified by their choice as anyone.

"My cousin."

The king turned, his heart leaping up at the sound of that beloved voice. It was Kurunta, his head emerging from the trap in the roof. The wind sent his black hair flying into his mouth, and he laughed as he spat it out. The king laughed with him.

"I haven't heard that sound in weeks," said Kurunta, baring his white teeth in a smile that carved long dimples alongside his mouth. He crawled out of the trap and approached his cousin a little cautiously because of the ice, his arms outstretched, and they embraced. The king found it hard to detach himself. In that embrace was more warmth and uncritical support than he could count on elsewhere in his entire kingdom.

"Not much to laugh about lately, cousin," Tashmi-sharrumma said, but he could barely suppress his crooked grin. "Thank you for coming to the coronation."

"By the thousand gods of our ancestors, Tash. Did you think for a minute I wouldn't? I know, I know; it's winter."

"A lot of your fellows haven't made it."

"They'll come as soon as the snow melts. You do believe that, don't you?"

The king made an ambiguous gesture with his shoulders and hitched his furs up around his ears. In fact, he feared that some of the vassal kings would refuse to recognize him. "How are things?"

"With me? Well, as always. Anitti and the children are all well. You look..."

"Kingly?"

"Wrung out." Kurunta clapped the king on the arms with both hands. "Don't forget to eat, eh?"

"I haven't gotten much sleep," the king said.

"Only too obvious, old friend. You should have seen yourself at the funeral banquet."

Unaccountably, Tashmi-sharrumma felt his nose burning. He told himself it was the wind. But Kurunta drew him against his hip as one might a child.

"I know," his cousin said quietly. "It's hard."

Kurunta was four years older than the king. When

they had been children, his first role was protector of a shy, homely younger boy against the brutal rough and tumble of the royal children. Somehow, over the years, their relationship reversed—Kurunta was the cheerful, outgoing scapegrace; Tashmi-sharrumma was pious and dutiful and often kept his elder cousin out of trouble. Yet under the surface, they weren't so unlike. They were both misfits. He had found in Kurunta—Ulmi-tesshub, as Kurunta was known before taking a throne name—that much-longed-for soul mate who would listen to his most intimate thoughts without mocking. Kurunta had been able to make him see the absurdity of those small sufferings that loomed so large in the mind of a child. The king wondered if his mother had paired them up for precisely that reason: to lighten his own gravity, to give an overly serious boy a chance to laugh. Kurunta could still make him laugh.

They stood side by side, the wind whipping their skirts, their furs drawn tight around their shoulders. Neither looked at the other, as if that would risk awakening something too strong for them both. Their gazes traveled across the vast whiteness of the rocky plain, a lonely, frozen scene. Tashmi-sharrumma could feel Kurunta's presence at his side, radiating warmth even through the wool and furs. Tashmi-sharrumma's gratitude was so great he longed to put his arms around his cousin, but the king was not a demonstrative man. Such displays embarrassed him. And now, as king, he was unsure of what he could and couldn't do with propriety. There were so many rules of ritual purity and etiquette—even his personal life had become a quagmire of potential offenses.

Kurunta seemed to perceive how ill at ease Tashmi-sharrumma was, and as usual, he stepped in with good cheer. "I don't think I've ever actually congratulated you, cousin. Welcome to the fellowship of kings, from one who is an old hand!" He grinned, made a circlet of his forefingers and thumbs, and pretended to place it on Tashmi-sharrumma's head. Kurunta had been a viceroy, king of Tarhuntassha, for fifteen years.

"Do you ever get used to it?" Tashmi-sharrumma's lips pulled into a wry smile, but a tide of misery rose in him. Perhaps it was the memory of the happiness he and Kurunta had shared as younger sons of kings, which was forever over now, buried under a mountain of care.

"It's not so bad being a viceroy. Someone else is always ultimately responsible for things." Kurunta tactfully refrained from adding *and that someone is you.* "Plus, the weather's not so harsh in Tarhuntassha. I'd forgotten what a bitch our beautiful capital is. Can't say that I miss it."

"I love this weather."

"You would, Tash. You were always a grim lad. Give me Tarhuntassha any day."

Tashmi-sharrumma had to look at his cousin's face before he realized this was at least partly a jest. He threw back his head and laughed. Then his expression grew sober. "Do you remember when we were children that you once said you would support me no matter what? Even against your own brother?"

"I do," said Kurunta, turning serious. He fixed the king with his gaze, and Tashmi-sharrumma realized that his cousin had not aged as much as he. Even at forty, his hair was dark, his cheeks almost unlined. The two men were clearly related, with their long, lean faces and heavy-lidded eyes, but Kurunta was handsome, perhaps the handsomest man Tashmi-sharrumma had ever seen, with dark, expressive brows and perfectly sculpted lips. The king himself was like a paler, harsher copy by a poor artist whose hand had slipped somewhere around the mouth. And now they appeared to be more or less the same age, as they had long felt themselves to be.

"What was the occasion, do you remember?"

"I think Uncle Hattushili was trying to get Urhi-tesshub extradited from Mizri. And I said I didn't care what happened; I wanted to be your man. And even if you weren't the official choice for king, I would always support you. I swore that to the Oath Gods."

"You know," Tashmi-sharrumma said pensively, "I sometimes think that's why they made me *tuhkanti*. My parents, I mean. Nerikkaili is the obvious choice in every way, but you supported me."

In his typical joking manner, Kurunta made a comically impressed face. "Why, how flattering, cousin. I had no idea I was so important."

"You are," murmured the king with a little too much feeling. He let an embarrassed sigh escape him. They were silent again for a long moment.

Kurunta said finally, in a quiet voice with a slight hard edge that the king couldn't quite interpret, "Don't sell yourself short, Tash. You were a plenty obvious choice. You were good at everything."

Tashmi-sharrumma thought at first his cousin was mocking him. "Me? Everybody thought I was a half-wit."

"No, they didn't. You're not a quick responder, I'll grant you, but you just want to think things over first. You

47

were good at letters, at music, at sports. I couldn't beat you at anything."

"But you did. All the time. I could only dream of being like you."

Kurunta looked at him sideways and gave a little chuckle as if to say *hopeless*. "I was four years older. I should have been able to outrun or outwrestle you without breaking a sweat. No, my dear. Why do you think your brothers disliked you so much?"

"Because my mother pushed me ahead of them? Because... because I wasn't very likable?"

Kurunta laughed and drew his cousin to him in a quick embrace. He chided Tashmi-sharrumma affectionately. "You idiot. How old are you—thirty-five? And so naive? Maybe you *are* half-witted!"

He's teasing me, thought the king humbly, *to make me feel better. He's always done that for his Tash.* No one—including Tashmi-sharrumma himself—had ever been able to say anything against Tash without Kurunta flying to the rescue. *That's real fidelity,* thought the king, tenderness warming him inside like a brazier of hot coals. "Your oath—do you still feel the same way?"

"Of course, man. Do you need to ask?"

"I just wonder lately how much oaths mean to people. You heard how all those men at the funeral banquet swore to support me, but I ask myself how many of them meant it. Look how many vassals didn't even show up. Nerikkaili— what must he think? Lurma-ziti—would he stand up for me?"

Kurunta shook his head affectionately. "Just like you to get all twisted up over something arcane like that. I'm afraid I can't answer your question. Ask what's-his-name, the priest of Arinniti."

"Tattamaru? He's my mother's votary."

Kurunta gave a snort of laughter. "If you plan to omit from your list of trusted councilors every man who is in love with your mother, you won't have many left."

"Perhaps only my wife," said the king, between sarcasm and seriousness. Then he brightened. "Oh, I have some wonderful news. I had almost forgotten to tell you. But don't say anything yet; there will be an official announcement at some point. Ellat-gula is expecting. Maybe a son this time, eh?"

Kurunta whooped with joy and embraced his cousin. "You sly dog! Been busy, have you?" The two men laughed happily in one another's arms.

Tashmi-sharrumma clung to Kurunta for a moment longer then drew away. "It's a good omen, right?" the king said, almost afraid to believe it.

"The best, Tash. Long life to you and your descendants, My Sun."

The king had a momentary vision of his late father, whose very long life had rendered him incontinent and bedridden at the end, mostly blind, and suffering from sores that never healed.

"Maybe not too long." Tashmi-sharrumma sighed, hoping the gods had heard.

"You'll be a great king like Uncle Hattushili; just you see."

"What does that mean exactly?" murmured Tashmi-sharrumma half to himself. The last of his joy drained out. That was a question that had been weighing on him heavily since he had been named *tuhkanti* nine years before, and in the last few weeks it had begun to crush him to the ground.

Kurunta looked up at him, his expression puzzled and a little amused. "What does what mean?"

"To be a great king."

"By the gods, Tash. Is this such a mystery? Like your father—lots of conquests, a power to be reckoned with among the other Great Kings. A strong ruler, respected—demanding respect—and successful. The defender of his people."

Tashmi-sharrumma gnawed his lip, reflecting, until Kurunta snorted with laughter. "Maybe you are slow after all. Doesn't seem like such a difficult concept."

"I don't know. You didn't mention any of the traditional virtues. Clemency, justice. I mean, the king is a man chosen by the gods to be their vicar, isn't he? Doesn't he owe them an effort at virtue?"

Kurunta eyed the king, his mouth trembling with suppressed laughter. He said only, "Yes, of course, O High Priest of all the Thousand Gods."

"I'm serious. Isn't that his first duty?" Tashmi-sharrumma shot a look at his cousin from the corner of his eye.

"His? Don't you mean yours?"

"Tudhaliya's. I still don't feel like that's me. But listen, Ulmi. How can the king defend his people if the gods abhor him? Virtue is his very first duty, or nothing else matters. It's got to be."

"I'm not the person to ask," said Kurunta with a grin. "I've got to say, pleasure attracts me more than virtue."

"But you're a good person. Kind. Faithful." The

king's gaze grew soft with affection, then he looked away, discomfited by the depth of his feeling.

There was a moment of friendly silence. Suppressed amusement making his voice juicy, Kurunta said, "Speaking of my virtue, do you remember that time we stole some chariot horses?"

The king, who remembered only too well, protested, his face burning with embarrassment. "Not exactly stole…"

"No, true. Just *borrowed*." Kurunta laughed richly, shook his head, and slapped his thighs, still seemingly tickled by the memory of everyone's consternation even after all these years. "What a coup! You were the last one anyone suspected!"

"Yes, well…" Tashmi-sharrumma grinned, but his face was burning. "They found out."

"Nobody whipped you. They knew I was the instigator. But that took some real daring, didn't it, Tash? Those stallions were real devils, and we were only—what, ten? Eleven? Well, I was."

His cousin looked down, his smile fading a little. "I'm afraid the grooms were punished. I felt bad about that."

Kurunta shrugged. Another silence fell, not so comfortable. The wind changed direction and sent their hair flying into their faces. The viceroy reached over and drew the brown strands out of the king's mouth then leaned toward him and kissed him on the lips. Tashmi-sharrumma jerked away, his heart pounding in confusion. He could feel heat flooding into his face.

"What's wrong?" asked Kurunta a little defiantly, his dark eyes fixed on Tashmi-sharrumma's.

"I just…" the king stammered, suddenly unable to swallow.

"Don't like me anymore?"

"No, Ulmi, of course not. There are just so many rules now." The king made a point not to look at Kurunta. After a moment he turned his head away altogether. He found breathing hard. A kind of panic was overtaking him. "I never know what I can… I spend half my time getting purified from something these days."

"You'll get all pruney, I suppose. Can't have that." Kurunta was grinning, but he didn't look happy. His dark, winged eyebrows were drawn down in annoyance. Tashmi-sharrumma threw him a quick, pleading glance but said nothing. He wanted to, but he couldn't. He was choking with some emotion that was strong, painful, and frightening. The two of them stood, not looking at one another, and a tinge of frost began to settle over them.

"So you think I'm going to pollute you, do you, Tash? I'm a king's son, too, you know. And virtuous besides." There was a definite hard edge to Kurunta's voice.

He's angry, the king thought helplessly. "I know. Of course not. It's just…"

"Just what, exactly?"

"I dare not offend the gods, Ulmi. I'm already…"

"Oh, offend the gods, eh? And why would they care? Why is a kiss worse than a hug? Or for that matter a blow?" Kurunta growled the last word, sounding increasingly angry.

Tashmi-sharrumma knew how temperamental his cousin could be. They needed to talk about their relationship, but anything he said would anger Kurunta. Impotent gloom descended over the king.

"I... I..."

"Just stop, Tash. I don't want to hear any more lies."

All my relatives have such quick tempers, thought the king helplessly. Dear gods, even his father. He remembered the aftermath of the horse-stealing episode. True, he had not been whipped physically, but his father—his father, the Great King, whom he so seldom saw, whose love he craved like life itself—had flayed him with words: *stupid, unworthy, dangerous, endangering others. Are you going to let someone else tell you what to do when your own conscience protests?* The little prince had wanted to cry, "Father, don't be mad. I'm only seven," but he hadn't. The sole way he knew to disarm the anger of others was by staying silent, letting the arrows fall into the water. He hoped now that Kurunta's fit of pique would pass quickly if he said nothing. It always had before.

After a long moment of excruciating discomfort, the viceroy of Tarhuntassha strode to the trap and climbed in silence down the ladder, his cloak of wolf fur billowing. Finally, his black head disappeared. The king remained alone in the chill wind, sucking unhappily on his teeth.

"My Sun!"

Tashmi-sharrumma looked up, the hair that had torn itself loose from within his upturned furs lashing his face. His heart lifted with the momentary hope that Kurunta had returned. But it was not his cousin. Hope faded. Instead, the king's secretary, Tarhun-miya, trotted toward him along the roof, his skirts and cloak snapping in the wind. "The

Lords of Hatti are seeking My Sun. They say you called them to a meeting, yet you're nowhere in sight."

"Tell them I'm coming."

The king abandoned his somber thoughts and followed his secretary down the ladder.

The council room was dark, shutters and hangings drawn against the cold. The lamps were lit in broad daylight. His eyes still dazzled from the snow, the king paused for a moment before his sight gelled, hearing rather than seeing the chairs scraping back as the assembled men rose. Nerikkaili was there with his big shoulders, big belly, big jaw. He was so big he seemed to suck the air out of the space. Hishni was there in his white uniform, a patch of snow in the lamp-lit darkness. Lurma-ziti, the hunchback, was there with his black eyes that missed nothing. They were mature men, old enough to have been the king's father. Of his full brothers, Tashmi-sharrumma saw Huzziya and Shanda-kurunta, slim youths who were both governors of border districts. Walwa-ziti, the chief of scribes, was there, and Alalimmi, a cousin, a field marshal in the Upper Land. Also Ini-tesshub—the viceroy of Karkemish, with his iron-gray hair and lugubrious face—and Tattamaru, some kind of relative by marriage on the king's maternal side, Great Shepherd of Arinniti and chief of the heavy-armed guards. Tattamaru's two brothers were with him; Tashmi-sharrumma didn't remember their names. They had all sworn their loyalty to him.

The king's gaze sought one face above the others: his cousin's. And there Kurunta stood, in the second row of the Lords of Hatti among the viceroys and diplomats. He was too far away and too much in the shadows for Tashmi-sharrumma to make out his expression with precision, but there was a smile across his face; that much was clear. His anger had passed. A great load of anxiety lifted from Tashmi-sharrumma's chest and flew away. *The one person I can trust among all these*, thought the young king, his heart thawing with relief. Kurunta, the only one who genuinely wished him well—except for the *tawananna*, who stood beside his throne. *If I can trust her.*

The king dropped into his chair. "Be seated, my brothers."

Chairs scraped and rumbled as they took him at his word. The secretaries stood around the edges of the hall, ready to record upon their waxed wooden tablets anything the councilors might say.

Nerikkaili stepped forward first, as was his right. "My Sun, the gravest issue confronting you is the rising of the Assyrians. Ini-tesshub can attest to that."

The gray-haired viceroy of the East nodded grimly, his long face more funereal than usual. "They're up to no good, My Sun. There's activity along their border with Hanigalbat and also in the mountains to the north. The Forty Kings of Nairi Land have declined so far to cooperate, but if they decide to change their policy, we'll lose our access to the copper and silver in the Red Mountains. And the quickest path directly into our heartland will be exposed."

"But," Nerikkaili interrupted, "Hanigalbat is the more immediate problem. King Shattuara seems to be wavering."

"Not still determined to break loose from his masters?" asked the king.

"We can't tell, My Sun." Old Nuwanza's voice was shaky with age, but his opinions were as forceful as ever.

He had been field marshal under three kings. "He changes his story with every communiqué. He says he's like a man who owes money to two creditors—he has to pay off the more threatening one first. He wants us to come fight for him, but he fears that if we fail, the Assyrians will wipe his puppet kingdom from the black earth. And by the thousand gods, he's right."

"That would be quite an insertion into the internal affairs of a sovereign state, My Sun. One could hardly blame Tukulti-ninurta for viewing us with a jaundiced eye if we were to do so," said the vizier Walwa-ziti, who was the *tawananna's* man. That had to be her position, realized the king. "The only thing that can save Hanigalbat is a diversion to their south. Turn Assyria's attention to Karduniash."

"We have a treaty with Karduniash, just as we do with Shattuara."

His mother spoke out, one lone treble voice among the grumble of men. "It was expedient at the time, My Sun, but now things have changed. If the Assyrians can be distracted by designs on their southern neighbor, they'll not be likely to take over Hanigalbat."

"For the moment."

"Karduniash is formidable. It will consume much gold and many men to bring down. Once they've conquered it, they'll have to work to keep it. It won't be the distraction of a moment only. The best policy for us is to foment disagreement between the two Kingdoms of the Rivers."

She would not easily let go, Tashmi-sharrumma saw. "Abandon our allies? Throw them to the wolves to save ourselves?" The king knew he was echoing the phrase of Ellat-gula.

Ini-tesshub said, "If Hanigalbat falls, My Sun, there is no longer any buffer between Assyria and the easternmost provinces of our empire. Karkemish itself is right on the banks of the Puruna"

"Is a treaty sworn in the presence of the Oath Gods worth nothing, then?" the king asked calmly, as if he really wanted to know a juridical fact. But he was thinking, *How much does the loyalty oath these men swore only a fortnight ago mean to them?*

The *tawananna* spoke to him in the tone of a teacher, looking with patient, smiling affection right at him, and not at the assembled Lords of Hatti. "The welfare of the kingdom of Hatti is the most important thing of all, My Sun. We must let the Babylonians take care of themselves."

As if he had not been privy to the political discussions of his father for nine years. As if he had any doubt about what was most important. *But the only way to make the kingdom secure is to win the gods' favor.* He could not renege on oaths and be a king blessed by the gods.

He stared at his mother, careful not to reveal his feelings. Let the assembly interpret his expression as they would.

He saw her smile deepening and growing intimate. *I know what you are thinking*, it said. *I know you'll understand that my advice is always best.*

He looked up, still impassive. "What else, my lords?"

Alalimmi rose. He wasn't very tall but had the broad shoulders, corded neck, and potent chest of a bull. His eyes were a little squinted, as if staring into the sun on the battlefield for forty years had permanently marked him.

For a man of his size, he had an unexpectedly high-pitched voice, which earned him the friendly taunts of his peers.

"There's a rumor that Prince Urhi-tesshub is plotting again, My Sun—that with the death of the late king, he has chosen to come back to Hatti Land. And that he may once more be seeking the aid of Assyria—or Karduniash—to return him to the throne."

Karduniash in league with Urhi-tesshub again? There had been whispers to that effect when Hattushili was newly consecrated, but now… If Ellat-gula's brother was interested in overthrowing Tashmi-sharrumma, what were her own thoughts on the matter? Urhi-tesshub on the throne would mean the end of her ambitions.

A buzz of murmurs and even curses greeted this bit of gossip. Kurunta's voice cut through the babble—"I know nothing of this Babylonian business, My Sun"—and the implication was dismissal. If it had been true, he would have known of it. Urhi-tesshub was his brother, after all.

The king nodded, relieved. He could feel tension abandoning his body and realized how unnerved he had been by the magnitude of the problems facing him.

"But," Kurunta added in a lower voice, "he's been spotted in Kizzuwatna."

There was an immediate reaction among the Lords of Hatti—a few *aha*s and more than a few snarls.

"I'd like to think anyone who sees him would turn him in, but it's been thirty years. He must have changed," said Nerikkaili, who knew his cousin as well as anyone.

Kurunta nodded. "I'm his own brother, and I've never actually seen him except from afar. I know *I* wouldn't recognize him. It'll be easy enough for him to hide."

"Let's assume Urhi-tesshub is always plotting," said the king. "Keep your ears open."

They talked about many things—the problems that faced the empire were without end. The West was restless. The crops were poor. There was an earthquake in the northwest. A bridge was out in Shanahuitta.

Finally, the briefing was over. The king called out to his brother Hishni, who was moving toward the door in company with Lurma-ziti. "A word with you, brother."

Hishni was a stolid, soldierly type, with a neck wider than his lantern-jawed face, and had begun to grow a little jowly. He had been unkind to the king in his childhood, but not with any particular malice. He had just been the henchman of Lurma-ziti, who had had malice enough for two. Tashmi-sharrumma had made an effort to show he held no grudge.

"My Sun." Hishni turned and approached, as respectful as if there were no history between him and the king.

"I want you to be the chief of my *meshedi* guard, Hishni."

The older man bowed. This post had been Tashmi-sharrumma's under their father, and Hattushili's before that under the reign of his brother Muwatalli. Assigning it to Hishni was a sign of the king's absolute trust in him. "My Sun does me too much honor."

"You'll swear your oath tomorrow. Then you can begin to recruit and take your place in the barracks." The king smiled his dry, fanged smile. "Your wife may not be happy."

"She'll welcome the favor of the king, My Sun, whatever her personal inconvenience. Thank you for your confidence."

"Be worthy, my brother."

Tashmi-sharrumma snapped his fingers for Pirwannu, the valet, who approached with the fur cloak he had been holding and slid it over his master's shoulders. The *tawananna* directed her brisk steps toward the king, but he turned his back and pretended not to see her. He did not want to talk to her until he had had time to think about the game she was playing. Kurunta was nowhere in sight. The other men were departing from the audience hall into the blinding whiteness of a winter day, and the king, too, made his way into the cold afternoon.

CHAPTER 3

S PRING HAD SPREAD ITS FRAGILE beauty over the harsh highland plains. Briefly, the gray rock was frosted with green, despite the lack of rain. The apple blossoms were appearing on the trees like frothy snow melting in the orchards, but the pasturage was yet thin. The flocks would go hungry unless the Storm God should relent and empty his clouds soon. Weeks had passed since the equinox, New Year's Day, and the temperature was climbing. Yet still it did not rain. The Keepers of the Royal Storehouse had met with the king and warned him that if the crops should fail again, there would be a famine. Tashmi-sharrumma had written to the Great King of Mizri and begged—as proudly as possible, but begged, nonetheless—to buy grain from that land of riches. There the river rose to water the fields. No one had to wait on the good pleasure of an angry Storm God.

The king, who had been a priest of Sharrumma, the Storm God of Nerik, since his youth, wondered what he had done wrong. The sowing festival of Purulli had been carried out with scrupulous care. The people had been able to celebrate one last carefree spring, with acrobats and actors, roast lamb and *walhi* drink in abundance, all at the king's expense. Perhaps they hadn't even realized that they were barely skirting starvation. He considered taking an oracle but dreaded what it would reveal. The wrath of the gods had already begun to fall on him.

Tashmi-sharrumma climbed down the ladder, which creaked under his weight. The council hall was empty, dark, cool, and smelled of damp stone. There was no sound but the click of his shoes upon the flagging, and he passed into the courtyard, where scribes and servants busily crossed back and forth. When they realized it was their king who had come among them, they knelt hastily. He heard "Hail, My Sun" here and there but walked on. He had cultivated a long stride with downcast eyes, a posture that suggested, *Pay no attention to me; go on about your business.* But no one wanted to be the first to rise until he had gone away.

In the door that led to the royal apartments, he encountered his mother. She was pale, her lips grim. Her eyes fixed upon his almost accusingly. Without so much as a greeting, she said, "Shattuara has risen against Assyria."

"We knew this was coming." But anxiety tightened his stomach, perhaps as much in anticipation of standing up against his mother as standing up against the Assyrians.

"He pleads for our aid. What shall we tell him?"

"We'll come," said the king.

"Tashmi-sharrumma, this is foolish, and you know it. If you had encouraged Shulmanu-asharedu to think he could attack Karduniash with impunity, he would have let Hanigalbat go."

"We have a treaty to defend Shattuara, my mother. And

also the king of Karduniash. You yourself drew it up fifteen years ago." The king realized he had made this same point over and over, but his mother was not about to yield. He licked his teeth, smoothing out the ripple of irritation that passed under his skin.

"Here's where your inexperience shows, son. Things have changed. Karduniash and its king are no longer our real friends. Whereas we need Hanigalbat as a buffer—"

"And so we'll defend it."

"And so we *should* have deflected the Assyrians' designs on it by discreetly offering them Karduniash instead. They can only attack so many fronts at once. If you would ever just listen to anyone—"

"To you, you mean?" he said in a carefully neutral tone.

She was becoming angry now, her cheeks burning like bright coals, her dark eyes lit with self-righteousness. She was like a statue of Shaushga, goddess of love and war, whose priestess she was. He comprehended why the entire court was under her spell.

"Yes. To me. To the *tawananna*. To forty years of experience at the side of your father, who was a great statesman."

"If a king's untrue to his word, what will befall his lands, Mother? Who will trust his oath?" He wanted to say, *It is you who have taught me this, you who have made me understand how the gods honor uprightness. Why are you changing now?* He wanted to say, *Remember what happened to my great-grandfather Shuppiluliuma after the Egyptians killed his son. He put them to death, broke his treaty with Mizri, and invaded their vassals. What mortal wouldn't have felt the desire for vengeance? And even so, the gods struck him and his* tuhkanti *down with plague, which ravaged Hatti Land for twenty years.*

But he remained calm, sinking into that imperturbability that was his defense against someone else's anger. He was not an agile fencer with words, like the *tawananna*, but he could swallow her anger as the water swallows fire. He simply would not ignite.

"Then you have a war on your hands, my son. A war that could have been avoided. And an army must be fed. It will take men from the fields, too. You're making a bad situation worse."

He said neutrally, "The results will tell us whether it has been a bad decision, my mother. Let the Gulshesh grant victory where they will."

She compressed her lips, exasperated, and turned away from the king, staring at the wall. He watched her and thought how dangerous her beauty made her. How quick people were to forgive the beautiful, how quick to condemn the plain.

After a moment, during which she sought to compose herself, the *tawananna* took her son's hands and said more kindly, in that rich, confidential voice she used to such artistic ends, "My sweet child, don't think you need to rely only on yourself. Even kings must have advisors. You know I mean you only good, as I ever have. Don't feel you have to turn away from me now or be less of a man." She pressed his ringed knuckles to her lips and stroked his breast as if to pacify an animal.

He stared down at the top of her veiled head with its pointed miter.

"Why was this communiqué not brought to me first, Mother?"

She looked up at him, hardened again, and said defensively, "No one knew where you were, My Sun."

No, he agreed in silence, not altogether happy about it yet unwilling to change. *I am well concealed.*

Four weeks had passed—the time it took to move an army from one border to another across the formidable Red Mountains. Another plain now stretched out below the king's gaze. A river forked across the dry red earth freckled with spring flowers that had not heard about the drought that seemed to afflict the entire world. A walled city huddled against the bank of the easternmost branch: Taite, the capital of Hanigalbat. At its feet, the sprawling army of Assyria spread like a bloodstain. Those with better eyes than his own told Tashmi-sharrumma that there were tens of thousands of soldiers, chariots, and horses encamped below. Vultures were already hanging in the sky overhead like spiraling motes in an unfiltered beer that has been stirred. Having feasted upon the victims of the siege, they now awaited the banquet that this confrontation of two great powers would prepare for them. Farther away, smoke rose from other towns already taken and torched: Amashaku, Shadikanni, holy Kahat.

The Hittite army hunkered in the foothills overlooking the heartland of old Hurri, now the Assyrian vassal state of Hanigalbat. Tashmi-sharrumma had come to honor his treaty with Shattuara, its rebel king. But it was spring— many of the men he called up had been unable to leave their lands at sowing time, or else the kingdom would have starved. Of his vassals in the West, few had deigned to join him, pleading one or another excuse. He wasn't so fatuous as to believe them. Their absence was a protest against his illegitimacy, and the king suspected this was a reflection of Urhi-tesshub's return to the borders of Hatti Land. Dissension was brewing now that the deposed king had reappeared to offer the disaffected a rallying point.

But that problem was not what preoccupied the Great King at the moment. He was calm and concentrating on what he would face in a matter of hours—the counter-siege of Taite.

He felt at home on the battlefield, the dancing ground of the Lord Wurukatte. The weight of bronze scale armor on his shoulders, the heft of a battle-ax in his hand, the smell of an encampment of thousands of men and horses—these were familiar to him since his first campaign at the age of twelve. Here a man was not judged by his fluency in words but by his deeds. The king wasn't much of an archer—his eyes weren't keen enough—but with a sword or an ax, he was an effective warrior.

Except now his advisors had warned him that his days in the press of battle were over. They could not risk the death—or worse, the capture—of the sovereign. So, resigned if not happy, he would wait up there in his chariot, directing things, while his brothers and cousins led their troops into the fray, encircling the Assyrian besiegers, setting free Shattuara and his badly outnumbered men. It would be the first time the king's youngest brother Hannutti would take part in a battle.

May Ishtushtaya and Papaya, the Ladies of Destiny,

66

guard him, thought Tashmi-sharrumma, remembering the exaltation and terror that had blazed within him in his own first battle.

"My Sun, the troops of Sheha River Land have arrived," said old Nuwanza at the king's elbow. He and Lurma-ziti would remain with the king during the battle—Nuwanza was too aged to fight, and Lurma-ziti was too sickly—but they were clever at strategy. Lurma-ziti, arms crossed, sucked his yellow teeth and watched the Assyrians below, wordless. The king had made a point of treating his brother with respect. Of all his familial histories, the past he shared with the hunchback was the most poisonous.

Alalimmi spat on the ground. "Let's hope some more of those godforsaken Western vassals show up. We don't have enough troops otherwise. Alantalli of Mira only sent fifty men, the dog turd. What an insult! And he didn't even come with them. It's going to be touch and go."

The priest Tattamaru also stood among the royal officers. In addition to his other titles, he was commander of the left wing. He appraised the sun, which was still low but might be in the Hittites' eyes by later in the morning.

Nerikkaili was absent. As *tuhkanti*, he would never take part in the same battle as the king. Tashmi-sharrumma's brother and the *tawananna* would watch over the kingdom from Hattusha as they had done for many years while Hattushili had been on campaign and the king himself had still been young. Tashmi-sharrumma thought uneasily of his pregnant wife back at home and wondered how many of her suspicions of her mother-in-law were true. For sure, the willingness to throw the treaty with Karduniash to the winds had proved to be a fact. He prayed Ellat-gula was safe. Perhaps she had already gone to the summer palace in Shapinuwa. For once, he hoped her mother and cousin would stay beside her.

"Then we'll have to fight all the more valiantly." Kurunta was full of cheerful bravado, as usual. He was at the king's side, of course, and had brought seven thousand troops with him from Tarhuntassha, despite the pressures of sowing season and the exemption granted him by the former king.

"I'd rather have more men and less need of desperate bravery," said Ini-tesshub, lugubrious as ever. But Tashmi-sharrumma knew this cousin would acquit himself impeccably, for if anyone had reason to want to see the Assyrians stopped, it was he, the viceroy at Karkemish, the easternmost border of Hatti Land.

"How late can we wait to see who's coming?" the king asked.

"Not much more, My Sun," Tattamaru replied. "The light will be in our eyes if we delay much longer. I counsel an immediate advance. Let's hope our downhill momentum gives us the edge."

Surprise would be an even better advantage. "Do they know we're here?"

Alalimmi nodded. "They had horsemen out earlier, scouting the foothills. They know something's going on. Some of the locals have probably reported our movements."

"Then set up your flagmen, Lurma-ziti, and the rest of you, get going. May Wurukatte watch over you."

The officers saluted their king and strode away. Whistles, shouts, and finally the sound of drums signaled that the army was mobilizing.

"If there's a change in formation, watch for the flags," Nuwanza called after the officers in his tremulous voice.

The king heard the noise of the vast horde swinging into action—the clatter and neigh of horses, the creaking of harness, bronze-shod chariot wheels rumbling over the stony earth, raised voices, and the pounding of feet. Drums and flutes struck the cadence. There was nothing like it to send a shiver of fear and exhilaration up a man's back, Tashmi-sharrumma thought, his heart stepping up a beat. It was like the moment when the musicians all picked up the tone of the middle string—the one they called *Ea-its-creator*—and it passed from instrument to instrument. Nothing could stop them now. The action had begun and had taken on a life of its own. The spindle of the Gulshesh had begun to twirl, their thread stretched out across the plain. *Where will we all be when it's cut?*

It took nearly half the morning for the vanguard of the Hittite troops to appear on the plain below. They flowed downhill like a white-clad tide. Below, the Assyrian besiegers clustered around the walls of Taite. Tashmi-sharrumma squinted against the sun, his breath coming fast with the exquisite tension of anticipation. He knew the chariot forces would make the first attack, and the massive three-man war chariots of Hatti Land were fearsome. Before the opposing chariots could even get into position, they could smash a camp or an infantry line.

From here, upwind, the vehicles were almost silent. The war cries and the rumbling of the wheels as the chariots picked up speed were reduced to a distant rumor. There were few chariots to oppose, since the Assyrians were gathered for a siege, with foot troops, war machines, sappers, and torches. Their camp was surrounded by leather-covered hurdles, yet those would go down like wheat before the harvesters when the line of galloping horses hit them.

But near Taite, the tide of chariotry seemed to break and stagger. Uneasiness fluttered in the king's heart, not yet quite dread.

"The ground must be uneven," muttered Lurma-ziti, his mouth fixed in its permanent downward crescent. "The charge is slowing down."

The infantry caught up, the foaming white of a cataract. It swirled around the darker red and brown of the Assyrian troops. Tashmi-sharrumma saw tiny blooms of color, which were the banners of his vassal states. Bronze weapons sparkled under the sun. The colors and the white merged, surged, shifted. Danced backward and forward. The king thought he could just hear the distant cries of the wounded. Some distance away, another body of white seemed to hold itself in readiness.

"Signal the men of Tarhuntassha to attack," said the king in a level voice. But his knuckles upon the chariot rail were blanched with tension.

Lurma-ziti yelled at his flagmen, and they passed their signal. Below, the waiting troops, seven thousand strong, surged forward at what seemed from here to be a funereal pace. But soon they, too, had joined the melee, Kurunta leading them. If anyone could save the battle, it was Tashmi-sharrumma's valiant cousin. Still, the onslaught had less impact than he had hoped. The colored uniforms seemed to be as numerous as before, the white less so. Much white seemed spread upon the earth. For the first time, something close to fear snaked though the king's belly. Kurunta was not immortal.

Suddenly, there was a flurry of action along the wall. A few of the city's defenders sallied from one of the posterns. But instead of attacking the Assyrians, they made a dash for it. One chariot streaked away, rocking and bobbing, into the foothills, while the others covered its retreat, sacrificing themselves. Red and brown uniforms closed over them.

"Shattuara is escaping, the cowardly dog!" snarled Nuwanza. "He begs us to come and fight with him, and while we try to save his kingdom, he sneaks away."

"Fight *for* him, you mean." Lurma-ziti's contempt was so thick a sword could cut it. He spat on the ground.

The king watched, his stomach sinking like lead, as his troops were cut down and down. It had only taken half the day. His hope of a quick victory had evaporated like mist as the sun rises. At last, he said without much expression, "Call off the men. Tell Alalimmi to request a meeting with their commander. We'll negotiate a surrender."

Tashmi-sharrumma's defeated army had limped back to Karkemish. There was not much joy among the Lords of Hatti. Shattuara had played them for fools, and Shulmanu-asharedu's troops had humiliated them. A spring storm had broken over their heads as they dragged west, drenching the men and horses. They looked as dispirited and beaten as they felt, crawling back into their own territory across the River Puruna. The Assyrians had swallowed Hanigalbat whole. They were now direct neighbors of Hatti's easternmost provinces.

The cold, licking flames of fury raging within, the king longed to shut himself up and brood. He was furious with himself, with his disloyal vassals, and with the famine that lay upon his land and demanded that the civilian levy stay home and sow or die. He was furious with his mother, who was right and would gloat and say, *See? You need my advice, my son.* He was furious because he was still clean and fresh as his filthy, exhausted, blood-streaked men pulled themselves back up the hill to confront him. His brother Huzziya had had an arm broken by an ax blow, blood running down his sleeve. And little Hannutti's first battle had been a rout.

But he couldn't endure what anger did to him, how it twisted his stomach and made his temples pound. It pushed him to words he would rather not have said, deeds he would rather not have had on his conscience. He willed it to become mild, like a dog brought to heel. He forced himself to grow calm, wiped fear and shame from his face, and walked among his men tranquilly, praising their courage, allotting them extra rations.

Only in the presence of Kurunta did he permit himself to reveal the depth of his frustration. They were standing in Ini-tesshub's throne room, which was now empty and dark. The king ground his teeth. "I don't understand, Ulmi. The oracles gave us the victory. How can we be punished for keeping to our oaths?"

Kurunta heaved a sigh of resignation. He put a supportive arm around his cousin's shoulder and squeezed. "You're the priest, Tash. I don't know why the gods do what they do. All I know is we were outnumbered, and the terrain turned out to be a lot more uneven than we could see from the hilltop. It doesn't mean you've done anything wrong."

"When I saw how few we were going to be, I should have called off the attack," the king said. "It would still have let the Assyrians know we were watching them and perhaps would have scared them. Maybe that would have been enough."

"Well, look at all these rings." Kurunta took his cousin's hand, changing the subject with transparent abruptness. "Since when have you started wearing rings?"

"Since Pirwannu started putting them on my fingers." The king sighed, forcing himself to set aside his gloom and relax his jaw.

"This is your royal seal, eh?" Kurunta singled out the knuckle where a heavy gold signet weighted the king's finger. "That means *Great King*, I think. And these things—that's your name? I should have paid more attention to our tutor, eh, Tash?"

Tashmi-sharrumma managed a smile. His cousin had never had the patience for studies. The king, on the other hand, had plugged zealously away at reading and writing until his mother had forced him to stop, saying it would ruin his already defective eyesight. He loved the idea of speaking to someone through tiny symbols and not face-to-face. He thought that he would happily have been a scribe.

Kurunta, apparently seeing that his efforts to cajole the king out of his funk were bearing fruit, grinned. "Luckily, my name is just written with a picture of an antler, eh? Even I can learn that." He caressed Tashmi-sharrumma's hand lightly before restoring it to him, and the king's dejection began to cool into fatalism.

But Tashmi-sharrumma couldn't long ignore the serious present. To the east, the Assyrians were stripping the treasures from the cities of Hanigalbat and slaughtering its people or marching them away into slavery. Perhaps tomorrow it would be his own subjects in Karkemish or Halep. Day after tomorrow, maybe Nesha and then Hattusha itself. The Forty Kings of Nairi Land were almost all that stood between Hatti and what was now Assyria. "Our cousin Ehli-sharrumma rules Ishuwa, in the mountains north of Nairi Land. Do you think he can be trusted to hold the line if the Assyrians start to move on Nairi and the Forty Kings go over?"

Ehli-sharrumma had been loud in his disgust at Taite, the king remembered, and loud in his blame of Tashmi-sharrumma's generalship.

Kurunta seemed to know where the king's thoughts had taken him. He said sarcastically, "What's he got to complain about? If he'd brought more troops, maybe things would've gone differently."

A discreet cough made the men look up. Tarhun-miya, the king's secretary, stood in the doorway. With his retreating hair, sloping forehead, weak chin, and long, pointed nose, he had the profile of a woodpecker. But he was a skillful and intelligent scribe who knew just when to speak and when to be silent.

"My Sun," he called out. "Your uncle, the king of Sheha River Land, is looking for you. Will you see him, or shall I tell him to wait?"

"Send him over," said the king.

Kurunta murmured, "Should I go?"

"No, no. He'll want to see you, too."

Mashturi of Sheha River Land was one of the very few Western vassals whom the king could trust. He was

Kurunta and Tashmi-sharrumma's uncle by marriage. But he had no children. Tashmi-sharrumma dreaded the day when he would have to appoint another to shepherd the gods' people on the shores of the Western Sea. It would be too easy for such a man to find in the Ahhiyawans a more powerful protector than some Great King far away in the interior.

Mashturi appeared in the doorway, a barrel-shaped old man whose gait was no longer steady and whose hair was sparse on his shoulders. His homely old face split into a grin. "My Sun!" he cried. "I am here to swear my loyalty oath." Mashturi attempted to kneel, but Tashmi-sharrumma prevented him.

"In good time, uncle. You've already demonstrated your loyalty by heeding the call for troops. Let's sit down."

He led the old vassal to the dais, where the two of them seated themselves on the edge, below Ini-tesshub's throne.

Kurunta followed them, smiling. "Uncle, you're in fine shape for your age." He looked around for a place to sit beside them. "Am I meant to sit on the throne, then?" he joked.

A chill ran up Tashmi-sharrumma's neck, but he said casually, "There's room beside me, cousin, as always." He scooted to the side, and his cousin settled himself hip to hip with the king.

"Look, son, don't take that defeat too hard. No king wins every battle," Mashturi said.

"Of course not," said Tashmi-sharrumma smoothly, but he could feel the heat of mortification in his cheeks. "How is Aunt Masshanauzzi?"

"Well enough." The king's uncle shrugged, his eyes,

filmy with age, not optimistic. "She's old. What can I say? Little things start going wrong, same with all of us. But nothing big. We're doing all right. The crops don't look promising, though."

"No," Tashmi-sharrumma agreed, his lids lowered. The fear of famine haunted him. Hatti Land was rocky, suitable only for sheep, the weather harsh. It depended for its life upon the success of its vassals' harvests. "Thank you for coming all this way. You're the one man I can always count on." He turned a little and smiled back over his shoulder at Kurunta.

"But of course you can count on me, son. I was your father's most enthusiastic supporter back in our day. I'll follow his boy wherever he leads; you know that."

A somber shadow darkened the king's gratitude for a moment. He had to speak of what was gnawing at him, if only to clarify his own thinking, but he wasn't sure just how to approach it.

"Uncle... you'd sworn your oath to Urhi-tesshub, had you not?"

The old man looked a little wary but thrust out his chin, not ashamed. "No, never did. He was only the son of a second-rank wife—begging your pardon, Ulmi-tesshub. There was no reason he should've come to the throne when Muwatalli's own brother, born of a queen, was alive. To me, your father was clearly the legitimate heir, Tashmi-sharrumma. And I wasn't the only one who felt that way."

"But didn't Muwatalli specifically appoint his son as *tuhkanti*? How did you and the others get around that?"

"There are laws, son. A king can say whatever he wants, but that's the beauty of Hatti Land—we have laws. First-rank sons, if there are any, take precedence over second-rank sons. Sons of a concubine can never be king. Simple enough."

"My father wasn't even the oldest brother of Muwatalli."

"No, but he was the best by far. And who cares whether he was older? Hattushili may've been the youngest, but he was plenty smart, an impressive general. You couldn't stop him. Despite his health problems, he just kept coming, no matter what. He was a great king."

Clearly the most ambitious of the brothers, at least. But Mashturi was right; there were no laws saying the eldest son had to be the heir. There had been some rule to that effect long ago, but in fact, the eldest was not always the best, and that counted for something. A king should have the right to pick his own heir. Tashmi-sharrumma chewed thoughtfully on his uncle's words, wishing he could see Kurunta's face. As far as the king was aware, his cousin wasn't sensitive about being second rank. *I would know if he were.*

"Mashturi, all I have is daughters. What if I were to die before having a son by my queen? My heir is Nerikkaili. He's second rank. Would you accept that?"

The old man purses his wrinkled lips in thought. "If there weren't anybody else, I guess so, son. Why?"

"Because it seems to me," said the king slowly, formulating his thoughts as he spoke, "that a vassal should accept his suzerain's choice of heir without weighing it. If Muwatalli said Urhi-tesshub was his *tuhkanti*, you should have fought for him, against… against my father."

Mashturi's woolly eyebrows flew up in astonishment. "But he might not have become king if I hadn't supported him. And Urhi-tesshub wasn't a good king, believe me.

He made a lot of mistakes. He was too quick to reward his friends, and he was vicious to your father, after all Hattushili had done for him. Urhi-tesshub forced him to rebel, Tashmi-sharrumma. You're too young to remember what it was like."

That much was true; the king had only been five at the time. But the picture of Mashturi's loyalty was becoming clear. He supported the man he believed to be the best, legitimate or not. And then he was loyal to that man's descendants... until... unless...

At least he had been honest enough not to swear to Urhi-tesshub. When the time had come to decide, lots of people who had done that still sided with Hattushili—the capable middle-aged uncle with a lifetime of favors to call in.

"He was consecrated," the king said. "The gods had accepted if not chosen him—Urhi-tesshub, that is. Murshili son of Muwatalli." That was the throne name of Urhi-tesshub, which was never to be spoken. After a moment, he added, as if to himself, "My father was not the legitimate king. He was a usurper."

Behind him, Kurunta hissed in warning, "By the gods, Tash!"

Mashturi's kindly old face grew red and stern but with the benevolent wrath of the parent of a slow child. "They fought it out, son—judicial combat. Hattushili won fair and square. Whatever the gods accepted at first, they spoke loud and clear on the battlefield."

Tashmi-sharrumma started to contradict him but felt his cousin's hand clamp upon his shoulder.

"Thank you for your honesty, my uncle," the king said

instead, smiling at Mashturi, hoping to soften the old man's outrage. "My secretary will bring you the text of the oath soon, and you can swear it before those Lords of Hatti who are here."

The old man struggled to rise, and the king helped him up. Tashmi-sharrumma saw from Mashturi's good, open face that he was not offended. Mashturi bent and kissed his sovereign's hand and started to back out, suddenly formal, but Tashmi-sharrumma waved him on with a friendly brush of the hand.

When he had gone, Kurunta let out a huge breath. "Tarhunta have mercy, Tash; you were talking to a vassal like that! Your father wasn't legitimate? What's gotten into you, man?"

Tashmi-sharrumma knew very well he had said too much. He should have hashed all this out in his own heart, not in front of his uncle. Disgusted with himself, he murmured, "You're right."

But Kurunta took him by the shoulders, adding more kindly, "You're really obsessed with this legitimacy, aren't you? Tash, stop thinking about it. Don't think so much. That's for people on the outside wanting in. Here you are, on the inside. Just be the king, all right?"

Tashmi-sharrumma nodded then raised his gaze. He and his cousin were of a height. They looked into one another's eyes.

"Don't think so much, eh?" Kurunta repeated gently, a mischievous grin twitching at the corners of his mouth. "You know, I love your mother, but she really made a mistake when she had you trained as a priest."

The king smiled, as he was intended to, but could think

of nothing to say. He looked past the other man into space and let his breath out slowly through his nose.

Kurunta said, "That business at Taite really got to you, didn't it? Listen, in a few years, after you've done all sorts of good things for the kingdom and won a lot of battles, no one will even remember this. You'll be a wonderful ruler."

Tashmi-sharrumma sighed and brought back his gaze. "Perhaps." And then he said, "You heard what Mashturi said about judicial combat."

"Look, I don't think the Assyrians figure into the minds of the Gulshesh. Nobody, least of all the thousand gods of Hatti, think you were less deserving of victory than Shulmanu-asharedu and his sheep fuckers, or somehow less legitimate. Just get this affair out of your mind. You were outmanned and hit uneven terrain that derailed a chariot charge. There's no message here, all right?"

"All right," said the king. But he didn't believe it for a moment.

CHAPTER 4

S UMMER HAD SET IN WITH all the desiccated fury
foreshadowed by the waterless spring. The air hung
in a shimmering curtain over the mountain fastness
of Hattusha, heat radiating from the dark stone. The citadel
seemed altogether too close to the sun, as if it had been held
up as a burnt offering to the Lady of Arinna. The courts
were blistering. The chambers, with their small windows
built to keep out winter's cold, sweltered breathlessly.

The queen was lying in, shut miserably into a dark,
airless room occupied by generations of parturient queens
before her. It was fetid with the smell of her sweat and that
of her handmaids, midwives, and the Babylonian doctor
her brother had sent. The smoke of propitiatory herbs had
fogged the upper corners of the room and made the eyes
water. Perpetual chanting rumbled from the Babylonian
Gula priests beside her bed, and a group of Old Women
beat softly on a little drum, punctuating their prayers
with grunts that imitated the pushing of childbirth. Lady
Patiya, the queen's mother, murmured to her soothingly in
Akkadian and wiped her brow with a cloth soaked in cool

water. From time to time, the *tawananna*, who was chief midwife for the royal children, had to shove her and the other foreign ladies aside to carry out her business. Tempers had grown short more than once.

Outside, in the women's court, Ellat-gula's husband paced, looking very large and very lost among the scurrying Babylonians. The *tawananna* stepped to the door and breathed the open air greedily. She had done all she could as midwife until the gods decreed it was time for the child to come out. She saw the king dragging himself back and forth, picking at his cuticles, and called out, "Not yet, my son. You can relax for a while. She's had a few contractions but isn't yet in labor."

He looked up with his heavy-lidded, blank expression that masked anxiety, his long face glistening with perspiration. "Everything going well, then?"

Puduhepa wiped her hands on her smock, beckoned him into the shade, and pursed her lips at him so that he had to stoop to let himself be kissed. She patted his arm. "Yes, fine. You already have three children, my dear. This one will be no different."

But this one, the first born to him as king, was his omen, she knew.

He can be very religious sometimes, she thought with an inward sigh. That was the way she had brought him up, but—although, as a priestess, she should not admit it—his piety had become burdensome. His whole childhood had been spent during the big reform of cult she and her late husband had undertaken as a part of their effort to buy the favor of the gods for a usurper. Their eldest son had taken it all in so earnestly; he had been an earnest child in every way. He probably would have been happier as a simple priest.

The king was still staring at his wife's door. Puduhepa gazed at him tenderly. Always a good, docile boy. But he was taking kingship too seriously and seemed to have little joy in it. She hoped he would find equanimity. If Ellat-gula gave him a son, that would make him happy, drive from his mind those obsessive fears about his legitimacy. She and Hattushili had been at enormous pains to establish their own right to the throne; perhaps they had infected Tashmi-sharrumma with doubt. He was much more sensitive than most people realized.

Much more easily managed.

A howl resounded from within the lying-in room. The king went rigid, straining toward the door; he cast questioning eyes at his mother.

But she smiled reassuringly. "More contractions. We'll know when labor starts. Why don't you go on? It could be hours. I'll send someone for you as soon as there's a change."

"You think it's safe?"

"Of course, of course. I've done a thousand of these, my dear."

The king loped away with his long-legged, nearsighted stride. The wool of his blue tunic was dark with sweat, and his long hair stuck to it, but he was broad shouldered and trim hipped with the rangy grace of an athlete. *He's a good-looking boy from the back*, she thought with a mother's fond pride.

＊

Restless and not knowing exactly what to do with himself, Tashmi-sharrumma headed back to his chambers. He'd been unable to figure out how to deal with his wife's fears regarding his mother, and so he'd done nothing. Now the suspicion haunted him that perhaps the *tawananna* would attempt some sabotage of the birth.

His secretary was sitting on a bench in the shade outside the door. Tarhun-miya popped to his feet as the king approached.

"My Sun, the *tuhkanti* and the chief of the *meshedi* were just here looking for you. I told them you were in the court of women, so your eunuch took them away. Shall I...?"

"I'll find them, Tarhun-miya. Thank you."

"Has the queen...?"

It was out of line for the secretary to ask, but his master answered nonetheless. "Not yet."

Tashmi-sharrumma turned back toward the public part of the palace complex, hoping to see the tall Zuzu's head somewhere above the servants and scribes who fell to their knees at the king's passage. He encountered his brothers, standing in the shadow of the throne-room porch, talking. They straightened as he approached and bowed, their fists to their chests in salute. Nerikkaili, he observed, was acquiring a bit of a paunch.

"Hail, My Sun," said Nerikkaili with what might or might not have been a tinge of sarcasm to his deep, fruity voice. "We were just saying that a messenger has arrived from our sister in Amurru, and we wondered if you had heard him yet. Tarhun-miya said you were haunting the court of women."

They all laughed knowingly as men who had awaited

children—and had been anxious for an heir. But perhaps Nerikkaili would not be so anxious for the birth of Tashmi-sharrumma's heir.

"The queen, has she...?" Hishni began. He and Nerikkaili already had grandchildren, joyous little denizens of the big royal nursery.

"Not yet. The *tawananna* promised to tell me when she goes into labor."

"She sent you away, eh? Under her feet, no doubt." Hishni chuckled.

"The *tawananna* is a capable woman," said Nerikkaili a little smugly.

It occurred to Tashmi-sharrumma that these half brothers were the same age as his mother, and they had known her for longer than he had lived. He had often heard that proprietary tone when Nerikkaili spoke of the *tawananna*. The king wondered what they had thought when their father had married her. He wondered if her beauty had been a distraction to a pair of young princes— and if it was still a distraction. He wondered if they had resented the ascendance of her first-rank children. He could actually remember meeting their mother, who was old at the time, one of his father's secondary wives, an aristocrat of some Luwian-speaking family, no mere concubine. She might have been queen just as easily as Puduhepa, a Hurrian priest's daughter from Lawazantiya.

In the gods' sight, family loyalties took precedence over all others, yet the bonds within his own family were so complex that he couldn't imagine what the lines of allegiance might be, except to the king, who was both kinsman and suzerain to all these brothers and cousins and uncles who abounded in Hatti Land. The king was the spider in the center of the web.

But which man, in the sight of the gods, is really the king?

The three brothers found Zuzu and the messenger at the entrance to the court of women. Still in her smock, her hair tied up in a scarf, Puduhepa had come to the gate to hear him read the tablet her daughter had sent from Amurru. The *tawananna* looked like any mistress of a household. This comfortable, maternal aspect of hers was almost her signature. *Is it meant to identify her with Hannahannah, the divine mother, or to distract from her own machinations?* The king could testify that she'd been a good mother, but more and more, he felt uncertain that her goals and his were the same.

"My Sun. My princes." She greeted them, smiling, her face rosy with heat. "Gasshulawiya has written to remind us that her youngest daughter is marrying the king of Ugarit in the fall. You were very eager for this to happen, weren't you, my dear?"

The king nodded. They had to solidify that coast. "They'll relay the grain from Mizri in their ships. If anything disrupts the line of grain ships…" He trailed off. The results were so awful to contemplate that he would not say aloud the inauspicious word: famine.

"My wife is an Amurrite," Nerikkaili said, "although she doesn't have much influence on her father anymore, I guess. It's all about the new queen's children now. The old king of Ugarit was married to an Amurrite, too, wasn't he?"

But Tashmi-sharrumma was still pondering his brother's comment about the new queen's children and what that meant in Nerikkaili's mouth, and the conversation continued without the king.

Puduhepa nodded. "Yes, she's still their *tawananna*, or whatever they call her. We need to keep things peaceful all along the coast for as many generations as possible. The Assyrians, damn their black hearts, have actually been feeling out those coastal kings—"

"Poaching our vassals!" cried Hishni.

"Rich little kingdoms, even apart from their value to us as part of a shipping route from the south. The king is right: they must be kept loyal at any price. Perhaps you should plan to attend the wedding yourself, My Sun." She raised her eyebrows at her son as if awaiting his response.

Tashmi-sharrumma, rousing from his reverie, assented with a silent tip of the chin. Gasshulawiya, two years older than he, was his favorite sister. She was kind and steady and had made of her eccentric little old husband a solid vassal. The king looked forward to seeing her again.

The *tawananna* added, addressing him, "And your Ehli-nikkal, my son. She must be near marriageable age. Why not think about giving her to one of the sons of the king of Ugarit?"

For nearly forty years, Puduhepa had woven her web of marriage alliance throughout Hatti Land and beyond, creating lines of allegiance that had become ever more complicated. Tashmi-sharrumma's betrothal to a daughter of a Great King, while Nerikkaili was only given the child of a vassal, had been one of the first signs of his own ascendance. He had been oblivious as his mother had guided him upward and over the heads of his brothers.

"Good idea," Nerikkaili rumbled, shooting the

tawananna an appreciative lift of the eyebrows. "Ugarit is a rich agricultural area, too."

"Speaking of agricultural areas," Hishni said, turning to Nerikkaili and the *tawananna*, "the fields are all blasted in the Lower Land. I've never seen anything like it. When we passed them last spring it looked as if someone had turned fire on them. And that's the breadbasket of the empire. Hardly any olives or pomegranates in Kizzuwatna."

Puduhepa shook her head, grim—Kizzuwatna was her homeland. "We need that grain from Mizri. We must keep the coastal towns loyal, for sure."

"And especially Tarhuntassha," Hishni added. "The grain will be off-loaded there, won't it? It would be a disaster to lose it on our very doorstep."

"Don't worry about Tarhuntassha. Kurunta will be loyal no matter what," said the king.

But Nerikkaili shrugged. "Loyal, but our cousin isn't very—how to put it—steady. If he tries some lunatic heroics that go bad…"

"He won't," Tashmi-sharrumma snapped. *You're jealous, my* tuhkanti. But he himself was as prejudiced against his brother as Nerikkaili was against Kurunta. How could the king forget the unkindness of the adult Nerikkaili to a little half brother? Tashmi-sharrumma tried to show him favor, trust, and all the things the prince deserved, but he couldn't easily purge it from his memory. And that troubled him. It made being fair to his heir very difficult, and he wanted to be fair.

Rather than leave his sharp words reverberating, Tashmi-sharrumma added, "If those brigands from Lukka

Land get in on the act, we may need to help Kurunta fortify Ura."

"Alashiya is a bigger danger," said Hishni. "They'll attack while the ships are at sea."

"I'll write to their king myself," the *tawananna* said, as if oblivious to the hostile undercurrents swirling around her. "We're old friends. And I'd better do that right away. When his son succeeds him, I won't have any more leverage."

She turned to the king. "I think we need to make a new and more advantageous vassal treaty with your Kurunta. Make him feel valued. We can't lose him now."

He feels valued, thought the king, a little defensive. *His is one vassal's loyalty we don't need to worry about.* Aloud, he said nothing, just ran his tongue placidly over his teeth.

"We'll talk about it," his mother promised, squeezing his hand. "I have my ideas on the subject—"

A scream severed her words. The men froze. This feminine mystery of childbirth embarrassed them as if they had overheard forbidden sacred rites. Another shriek resounded that made Tashmi-sharrumma's hair stand on end. He gripped his mother's arm, sucking in his breath. Puduhepa shooed her stepsons away and pulled the king to the side.

"Go on, now, you two. They need me. Tashmi-sharrumma, stay outside in the court until I call you." She turned and flew off, all professional competence. Horripilating pants and wails arose from within. The elder princes departed eagerly, and Hishni called over his shoulder, "The Hutellurra guard her, brother."

Alone, the king stood in the emptied court of women, his heart hammering in his chest, dread making his breath short. He had killed men in battle and seen his own troops fall at his side, crying out their agonies, but these preternatural screams were worse. He closed his eyes and forced himself to place his soul calmly in the hands of the Ladies of Destiny. This was not the first child he had awaited—but it was the first child of the *king*.

After a long time, Amatalla, the queen's cousin, emerged, red-faced and smiling. "My Sun, come see."

Tashmi-sharrumma stumbled into the room, feeling he had displaced the last of the air from within the walls. Crowds of people dropped to their knees, murmuring "Hail, My Sun." Babylonian handmaids, priests, and midwives, with their oily black curls, bobbed and bowed. Patiya, his mother-in-law, hovering at her daughter's head, snatched the king's hand and covered it with kisses. White and drained but triumphant, Ellat-gula smiled beatifically, and on her breast, nestled in her crooked arm, swaddled in clean white linen, lay the baby.

"My Sun!" His wife beamed up at him. "I have given you a son!"

They all stared at him, hanging on his reaction.

Joy bubbled up inside him, an irresistible spring, and Tashmi-sharrumma began to grin like a giddy idiot. *A son! An heir!* "Gods be praised. Thank you, my dear."

The Babylonians smiled at each other. Their position was safe now. The king bent and took his wife's face between his hands and kissed her damp forehead. Her ladies had made up her lids, brushed her sweaty hair, and splashed her with sweet oils. There were dark circles under her eyes nonetheless. He smoothed her eyebrow with his thumb. Tashmi-sharrumma felt something very like tenderness for her, his little warrior who had fought back death and won a son for him. He swallowed hard, and his nose prickled.

"Thank you," he whispered again. Ellat-gula handed the child up to him, and the king took his son awkwardly in his arms. Patiya drew back the swaddling bands so he could see that it was in fact a perfect boy child. The baby was wrinkled and red, his face screwed up, his little fists waving, the nub of his umbilical cord ugly and purple, but he was the most beautiful thing the king had ever seen.

His son. His heir. At last. The gods had not refused him this blessing. Surely this was a sign of their approval. At the end of the days of seclusion, the priests would lay the child formally in his lap, but everyone understood that he had acknowledged him, his little *tuhkanti*.

After a moment, during which the king reclaimed his self-control sufficiently to speak, he asked, "Where is my mother?"

"She wash her. All covered in bloody," Patiya informed him, a smug note in her voice. Satisfied. Victorious. So had this been a coup on the part of the Babylonians, he wondered—to present him the child while the *tawananna* was absent? It seemed the petty machinations would never cease. He wanted to order all the hangers-on away but didn't know who was needed and who was not, and he decided to wait until his mother's return.

Just as he had made that decision, she entered, saw the child in his arms, and smiled warmly at him but shot Patiya a murderous look. "Everyone out now, except the queen's maidservant. There you go. Yes, you. She needs to rest. Out. Out. Go on."

"I am mother!" squealed Patiya in outrage, but she

hustled out, Amatalla in her wake. Ellat-gula was too tired to protest. She held out her arms for the baby, and her husband laid him gently against her breast. Mother and son fell asleep together, smiles on both their faces.

Puduhepa drew her son outside, her jaw tense with anger. "Did you touch the queen?"

Tashmi-sharrumma was taken aback by the question and by her fury. This was the happiest day of his life, and she was quivering with rage.

"I... kissed her, yes." He wanted to say, *I thought you'd like that.*

"Then go take a bath, and call the Old Women," she ordered, nearly spitting. "You're polluted."

He stared at her blankly, not knowing what to think. "Why?"

"You touched a woman who has just given birth, Tashmi-sharrumma. Aren't you a priest? You should know that. Those Babylonians should certainly have known. They *did* know. They trapped you, you poor, besotted fool. What if you had made an offering of thanks in a polluted condition? Do you see what I mean about being no friends of Hatti?"

Her harshness stung the king, but he had to agree that he should have known, and his near brush with sacrilege left him shaken. His wife had had four children before today, after all. His joy was chilled as if it had fallen into the snow. *Politics, even here?*

His mother continued to mutter as she propelled him across the courtyard of women. "I'm surprised they didn't circumcise him while I was out of the room. Wouldn't that have been nice?"

"Circumcise him?" The king felt slow and stupid, unable to keep up with the venomous pace of the *tawananna*'s accusations. She was so much better versed in outrage than he. "We don't circumcise babies."

"No, but the Babylonians do. Would that render him ineligible for kingship, like castration? I don't know, but I'll bet it crossed her mind."

The *tawananna* and Ellat-gula had gotten off on the wrong foot as soon as the younger woman had appeared in Hatti Land with her entourage of handmaids, diviners, astrologers, and relatives. The treaty with Kudur-enlil had seemed to promise the Babylonian equivalent of a first-rank daughter for Puduhepa's son, but as it turned out, the bride had been the child of a concubine—a lowly dancing girl, no less. It had almost provoked an international incident. Tashmi-sharrumma imagined that the fourteen-year-old bride had had a pretty unpleasant surprise herself when she saw her new husband. Mindful of this, he had tried to be kind to her and had been rewarded by something close to real friendship.

The *tawananna* pushed him through the gate, saying, "Go take a bath" between gritted teeth.

The king, feeling very much like a chastised little boy, made his way across the outer, public court, seeing only his feet stepping in front of him, one after the other, in his red shoes. They were ceremonially sewn from the hides of sacred cattle slaughtered according to strict ritual. This was his life now—a teetering walk across a dangling footbridge over a gorge, with the wrath of the gods on either side.

He perceived kneeling courtiers around him, and looked up to see their curious faces, trembling on the edge of joy but not daring to trust the rumors until he confirmed them. He knew they had to be thinking, *But the king looks so unhappy*.

He forced himself to smile then defiantly let the smile become real, exposing his ugly teeth. "A son. An heir."

⁎

"Now, my dear, about that new treaty with Kurunta."

Puduhepa had removed her smock and scarf. She was no longer the midwife and mother but the *tawananna* once again. Her son, still glowing with a faint smile at the thought of having fathered an heir after all these years, sat before her on the dais of his throne, his knees sticking up, his forearms resting on them, his long hands dangling. They were alone except for Mahhuzzi, who had brought the copy of the treaty. He stood discreetly behind his mistress, arms folded over the tablets, which he pressed to his skinny chest. Around them stretched the forest of wooden columns that supported the ceiling of the vast, shadowy hall.

"I think you need to offer him some major new concessions."

"What's left that my father didn't already offer him? Kurunta ranks with the viceroy of the East. He's second only to the *tuhkanti*."

"Well, for one thing, he has usufruct of a number of cities without directly owning the population—"

"Owning?"

"For taxes, I mean. It's a legal distinction. But this gives him more—"

"I can't imagine him caring." The king looked up at her with his sleepy, impassive gaze.

"Well, of course he cares, Tashmi-sharrumma. It's more revenue for him."

"And he needs more revenue because…?"

She rolled her eyes in exasperation and enunciated with greater precision. "Gold, son. Don't be so unworldly. Everyone needs it. His mines are played out, you know, and we're asking him to off-load a lot of grain."

The king lowered his eyes and sucked his teeth thoughtfully.

"So," his mother continued, "we can also add salt rights in the areas where he has had none. There are some occasions when he has levy duties, which we can probably forego. You can be pretty sure he will respond anyway."

"Why all this rigmarole, Mother? We don't have to worry about Kurunta."

"My dear, do you really realize how important his goodwill is to the shipping of this Egyptian grain?" Puduhepa faced him, her eyes wide with incredulity. "We have no deep-water ports on the south coast except his. If he fails us, the kingdom will literally starve."

"And why would we expect him to fail us? He's been like a brother to me since childhood."

She gave a contemptuous snort. "Yes, well, he's had a little incentive, too, Tashmi-sharrumma. You surely don't think your ascent to power has been pure luck, do you?"

She saw him skew his jaw mutinously and added in a more tender tone, "I know he loves you, dear. That's genuine, of course. But Kurunta isn't quite so idealistic as you."

"He'll be hurt. He'll be offended. I would be."

"Didn't you hear me? Kurunta is *not* you. He likes his

pleasures, and they're not free. He'll be pleased you thought about this so he doesn't have to ask."

The king looked up and saw his mother's secretary, whose close-set little eyes darted from face to face as they argued. "That's all, Mahhuzzi. You can go," he said.

"No, wait a minute," his mother countermanded, gesturing her secretary back.

"That's all, Mahhuzzi. You can go," the king repeated impassively, but he looked at his mother, not at Mahhuzzi. Her face grew hot with anger. *Why is he trying to embarrass me like this? He insists on living in his godly little world, where everyone is pure of heart and motivated by the highest ideals, then he treats me with complete disrespect and undermines my authority.*

The secretary shot a quick glance at his mistress, but he dared not disobey the king. He bowed and scuttled out of the throne room and down the external stairs, letting a long shard of spring sun skewer the room before the door slammed closed after him.

Puduhepa fixed her son with a glare that could have melted iron. "What was that all about, please?"

"He shouldn't hear us disagree."

"Since when were you so scrupulous about showing the world our policies disagree, Tashmi-sharrumma, my dear? Eh?" She gave him a meaningful and reproving look. "This is not some little childhood game, where you can pay Kurunta in pistachio nuts. He's a grown man; he needs grown-up incentives. You'd better take this treaty seriously; I'm warning you."

"I take Kurunta seriously. He's a man of his word." After a moment, the king added a little tartly, "Why not stop forbidding him access to his father's Stone House if you want to make him happy?"

Puduhepa rolled her eyes. "Dear gods, Tashmi-sharrumma. Can't you figure out why? All he needs is to start meditating on the fact that he is Muwatalli's son."

"Well, he is."

"It's not on the table, son. Anything else. And lots of it."

The king looked down, his face almost sullen. "He'll be offended."

The *tawananna* threw up her hands in resignation, but anger simmered hotly in her cheeks—she was anything but resigned. "Have it your way. But just remember the stakes. If he feels you don't value his loyalty…"

"We're friends, Mother. He'll be faithful without a bribe."

Her voice rising in exasperation, she said, "By the thousand gods, child. You should be doing everything in your power to assure he will stay friends with you. Do you understand me? Everything in your power. Are you doing *everything* in your power?" She tried not to be too explicit, but one could never be sure what Tashmi-sharrumma understood. He had strange blank places in his intellect, especially where it intersected with his emotional life.

Finally, the king began to look irritated, his lips tight and his eyebrows grim. He hoisted himself to his feet and towered over his mother for a moment, grinding his jaw. Then he turned away and stood for another while, indecisive, as if he were arguing in silence with himself. At last he came back to her, his face expressionless as a stone.

"Give me the treaty," he said.

She couldn't repress a smile of victory. "You won't regret this, my dear."

Her smile widened, warmed, until she was melting with motherly tenderness. She put her arms around her son, who stood unresponsive, his face an unreadable blank. Gods knew how annoying she found this stony impassibility of his, but it was better than open rebellion. And he had, after all, yielded. Her dear, obedient boy.

"So you'll present it to him?" she pressed.

"Yes."

"And make it sound genuine, like it's your own. Don't just say, 'Mother made me do this.' Make it sound like you mean it."

"I said yes." He stared off into space.

She rubbed her cheek against his chest and stroked his back, which was rigid under her hand. "Trust me, my dearest. I know Kurunta."

He grunted.

"Let's have this written up in duplicate on a nice bronze tablet, one for him and one for our chancery... and some copies for the temples."

"Whatever you want, Mother." He sounded vaguely sarcastic. It had always surprised her that someone so earnest and pious could be so sarcastic when he let himself. She realize that her son was not a simple man. She puckered her lips and craned up toward him, forcing him to stoop and offer his cheek to her kiss.

CHAPTER 5

THE JOURNEY TO UGARIT TOOK nearly a month and, at that season of late summer, could hardly have been more miserable. But the Lords of Hatti agreed that it was important to bless the alliance of Ugarit and Amurru with the royal presence. The caravan set off across the River Marrasshantiya, past the ancestral town of Nesha—which had given its name to their language, Neshite—down through the languishing olive orchards of Kizzuwatna and the formidable mountains that guarded the Lower Land to the east. They passed through the narrow gorge called the Sea Gates and skirted the coast as far as Yadiya then cut inland to Karkemish on the Puruna. There the king would confer with his viceroy of the East, Ini-tesshub. They would not arrive in Ugarit until the local New Year's Eve, the day before the autumn equinox. The wedding was set for three days later—just long enough for the weary travelers to recuperate.

So the horses wouldn't have to pull them over the steep mountain tracks, the chariots were packed upon ox-drawn wagons. The king and his brothers, cousins, uncles, eunuchs, and secretaries also rode in hard, rattling carriages, proceeding no faster than the foot soldiers who walked alongside the train. Conversation had stopped leagues ago, and the princes and their attendants were liquefying in their woolen tunics. They had braided their long hair to keep it off their backs and were quick to snarl at one another.

The king was content not to talk. His thoughts were in Hattusha with little Arnuwanda, his son. He had named the child for the heir of the first Tudhaliya—the original Arnuwanda had been a great religious reformer. The *tawananna* hadn't been much pleased by Tashmi-sharrumma's choice, would rather have seen a fourth Hattushili. But this was a name the late king's son was seeking to avoid, despite his devotion to his father. For many in the kingdom, Hattushili was the name of a usurper.

Not many leagues before the royal party's arrival, a messenger in a light one-man Hurrian chariot was spotted ahead on the road, galloping toward them at breakneck speed. The caravan drew up, ponderous and uneasy, and soldiers positioned themselves in the vanguard. The king jumped to the ground, sword in hand, his brother Hishni and the twelve *meshedi* on duty immediately surrounding him. Seeing himself cut off from the king, the messenger cried urgently, "A message from the viceroy, My Sun. Important message for your ears alone."

"Follow me." Sheathing his sword, the king gestured the panting messenger to the edge of the road in his wake. For his ears alone or not, guards followed with a two-fisted grip on their spears—one could never be sure if someone was the viceroy's real emissary. But the man fell to his knees and passed the king a tablet sealed with Ini-tesshub's seal.

Tashmi-sharrumma held it close to his face and read it silently. Finally, he looked up at Lurma-ziti and Huzziya, who were waiting, wide-eyed with curiosity, at his side. Tashmi-sharrumma could scarcely contain his elation as he announced, "Shulmanu-asharedu is dead."

Young Huzziya let out an undignified whoop, and a babble of savage satisfaction broke out all around. This was the shit-eating Assyrian king who had defeated them at Taite, and he had gone beneath the black earth while their own king stood among them in good health. Here was the judgment of the gods! Although he didn't consider himself a particularly vindictive man, Tashmi-sharrumma found this news filled him with delight. Another excellent omen.

The remaining leagues to Karkemish passed quickly. The men were talking again, speculating, cursing, laughing, cracking obscene jokes at the late Assyrian's expense. Tashmi-sharrumma wondered about Shulmanu-asharedu's successor and what manner of man he would prove to be. Perhaps things would look up between Hatti and Assyria. Perhaps the gods had relented in their anger. Good things seemed possible again.

In a clattering, clopping, rumbling, lowing procession, they entered the city. Karkemish—dun walled, high upon its artificial mound—was reflected in the Puruna, whose serpentine blue waters were as wide as a minor sea. On the opposite bank, where Hanigalbat had once lain, stretched Assyria.

Ini-tesshub greeted them, as cheerful as he was ever likely to look. After the formalities of welcome, he confided to the king, "My Sun, our ambassador to Assyria is here. It's he who brought the message that you've just received.

Perhaps you would like to speak to him, hear what else he has to say about the situation to the East. Or perhaps you would prefer to eat and rest first?"

"No, that can wait. I want to talk to the ambassador. Who is he?" said Tashmi-sharrumma, raising his eyes to his cousin.

"Mashamuwa, My Sun. He has been in Asshur since before your coronation, so perhaps you've never met him. He is a member of my wife's family. A sound man, fluent in Akkadian. We can trust his perceptions, I think."

Ini-tesshub installed the king and his brothers in a council room and brought in Mashamuwa. Like his relative the viceroy, the ambassador was tall, lean, gray haired, and dry as a stick. He had a nose that looked as if it could cut cheese. Tashmi-sharrumma, who granted his trust only cautiously, liked him immediately.

"It was a sudden demise, My Sun," Mashamuwa told the king. "And then Shulmanu-asharedu's son Tukulti-ninurta was enthroned in what strikes me as unseemly haste. There are rumors at court that the late king's death may have been hastened along by human agency." He compressed his lips in an evil grin.

"What sort of man is the new king?" *Apart from a parricide.*

"Proud, impetuous. He's only a boy—well, thirty or so. A dangerous boy, I think. He fancies himself a legendary conqueror like Sargon of old. He does have a sense of humor, although a cruel one."

"We must be firm with him from the start, My Sun," urged Ini-tesshub. "As you know, I've long been trying to set up a meeting between Mashamuwa here and the Assyrian ambassador to talk about details of a mutual nonaggression pact, but Shulmanu-asharedu just strung us along. He rescheduled the meeting time after time, upon every kind of pretext. I don't think he was ever serious, at least not after, well… after Taite. We mustn't let his son think we'll put up with this indefinitely. We must come right out and tell him we know what he's up to and won't tolerate it."

"On the other hand," said the king mildly, "this son may be a completely different sort." *We should deal with him straightforwardly until he gives us reason to doubt his sincerity. Perhaps a show of friendship can change the relationship of our kingdoms.* "Have we any common enemies?"

Ini-tesshub and the ambassador exchanged uneasy glances.

Lurma-ziti, hunched under his twisted shoulders, was watching them like a hawk and called them out. "So what do *you* think, since you don't seem to agree with Our Sun?"

The viceroy admitted, "I've dealt with them for a long time at very close range, cousin, and this much I know about the Assyrians. They're duplicitous on principle. I would never believe any protestation of friendship from Tukulti-ninurta or any other King of Kings."

Tashmi-sharrumma sucked his teeth thoughtfully and said nothing.

Ini-tesshub leaned forward. "My Sun, I have another piece of bad news that further weakens our position against the Assyrians. Ehli-sharrumma of Ishuwa is showing definite signs of shifting his allegiance to Assyria."

"By the thousand gods of Hatti!" cried Hishni. "He controls the copper mines."

Tashmi-sharrumma could hardly conceal the flash of

horror that must've flitted across his face before he was able to recompose himself. Lurma-ziti had seen it; his wicked black eyes missed nothing. *No doubt*, thought Tashmi-sharrumma, *my brother is filing away this bit of information about his king.* He realized he had no idea where Lurma-ziti's loyalties really lay. The hunchback seemed to collect other people's weaknesses against some future use. As a young man, he had been particularly unkind to the child Tashmi-sharrumma, exercising a kind of malicious strategy tailor-made to his victim's flaws. The king had to admit his brother was a skilled tactician, but his outlook on the world was warped. *Perhaps the unfortunate lot life has dealt him has embittered him,* Tashmi-sharrumma told himself. Lurma-ziti was the king's only rival in ugliness, but it was his angry, belligerent expression, as much as anything, that marred his face.

"So much for family loyalty, eh?" Lurma-ziti snarled. "He deserves that barren wife of his."

"He also secures the northeastern border of Hatti should Assyria penetrate Nairi Land."

"I'm afraid the defeat in Hanigalbat has jolted him," said Ini-tesshub, looking apologetically at the king. "He feels he's vulnerable, that we may not be able to defend him if he's invaded. He's told me this frankly."

"Let him have it, My Sun. Him and Tukulti-ninurta, too. Tell him we're tired of playing nice." Hishni was ever the bluff soldier, but Tashmi-sharrumma wondered if in fact he really had no depths. He was harder to read than the suave, cynical Nerikkaili or the spiteful Lurma-ziti.

The king said, "Remember how Urhi-tesshub angered everyone by insulting Shulmanu-asharedu when the latter came to the throne? It was called a lack of diplomacy. Evidence that he was a bad king."

The others looked uneasy, a little rebellious. They sucked their lips, pursed them, examined their fingernails. No one wanted to contradict the king. Finally, Ini-tesshub, who outranked the others, said gently, "That was then, My Sun. Times have changed. Assyria is a real threat now."

"We'll discuss this again later. See you at dinner, my lords."

The king retired to the chamber Ini-tesshub had prepared for him, a place with a splendid view of the river and the rolling, scrub-covered highland beyond. *Assyria,* thought Tashmi-sharrumma, somber. *Assyria, a stone's throw away.*

He stared out the window, but his gloomy thoughts were elsewhere. The same depressing theme as always was playing here in Karkemish: *then* we kept our word; *now* we must break it. *Then* we were civil to our peers and gave them credit for decency; *now* we must insult them and rattle our swords. *Then* we believed in ruling according to the gods' precepts; *now* only expedience reigned.

He stood there for a while, brooding on the mutable nature of virtue, then he summoned Tarhun-miya and dictated a letter to the new King of Kings: "Good luck on your new reign. This is a fresh chapter for our two countries. You can count on us to be helpful. But don't forget how dangerous the mountains to the north of Nairi Land can be—lots of wolves." Tarhun-miya would make it elegant. The king hoped this was clear enough to satisfy the more belligerent among his advisors and perhaps tickle the cruel sense of humor of his new counterpart to the East.

It was a short night, and even before the Lady Arinniti had revealed her golden face, they were on the road again, heading back to the coast by way of Yadiya, trailing through the Mukesh Gap and southward down the side of the sea. They pitched camp north of the capital at the Ugaritic town of Shalmiya and sent word to King Ammishtamru of their arrival. The day had been consumed with unpacking the chariots from the wagons and reassembling them. The horses were rested, the harnesses shined. The king's valet prepared his ceremonial garb for the entry into Ugarit.

It was a festive occasion and also a reminder to the people of the coast that they were an honored part of the Land of Hatti. *Keep them happy; give them a spectacle,* Tashmi-sharrumma told himself more than once. Young as he was, he was tired, aching, and had a headache from the glare. The older dignitaries, the soldiers who had walked all these many leagues, the out-of-shape secretaries and household staff had to relish this day of less harried activity even more.

Unflagging old Zuzu had already trudged up to the city to confer with the local palace officials about matters of protocol. They would have to sweep the gate before the Great King entered, do whatever people had to do to fulfill the mountains of ritual requirements for such occasions. Tashmi-sharrumma found himself remembering the more or less carefree days of his life as a mere prince with increasing fondness.

The procession formed up before daybreak, and by the time the sun had fully risen, the outriders of the caravan had begun to enter the city of Ugarit. It was a steep road from the coast up to the white walled city on its hill, and the horses were blowing. The king could see before him, devoid of particular detail, a long, glittering serpentine of movement and color and flashes of bronze that wound through the olive groves. Ammishtamru's soldiers, alternating with Tashmi-sharrumma's own, lined the road, a festive necklace of white and red, holding back the cheering populace. Little local girls dropped flowers; the cantor and singers and bands and dancers frolicked and cried, "hail" on a thousand different tones.

Sweltering in his regalia—long tunic with a heavy, trailing, gold-embroidered cloak and the red-and-gold crown upon his head—the king rode near the end of the procession, standing straight and unmoving on the platform of his chariot like a statue of a god. The twelve Golden Spearmen and twelve *meshedi* guards walked alongside him in double rows, while his brothers and other princes of Hatti rode ahead, and rows of dignitaries with batons of office proceeded on foot. Then came Tarhun-miya and the other secretaries and lesser officials, walking three by three.

The sun was high in the sky by the time the Great King's entourage had passed under the massive Royal Gate into the palace grounds. Here his guards formed a hedge between his chariot and the entrance to Ammishtamru's residence. The russet-bearded vassal king awaited him there, beaming widely and holding forth on the depth of Ugarit's loyalty. Tashmi-sharrumma was ceremonially passed from the care of his guards to those of his host and the palace staff. He was escorted to his chamber, and a golden spear was laid across the doorsill to mark the imperial presence. And except for Pirwannu, the king was finally alone.

The silence of the cool upper-story room flowed over

Tashmi-sharrumma like balm. The valet removed the king's skullcap, and he felt the air on his scalp for the first time since dawn. He shed the gold jewelry and heavy ritual garments that had configured him to Ishtanu the sun god—god of justice—and clad only in a clean linen tunic, he stretched out on the bed. A lukewarm breeze ruffled the sheer curtains. The morning sunlight, sweetly filtered, drifted in from a garden. It was a beautiful area here along the coast, soft and feminine, perfumed with flowers and the smell of the sea, unlike the harsh, sunbaked, rocky fastness of Hattusha. Even the air seemed gauzy and not quite transparent.

His mother had told him that the men of Ugarit were luxury loving and deceitful, as inconstant as their sea. Gold was all they cared about. The only way to secure their loyalty was to buy it. Ammishtamru, their king, was one of the vassals who had sworn his oath over the summer, but spending a few days under his roof would allow Tashmi-sharrumma to get to know him better. The Great King, too, would become a real person to him and not be just a golden idol with a name. Well worth a little exhaustion.

He was lying in a half-conscious state of relaxation, feeling his headache pulse with gradually less maleficence, when a knock on the heavy door resounded.

The king sat up abruptly and swung his bare feet to the floor. "Come in."

Zuzu, his face puckered with anxiety, stood flustered in the opening. "My Sun, a messenger is here from your mother the *tawananna*."

"Send him in." Sleep had fled Tashmi-sharrumma; fear

made his heart beat wildly. What could be so urgent? *My son... please the gods, nothing has befallen little Arnuwanda.*

The messenger was filthy and dripping with sweat, his face as red as a pomegranate. The gods knew how many relay horses he had driven into the ground. He dropped unsteadily to his knees and fumbled a tablet from his courier bag. Even as he extended it, he repeated the contents from memory.

"The *tawananna* Puduhepa in Hattusha to her son Tudhaliya, Great King, in Karkemish or Ugarit. The people of Lalanda have risen against us and killed our governor. I have sent Alalimmi and Nuwanza with what remains of the standing troops here. Proceed immediately to the siege. Vassals in the Lower Land have been alerted and will join you as you pass. Waste no time."

The bottom dropped out of the king's stomach.

The West was rising.

Lalanda was, properly speaking, only a town, but it was one of the border fortresses against Lukka Land. Tashmi-sharrumma had just almost named his younger brother Huzziya to be the governor there; thank the gods he had changed his mind and put him in a safer place. *Although are there safe places any longer?*

He tried to picture Lalanda in relationship to Tarhuntassha and realized it was not that far from its border or from the port town of Ura, upon which the entire scheme to import Egyptian grain hinged. *Waste no time.*

He turned to Zuzu. "Tell the Lords of Hatti that we ride to Lalanda at dawn in the chariots, taking the guards and soldiers only. The wagons and officials and servants will set out as soon as they are able, to return to Hattusha. Send me Ammishtamru."

He signaled his valet, who bought him his red shoes with their curled toes and levered them onto the king's feet. Pirwannu clasped gold bracelets on his forearms and from his ears, suspended great golden disks. Tashmi-sharrumma scratched at his face and realized it was far from well shaved, but he'd deal with that later, before the banquet. Now he had to make his apologies to his host and attend to the promised audience. He would not see Gasshulawiya, he realized to his sorrow. It had been nearly twenty years since she had gone away.

The audience went well enough. Tashmi-sharrumma was distracted and scarcely conscious of the cases laid before him, yet somehow, he managed to give a satisfactory judgment without seeming too much of a dullard. Ammishtamru, at his side, was clearly disappointed that his suzerain wouldn't ornament his wedding ceremony but bore it with good grace. Hattushili had put him on the throne ahead of his older brother, and the Ugarite seemed gratefully loyal to the former king's successor. He would take a lot from the Great King without complaint.

That evening, the king of Ugarit hosted a splendid banquet, which Tashmi-sharrumma felt obligated to attend even though the prospect of an early-morning departure made him long for an early hour to bed. He wasn't a man who paid much attention to what went into his mouth, so he was indifferent to the dainty dishes paraded before the guests. Still, he reminded himself to make appropriately appreciative comments from time to time. The musical entertainment, he had to admit, was sublime—Ammishtamru had rounded up some superb players and singers. For most of the duration of the meal, Tashmi-sharrumma was lost in the music, smiling blandly and silently around him as if he knew what people were saying to him. The level of noise and the amount of wine being served provided a certain excuse for not responding. It occurred to him that most of the first year of his reign had been spent in a similar state of glassy-eyed exhaustion.

Well before dawn, the king and his brothers and cousins and uncles mounted their ceremonial chariots and drove their prettified horses out the gate with considerably less pomp than when they had arrived. They would soon need sturdier relays, but they couldn't travel at the pace of an oxcart to spare the beasts. Lalanda was two, perhaps three weeks away even if they went at a steady clip. Tashmi-sharrumma heard the four great doors clanging shut behind him as they clopped down the steep road in the semi-darkness. It was, he feared, a descent into darkness indeed.

They were still clinging to the coast and hadn't even reached Yadiya when a rider overtook them with a message from the viceroy. Ini-tesshub had arrived for the New Year's celebration the evening of the Great King's departure, only to find Tashmi-sharrumma gone and Ugarit in the midst of a civil war.

Civil war? The king reeled inwardly but maintained a calm exterior.

"What?" squawked Lurma-ziti. "We were just there."

"Yes, my lord," the messenger panted. "It was the king's brothers that started it. They struck during the New Year's liturgy that very evening. The king was acting as high priest, and they were standing behind him, and they and their men broke out their arms right there with the sacrificial fire burning and everything. The whole plaza was full of fighting. But the vizier got a messenger out, and he ran into the viceroy right at the gate. And then my lord Ini-tesshub and his men came in and put down the rebels."

Hishni cursed softly. "What would the bastards have done if we hadn't left early? Maybe you should travel with more guards, My Sun."

But everyone knew that only twelve *meshedi* were ever together in one place, and there were always twelve Golden Spears to neutralize them... because no one fully trusted them or anyone else who stood around the king with weapons.

Tashmi-sharrumma found himself unnerved, his heart sitting queasily in his throat. Regicide was a frightening epidemic that could spread from kingdom to kingdom, and the king had plenty of enemies. He remembered the king of Ugarit's brothers—two charming men with whom he had dined only yesterday. There had never been any hint of animosity between them and Ammishtamru. Tashmi-sharrumma feared he was not a skillful reader of people's intentions, and this could be a fatal flaw.

"What was it about, do you know?" he asked the messenger.

"The king of Ugarit is a younger son. Apparently, his elder brother thought *he* should have been king."

The Great King said nothing. He was aware that Lurma-ziti and Hishni avoided looking at each other. After a moment, he spoke to the messenger. "And what sentence did Lord Ini-tesshub impose on the rebels?"

"He exiled them to Alashiya, My Sun, because he said he thought that's what you would want. He said if you wanted them put to death, he could do it afterward, but if he executed them first, you wouldn't have a choice."

"Fair enough."

The experienced Ini-tesshub knew the traditions of Hatti Land as well as anyone in the royal family—the abiding principle was always clemency. The Assyrians might maim and torture, but in the land beloved of the thousand gods, clemency was queen of virtues, consort of justice. The king was not a highly flammable man like the enthusiastic Kurunta, but the ideal of justice had fired him since childhood. The gods blessed the clement, the just. An ugly man might be made beautiful by the practice of justice. And clemency was its bride.

As if he had read his mind, Lurma-ziti asked, "But what happens when it's unjust to pardon, eh?"

"Would you not pardon an erring brother, Lurma-ziti?" said the king quietly, the memory of certain childhood chastisements at the hunchback's hands only too vivid. "Then you're not just."

Watching the king uneasily, Lurma-ziti fell silent, no doubt wishing he had kept his mouth shut.

The royal party pressed on in a somber mood, leaving behind the humidity of the coast and striking inland across Kizzuwatna. At Tarhuntassha, Kurunta's capital, they took on fresh horses and relays and exchanged their ceremonial chariots for war vehicles. Kurunta had already gone on to Lalanda with his troops, but old Mashturi was there, waiting for his suzerain. Mashturi seemed eager to assure Tashmi-sharrumma by this gesture that their discussion of some months ago had not caused any disaffection. The king found his uncle measurably enfeebled since last winter, and remembered with a sinking heart the long, slow decline of his father. Hattushili and Mashturi had been much of an age. Tashmi-sharrumma wondered who would make a suitable replacement on the throne of Sheha River Land when the old man went under the black earth.

They were passing ever farther westward now, into the area called Kuwaliya, a sort of no-man's-land that both did and did not belong to Hatti. Usually, it played the vassal, but there was no formal treaty. To the south lay Lukka Land, a mountainous stronghold of brigands and pirates with no real government. Attempts to suppress the Lukka had never succeeded, and the Great Kings had learned to let them be, as long as they were not too disruptive. Kurunta had had to deal with them constantly almost since the day he had taken his throne. Now, with the grain ships docking at Ura, the policy of benign neglect might have to change. The opportunities for piratical blackmail were too enormous.

To the west lay Mira.

"What's Alantalli up to?" the king asked his uncle one evening as they sit down to a hurried dinner in the field.

Mashturi pursed his lips and lifted his shaggy white eyebrows. "Nobody knows, My Sun. He's kept quiet for the last few months. That doesn't mean he isn't up to something, though. He claims he wants to set the Luwians free to be their own masters again, but I wouldn't be surprised if he's talking to Ahhiyawa. They had an emissary at Millawanda during the summer."

Of course, thought the king blackly. Millawata—or *Millawanda*, to Luwian speakers like Mashturi—was a veritable colony of the Ahhiyawans right there in his own territory. They had abetted the rogue Piyamaradu and helped to humiliate Hattushili by whisking the defiant prince away to Ahhiyawa by ship, knowing the Hittites couldn't follow. The very thought of Millawata was wormwood to any son of Hatti Land. And now Tashmi-sharrumma's own vassal Alantalli was cozying up to it.

"Wouldn't be surprised if he had a hand in the rebellion at Lalanda," Hishni growled around a mouthful of meat.

Lurma-ziti, who had been ailing en route, was in an even darker humor than usual. "Burn them all down, and sow their fields with salt. Nothing else teaches these sheep fuckers a lesson." He belched painfully. "While we're here with a full army. Why not?"

Mashturi chuckled a little and waggled his eyebrows. What he really thought of the idea was unclear. Perhaps he would have loved to cleanse the earth of the dangerous rivals who surrounded his small kingdom. But Tashmi-sharrumma doubted that his men could burn them all down even if they wanted to. The West was sparsely settled, full of god-haunted peaks and narrow valleys running with perilous water. An army could be swallowed up in such terrain while the natives, who knew it well, rained down death upon them from the forests. It had happened many times—many, many times. The West had ever reduced to ashes Hittite imperial ambitions. The king remembered his father's perennial frustration, how it had embittered his old age.

Better to keep the Luwian-speaking inhabitants happy,

treat them well. Make an occasional show of force just to remind them to be on their best behavior. Lalanda may be just such a show of force. Perhaps it will recall to Alantalli his duties.

Or perhaps, the king realized, he was simply indulging in wishful thinking.

CHAPTER 6

BEFORE THEM HUNKERED LALANDA. IT was only a small town, a foursquare little mastiff of a fortress with scalloped crenellations, set on the wide, rolling plains that were the skirt tails of the mountains. The dry summer had left the fields and grazing lands blasted. It wasn't going to take much to reduce the town by hunger. The sprawl of army that surrounded it was Tashmi-sharrumma's own; the town itself showed no sign of treachery and death. A serene fall sky vaulted overhead. Cool wind whipped their standards and lashed unplaited hair.

Ever the first to heed the call for troops, Kurunta had been there for two full weeks. He opened his arms to the king as soon as the latter alighted from his chariot, and Tashmi-sharrumma embraced him, the king's chest filling with the warmth that Kurunta's presence brought. The two men pounded one another on the back, and Tashmi-sharrumma hung there a moment longer than necessary before they drew back.

Kurunta held him at arm's length to gaze upon him. "Cousin!" he cried, a grin of joy lighting up his handsome face. Armor set off his beauty like nothing else. He had the look of Wurukatte in the flesh. It seemed like a splendid omen. "The *tawananna* sent word about the uprising in Ugarit. We were worried for you, but then they said you'd already left before the blood began to flow."

"We got out in good time. Ini-tesshub has things well in hand." The king opened his mouth to interrogate Kurunta about the situation at Lalanda, then he saw Alalimmi and Nerikkaili standing behind the king of Tarhuntassha. "My brother. Cousin." Tashmi-sharrumma nodded to them, and they clapped fists to chest in a quick salute.

Nerikkaili's presence was a reminder to them both that he was no longer *tuhkanti*. He now ranked behind Kurunta, a viceroy. Nerikkaili held out a tablet. "The *tawananna* sent this with me, for your eyes, My Sun. Requires no reply." He had a peculiar little smirk on his fleshy face. It might have been embarrassment at having witnessed something a trifle too intimate, or bitterness just barely conquered. Or was it somehow related to that expression his face took on when he spoke of the *tawananna*? But Nerikkaili had been a diplomat for longer than his half brother's lifetime. He revealed nothing he cared not to.

The king took the letter and read in silence—no doubt to the others' disappointment. Then he snorted and shook his head, a grin of amusement twitching at the corners of his mouth.

"Nothing bad, My Sun?" asked Hishni, openly curious. "All is well?"

"My mother tells me she has procured a dozen clean and attractive slaves to be my new stable of concubines. She says she knows I like them plump and dark haired."

The men all laughed uproariously, rocking back and forth and slapping their thighs. It occurred to the king that they might not be laughing at the same thing. He and Kurunta found the officiousness of the *tawananna* amusing. But the other princes might be mocking Tashmi-sharrumma's disinterest in women. In fact, maybe Kurunta was, too. The viceroy, of all people, should know.

Tashmi-sharrumma's amusement went a little cold. He felt the habitual cringe of unease at being the object of other people's inspection.

"Ever one for details, the *tawananna*," Nerikkaili said, chuckling. Kurunta had laughed so hard he had to wipe his eyes, and he continued to erupt from moment to moment.

"I'll be right there to protect you, My Sun," declared Hishni, and a fresh wave of laughter rocked the princes.

But Tashmi-sharrumma was starting to wonder about that jab at his affection for Ellat-gula.

⁂

Later that evening, Kurunta was seated with the king in the royal tent. They'd been drinking a little after dinner, companionably, and talking in an informal way about the political situation in the West. Tomorrow, the king would have a plenary discussion with his generals, but in his usual fashion, he had said he wanted to acquire a better-informed personal grasp of things before he opened his mouth publicly.

It's good for us both to spend a little time together, thought Kurunta. *It's been far too long.* He had hardly so much as spoken to his cousin since Taite. Tashmi-sharrumma had always had one of those long, bony faces that looked older than its years, but he was downright haggard these days. Poor ugly old Tash with his snaggly teeth and tired, guarded eyes. He was so determined to do the right thing all the time that he exhausted himself arguing it over in his head. He had always been that way, thought Kurunta affectionately. One always had the feeling that life was a lot of effort for him, when mostly it was so simple.

But tonight the king seemed relaxed. The battlefield was something he understood; there were no requirements to be eloquent. Kurunta knew how much his cousin loved him and the peace Tash found in his presence, and he was glad he could help him in this way. Or any way. He was only waiting for a call, the gods knew.

Yet Kurunta's instinct for the subtler emotional vibrations told him something was wrong. It seemed that with Tash's consecration, their friendship had already been tarnished somehow. Well, the demands on his cousin's time were greater. But there was a slight distance. As if—and how very Tash this was—the new king feared their friendship was a luxury he must sacrifice. That refused kiss still rankled. The king was loth even to touch him now, as if his cousin had been some commoner who could pollute the high priest of Hatti's gods. And yet Kurunta sensed the longing in him. They needed each other more than ever. Because the king, afraid of pleasure and shut up in his own mind with his cruel sense of duty, was really and truly alone from now on—a golden idol on a high, lonely pedestal. Because Kurunta, who was by no means afraid of pleasure, was alone, too—the "brother" who wasn't a brother, with no family of his own.

At least they'd had a few hours of merriment about

the harem girls—and Puduhepa, that maternal force of nature—before the looming demands of war and defecting vassals closed in around them once more.

Kurunta had reminded himself of the *tawananna*'s letter, and before long, he couldn't suppress his snickers again. Tash looked up at him inquiringly, and the two of them broke out laughing, each knowing what the other was thinking.

"How about a nice, plump, right-handed, dark-haired girl with a dimple in her chin and a chip off her left front tooth? And a hangnail on her right thumb? Ha-ha! 'Ever the one for detail,' as our Nerikkaili observes," roared Kurunta.

"And fluent in three languages. Only my mother could find twelve of them." The king tried to drink while he was laughing and choked on his beer. Kurunta was still hammering on the royal back when Zuzu cleared his throat at the entry flap.

"A tablet from the capital, My Sun."

"Who from?" The king coughed, brushing beer off the front of his tunic where he had sprayed himself.

The eunuch admitted a messenger, who knelt and abased himself before offering his sovereign the tablet.

Tash read it silently, his smile paling and turning gradually into a grim line. "Messenger, leave us. But don't go far. I'll have a response." He stood there staring at the tablet for a long time.

Kurunta waited for him to speak, but finally, thinking the king must have forgotten his presence, said, "What news, cousin?"

"It's from the queen. She says my mother is making her life miserable, trying to take Arnuwanda away from

121

her. She… she says the *tawananna* has written to her counterpart, the queen of Assyria, urging her to encourage her husband to attack Karduniash."

"By the thousand gods of Hatti! I thought you said you had an argument about that policy and you set her straight."

"Nobody sets my mother straight unless she wants to be set straight." The king smiled dryly then turned somber. "But to go behind my back like that, to defy my stated policy openly…"

Kurunta shook his head, not sure what to make of the letter. He was an admirer of Puduhepa. Who wasn't, who had enjoyed her favor? She was the mother he had never had. She had treated him in every way like one of her own children, just as she had treated her husband's numerous lower-rank offspring. She had showed him uncritical affection, had been proud of his little triumphs, and had corrected him gently when his mischievous nature got the best of him. She had given him his wife, had given him his best friend. And there was no denying her brilliance, her energy. If she had been born a man, what a king she would have made.

But this… what was he to think?

"I'm speechless," he admitted finally.

The king laughed bleakly. "Well, that's some kind of miracle," he said, but then his face softened, and he added with great tenderness, "You love her, too, I know." He dropped his eyes to his hands, with the tablet between them. Somehow even his hands looked desolate. "I tell myself she's become accustomed to running the country during my father's illness. That can't just be turned off like an irrigation channel, you know."

"Of course not. And maybe Ellat-gula is exaggerating."

"Maybe." The king fell silent. His expression had gone blank. Kurunta knew that this was his mask against hurt or fear, and his heart was wrung for him. "Otherwise, this is treason, isn't it?"

"Oh, Tash, you know that whatever she does, she thinks it's for your good. She'd never knowingly betray you—any more than I would."

"I don't know what to do, Ulmi. She's my mother. I can't arrest her for treason."

"Of course not," Kurunta assured his cousin. "She's had a lot of freedom to set policy for years and years, and she thinks this is in your best interest. What do you do? You get a good night's sleep, and tomorrow, you take back Lalanda. Talk to the *tawananna* face-to-face when you get home to the capital. You'll work it out, I'm sure. Don't overthink it, eh?"

"Ellat-gula says Mother's trying to take little Arnuwanda away from her."

"You know how the *tawananna* is; she wants to put him in that big, happy nursery with all the other royal children. Probably Ellat-gula's not used to that sort of thing. Who knows how they do it in Karduniash? But I'll bet there's nothing sinister at all here, Tash. You've got to trust people. Has she ever done anything to hurt you on purpose?"

The king continued to stare down for a moment as if he were in fact combing through his memory for offenses. Finally he said, "Yes. No."

"Well, that's perfectly clear," Kurunta said with tart

good humor. He laughed, clapped the king on the arms. "You do overthink things, cousin. I take it you mean no, then. Tell the messenger you'll discuss this with the *tawananna* in person when you get back. And now, I recommend bed. Unless you have further need of me"—he grinned suggestively, although he had little real hope—"I'm off to my tent. Good night."

"Wait, Ulmi. Don't go yet. I wanted to tell you something."

Kurunta was bone weary. Tash must have been too; after all, he had been traveling nonstop for two weeks. But the viceroy turned back to the king and, fists on hips, said cheerfully, "All right, My Sun. Your vassal can refuse you nothing. What is it you want to talk about?"

"Don't say it that way. Because… that's exactly what I wanted to talk about." Tash cleared his throat. "I want to make a new vassal treaty with you, Ulmi."

Kurunta cocked his head, thinking perhaps he had misunderstood. "Oh, you do, do you? Why? What's wrong with the old one?"

"I would like to give you some more cities, push back the frontiers of Tarhuntassha a little. Salt rights. Maybe give you more military exemptions, and—"

"Let me visit my father's Stone House?"

Tashmi-sharrumma hung his head. "I…"

"I thought not. So why, Tash? What's this all about?"

"I know my mother made my father include a clause that only children of Anitti could inherit from you, but her father's not so loyal suddenly. I want you to be able to name your own heirs."

"Like a Great King, eh?"

"Exactly. Why not?"

There was something in all this that bothered Kurunta. Its suddenness, for one thing. Just as they needed his port for the Egyptian grain. And the extremity of it. And the wary look on his cousin's face, his eyes that slid off to the side. There was some hidden intention there. Not willful dishonesty—he thought Tash was probably congenitally incapable of lying outright—but something that made the king ashamed.

"So has something happened? Other than Anitti's father."

"No."

Suddenly, Kurunta felt a burning stream of anger rising up his gullet. His cousin was seen by others, no doubt, as a secretive man. He certainly did not reveal much about himself—his positions, what he felt, what he liked. But Kurunta had been almost a second self to the king since they were children. Tashmi-sharrumma had exposed everything that he knew of himself to Kurunta, good and bad. Not that there was so very much bad; he was, in fact, a good man. If anything, he was painfully well intentioned. More than once, the king had hinted—because he tended to be oblique—that it had been a great relief not to have to hide from his cousin.

And yet here he was, reshaping their very relationship, putting a market value on it... and refusing to tell him why.

"You're trying to buy me," Kurunta said, his face growing hot. "What by all the Lords of the Underworld is this about? Alantalli? The grain?"

"No. You're just... worth more. To me. My father's

terms seem insulting." Tash was shifting about uneasily. He couldn't prevaricate with any skill at all.

Anger was starting to collect around Kurunta like heat around a brazier. His voice was a little dangerous. "You're lying, cousin. This may be the first time in your life, but I know a lie when I smell one."

The blank gray eyes again. Tash's eyes were the dark gray of storm clouds, and they had always joked that he was consecrated to the Storm God of Nerik from the womb. Kurunta had never seen lightning in those clouds, but he was seeing something now he didn't like.

"I-I thought you'd be pleased," stammered the king.

"That you're trying to buy me? Is that the kind of man you think I am?" His cousin was such an exceedingly bad liar that Kurunta's anger was all but disarmed. Sorrow for poor old Tash welled up in him like a hot spring. Though perhaps not for the consecrated king, who had cities and boundaries and salt rights to hand out.

There was a very long moment of aching silence.

"I need you, Ulmi," said the king at last.

"Well. Now we're getting somewhere. But is it really me you need, or is it Tarhuntassha?"

"You. Both."

"No, I think it's this way: Tash needs me, but the king needs Tarhuntassha."

Tashmi-sharrumma hung his head for a moment and swallowed repeatedly as if he couldn't breathe well. When he raised his head, Kurunta saw misery in his eyes. They were both standing now, face-to-face, almost chest to chest, equals in every way but rank.

"I can't help being king. The gods chose me." Tash's voice was barely a murmur.

"More like your usurper father chose you. Your wildly ambitious mother chose you." Kurunta was uttering treason now, but he knew Tash would recognize his own words to Mashturi. There was enough anger in the viceroy to fuel this unkindness. "Let me tell you something about yourself, My Sun. You don't trust anybody very much. You need Tarhuntassha, and you don't quite trust my love for you enough to believe that I'll be faithful simply because I'm faithful. You think you have to bribe me to support you because I won't find your friendship sufficient. Perhaps it's *you* you don't trust."

Kurunta breathed hard for a moment as if to fan the coals of his grievance. As soon as they cooled, he would become his usual easygoing self, but he needed to say these words. The king's face was white as linen under its ruddy sunburn. He needed to hear these words.

The silence between them seemed to stretch on for days. Finally, Tash nodded. He said nothing, hung his head, his arms, awkward, at his side. *Embrace me,* Kurunta willed him silently. *Touch me; make a gesture so I know you care about me at all. Don't you know what I* do *want?* But the king made no move. Kurunta looked briefly at the straight white part in the top of Tash's hair, which had fallen over his shoulders and hidden his face. Then the king's cousin turned on his heel and, against all protocol, strode out. His anger wasn't dissipating after all.

⁂

The next morning, the king and his advisors met with

the loyal officials who had escaped from Lalanda. Their spokesman was the late governor's chamberlain, a fat eunuch with a walleye. He explained excitedly how a confederacy of the local aristocrats broke in while everyone was asleep and slaughtered His Lordship right before his eyes.

"Or one of them, at least," sneered Lurma-ziti under his breath. He looked gray and wasted.

Another palace servant gave a different version: the locals had asked for a moment of the governor's time and walked boldly into the audience hall with their daggers hidden in their sleeves.

The upshot was they had done away with the governor, declared their independence from their overlord in Hattusha, and were joining with the king of Mira. Tashmi-sharrumma wondered if he could expect the Mirans to turn up at any moment for a counter-siege, but in fact, it hardly mattered. He had assembled here a very large army. So many of the troops from the capital had accompanied Nerikkaili and Alalimmi and Huzziya that the king wondered if Hattusha had been left undefended. All this was certainly at the *tawananna*'s orders. Was she purposely jeopardizing his wife and son?

Stop it. Kurunta was right—you trust no one.

The thought of Kurunta was like a dagger in his own heart. The king of Tarhuntassha stood only a few feet away, among the other brothers and cousins and uncles who had brought their troops to the siege. He smiled and jested with the rest, but there was a substrate of darkness in his grin. The viceroy was tense and unhappy—or worse, tense and angry.

The king had insulted Kurunta with the *tawananna*'s

plan to buy his loyalty—as he had known he would. And yet Tashmi-sharrumma had let himself be pressured into presenting it. Even then, he could have said to Kurunta, "This is her idea, not mine. I would never put a market value on your love." But he was not the sort of person to blame others for an action he'd been too spineless to avoid. And so the wound festered. He was trapped, helpless to rectify things because although he wasn't proud, he was stubborn. He had told his mother he would present her new treaty as if it were his own, and now he would stand by that word. The longer the lie of omission went on, the more irreparable it became.

Tashmi-sharrumma found he had to exert an enormous amount of effort to control his own face, to keep his voice cool and level. He was the leader of a great army, and he had to be clearheaded—lives depended upon him. He shoveled out the ordure of his private life and sank into his habitual battlefield calm.

"Send a herald to the walls, Nerikkaili, to ask them to surrender. If they accept and swear an oath to be loyal henceforth, tell them they'll be granted an amnesty and returned to my full favor. If they refuse, we'll attack and destroy them."

"You think they deserve such a choice, My Sun?" the king's half brother growled. "These are not honorable fellow kings but a bunch of rebel vassals, the scum. They're showing what they think of oaths already."

"This is our tradition, brother. Clemency is a great virtue."

"What's to keep them from swearing and then turning on you as soon as the last of the army is out of sight? They've already broken their vassal treaties," asked Alalimmi in his incongruously boyish voice.

"Then they're forsworn, but we've behaved according to justice. The gods' wrath will fall upon them, not us."

Nerikkaili and Alalimmi exchanged a quick glance, then the prince observed dryly, "It's been a long time since anyone took that seriously, My Sun. Of course, I'm not a priest..."

"But I am, Nerikkaili," said the king with his unreadable look. Nerikkaili froze for a moment, as if not sure whether the king was angry or only being self-righteous. Kurunta watched, his mouth twisted skeptically. His half-closed eyes seemed to say, *You trust these traitors but not me?*

In the end, the issue was moot. The defenders rejected the offer of amnesty, and the king began preparations for a siege. The priests sacrificed a sheep, spread out its liver, and took the oracles, which were propitious. The gods offered them victory, but they still had to earn it.

Old Nuwanza, veteran of many sieges, had taken the liberty of cutting down a tree en route and fashioning a ram. A squadron of soldiers, scurrying along under light leather shields, rolled it to the city gate. The slow, rhythmic, gut-churning noise of its battering began.

Boom. Boom. Boom.

The rebels shot a volley of arrows down at the men. But they were too well covered, and the archers only exposed themselves to return fire.

The king stood in his chariot with his officers around him, just out of reach of the enemy's shots. He wore his long coat of bronze scales and a tall miter-shaped helmet with earflaps and a trailing plume that lifted in the fresh morning wind. Beside him, the banner of the double-headed eagle rippled and snapped. The fall day was crisp, the blue sky immaculate. His sweat dried on his cheeks almost as soon as it rolled down. The king flexed his nostrils and took in the keen smell of autumn. It was a fine day for a siege.

Boom. Boom. The noise of the ram reverberated in his viscera.

The king saw that his engineers had sufficiently attracted most of the men on the wall to the gate. His archers were already shooting high into the city with fire-tipped missiles. He gave the order for scaling ladders and grappling hooks to be brought out.

Tashmi-sharrumma longed to be in the fray—to haul his weight up the wall, hurl himself over the ramparts, and leap into the streets like a stooping bird of prey. He was tingling with the kind of nervous tension that battle brought—a sense of purposefulness, a clear goal toward which every sinew was bent. No overthinking now. No nuances. No horribly miscalculated words. Only action. The moment was rich and sweet as a swig of *walhi* drink.

At the king's side, Nerikkaili shouted over the din, "There aren't many of them, I think."

Alalimmi nodded agreement and hawked and spat on the ground. The wind was blowing dust upon them from the drought-stricken fields with a force that stung the cheeks and made eyes squint. The king reveled in it.

Boom, boom, boom.

"I don't think they'll hold out long at all, My Sun," Nuwanza yelled in his cracked old voice. "They've already been penned up here for nearly two weeks. The eunuch says their supplies of food were at rock bottom already."

He must have been a very poor governor to let his supplies become so reduced. The king tried to recall whether he had received a report from the man in the last year, but there were so many, many messages passing through the chancery from every corner of the empire that his attempt to recall them was fruitless.

All at once, the ramming ceased. Cries arose from the battlements. The men of Hatti were pouring over, almost unresisted. A wave of white surged toward the wall. Someone threw open the gate, and the white wave poured in. Lalanda was theirs. The officers and their king exchanged a wild grin of exhilaration.

"Gods be praised!" cried the king in glee, and Tiwatipara, his charioteer, whipped up the horses. The other men followed eagerly. Wurukatte had given them a victory almost without cost.

It turned out that most of the garrison was loyal. They had been overwhelmed in their sleep and slaughtered or tied up by a handful of partisans of Mira. These leaders and their henchmen, far too few to defend the fortress from the Great King's attack, were nonetheless an insolent and unrepentant bunch. Excepting foot soldiers, there were twenty-one of them, mostly minor lords from surrounding towns and all of them young. They shouted defiantly that Hatti's reign was over and that the Luwian lands would come into their own now.

Kurunta, whose troops—being those of the ranking viceroy—had shackled the prisoners and brought them before the king, lost patience with their smirking bravado and snapped at his men to rough them up a little. Although he found such unnecessary violence unworthy, Tashmi-sharrumma did not contradict his order. This was not the Kurunta he knew. He saw that his cousin was still in a black mood; perhaps this petty vengeance relieved him. The king wanted to do nothing to redirect Kurunta's anger toward himself; it already sat lodged between his ribs like a spear point, poisoning his enjoyment of this victory. The exaltation of the battle was chilling down fast.

How could I have miscalculated my cousin's reaction so badly? The terrible suspicion overwhelmed him that he might have ruined everything, both for "Tash" and for the king.

When they returned to the camp that evening, they found that Tashmi-sharrumma's brother Lurma-ziti had died suddenly. He had been ill, it was true, but there was nothing unusual in that—of all Hattushili's sons, he had had the greatest share of their father's poor health. He had been among them only that morning, with his caustic tongue intact. But instead of proceeding to the walls of the town with his relatives, he had taken to his bed. And by evening, he had gone under the black earth. He had scarcely been older than fifty. They cremated his crooked, emaciated body there on the plain of Kuwaliya, along with the few soldiers who had died in the siege.

Although there had been no love lost between him and his half brother, the king saw in this a grim omen. He watched the flames of the pyre shooting up, carrying the soul of a king's son to the gods, and wondered what those gods thought of Lurma-ziti. His own memories of the man were too painful to indulge; he had fought them down for twenty-five years.

But in spite of his reluctance, a remembrance forced

itself upon him. Lurma-ziti had promised to show his very little brother how to hunt squirrels. He had led him out into the forest, told him to hold the leather game bag while he himself stepped off into the trees to beat the animals toward the boy. Hours later, as the sun went down, a frightened and humiliated Tashmi-sharrumma had realized that he had been abandoned alone in the woods. His father's men had rescued him, but instead of berating Lurma-ziti for his cruelty, they had mocked the little boy's innocence.

An even worse memory surfaced from when he was ten and his half brother was twenty-six. Lurma-ziti's back had not been so twisted in those days, and his health had been rather better, but fortunately for the little prince, he hadn't been a strong man even so. Yet still, he he had been an adult, and Tashmi-sharrumma was only a child. Under the guise of teaching the boy to fence, Lurma-ziti had challenged him to a fight with wooden swords. The elder prince had assaulted the boy brutally, bludgeoning him with strike after strike, screaming at him to yield. But the stubborn child would not; he just kept trying to defend himself, even after he was curled up under the shield on the ground under a hail of vicious blows. Even though the others had no love for the boy, they had still called out to Lurma-ziti to stop before he killed Tashmi-sharrumma—to no avail. His brother had gone into a kind of rage, foaming at the mouth. It was Kurunta, a stripling of fourteen, who jumped on the man and dragged him to the ground. Tashmi-sharrumma crawled out from under the splintered remnants of his shield, black and blue, with broken fingers and a cracked ankle. He had never understood what had provoked Lurma-ziti's rage, but it had been utterly merciless.

The king found his breathing was becoming constricted and unsteady, and he forcibly banished this memory. He didn't want to think ill of the dead. But even more than that, he couldn't bear to feel again anything as powerful and wrenching as the hatred he had felt for his half brother that day. He had managed not to cry, but he was not able not to hate. And he had felt he was punishing himself rather than Lurma-ziti with the gales of fury, the silent storming and snarling that knotted him up inside. He was a peaceful-spirited boy. Where had that hatred come from? It was all too much for him.

The gods expected certain behavior, but they seemed to have no opinion on what one felt. Yet Tashmi-sharrumma was afraid he could never be just and merciful with such seismic anger coursing through him. He suspected that had it not been for the soothing love of Kurunta, even today he might have been a rancorous monster, caught up in a war of vengeance against his brothers. Instead, he had sworn at that moment that he would never do anything like that to anyone. He would not be so unfair, so merciless. To anyone. Ever.

The flames were so hot his face ran with sweat; he had to stand back from them. He remembered his father's pyre only a few months ago and how sorrowful he had been to think Hattushili was no longer with him. Now Tashmi-sharrumma felt nothing. The black earth had shrugged off Lurma-ziti like a fungus. The king felt neither hatred nor joy as he made himself pray for his brother's ugly soul.

CHAPTER 7

BY THE TIME THE GREAT King and his army returned to Hattusha, the first snow was falling, blurring the jagged rocks and crenellated walls of the city, stinging the northward-marching men in the face and beginning to pile up in the furrows and along the hardpan of the road. It was early. More bad news for the farmers. As the troops passed, the landscape was dismal in the extreme throughout the whole of the Lower Lands. Pasturage bare. Carcasses of dead sheep, stripped by the wolves, lying by the road. Fields blighted with drought. The snow was moisture, true, but it heralded an early winter and, to hear the augurs tell it, a harsh one. The joyful victory and even the ambiguous sorrow over Lurma-ziti's death were pushed roughly from the king's mind. All he could think of now was famine. It was coming.

Anxiety over the grain ships had come to sit permanently upon the king's shoulder like a vulture. He had received no word since their purchase. So many things could go wrong to delay the grain, and they needed it now. By the time winter had fully set in, the capital would be inaccessible. If the granaries were not filled in the next few weeks, the city would starve.

Worse was the matter of Kurunta, the key to it all. Would he sign the new vassal treaty, or was he so offended that he would renege? And if that happened, what would he do about the grain shipments that would be arriving in his port? Perhaps they already lay at anchor in Ura, and the viceroy was pouting and refusing to send them on. Tashmi-sharrumma felt he would rather have cut off a hand than suffer this lack of trust in his beloved cousin. But after all these years and all these confidences, he saw that he could be sure only of what he felt for the man, not what Kurunta was at his very core. The Kurunta he knew was light-hearted, empathetic, funny. True, he was capable of sudden changes, could flash to anger. But his wrath was over as swiftly as a spring flood rises in the mountains. The grim, implacable prince Tashmi-sharrumma had watched these last few days was not a Kurunta he recognized... and yet it was Kurunta.

I've touched him on a nerve, he told himself in misery. *I've hurt him badly, perhaps irreparably. Trust was his sore spot, and I never knew it.*

The princes ascended to the palace up the steep, rattling causeway, their horses laboring. They passed under the arched gate, through the darkness of the tunnel under the wall, and emerged into that other, hermetic world which was the royal citadel.

The *tawananna* came to see her son in his chamber almost before he could divest himself of his traveling clothes. He was unshaven and dirty, smelling vaguely of Lurma-ziti's smoke—and preoccupied. He would have preferred to collect himself before speaking to her. He would have preferred to talk to Ellat-gula—to understand more details about her charges, get a sense of how much exaggeration they contained—before confronting his mother. But Pirwannu had just brought him a clean tunic and slipped it over his head, tied the strings at the neck and knotted a wide belt around the king's waist when he heard Puduhepa's voice in the vestibule. She did not ask permission to enter. He heard her laughing with Zuzu in her rich, sweet tones, and then she had opened the door, and there she was. Cold air entered the room behind her, and the hair stood up on the king's arms.

"My son!" she held out her hands to him, beaming proudly. The *tawananna* spoke in Hurrian, her native tongue, the intimate private language she and her eldest son had shared since he was small. "The gods have granted you a victory!" She took him in her embrace and squeezed him for a long, delicious moment, and after a heartbeat, the king returned it. She was tiny; her head just reached his breast. She smelled of a sweet oil that he remembered from his earliest childhood—attar of roses. Somehow his memories were treacherously loosened by this perfume. He felt his resolve weakening.

"Lurma-ziti is dead," the king said.

"Yes, Nerikkaili told me. It's too bad, but his health was never good. Don't let that spoil the glory of this victory. This is a warning to all the vassals in the West and especially to that Alantalli. You've done really well, my dearest."

So far from basking in her praise, the king felt that he was in fact deeply undeserving. He hadn't done well at all.

"Why so glum, son? I didn't think you and Lurma-ziti were all that close."

"No. Although I didn't wish him harm." This was perhaps not self-evident to Puduhepa, who knew how the dead prince had tormented her son. He wondered just then why she had never called Lurma-ziti and the others off but instead left him to defend himself as best he could against the malice of grown men. With the help of Kurunta.

"He wasn't a very nice person, I know," she said, as if responding to his thoughts. "But we mustn't speak ill of the dead. Nerikkaili is going to tell his wife and schedule the funeral rites. He said you brought back the ashes."

Tashmi-sharrumma's jaw skewed in irritation. It irked him that his mother kept referring to Nerikkaili. She had clearly already spoken to him before approaching her own son, who was, after all, the sovereign. But he said nothing, just nodded.

The *tawananna* continued, oblivious to his annoyance. "Apparently, the Lower Lands are in bad shape, aren't they? All the reports we've received from all over the country are grave."

"No word of the grain ships?" asked the king.

"None, but Ammishtamru of Ugarit swears they've left his port. If they haven't already landed in Ura, they should arrive any day."

And of course that brought them to the inevitable subject of the new vassal treaty with Tarhuntassha. They could avoid it no longer. Puduhepa tackled it first, smiling, eager, confident that her son had conquered here, too. "Did you talk to Kurunta, my dear?"

His face frozen into its expressionless mask, the king nodded. He ran his tongue over his teeth. His mother stared up at him expectantly but received no response. Finally she prodded, "Well? When is he coming to sign it?"

The king could bear to look her in the face no longer and turned away. He tipped his own face up as if he were awaiting the snow, but in fact, his nearsighted eyes were fixed on the memory of a happier past.

"What's wrong?" His mother touched his arm, alarmed. "Is something wrong? You look very strange, son."

He faced her but declined to meet her eye except for the briefest moment. "I don't think he'll sign it. He was very offended at the whole idea. He's still angry at me after all these days."

"Angry? Why in the world? You've offered him enormously expanded concessions. This is all to his advantage. Did you say something to offend him?"

"Apparently. He said I was trying to buy his friendship."

The *tawananna* gave a huff of exasperation. "Since when is Kurunta so pure and virtuous? He's as jealous of his privileges as the next man, by the gods. You must have said something wrong, Tashmi-sharrumma. Tell me what you said."

But it was not what he had said so much as what he hadn't said, the king knew. He replied coldly, "Enough. He either signs, or he doesn't."

"But you do understand how dangerous it is to offend him at this particular moment, don't you? If he's angered, that grain could be sitting in his port right now. We have to get it before the winter sets in." She wouldn't let go, following him around as he headed toward his bed. He sat down on the edge, suddenly aware that he had reached the end of his energy. And he had yet to speak to her about Ellat-gula's letter.

She took a seat beside him, put an arm around his waist. The gesture was affectionate, but her voice was a little threatening. "You aren't going to let all your father's work fall apart now, when we need Kurunta so especially, are you, my son?"

So you were *trying to buy him all along. You used him, and now he thinks I'm using him.* Self-disgust that he had let his mother manipulate him like this overcame Tashmi-sharrumma. "I understand why he's angry. He's been dealt with shamefully."

She sprang to her feet. "Are you joking? We've showered him with favors. Is that shameful? You're mixing up your personal feelings with hard policy making. Everybody knows you're lovers."

"We're not lovers. Why would you think that?" His face was burning. He felt cornered and wanted to slash about. Then, suddenly enlightened as to the depths of her manipulation, he looked up at her with a crooked, accusing smile. "Did you want us to be?"

The *tawananna* put her hands to her face in frustration. She expelled a huge sigh, as if her trials were too much to bear. "Oh, Tashmi-sharrumma, stop lying to yourself. All those years—you think no one had eyes? What I want to know is, if you are no longer lovers, why not?" She stooped over her son and took him by the breast of his tunic. "Just keep thinking about the grain ships," she said slowly into

141

his face as if speaking to a simple child. "Just think about the fact that Kurunta is Urhi-tesshub's heir…"

The king laughed and gave a caustic shake of his head, amazed by her cynicism. She drew back, seemingly offended by his levity, and he dropped the pleasantry. "I'm thirty-six years old and the father of four children. With thirteen wives," he added wryly, reminding his mother of the new concubines she had foisted on him. "Don't you think it's time to stop meddling in my private life?"

"The king has no private life, my dear. When you figure that out, the need for me to 'meddle' will be over."

Clenching his fists, he thought to himself grimly, *Alas, nothing could be clearer*. His face was aflame with a mixture of embarrassment and anger, to think that the most intimate details of his life were the object of public scrutiny. It was what he hated more than anything.

Tashmi-sharrumma saw his mother open her mouth to say something self-justifying and headed her off, immensely relieved to change the subject. "Why have you been trying to undercut my policy with Assyria?"

She bristled, her neck arching in righteousness. "I am the *tawananna*, Tashmi-sharrumma. I have broad diplomatic powers. Beyond that, I don't really know what you mean by undercutting."

"I thought I had made it clear that I wanted to keep the alliance with Karduniash. But it seems that in my absence you've been pushing the Assyrians to attack them."

Her dark eyes snapped. "Who told you that?"

"No matter. It's true, isn't it?" He fixed her in the eye, challenging her to lie.

"It's Ellat-gula, isn't it? You still don't see through her."

"And let her bring up our son any way she wants. She's his mother, after all."

The *tawananna*'s lip curled in contempt, and her voice dripped with the same bitter serum. "Why, you're just her mouthpiece. It's pathetic. You were never very quick, but I didn't think you were stupid."

The king, stung, stared at her with glacial eyes. She faced him down, her mouth compressed, her nostrils white. There was a long pulsing space of silent confrontation, then she spurted out in fury, "Can't you just get mad like a normal person? You're like a big, cold carp. I wonder if we haven't made a mistake."

But then her face changed altogether; contrition flooded across her features, thawing them, making them beautiful again. She threw herself down on the bed beside him and put her arms around him, buried her forehead against his shoulder. He drew away slightly, hurt, not really knowing how to deal with such an outburst. Was he expected to comfort her? But it was he who had been wounded. He loved her; he didn't want to know that she had always held him in contempt, as she seemed to.

"Oh, Tashmi-sharrumma, my child. I'm so sorry. Of course I know you're not stupid—quite the contrary. There's just that sort of... obstinate innocence about you that can be frustrating. I'm so overwhelmed by all the burdens of the kingdom right now, my dear." She nuzzled her face against his arm and clung to him. The attar of roses ate away at his will. "The famine, the vassals defecting. And then all the details you show no interest in. You have to have concubines, my dear; it's been a year. Would you ever have done it if I didn't take it in hand? You should get a second-rank wife, at least one. It's your duty to have lots of children. You're not interested, I know, but you're young and strong. Look at your father. Despite his ill health, he was very concerned to provide royal sons and daughters for the diplomatic corps and to marry in alliances abroad. You see, it isn't just your private life, as you seem to believe."

"I can't do everything in twelve months. I've hardly been home." He thought of little Arnuwanda, whom he had scarcely seen since his birth. If Tashmi-sharrumma's mother was overwhelmed, how much more he himself, who had to lead the army and travel the country for religious duties in addition to everything else. But he despised this effort at excusing himself. He fell into a morose silence, staring into space over his mother's head.

"That's why there's a *tawananna,* you know, my dearest: it's just too much for one person. But you have to trust me," she said.

"Don't put Arnuwanda into the royal nursery with all my father's children and Nerikkaili's and everybody else's. I want him to know he's loved and not be picked on by bigger boys."

She looked up at him, her head tilted, as if she was marveling at a sight she had never really seen before. "But it's good for the little princes to grow up together. They form bonds that last them a lifetime."

"Yes, that's clear in our family history," the king said rather more icily than he intended. "Where do all the fratricides and usurpations come from, I wonder?"

Puduhepa laid her hand on the king's thigh and smiled with the wisdom of one who knows best. "It isn't good for a future ruler to be brought up alone, coddled by his mother. It spoils him."

"I wouldn't know."

The *tawananna* shook her son's leg affectionately. "You of all people, my dear, should see that. You were so solitary. You really needed some rough and tumble. You're much the better for it. You're a fine young man now."

"A fine cold carp?"

She made a noise of benevolent exasperation. "Forgive me, dearest. I was angry when I said that." She stroked his ill-shaven cheek. "You know how much I love you. And your father did, too. Surely you could never have doubted that."

He had *not* doubted their love, but in his childhood, it had been far away and infrequent in its doses. He had longed for their attention as for a ray of sunshine in the heart of the endless northern winter. He had not even been the *tuhkanti* until the age of twenty-five, just a younger son who had to share his father's affection with scores of little princes. Those rare occasions when Hattushili had taken him out to the battlefield—letting him ride in his chariot with him, explaining to him the different formations, the flag signals, the tactics of war—had been the purest joy. The thought of his father, that towering figure of his childhood, superhumanly powerful, glittering in golden scales, his long hair whipping, lord of the earth with his wonderful, strong, ugly face... Tashmi-sharrumma drew a shaky breath. It seemed impossible that he could miss anyone so much after a whole year. In his father's absence, his mother's attentions had taken on a feverish, demanding tone.

Puduhepa misinterpreted the shudder that went through his body.

"But you're tired, my child; you've been traveling for days. We can talk more tomorrow."

"Get him out of the nursery."

"We'll talk about it tomorrow. Good night, my victorious Sun." She kissed him brightly and bustled away.

He realized, with a sinking sense of his own impotence, that he hadn't made a dent in her.

The next day, the king surprised the servants in the court of women with an early visit to the queen. The air was bitter and dry, the sky the color of beaten silver. The wind from the mountains smelled like snow, but none was falling. The courtyard was mostly clear, with triangles of fine powder in the corners where the spiraling updrafts had blown it. Without being announced, he entered his wife's unlit chamber. She was still curled up in bed, bundled in tawny furs, her dark hair the only thing visible upon the pillows, and her body made a gently mounded mountain range beneath the covers. He shed his cloak and sat beside her, rocking the bed briefly, and she groaned a little.

He shook her shoulder. "Ellat-gula. Your husband is back."

"Tell him I'm sleeping," she mumbled.

He laughed. "No, it's me."

She opened her eyes, stretched her plump white arms luxuriantly, and curled her lips up in a satisfied, catlike smile. He leaned over and kissed her on the cheek.

"Welcome home, my conquering hero."

The king lifted a self-deprecating eyebrow. "Some conquest. They held out for about a fortnight with no active siege, then we rammed their gate and went over the wall, and that was it. There were only a few hundred of them all together. The leaders were a bunch of young idiots showing off for the king of Mira."

"You taught them a lesson, My Sun." She drew his head down to her, nose to nose. "Did you get my letter?"

He reared back up, all playfulness gone. "Yes. I talked to the *tawananna* last night. But she has an excuse for every action. I doubt if she'll change a thing on her own. Just keep Arnuwanda with you. If she gives you any trouble, I'll protect you."

The queen laced her fingers in the king's hair as if to ensnare him, but he drew away. Her tone grew petulant. "Your mother wants him in the royal nursery so she can win his heart. She wants to make him her creature, My Sun, like all the other princes of your house. She'll try to turn him against me, his own mother."

"I said keep him." Her whining irritated him. He felt helpless against his mother. He was far too honest—what did Puduhepa call him, obstinately innocent?—to be a worthy opponent of that master of guile.

"Did she admit she's trying to poison the alliance with my brother?"

"No. But I think she's guilty of it nonetheless." The king let out a sigh as inconspicuously as he could.

"Don't let her force your hand, My Sun."

"Don't worry," he said a little crossly, then revised his tone. "We'll renegotiate the treaty, then it will be my seal on it. She won't be able to break it."

Unconvinced, Ellat-gula sniffed, "I put nothing past her."

"That would be illegal since it'll be in writing. She won't dare do it."

Ellat-gula sat up in bed, the covers dropping to her lap. She was still lusciously fat from her pregnancy, with rolls of flesh at her waist, a soft, round belly that hung a little over her bush, and enormous breasts. Her black hair cascaded over her shoulders like shining water. Eyes bright and inviting, she tried to pull her husband over to her, but he stood up, shifting his gaze away, and stretched.

"I have a lot of things to do. Maybe tonight." Then he remembered with a sigh of weariness that he had to start his round of visits to the concubines his mother had bought for him. *A dozen.* "Or maybe in a fortnight."

The queen pouted, and her eyes grew baleful. She pulled the furs up to her neck. He admired her beauty but felt no desire. His congress with her was all about producing children. But she was lively and amusing and content with a minimal display of affection on his part. Her company was restful... or had been in the past. Lately, she had become demanding.

"I've waited for you all these weeks, My Sun. Don't you want another little prince?"

"Lots of other things have waited, too, my dear. For one thing, I want to see Arnuwanda," he said wearily.

"I'll have them bring him in."

He tried to protest and tell her he'd go to the nursery, but she threw back the covers and swung her feet to the floor. Tashmi-sharrumma discreetly averted his eyes from the display of white flesh; nakedness was shameful in Hatti Land. But not in Karduniash, it seemed. She padded to the door in her glorious bareness, despite his offer of his cloak, and called to her handmaids.

In fact, it was Patiya who appeared in the doorway. Seeing the king behind her daughter, she became all happy and excited, her hilarity rising in suggestive squeals. She grabbed her daughter's belly and made it jiggle, and the two women laughed uproariously. Ellat-gula wagged her dimpled fanny in a playful dance while her mother giggled and says, "Nice, eh, My Sun? Like Ishtar, eh? Full of babies."

Tashmi-sharrumma was suffocating with discomfort. He felt a trickle of sweat down his back. *Dear gods, such excruciating bad taste, these women.* He couldn't look at them. "Bring my son." He wrapped his cloak around his wife's shoulders, and she accepted it, smiling up at him archly, but didn't really conceal herself with it. He wanted desperately to flee the room, overheated as it was in every sense. The only thing he could think about was Kurunta and how their friendship might be ruined forever. All of a sudden, he understood his mother's suspicions. These Babylonians were utterly foreign; they just didn't think like the men of Hatti Land.

After a moment, Ellat-gula's cousin Amatalla carried in the baby *tuhkanti*, swaddled warmly in her arms. Only his little round face was exposed, red and disgruntled from the trip through the cold. He had wispy hair—dark, lively hair like his mother's. He was a beautiful child, with a pretty little mouth and eyes of an indeterminate color. He looked up suspiciously at this tall man, who was a stranger to him.

"Thanks to all the Tawara, he takes after you." The king smiled, his heart going out to the child. He touched the infant's cheek with his fingertip. Here was the future of his kingdom. Had Hattushili had this same feeling toward him, although he was only a younger son? He thought of all the burdens that awaited the child's shoulders. *Be wise, little boy. Be just.* The idea of Arnuwanda being brought up by these immoral Babylonians was disturbing. He felt that perhaps his mother had the right in this matter after all.

They had brought his three daughters as well. Taduhepa was just a toddler who ignored him, absorbed with her doll. Ehli-nikkal was thirteen, Hantawiya two years younger. Unveiled, both were still physically children. They were older than some of his sisters, yet they were total strangers to him, he realized, pained. After thirteen years living in the same palace, he could not have picked them out of a crowd. The older two were skinny girls, narrow and stick armed, with undistinguished faces and mousy brown hair. But the eldest made an earnest little bow and said in a surprisingly low voice for a young girl, "Be well, my father."

He found himself charmed. He smoothed her hair affectionately then did the same for the younger one, who looked almost frightened. *The shy one. We mustn't forget her.* "Thank you, my lovely daughters. Are you both well and happy?" "Yes, Father," they chorused.

"Is there anything you lack for?" *Yes,* he answered himself silently. *My love. You've hardly even seen me. You were small children the last time I so much as said hello.* Shame covered him.

"No, Father," said Ehli-nikkal, the spokesperson.

"Is everyone kind to you?"

"Yes, Father."

Does your mother look down on you because you are not beautiful? he wanted to ask. But no doubt it was enough that they were daughters and not sons. He wanted to be sure they were given in marriage to someone kind. He thought of his eldest sister, Gasshulawiya, who had been married away to a vassal almost old enough to be her grandfather.

Ellat-gula—who had, mercifully, covered herself—stepped up to the girls and wrapped an arm around each, pressing them against her sides like a goose with her goslings. The little one ran over and clasped her mother's legs, looking up adoringly. The queen's smile was genuinely loving, he saw with relief.

"They are very good girls," she said proudly. "They can spin and embroidery—how do you say that?—and they speak Akkadian as well as Neshite."

"I'm impressed. I think I have especially wonderful children." He saw the happy grin shy Hantawiya flashed her mother. Then they were led out, and in perhaps another five or six years he would see them again, if they hadn't been sent to Mizri or Taruisha or somewhere remote to fulfill the role of living peacemakers.

Alone once more with his wife, Tashmi-sharrumma found he had nothing to say. She smiled at him a bit slyly, an expression that was part triumph and part accusation. Acute discomfort and even revulsion seeped back into him as he remembered her little naked dance. He made his excuses and returned to the clean cold of the out-of-doors. He couldn't get out fast enough. Tashmi-sharrumma took long drafts into his lungs and expelled them slowly, watching the fog his breath left hanging in the frosty air, trying to cleanse himself of the Babylonian infection. He thought unhappily that he would have to say something to Ellat-gula. She should have a better sense of propriety after all these years. Perhaps bearing her husband an heir had gone to her head.

The king was en route to the chancery when he saw Tattamaru coming his way. The chief shepherd of Arinniti was a fleshy, good-looking man about Kurunta's age but a head shorter, who looked more at home on the battlefield with his units than at an altar of sacrifice. Tashmi-sharrumma experienced a certain sense of constriction in his presence, knowing that Tattamaru was his mother's partisan, indeed her kinsman.

The priest fell to his knees, and the king motioned to him to rise. Tattamaru's jowly face was strained and grave. He blurted out, "My Sun, there's some bad news I need to communicate to you. One of my confreres just came in from Arinna. The plague has broken out in the holy city."

"Iyarri protect us," the king murmured, a chill running down his back. *Plague!* What was missing from his misery but this? And of all places, the stronghold of the Sun Goddess herself, Wurushemu the Arinniti—she of Arinna, the Torch of Hatti Land.

"How many cases so far?"

"Only two, but with the winter weather setting in, everyone is cooped up together. It's bound to spread."

And in a few months, the king thought, *when spring opens up the roads, pilgrims will be flocking to the holy city and carrying plague back to all corners of the land. How long before it arrives in Hattusha? Arinna is less than a day's journey away.*

"Find out how we've angered the gods," the king instructed him grimly. "Have we neglected something?

152

Have we omitted to thank one of them? Is there pollution somewhere? Find out."

Are they angry because the son of a usurper sits in the arms of Halmashuit? He dared not voice that question. If they answered "yes," what should he do?

CHAPTER 8

THE FIRST SUNLIGHT OF SPRING had raked across the bleak mountaintops and gilded the battlements of Hattusha. The pure, sterile scent of cold gave way to a rich, damp, earthy smell. At last the winter was ending, at least in name—in the shadow of the walls and the crevices of the rock snow still lingered. The king couldn't remember such a winter ever. The plateau below the city should have been frothy with apple blossoms, but the orchards were still nearly bare.

Tashmi-sharrumma hoped the crops would be better this year, but it was hard to be optimistic. The Festival of Sowing, the Purulli festival, had taken on an almost desperate urgency. Two bad years—well, the shipments of grain from Mizri had managed to keep them afloat. But a third? A fourth? Hatti Land was never so very far away from famine. And soldiers had to be fed in order to fight.

Hanging in the back of his mind, like a spider bouncing on its web, was the thought that the gods were angry with him.

The day before the Purulli festival began, the Great

King met with the priests and the Lords of Hatti to discuss something of vital importance. They were closeted in the council room where the *panku*—the plenary meeting of all the palace personnel—used to meet, back when it had been an important deliberative body. Now it was only the king, his brothers, cousins, and uncles, and the priests and scribes. And the *tawananna*.

"My lords, my mother. There is still plague in Arinna. Do we go there or not for the festival?"

"There's plague here, too." Nerikkaili shrugged fatalistically. "But that's not a vote for going inside the sanctuary, My Sun. I think the outer gate of the city is far enough to satisfy the demands of the ritual—though I'm no priest."

"I *am* a priest," says Tattamaru, "and I agree. We can't take chances with the life of the king."

And the queen, thought Tashmi-sharrumma. Ellat-gula was pregnant again. But Tattamaru was his mother's man, and no doubt she would very eagerly take chances with the queen's life.

Walwa-ziti pursed his little red lips and looked skeptical in his cuddly way. "How can we be sure the goddess will not be offended if we curtail her visit? I say, seek an oracle."

"An oracle it is," the king told Tattamaru. They sent Tarhun-miya out with a message to the shepherds to watch birds and examine sheep livers.

"What about the others?"

"Do we want to risk plague in *any* member of the royal family?" demanded the *tawananna* with an expression of incredulity that said she would never condone such a thing.

155

"Anything that enters the palace compound will spread like a fire in chaff."

The king suppressed a dry smile. His mother's unfortunate choice of imagery seemed to imply that most of the denizens of the palace were useless waste. He said nothing.

"So we avoid Arinna altogether?" Hishni stroked his chin. "I'll abide by the oracle, but that surely looks like asking for the goddess's displeasure."

"All right. To the gate. What do you think, My Sun?" said Nerikkaili.

"You to the gate, me into the sanctuary, as usual, and—"

"With guards, at least," interrupted Hishni.

"The queen stays with you," finished Tashmi-sharrumma.

The *tawananna* leaned across the circle of chairs to the king. "But son, you're the one we need to protect the most. You don't seem to understand. Your life is infinitely important." She took his hand, and her persuasiveness turned on him like a sudden shower. In a soft and intimate tone, she said—as if the others were not present—"You don't have to play the hero."

No, Mother; you don't understand. The king suppressed with difficulty his annoyance at being treated like a child and said in a mild tone, "Nothing must jeopardize the favor of the goddess. Nobody's life is more important than that."

"Seems risky." Nerikkaili sucked on his lip in thought.

Come on, brother, thought the king sourly. *You wouldn't mind me dying, would you?*

"It's like sending the Great King into the front line of battle. I mean, no one doubts your courage, My Sun, but…" Nerikkaili shrugged. *But you're a fool to do it,* his gesture seemed to say.

"That's my will," the king said firmly, glancing sideways at the *tawananna* from under his lids. "That's my will. Whether the oracle requires it or not."

"You're sure, my lord…?" murmured Walwa-ziti. The others exchanged dubious glances. No one wanted to contradict him.

"Will the Lady of Arinna not be angry if we all enter her son's temple but not hers? Perhaps we should wait outside the gates of the Storm God at Nerik as well," Hishni said reluctantly. He looked to Tattamaru for support. "We could simply make this a change of ritual, not a slight."

But the *tawananna* was not so easily persuaded. "This is foolhardy, son. I beg you, don't do it."

And for the first time, Kurunta spoke from his corner. His face was as cold as last winter's lingering snow. "You won't change a mule's mind by beating it. Let him go."

As the Lords of Hatti dispersed from their discussion, the king walked along alone, his eyes on the pavement, too much the object of his relatives' annoyance for anyone to accompany him. He looked up to see his secretary hustling toward him, bobbing a hasty bow. Tarhun-miya must be returning from his mission to the oracular priests. His woodpecker face was stiff and scared, and he kept looking around him like a furtive animal.

"My Sun, a word with you, I beg." The scribe was so nervous he could hardly stand still.

The king drew him over against the wall of the public court and, suppressing the chill of anxiety that prickled up his neck, said as calmly as he could, "What is it? Bad oracle?"

The secretary dropped his voice to a whisper. "My Sun, as I was returning from the court of the oracle priests, I stopped for a moment to… to urinate against the wall. And as I stood there, I heard a voice whisper, 'King's secretary.'"

The king swallowed down a wry comment about pee oracles and looked closely at Tarhun-miya, who licked his lips. He was almost panting with distress, and his eyes were round as moons. He certainly wasn't being facetious.

"Then it said, 'I have a message for your master, and he must heed me if he values his life.'"

"What do you suppose this voice was? The Lord Sharrumma?" asked the king uneasily.

"It was a man, My Sun. A man. Someone was standing just around the corner of the wall, clearly, and saw me stop. And then he said, 'The king's brother is going to try to kill him in Nerik during the festival.'" Tarhun-miya stared up at the king with anguish in his face.

Tashmi-sharrumma felt his heart constrict, but he continued to speak in a level tone. "Which brother? Did the voice say?"

"No, My Sun. Just 'the king's brother.'"

"And how do you suppose this voice knew such a thing, Tarhun-miya?"

"I don't know, My Sun. He said a high official sent you this message. He said you would suspect the official, but he was not involved."

The king said to himself that all the high officials of the land had been in the council chamber with him, although this voice might well have been that of someone's servant.

"Thank you, Tarhun-miya. Well done. I'll deal with it."

His first instinct was to tell Hishni to provide extra guards, but then, Hishni was the king's brother. The king stood for a moment, blank faced, despairing. Whom could he trust? None of his myriad brothers, neither the full first-rank ones—Huzziya, Shanda-kurunta, even little Hannutti—nor Nerikkaili and Hishni, his second-rank half brothers... nor any of the many sons of his father's lesser women. Six months ago, the clear answer would have been Kurunta. But he felt he no longer knew Kurunta. The viceroy of Tarhuntassha had turned into another person, sullen and implacable. True, he conversed and laughed with the others, but he never so much as approached the king, never tried to have a word alone, barely spoke in his presence. And even then... with a wince of pain, Tashmi-sharrumma remembered the chilling tone of his cousin's voice in council, dismissing all attempts to convince the king to be prudent.

Kurunta had even begun to look harder, long lines bracketing his mouth and pinching a pleat in his forehead. The king realized how much of the man's beauty was the open goodness of his expression—cheerful, mercurial, mischievous Ulmi. He was gone, and his loss was a death. Tashmi-sharrumma wondered just how bad it would be if someone *were* to assassinate him tomorrow. How many problems it would resolve... and yet he didn't want to die.

He looked up and realized that the Lords of Hatti had all dispersed. The courtyard was empty. He stood alone.

He wheeled and headed for the court of women. The queen had to be warned not to stand near him in Nerik. But as he approached the gate, his mother peeled off from the shadows and strode toward him, her face flushed with anger.

"You must do something about that woman and her thieving cousin," she began, but he shushed her with a hand.

"I have something more important to tell you."

"How do you know it's more important?" she stormed. "I haven't told you my story yet!"

He revealed to her the message transmitted through Tarhun-miya.

Her face grew white, and her eyes became enormous; she clutched the breast of her son's tunic. "Dear Shaushga, who can it be? Tashmi-sharrumma, you must cancel the ceremonies."

"No."

"Dear gods," she cried, grabbing at her head, "plague is not enough; now someone is trying to assassinate you! We must tell Tattamaru to put extra Golden Spearmen around you, in case it's Hishni."

"Won't that tip him off if he's the one? There are always twelve *meshedi* and twelve Spearmen. Besides, I don't think it's Hishni. He has no motivation."

"Who, then? Surely not one of your younger brothers?"

A rush of annoyance at her deliberate obtuseness burned at his throat, but he said calmly, "I see you're avoiding the obvious answer, my mother. Who has more to gain than Nerikkaili?"

"Don't be ridiculous, my son. He's been faithful so many times when he might have risen against you."

"He'll be standing closer than any of the others."

"I think you misjudge him—"

"I would rather be guilty of misjudging him and stay alive than trust him and be dead. Help me warn Alalimmi and Tattamaru. A few soldiers among the participants may come in handy."

⁜

They clad Tashmi-sharrumma in an ankle-length purple tunic with a silver belt. Over his shoulders, the priests laid a heavy mantle of blue, dyed with lapis and embroidered in gold along the selvages. They arranged the folds in the bend of his left arm while he stood as passively as a doll. The chief of the royal smiths presented him with a long curled divining rod, like a shepherd's crook made of gilded bronze. The king closed his fingers upon it, the reminder that he must shepherd the people of the Storm God. And then the smith set in his right hand an iron spear. The artisan backed away, not raising his eyes to the ruler chosen by the gods to defend his people.

The priests laid upon the king's head the red leather cap with its seams elaborated in gold that was the crown of his people's sovereign. They buckled a curved, gold-hilted sword at his waist, its pommel a crescent moon. His wrists and ears and throat and fingers glittered with pure gold; he coruscated in the shadowy sanctuary like a reflection of the Sun God, the god of justice. But Tashmi-sharrumma was well aware that this magnificence was borrowed; he was the image of a god, but only the image.

His throat was dry, his thoughts somber. The ceremony had to go perfectly. The gods had to accept the festival with pleasure; they had to turn their compassionate eyes upon Hatti Land. Any impurity in their vicar, any cowardice, any injustice, could vitiate the entire ritual. He alone stood between the thousand gods of Hatti and the human world. And he knew that neither he nor his family was without guilt.

They led the queen in to him, caparisoned as resplendently as he in purple and blue. She was beaming, almost effervescent, with her swelling belly, as she took her place beside him on the dais. It crossed his mind that she did not understand the gravity of the moment, let alone the danger. He was, in fact, beginning to wonder uneasily if he had done the right thing by siding with her against the *tawananna*. Despite yielding to his wife in this way, his easy relationship with her had chilled. He could hardly enter her chambers without painful self-consciousness and the awareness of his falsity. Indeed, his relationships with everyone—with all of those few people to whom he had ever revealed anything of himself—had curdled: Ellat-gula, his mother, Kurunta...

He tried to look less grim for the sake of the worshipers who would soon surround him, but the forced smile melted off almost immediately. *What have I done wrong?*

He had spent the whole night in vigil wrestling with just such questions, determined to be honest with himself. But still he had no answers. He seemed to know himself very little. Perhaps his fear was stronger than his desire for the truth. And now he might be facing his last hours.

The marshals invited him and the queen to descend from the dais. The royal couple paced deliberately through the sanctuary of the temple of Sharrumma toward the gateway in the wall that surrounded the temple district as though containing a city within a city. The king adjusted his long stride to his wife's short, burdened ones. The shaven-headed priests fell in behind them. At the gate awaited the massive, decorated oxcart that served as the rolling temple of Sharrumma for the course of this divine pilgrimage, which would last for an entire month.

The god had been summoned into his statue by words of power. Hip high to a man, it was made of wood covered with silver and gold and studded with precious stones. It was the shimmering, mysterious vision of the deity who inhabited it—he who wielded the lightning as his sword, who tempered the power of the storms, who sent the rains.

He who decided whether there would be crops, and whether the people of Hatti would eat.

To Tashmi-sharrumma's weak eyes, dazzled as he emerged into the sunlight, the gleaming vision of his patron deity was almost unendurable. Blinking, he handed off the crook and spear to the priests at his side, dropped to his knees upon the carpet they had spread there for him at the foot of the cart, and prostrated himself, his hands before his face. This ritual was older even than his people; it had belonged to the Hattic tribes who had inhabited the land before the coming of the Hittites. The king hoped these ancient gods were amenable to the prayers of their conquerors.

"Storm God of Nerik, my lord, I am but a human being, but my father was a priest of Shaushga of Shamuha. My father begot me, but the Storm God of Nerik took me from my mother and reared me; he made me his priest and a priest of all the gods. He appointed me to kingship in Hatti Land," he prayed in what he hoped was a carrying voice. He had always dreaded reciting things aloud.

The words were formulaic, but he meant them with all his heart. If the gods were deaf to his pleas, things would go from bad to worse. It occurred to him that Ellat-gula was kneeling at his side but not lying on her face. Of course, she couldn't with her pregnancy so far advanced, but he hoped the gods would see things the same way and not be offended.

"So now I, Tudhaliya the king, who have been reared by you, O Storm God, am pleading: take the words of my tongue and transmit them to the gods. Do not let them turn their back to my words."

There was more, but it all meant the same thing. His ancestors had written these words—generations after generations of kings standing between a precarious land and its thousand mighty gods.

After he had completed the prayers prescribed, acolytes helped the king to his feet, and the procedure was repeated at the feet of the god Telepinu, Lord of Crops, and at the feet of ancient Inara, Lady of Wild Beasts. The carts rolled forward with a creak, a rumble of heavy wheels, the shuffling of bovine hoofs on stone. The king and queen mounted the splendid, two-wheeled carriage that would be their own transportation to the holy cities of Nerik and Arinna. Priests and acolytes walked at their side. The white-clad soldiers of the royal bodyguard—led by the king's own brother—and the Golden Spearmen in their saffron tunics and leather leggings surrounded the king's personal carriage. Behind were the carriages of the *tawananna* and other members of the royal family: lesser wives, his older children, even young brothers and unmarried sisters, a whole race of kings' sons and daughters.

Kurunta is back there with the other viceroys, vassals, and lord protectors, Tashmi-sharrumma thought, distracted. His cousin was still faithful in his duties, although they had no words together, friendly or otherwise. To see Kurunta beside him in the guise of a stranger and know that the viceroy could seek him out but chose not to was far worse than not seeing him at all. At least then Tashmi-sharrumma could still wonder if the whole ugly business was just his oversensitive perceptions at work. But it was real. They were no longer friends. The knowledge of his loss was a suppurating wound.

Other carts followed, loaded with gifts for the temples of the gods in Nerik and Arinna. Bulls and asses, sheep and goats destined for sacrifice were herded along, splendid in garlands and red ribbons. Priests, musicians, dancers, and acrobats swelled the procession.

They descended from the temple to the great vaulted gateway of the city itself in a rumbling, clattering stream that poured between the clay-colored houses and outcroppings of bare gray rock. People were hanging out the windows, crowded along the roadway, standing on the roofs of buildings, cheering the passage of their gods and their human rulers, throwing leaves and flowers. They looked forward to the month of feasting and celebrations Purulli promised. There would be plays and acrobatics, songs and dances. There would be lots of beer and *walhi* drink. They would be able to forget for a while that want was never far away in this bleak highland kingdom.

On the other hand, Tashmi-sharrumma couldn't forget the dwindling contents of the state granaries and the threat of another bad harvest that the endless winter had imposed upon them. He thought of the plague that had raged only months before in Arinna and the trap that one of his own blood would spring upon him. Beneath the gorgeous raiment, his heart sat like a numb stone in his middle.

This was as close as any citizens would ever get to their king unless they had special clearance and underwent an elaborate ritual purification. The king realized this was also as close as he would get to the people he had been chosen to shepherd. He looked around at them from his carriage, and they were only a blur of mouths opening in white faces and the multicolored splotches of feast-day clothes. Their laughter subsided into awe at the passage of his carriage and those of the gods and then became joyous once more as the royal children followed. They shouted out blessings for the young princes and princesses.

Perhaps they didn't even realize that he, their king, was only a man, dressed as he was in the robes of Ishtanu himself. *I'm kept so sequestered*, he thought ruefully. At least when he had been a prince, he could move around without two dozen armed men isolating him from his own subjects. If they had only thought about it, the greatest danger was not the populace but his family, riding at his unprotected back. There was no shield bearer in his carriage, just the driver, his faithful Tiwatipara, who was himself a lower-rank half brother. *Could he be the one?*

Enough. Away, you Fears and Terrors. No matter how much harm someone may wish me, surely he would never dare to act during a sacred festival.

But then he remembered the brothers of the king of Ugarit, and his back seemed to tingle, feeling its vulnerability.

It took the long procession the better part of the day to reach Arinna, the holy city of the Sun Goddess. The city was small, containing little more than the temple complexes and such workshops and markets as were required to support the priests and their families and those who came on pilgrimage. Once the votaries of Wurushemu entered her citadel, they never emerged, even to marry. Brides had to be brought inside to them. Only the artisans and merchants came and went. The winter's plague had cut deeply into the temple personnel, but because of the snow, few civilians had left the city, either. So far, the disease had been more or less isolated, had burned itself out. But now that spring was here and the season of pilgrimage had begun, all that could change.

The royal party camped on the still-frozen pastures at the gates of Arinna, and at sunrise, the king, accompanied only by his two dozen guards and the line of priests and priestesses who had come to greet him, entered the city on foot. No longer the image of a god, resplendent in purple and gold, he was clad in the humble white wool of a shepherd, his head bare.

They passed beneath the gate and through streets still dark and void of inhabitants, the only sounds their steps and the creaking of carts and the dull clopping of the animals. Somewhere, invisible, lurked the plague. The thought of disease stirred a painful tightness in Tashmi-sharrumma's stomach. He was certainly no coward, but memories of his father's later years of suffering haunted him.

Yet the plague did not linger; it claimed its victims quickly, and few escaped its greedy clutches. The king told himself that he was the chief priest of the Storm God of

Nerik, the Lady Arinniti's beloved son. Surely, she would not permit him to die in her temple. Still, his heart was pounding as he strode across the plaza that separated the civilian part of town from the temple complex at its center.

Normally, this would be a long, festive procession. Now only he and the wagonloads of gifts and sacrificial animals were conducted into the halls of the goddess. The Storm God's statue entered the sanctuary to pay a visit to his mother, while the human servants of the Arinniti climbed up to the roof of the temple, where the king would make offerings in the name of all Hatti Land.

The wind was blowing on the roof, still bitter well into the spring, making their priestly skirts dance and whipping the king's hair around his face. The acolytes began their preparations, but the celebrants sat in the waning darkness, watching for the first glimmer of light in the east. The king had all he could do to keep his fingers from drumming nervously. He had only carried out this ceremony once before in his own name. He breathed deeply and strove to calm himself, to place himself in the goddess's hands.

The sky was growing light. The two wicker tables were set up facing east, one for the Lady Arinniti and one for her son. On them lay the thick breads, the honey and oil, the pot of curds, the bowl of groats, and the thirty pitchers of wine.

The master of ceremonies gestured to the king to commence. He rose, swallowed his fear, and bowed to the dawn manifestation of the Torch of Hatti Land. He invoked her through the divine bull, Sheri, the spokesman of his people. As his hair slapped him in the mouth, he prayed the ancient calling down of mercy. Fighting the sails of his wind-whipped cloak, the king dipped the numerous breads in honey and oil and offered them to the goddess then poured out the curds and the groats; he libated the wine, each pour tendered to a different god or goddess, beginning with Wurushemu herself and all the gods of rain.

Now came the plea: "Give us a rich harvest, O Great Lady. Do not let your people starve," and silently the king added, *nor let your servant die of plague or sword this day. And show me how to regain Kurunta's friendship.*

Again he made a round of offerings to the thousand gods and a special invocation of the Oath Gods—he, the son of a forsworn subject. Finally, the thickly spread loaves were cast into the fire, and the food that symbolized the goddess's plenty was given back to her. The king's duties were complete. Tension drained out of him like a libation, and gratefully, he retraced his steps to the city gate. He fancied he must be staggering, although he knew his weakness was invisible to all but himself. Relief flooded him, though it hardly seemed justified—had he expected the plague to jump out at him like a man in a black cloak?

By that evening, Tashmi-sharrumma was tottering, exhausted beyond the physical demands of his day. He had scarcely dared to draw a breath from sunrise to dusk. He suffered the strained excuse for a banquet the royal family celebrated in common and retreated early to his own tent. Ellat-gula followed him in. She was impossibly jovial and made him put his hand on her belly to feel the baby kick.

"I'm exposed to the plague. You'd better stay away," he warned her with the irritability of the bone weary.

She jumped away as if she had been scorched. "Why

169

didn't you say so, my husband? Do you want to put your son in danger?"

He gave her a blank stare, but she declined to understand his mood. *She's changed since the birth of Arnuwanda*, the king thought, not for the first time. Her ambition was starting to overcome her prudence. She was becoming less restful, more demanding. Her high-pitched voice grated on his nerves, and he had begun to dread her company.

"Is that why the rest of us stayed outside, then? Oh, my poor husband. Are you going to get sick?"

"Hopefully not. Though if it brings a good harvest, I suppose that's the least I can do."

"Well, I'm going to my tent." At least she knew better than to propose jumping into bed with him and risk pollution on a pilgrimage.

"Wait, there's something I've been wanting to talk to you about for a long time. I just keep forgetting." In fact, he had hardly seen her since last winter except on ceremonial public occasions. "You mustn't go around naked that way. It isn't decent. Maybe people do things like that in Karduniash, but not here. It displeases me, all right?"

She looked hurt and offended and drew her cloak around her defensively. "In my own bedroom? With my own husband?"

"I don't like it. You're the queen; you should maintain some dignity. And I certainly don't want Arnuwanda to see you like that."

"Because the beautiful body of a woman is a bad sight?" Her little round face grew sad; she looked up at him in resignation and reached out to squeeze his hand. "I know you don't really like women, My Sun. It's all right."

"Why would you say that? By the thousand gods, Ellat-gula; you can hardly complain I've neglected you. You're carrying my fifth child." He had tried so hard to be kind and affectionate toward her, to touch her as he thought she wanted to be touched and not to make her feel he merely endured her. In his exhaustion, the criticism was more than he could face with equanimity. He knew his tone was harsher than it should have been.

"I know, my dear. But… oh, well. Ours was diplomatic marriage, after all. We can't expect to love each other, too."

"You don't want love; you want power," he threw at her, but he felt like a brute. Her face fell, and her eyes grew moist. Despite his best efforts, he had a terrible faculty for hurting people. He clenched his jaw to stop a sudden tremor in his lips.

"I want to help you rule Hatti Land, yes, My Sun. This is the mission the gods have given me when I marry you. Here women can do much to help their king, so why should not I? Even if it displeases you to think so, I am fond of you."

She had completely rephrased his words to make herself look like a martyr. Guilt shook its finger at him, and the queen's little hands against his chest, which seemed to say *I'm not mad at you, mean though you are,* made him feel all the worse. The king realized he couldn't tell when she was sincere and when she was acting. But worse still, he didn't know when he was sincere. He was twitchy with his own dishonesty. He couldn't breathe, as wildly uncomfortable as if fighting an enemy in the dark. Part of him was moved that she said she was fond of him; he would have liked to think his efforts to be kind had been convincing. Yet

171

what were they but a convincing lie? Now he wanted to yell, "Don't touch me; it isn't fair," but he knew that he longed for someone else to touch him. Instead, he said without heat, "You'd better go. We don't want to endanger the child."

CHAPTER 9

T HE NEXT MORNING, BEFORE THE royal procession could form up for the long day's trip to Nerik, the holy city of the Storm God, the *tawananna* burst into her son's tent.

"What have you finally decided to do tomorrow, son?"

Pirwannu was shaving the king, and the latter replied in the stiff diction of a man to whose lip a razor was being applied. "Enter the sanctuary alone and carry out the rites, as we all decided the other day."

"No, I mean about…" She raised her eyebrows and tipped her head at the valet as if to indicate that she couldn't speak in his presence. "You know, the threat…"

The king sighed, gestured to Pirwannu to retreat, and sat forward, half of his face still bearded with suds and his hair braided down his back to keep it away from the soap. His mother's anxious expression released into a smile, and she ran her hand tenderly across his temple. *This is not a good look on him,* she thought. *It makes his face seem narrower and bonier and more crooked than ever.*

"Everyone who is not my brother is on the alert,"

said the king. "Alalimmi has extra men in civilian clothes planted among the participants. We've written ahead to the priests of Nerik to warn them; they'll be on the lookout, too, and some of them will be armed. I don't know what else to do. Sharrumma will protect me."

"Tashmi-sharrumma, don't go alone into the city." Her voice was brittle with concern.

"Why? I'll be away from my brothers there."

"But the *meshedi* may be in on it. He may have coconspirators. What if some of the priests are part of this? We don't know if this is just one person or a whole group, if it's political or just personal—"

Tashmi-sharrumma grinned. "The king has no personal life, remember?"

"Don't be facetious, son. Your life is in danger."

"Do you get this worked up every time I go into battle?" he asked, continuing to smile in a brittle way.

She huffed in vexation. "Take this seriously, please. And yes, I do. Mothers suffer the torments of the underworld every time their sons buckle on armor and go off to play soldier, believe me. But someone has targeted you personally today. One of your own brothers. Someone you thought you could trust."

"Yet again," he muttered cryptically. And then, looking at her from under his heavy lids, he said, "I don't know what you want me to do. We can't fail to carry out the rites."

How irritating her firstborn could be, she thought, torn between tenderness and frustration. *He's so stubborn, so full of stupid male heroics. Yet he was always the cautious one as a child. It was Kurunta who had the harebrained schemes of glory—first one thing, then another.*

"All right, then. As long as some sort of protection is in place. But carry a dagger. Be alert."

"Yes, Mother."

She rose, kissed his forehead, and stroked his hair once again. *It's a shame he didn't get my darker hair,* she thought fondly. *His is a little mousy.*

Outside the tent, Pirwannu stood with his arms wrapped around himself against the cold, dancing from foot to foot.

"You can go back in." She smiled, all graciousness.

But her mood was far from cheery as she wended her way between the tents of her cousins, sons, and stepsons. The sky was beginning to grow lighter. She found the tent with the lightning bolt standard of Tarhuntassha flapping lazily at the entrance, and nudging aside the guard, she pushed the flap back, calling, "Kurunta, are you decent? I'm coming in."

The king's cousin was alone, eating a bowl of porridge at a small folding table. He looked up, recognized the *tawananna*, and rose. He smiled, but with a subtle lack of warmth. There was something haggard about his handsome face. Of course, the harsh lamplight was unflattering. Still, there seemed to be lines that had not been there even a few months ago. *But then,* she realized, *he's over forty—not so young anymore.* She thought of him as Tashmi-sharrumma's age, if not younger.

"My lady and better-than-mother." He grinned, arms outstretched. "What brings you here at this impossible hour?"

She embraced him feverishly. "Kurunta, my dear. I'm so worried about the king."

His smile chilled noticeably. "Don't be. He's a grown-up; he can take care of himself."

"Help him, please. Stay close, and keep your eye on his brothers. He loves you more than any of them."

"Does he, now?" Kurunta's eyes narrowed.

Puduhepa could feel the rigidity of his back under her hands. *But he must listen to me. He must.*

"He does. More than anyone else at all, I think." She stared up into his dark, long-lidded eyes and tried to read what mysterious anger was there. But he pulled away, picked up his bowl, and standing, finished spooning his breakfast into his mouth.

She followed him, desperate to melt his resistance. Her voice splintered with her urgency. "Don't let him down. He trusts you, Kurunta."

"Oh, does he, do you think?"

"Of course he does. Don't you believe that?"

"Let me hear it from his mouth."

"What's happened between you and my son?" She clutched at his arm, almost whispering. *These two are acting like children while the kingdom trembles on the brink of disaster. After all those years of cultivating the pair of them...* yet she was less irritated than sorrowful. Clearly, it cost them both dear. Anger of this magnitude came from a very deep place.

But Kurunta was not in a mood to explain. He jerked himself free of her hand. "Nothing," he said tersely. "Tash is his old self, as frozen as the Marrasshantiya in midwinter."

"He can't help the way he is. He doesn't deserve to die

for it," she cried. "And he *will* die unless you help protect him today."

Kurunta turned on her angrily, his face red. "I *will* help protect him, woman. Who do you think sent that message?"

"You?" The *tawananna* was dumbfounded. "And you called yourself a 'high official'?"

"Well, I'm a fucking viceroy, am I not?"

"But you're so much more than that to him, Kurunta. And why didn't you tell him yourself instead of this crazy business of anonymous voices?"

"Oh, I think he doesn't much want to talk to me." His whole body was stiff and quivering. He looked as though he wanted to tear something apart.

Then she remembered what the message said: *He will suspect me.* Her heart curled up with pain for this man. She had raised him like her own child, from the moment she had been a fourteen-year-old bride and her brother-in-law had entrusted his banished infant son to her and Hattushili while he went off to a war that might well have proved fatal. The king had not died, but he had never taken Ulmi-tesshub back. *Does he feel he was abandoned?*

"I'm so very sorry," she said softly.

He turned on her with an ugly laugh. "I'll bet you are. I'll bet you were getting anxious about those grain ships last fall, weren't you?" He was almost yelling. She clasped her hands in distress, and he lowered his tone. "Tell your son that I am fulfilling my duties as a vassal. I'll send troops; I'll report food supplies; I'll show up for councils and festivals. Don't worry about a thing. I know he's incapable of trusting anyone, but I won't fail him. Because of who *I* am, not because of who *he* is."

"He... he said the new vassal treaty offended you..."

"Offended? No! By the thousand gods of Hatti, I love it! I'll sign it, of course. Why not? I might as well get more land and exemptions and... and salt rights. I'm certainly not getting anything else from him, damn his black soul." Kurunta was practically emitting steam, he was so furious, stalking up and down in the confined space of the tent like a caged, black-maned lion.

"Oh, my dear, dear boy." She bit her lip. This was not a rift that would be easy to repair. She couldn't think what Tashmi-sharrumma had done to him to bring this on.

With a heavy heart, she turned to leave. As she opened the flap she remembered to ask, "Do you know which brother it is?"

"Tell Tash to ask me himself."

Cursing the temperamental obstinacy of her husband's nephew, she hustled back to the king's tent. It was now fully light. Tashmi-sharrumma was emerging, clad in his Ishtanu-like splendor—golden sword, red crown, and all. He stared blankly at her for a moment, perhaps not recognizing her. Then he said, "You'd better get ready. We're nearly leaving."

"My son, you've got to go ask Kurunta who the brother is. I'm almost sure he knows."

He gaped at her.

He's always so slow to react, she thought, frustrated to madness. "He's the 'high official,' son. Ask him! Ask him! It's as much as your life is worth."

Frost crept over the king's face, setting his features in protective ice. "I'm the king. If he knows something, let him come to me."

"Don't be so stupid!" she shouted. People swiveled their heads to stare then turned away in embarrassment. Tashmi-sharrumma's face grew dark, but whether it was in anger or shame his mother couldn't say. He pushed past her and disappeared around the row of tents, his long god train floating out behind him.

※

The king was almost shaking with anger and apprehension as he strode to the chariot ground. He drew a shuddering breath through his nose and let it out in a cloud of frosty steam, seeking in vain to calm himself. He couldn't trust anyone, that was clear. Kurunta knew who the would-be assassin was and wouldn't tell him? He should have had his cousin arrested as an accomplice. But then, if Kurunta was the "high official," he had already saved the king's life, and that would hardly have been a just response, no matter how satisfying it might have been as personal revenge.

He couldn't face the gods with these unworthy emotions churning in his gut. Tashmi-sharrumma breathed again, slower this time. The cold, dry air made his cheekbones ache; his eyes felt scalded. He hadn't slept for two nights. First the vigil, then the anxiety. How had his father lived for thirty years under this horrible burden?

The groom set out the footstool, and Tashmi-sharrumma mounted his carriage. He gave himself up to the Lord Sharrumma, let the peace of duty sink into him. If he was going to his death, so be it. He would fulfill his priestly obligations till the last moment. He fingered the hilt of the golden ceremonial sword at his hip. It symbolized his role as defender of his people. Would it be sacrilege to draw it in his own defense?

The carriages and animals began their day's journey. Nerik was even farther north, in lands vulnerable to the Kashkans. They would pass the summer palace at Shapinuwa. They would pass Hakpish, where Hattushili had reigned during the days of the divided kingdom. *It was here that my father's sins began.*

These were formidable highlands—woods and grazing land—and few merrymakers lined the road to see their gods and king pass. Chiefly it was sheep, looking up from the transient green of their stricken fields, watching for a moment of curiosity, then returning to their grazing. Over the harps and pipes and drums, Tashmi-sharrumma heard the rattling of the carriages behind him as they rumbled over the brittle road, cut into the living rock. His wife and mother followed most closely, their two vehicles abreast as long as the road was wide enough. Behind them were Nerikkaili and Hishni, then the three viceroys: Kurunta, Ini-tesshub, and the king of Halep. Then followed all the sons of Hatti's kings, who might or might not wish him ill. *Meshedi* and Golden Spearmen trudged at his side, protecting him from danger. *Or are they the danger?* Tattamaru had also assigned heavily armed guards, who march outside the bodyguards like a line of troops heading off to war. Suspicion hung in a cloud over the royal family, and Tashmi-sharrumma wondered if the treacherous brother had somehow gotten wind that his plot had been revealed.

When will he strike?

They reached the walls of Nerik, and the king was still alive. They made camp, and the king survived the night, although he had slept so little for the last few nights that his eyes were burning and gritty. His nerves were taut, as if on the eve of battle—but now he fought an enemy he wouldn't know until the attacker was upon him.

In the morning, the gates of the holy city of the Storm God swung open, and the king and his guards, along with the priests and priestesses of Sharrumma who had met them, entered. The gates clanged shut.

This has to be the moment. The king's hand hovered on the hilt of his sword. He glanced to his side and saw that Hishni himself had replaced one of the guards. His heart dropped. *It's Hishni, then. What does he stand to gain from my death?* But ambition wasn't always reasonable, he knew. It wasn't always the eldest son who seized the throne.

The king wondered if anyone else had noticed the exchange. Surely if he, who could barely see past the end of his nose, had observed, then others had. But no one dared disturb the ceremony.

They crossed the courtyard in a triple line, the musicians and singers accompanying them. The king's mind was furiously occupied with details of the battle to come. Could he count on any of the *meshedi*? No, they must all have been in on Hishni's plan. He couldn't have undertaken something like this alone and expected to survive.

Tashmi-sharrumma wasn't able to make out Hishni's expression—he dared not turn his head too conspicuously. Surely the drumbeat of his own heart had to be audible to everyone in the temple complex. *And may it long beat,* he thought wryly.

Shaven-headed priests shouldered the statue of the Sun Goddess to carry it into her son's sanctuary. The party of celebrants and guards moved toward the narrow staircase to proceed to the god's chamber. The piercing perfume of incense rose up the stairwell and hovered there in visible clouds. Surely, this would be the moment.

He would have liked to rearrange the order in which the party mounted the stairs, but there was no time. A sacred silence reigned that he could not lightly break. The priests began to climb. The king followed, his heart hammering in his mouth. Behind him came his guard—led, he was certain, by Hishni. Were the Golden Spearmen interspersing themselves with the *meshedi*, as they were supposed to? He knew he had broken a cardinal rule of a fight: he had turned his back on his enemy. His spine seemed to curl and tingle with expectation.

They were almost to the top of the stairs when suddenly there was a shout behind him. The king wheeled, heart pounding. He saw his brother lunging upward toward his kidneys with something glittering in hand. There was no room to draw a sword. Tashmi-sharrumma threw himself down on the attacker and grabbed for Hishni's arm, the king's weight toppling the two of them. Only the press of the guards below held them back from falling down the stairs. The two brothers grappled, grunting and cursing. Tashmi-sharrumma hung, head downward, his hair in his face. His wrist trembled under the strain as he forced the arm with the knife away from his throat by sheer effort. Hishni was heavier than he but fifteen years older, and he was below the king, who had the momentum of his leap. They were so close Tashmi-sharrumma could see the man's sweating, snarling face. Below them, the *meshedi* and the Golden Spearmen were drawing their weapons upon one another. The king heard the screech of bronze on bronze, cries of anger and warning, blows. The priestesses screamed in horror. His own breath sawed loudly in his ears.

Then the guardsmen and priests dragged the brothers apart. They set the king on his feet and manhandled Hishni down the stairs with his arms pinned behind him. Temple guards came running. The king heard someone cry, "Sacrilege!"

Panting, Tashmi-sharrumma descended the stairs to confront his brother. Clearly whatever support the captain of the *meshedi* had expected from his men was too late and too little. The few of them who had drawn their swords against the king —and dear gods, some priests—were being held by the others. Heads hanging, they refused to meet his eye.

The king stood over his brother, his face grim, his chest heaving.

"What's this all about, Hishni?"

"If Nerikkaili didn't have the stomach for it, why shouldn't I?" the captain of the *meshedi* sneered, addressing himself to those around and not to Tashmi-sharrumma. "Lurma-ziti and I had planned to do this from the start. Why should that smarmy son of a bitch be king? He's letting the whole empire fall apart!"

Tashmi-sharrumma thought to himself dryly that this explanation left a lot to be desired. He'd have to interrogate Hishni later. But it was clear that he had appointed as chief of his bodyguards a man who had already resolved to assassinate him.

"Tie him up, temple guards, and keep watch over

him. We have to finish the liturgy. One of you, go tell the *tawananna* what has happened."

The priests, unnerved and scandalized, trudged on up the stairs, and the king followed them alone.

At last, the gates of Nerik swung open. The king led the procession out and saw his relatives and servants clustered around the opening in a state of anxious expectation. At his appearance, a ragged cheer of joy went up. His mother and wife rushed forward and fell upon him, weeping and making extravagant feminine displays of relief. He extracted himself in embarrassment and called to Tattamaru, "Schedule a cleansing ritual. We've polluted the temple."

Despite himself, his hands were twitching all the way up to his elbows as if he had cupped a buzzing insect in his fists. His cousins, brothers, and uncles crowded around, shouting, gabbling, laughing, and clapping him on the back. Somewhere, Kurunta must have stood, but the king couldn't see him.

"Are you hurt?" his mother asked, still clinging to his arm. "I can't believe how foolish that was. You were so brave, my son."

The king was grinning all over in spite of himself, giddy with relief. Under his clothing, he was drenched with perspiration, even though it was a cold spring day. He was quite aware of how dangerous his position had been, but there had seemed no way to stop the plot until they knew who was behind it. Hishni, of all people.

Alalimmi asked, "What shall we do with him, My Sun? Behead him here, or take him back to the city for punishment?"

"Let me think about it," said the king.

Before he could make off back to his tent, his mother intercepted him. Up close, he saw that her eyes were red with tears, but her expression was fierce, triumphant.

"Make an example of him, Tashmi-sharrumma. Have him beheaded publicly, the ingrate. You want to send a very clear message to all those other wretched princes who have fed at your father's trough for their entire lives and now are not ashamed to attack his legitimate heir."

Men like my father, who served his brother loyally... and then chased his nephew from the throne. "Perhaps we of all people shouldn't talk too loudly about legitimate heirs, Mother."

She opened her eyes wide but didn't argue, maybe because he had just escaped death. "Think about the political dimension, is what I'm saying."

"We're not Assyrians. I plan to exile him."

"What?" Her eyes went round with horror.

"Exile. Send him away. That's what my father did to Urhi-tesshub."

The tawananna's face was blooming scarlet in disbelief. "And thirty years later, he's still skulking around, causing trouble. No, no, my son; you need to take off his scheming head. The people will rejoice. It will show you're a strong king."

"And what will show that I'm a merciful king?"

The *tawananna* rolled her eyes. "Dear gods, Tashmi-sharrumma. Here you go again. At least blind him. Clemency is a lovely concept, but—"

"A virtue beloved of the gods. The same gods who spared me today," he interrupted, controlling his irritation with difficulty. "Remember my ancestor Telepinu, when he

185

had to face the murderers of some of his family. He said, 'They did evil to me, but I will not do evil to them.' The gods blessed him for that."

But the *tawananna* plowed on as if she hadn't heard him. "In the real world, it's strength that people admire. And fear, which is not a bad thing. Nerikkaili says—"

"What does our dear Nerikkaili say?" He knew his voice was metallic with sarcasm, but after his near brush with death, he was too weary and taut to control himself any longer.

"Oh, stop it. He had nothing to do with today's events. Why are you so hostile?"

"Why are you *not* hostile? And who knows if he had anything to do with it? He was your son's main rival for the throne. Where would you have been if it had been he and not I in the lap of Halmashuit?"

The *tawananna* heaved a sigh of exasperation that came a little too close to open anger. Her eyes glittered, and not with tears.

"Go and rest. You're obviously tired," she said sourly.

As he walked away, he remembered some words his mother had spoken months ago, on another day when she had been fed up with his naive devotion to justice. *Maybe we made the wrong choice,* she had said. *What did she mean,* he suddenly wondered... *and who was "we"?*

They all returned to their camp, and the next morning, the procession started back to Hattusha.

The king and his mother had been arguing all morning. She had wanted to conduct the interview with Hishni herself.

Tashmi-sharrumma had finally turned his back on her and left. He had cleared the council room and was lowering himself to his throne when the heavy doors clanged back, and a shaft of light cut through the semidarkness. Puduhepa strode up the columned aisle, still nattering at him. Nerikkaili trailed her, looking slightly embarrassed.

"I tell you, My Sun," the king's mother warned as she stalked through the room toward him, "Hishni won't speak honestly to you. Let me be the one to interrogate him." It was as if there had been no interruption in their conversation.

"It's my duty, Mother," the king said wearily.

"Duty." She made a skeptical puffing sound. "What good will it be if he doesn't tell you anything?"

"What if we make it a family delegation?" Nerikkaili proposed.

The king tried hard not to reveal his annoyance at this idea. How had his half brother managed to insinuate himself into this? He said dryly, "Why?"

"Because this whole business seems to be based on someone's idea about second-rankers versus the children of the *tawananna*, and I think I deserve a chance to represent my own position here and not be spoken for by Lurma-ziti and Hishni."

"He has a point, my dear," Puduhepa told her son. "Besides, Nerikkaili is an experienced diplomat. He knows how to read between the lines of what people say. I would value his counsel."

The king saw he wasn't going to get his own way. He had wanted to speak very quietly with Hishni, perhaps lay his brother's animosity to rest by a show of forgiveness. But he knew this would by no means happen in the presence of his mother and Nerikkaili. The latter, in particular, had an interest in looking harshly opposed to Hishni and the plan to assassinate their brother. Tashmi-sharrumma decided it was enough if he managed clemency over execution. He couldn't ask for too much.

He was more constrained than the would-be assassin.

Alalimmi had handpicked some guards from the *meshedi* and the Golden Spears to protect the king during his interview with the miscreant. And now Hishni was brought in, his hands bound behind him, his feet shackled so he could hardly shuffle. His captors had clearly roughed him up: his eyes were blackened and his nose bloody, but his expression was stoic.

"Hishni," said the king patiently. "Explain yourself."

"You're not the lawful king. Why should a younger son be on the throne? There were three of us before you, and we're old enough to be your father." His tone was contemptuous but not angry. He was no fanatic, just an unimaginative man led by others. *Lurma-ziti was almost certainly the ringleader of this. And he's beyond our reach.*

Nerikkaili interrupted angrily in his deepest, most authoritarian voice. "Our father appointed Our Sun to be his heir, Hishni. Who are you to oppose him? If anyone should be angry, it's me, and I'm not. So what's your complaint? You wouldn't have been on the throne anyway."

"It's the justice of the thing," Hishni cried. "She's always pushed the boy ahead of us in everything. Is he really the one the gods have chosen, or is he just lucky enough to have a scheming mother? Isn't everything falling to pieces under him? Isn't it? Is that the blessing of the gods? We all know that he was Kurunta's—"

"How dare you," growled the *tawananna*, her black eyes dangerously slitted. "Can you doubt for a minute that your father wanted Tashmi-sharrumma to be his heir?"

"And you and Lurma-ziti thought one of *you* would be a better king than our brother? Ha!" Nerikkaili's face was crimson. "What a choice: petty jealousy or stupidity."

"Well, if *you* had agreed…" the prisoner said.

"Did you ask him?" asked the king quietly.

"No, he didn't," Nerikkaili and the *tawananna* said simultaneously.

The king stared at them for a long, uncomfortable moment, then he turned back to Hishni.

"Did you ask him?" he said again.

"No. We… we asked our cousin Kurunta."

The king felt his stomach drop breathlessly. A painful fluttering began in his heart. He mastered his fear and raised his eyebrow in a calm gesture of curiosity.

But before Hishni could explain, Nerikkaili surged at the prisoner with balled fists. "You damned blood traitor. Are you so disloyal to our father? As if that dandelion-puff Kurunta would be a better king than any of our father's line," he snarled. The *tawananna* put a calming hand on his arm, while Hishni shrank away from his fists.

The king watched all this with a sense of unreality. He crossed his own arms because his hands had begun to tremble. "When was this?"

"I mean, we didn't actually ask him. Lurma-ziti was supposed to do that, but then he died. Then I was the only one left. But that was the plan."

The thought was pulsing inside the king's head that it had been Kurunta who had warned him of the plot and said that he, Tashmi-sharrumma, would suspect him. *The poor man; he warned me to save my life. They tried to seduce him to their cause, and he wouldn't yield. Did Lurma-ziti really ever speak to him? But Lurma-ziti's been dead for months. Why did my cousin wait so long to say anything? Why all the business about the anonymous voice? Why wouldn't Kurunta tell me who the assassin was? Is it possible he really didn't know?*

"Put this disgusting traitor to death, My Sun. After all the favor you have shown him, to turn on you like that. Impalement is too good for him," Nerikkaili cried, his face hard and crimson.

"Do you want him silenced?" the king asked softly.

His brother's eyes popped with shock and anger. The *tawananna* made a horrified exclamation. There was a moment of stunned silence during which Nerikkaili seemed to grapple with his outrage. Finally, he said in a barely controlled voice, "I'm on your side, My Sun. Remember?"

As far as the king could see, there was no one on his side. He had never found himself so crushingly alone in all his solitary life. Here he had tried so hard to forgive his half brothers their unkindnesses and treat them justly, even favor them. He had put his life in Hishni's hands to show how he trusted him. And the gods knew he was not a trusting man by nature—he had made an act of will and done violence to himself in this forced display of confidence. Yet here they all were, conspiring against him for no other reason, it seemed, than because they didn't like him. Dear gods, they still remembered his relationship with Kurunta, after all these years, and held it against him? Nerikkaili couldn't possibly be as pure as he protested. And look at the king's own mother, defending Nerikkaili as if his honor were hers. *What's going on there?* he wondered, not for the first time.

Dear Sharrumma, give me light. He felt the slow thumping of pain in his temples as a headache that had been threatening him since he awoke decided its moment has come.

He stood squarely before Hishni, loomed over him— the elder brother was not so tall as Tashmi-sharrumma, although he was broader. The prisoner recoiled a little, expecting a blow, perhaps, but his expression was resigned. He was no coward.

"I condemn you to exile," the king said calmly. "Go away, and don't come back."

"But son," his mother protested, her big, dark eyes starting from her face. She was trying to signal him something without words, but he declined to understand.

"Take him away," said the king, speaking past her to the guards. "Accompany him to the border of Nuhasshe, and turn him loose."

The soldiers hustled the hobbling prisoner out the door, while the other three stood there, frozen into a tableau of animosity. As soon as the door closed, the *tawananna* burst forth in fury. "Have you lost your mind, my son?"

Tashmi-sharrumma shook his head in slow negation. The headache was closing in on his eye sockets now. He longed to rub his eyebrow ridges but felt it would have been a gesture of weakness. The king wanted desperately for this moment to be over. He had a lot to digest.

"Make him listen to reason, Nerikkaili," shrilled the

tawananna. "He can't turn that man loose again. And Kurunta is in on this? Shaushga protect us all!"

"I think you've made a mistake, My Sun," growled the king's brother.

"Should I put to death every son of Hattushili in case they might betray me, brother?" Tashmi-sharrumma said a little more caustically than he intended to. Nerikkaili fell silent, his face flushing.

The king turned to his mother. "Kurunta is not in on it, Mother. You heard Hishni—Lurma-ziti died before he could say anything."

But Nerikkaili wanted to be heard. He forced himself in front of the king and thrust his red face, jowls quivering, under his brother's nose. "I wish you'd stop hinting that *I'm* somehow implicated in my brothers' plotting, My Sun. Have I ever given you any reason to suspect my loyalty? Have I? Can you say that I have?"

"Nerikkaili, no one has accused you of anything." The king reined in his anger and spoke in a mild tone. He even managed a slight smile.

"Then, with My Sun's permission, I'll take my leave," the eldest son of Hattushili said levelly, drawing back.

The king nodded. His brother bowed his way out, his broad back rigid, his steps a little firmer than necessary. He closed the door with extreme care behind him.

"Tashmi-sharrumma, you've made a terrible mistake, and I don't just mean insulting Nerikkaili, although that's a mistake, too." His mother closed in on him, her face fierce and scarlet.

"I've made many, no doubt," he replied without expression. "Apparently, the worst was to be born."

192

"What does that mean? Are you referring to your brothers' animosity? That's no fault of yours, my son." She turned motherly all of a sudden and put her arm around him. "That awful Lurma-ziti—he's behind this. Hishni isn't smart enough. He hardly knows why he's acting."

"So why punish Hishni with death? We're not Assyrians."

"He'll be back, son. This isn't over. It's never over until they're dead. I wish you would figure this out. I don't know what you're trying to prove." She rubbed his back. "My poor dear. Don't feel this is some deficiency in you. Every king has things like this to deal with."

He finally gave in and massaged his eyebrows with a finger and thumb. Her fragrance soothed him, but what he really wanted was Kurunta. "You and Father shouldn't have favored me so openly."

"Dearest, you were the one your father wanted to succeed him, but he had to wait until you were old enough to announce you as his heir. There were so many things we had to prepare you for. It wasn't favoritism; it was just practical necessity."

"It made all the others hate me." This was as close as he had ever come to expressing self-pity about his bullied childhood, and he regretted it instantly.

His mother caught the pain in his voice and looked up into his face with tenderness beaming from her eyes like the sun of spring—warmth after the winter of her chastisement. "My poor baby," she murmured without any sarcasm.

He pushed away from her and gave her a sardonic grin, his no-nonsense self again. "Next time I sentence an assassin, I meet with him alone."

She laughed. "I hope to all the gods there is no next

time. You should talk to Kurunta, though. Confirm that they never really approached him."

Kurunta. The king needed to talk to his cousin, all right. But he could hardly bear the thought of facing Kurunta after that awful scene over the treaty. And how could he ask the viceroy, "Were you somehow involved in the plot you finally revealed?" *He will suspect him...*

Instead, Tashmi-sharrumma asked his mother, "Who are the 'we' who made a mistake in choosing me?"

"What? I have no idea what you mean, son."

He nodded and made his way to the door, leaving her to wonder whatever it was she wondered.

CHAPTER 10

"**H**AVE YOU HEARD, COUSIN? OUR Sun has called for us all to swear a new loyalty oath to him and his son," said Nerikkaili.

He and Kurunta were in the latter's palace on the undulating plains of the Lower Land. Nerikkaili had been sent to accompany another load of five hundred *parishu* of grain from Mizri, shipped by Ugaritic vessels to the port of Ura, in Kurunta's viceroyalty. The king's brother had spent the day supervising the transfer of the wheat, freshly arrived from Ura on donkey back, into oxcarts, which would depart for the capital in the morning.

Nerikkaili drained the cup of *walhi* beverage he had been nursing and took the liberty of pouring himself another. "It's a beauty, with things like, 'Even if all the dogs abandon me, you must swear to support me.' I think he's gone a little mad."

At his side, Kurunta gave a bitter laugh. "Oh, I'm ahead of you, cousin. I've already been asked to sign my new vassal treaty."

Nerikkaili smirked. "I suppose it's the result of Hishni's

idiotic assassination attempt. For a soldier, he surely didn't plan that one very well."

"No," murmured Kurunta vaguely, cradling his cup in his hands.

"I'm sure it was Lurma-ziti's doing; he genuinely loathed Tashmi-sharrumma. Hishni was just his cat's-paw." Nerikkaili took a long swig of his *walhi* drink and wiped his lips with the back of his hand.

"No doubt." Kurunta wondered why Nerikkaili was telling him all this. They'd never been very friendly. But the Great King had instructed his viceroy to host the emissary. *The Great King instructs,* thought Kurunta bitterly. *That's the way it is now—he gives orders, and I obey. Once we were equals; once we were friends. We would have given our lives for each other, and nobody would have said, "Put your seal on this tablet in front of twenty witnesses so I can prove you actually swore before the Oath Gods to be my friend, you vassal."*

Nerikkaili continued, "Hishni said they had planned to involve you. Know anything about that?"

Kurunta looked up, mouth gaping and eyes round. "What?" His astonishment was so genuine that apparently the king's brother felt his question had been answered.

"So now Tashmi-sharrumma's afraid everyone he meets is going to double-cross him. But what I don't see is why someone wouldn't just go ahead and swear and then break his oath. That's what people always do. That's what my father did. The Oath Gods don't take it all that seriously, it seems to me."

"Maybe the oath-breakers' descendants are punished," said Kurunta, thinking of Tash's tortured conscience.

"That's what they say, yes. I wouldn't know; I'm not a priest."

"And you're not forsworn." The king of Tarhuntassha grinned maliciously. He enjoyed Nerikkaili's dry smile. "Never been tempted yourself, cousin?"

"To break an oath?"

"To enjoy the consolations of Halmashuit."

The prince snorted. "I'm nearly sixty. Any ambitions I might ever have had in that regard are long past."

"You have sons."

"Yes, well, when I see how my brother has aged in barely more than a year, I pray my sons never have the misfortune to sit on the divine throne. He looks pretty ground down." The prince chuckled darkly. "But then, he never did look like much, did he? There seems to have been some sort of tradition in our family that the homeliest man in every generation is made king."

Kurunta felt an ugly flutter of satisfaction at these unkind words but it was quickly overtaken by offense. The king's face, whatever its merits, was the object most dear to him upon the black earth. How many times had he defended it against the cruelties of Tash's own brothers? But those years were long past. His devotion had won him nothing.

"And if I were king," continued Nerikkaili with a snide grin, "it would be he in the diplomatic corps. Imagine our dear brother arguing a treaty. He doesn't exactly have a tongue of gold. Although in all fairness, I have to admit he isn't stupid."

Oh, but he is. He's done a very foolish thing.

"Well, I won't impose upon your hospitality any

longer, cousin." Nerikkaili yawned. "The wagons should be loaded, and we'll be moving out in the morning. I'd better get to bed... with your permission." The prince rose and stretched. The old boy was getting quite portly, his big jaw buried in a double chin.

Kurunta got to his feet as well and smiled genially. "My house is your house, Nerikkaili. You don't need my permission to go to bed. Unless you want me to join you!"

They laughed.

"Wrong brother." Nerikkaili smirked. "Well, good night."

The prince headed unsteadily off to his apartment, and Kurunta dropped back down into his seat. He sat for a good long while, deciding whether he would be angry or not. He was more than a little drunk—he and Nerikkaili had been putting away the sweet, deceptively powerful *walhi* drink for a long time. They'd talked about one thing and another but especially the king. Kurunta had thought that perhaps Tash could have seen his way to thank him for the tip that saved his life, but perhaps Puduhepa hadn't even told him the identity of the "high official." Anyway, what were the chances the bastard would ever talk to Kurunta again? *And now Hishni has implicated me. By the thousand gods, what an imagination.*

Kurunta had thought to lure Tash to him by the promise of revealing the assassin's name—not that he had really known it. He had only learned of the plot at all through a chance overhearing of words in a corridor. The plotters had apparently been en route to talk to him. Such delicious irony.

Still, everyone said the same thing about the king: he

was getting more and more withdrawn and suspicious. Without his sociable alter ego to keep him kneaded loose, this had been sure to happen. And then there was, of course, the assassination attempt. But it was vintage Tash, anyway. Exposing his feelings to anyone was so painful for him you'd think someone was pulling out his liver the whole time.

What feelings? Now the familiar lurking anger began to mount in Kurunta's heart again. *Tash has no feelings. He's probably never had any feelings for me at all. I've hinted, I've begged, I've crawled, but has he ever chosen to understand?*

Here was the comedy: everybody else joked about them as if they were lovers.

If only he were so lucky.

Kurunta remembered, with a mixture of anguish and tenderness, the years in which that relationship had been a fact and—he bared his teeth with bitterness—the end of it all. He had just been appointed viceroy and was due to leave for Tarhuntassha. He and Tash had found one another for what might be their last lovemaking for a long time, in the royal stables, among the sweet-smelling hay, the softly nuzzling horses. Wrapped in each other's young limbs, Tash all long and graceful, his thick brown hair all over his face, close to beautiful in his ecstasy. And then the odious royal half brothers had burst in on them.

Smirking as usual, Nerikkaili had observed, "Well, well. If it isn't the turtledoves."

"Which one of you birds lays the eggs?" that twisted piece of crap, Lurma-ziti, had added.

Kurunta had scrambled to his feet and lunged at Lurma-ziti with murder in his heart, but Tash had pulled him back. "Don't give him the satisfaction." As if Tash didn't care—as if he were above caring about such things.

Then they had discovered that Lurma-ziti had cut up their clothes with his dagger. And the two young kings' sons had had to sprint—naked as criminals or slaves—through the Upper City and up the excruciatingly long and visible causeway to the palace citadel. Around them had rung the laughter or scandalized cries of half the capital.

Never again after that could Kurunta soften Tash up enough to take off his clothes. It was as if he was afraid to give his brothers such a handle on him. Well, no wonder he was bent; that lump of shit Lurma-ziti would take anything Tash loved and beat him over the head with it until the boy's soul bled. It would have been bad enough if he'd caught his younger brother with some girl. But to find him with Kurunta, whom Lurma-ziti detested and envied, was all the worse. If it had been he, Kurunta, as victim, he would have torn out Lurma-ziti's throat. But Tash had just started putting on the armor, piece by piece. And then he had rejected this. And then he had rejected that. And before long, he was just *Anna* and *Atta's* perfect little workhorse, no fun at all.

By Tarhunta, Kurunta thought, tears of rage trembling on his lashes, *how I hate that Lurma-ziti and what he's done to Tash.*

And look at what Lurma-ziti's taken away from me as well. All his frustrated love for the king had melted into his hatred for the king's brother until he hated them both. The viceroy's life had become a putrefying bog of misery and resentment.

Kurunta was becoming maudlin, he knew, but that

couldn't be any more painful than the simmering bitterness that had been his daily bread for six months. Now Tash wouldn't even accept a kiss. As if they mean nothing to each other.

Kurunta examined the inside of his cup, but it was empty. He upended the dregs of the ewer into it and carried it with extreme care to the door. His face was burning, and he wanted a breath of air, even the frigid air of a delayed spring.

What he found was the chamberlain on his way to accost his master. They almost collided in the doorway, and the viceroy sloshed sticky *walhi* drink on his clothes. He cursed.

"Oh, my lord, forgive me," the servant stammered, bowing low. "But your father-in-law is here to see you. He has another man with him he says you'll want to meet."

"Oh, does he? Oh, will I? What fun. Send them in." Kurunta thought, *The old man is under interdict. I wonder what he's doing here. If Our fucking Sun knew, he'd be in serious trouble.* And then he asked himself if he should turn Alantalli of Mira in to the Great King. Would Tash be grateful finally?

Alantalli was a small, thin man, a Luwian speaker who pretended to know no Neshite—although he assuredly did; how different were the two languages, anyway? He had a shiny, bald head and a bent-looking nose. Mercifully, his daughter resembled him but little. Kurunta asked himself how such an uncharismatic fellow planned to ignite any passion for rebellion, if that was really his goal. Following Alantalli was a big, broad-shouldered, still-attractive personage in his fifties or sixties who had the appearance of being a member of the royal family—their look was hard to counterfeit. *Who is that?* He had no recollection of ever seeing the fellow before. Some uncle, back from a diplomatic posting on the farthest borders, perhaps.

"My father." The viceroy embraced Alantalli with a cool touch of formality. He didn't want to look too chummy with the rebel vassal, but he did speak in Luwian for his father-in-law's benefit.

"Son. May the gods bless you and your family."

"Even my cousin?" Kurunta grinned pointedly.

Alantalli tilted his head as if to acknowledge a shot well played. "I wish your cousin no harm as a man," he protested, a master of evasion.

The big uncle behind him suppressed a smile.

"So what brings you to my house at this hour, my father? Shall I wake Anitti and the children?"

"No, no. I've only come as an intermediary. I've brought you my friend, here, a man of whom you have no memory but who has a long history with you."

Kurunta's curiosity was piqued. He eyed the fellow carefully, but his faculties were not at their most acute. Beyond a general familial resemblance, he still couldn't guess the visitor's identity. He called a servant to refill the *walhi* beverage and became aware suddenly that his tunic was stained. Not the most impressive beginning for a reunion. He wondered if he had ever had sexual congress with this older relative who, despite his age and iron-gray hair, was more than attractive. He had presence.

"Come, my visitors. Let's take a seat and make ourselves comfortable." Kurunta led the way back into the room and offered his guests chairs. Alantalli perched upon the edge like a kestrel, while his companion spread out at his ease. Kurunta poured the two men a cup of *walhi* beverage and added some to his own beaker. "And you are…?"

"You don't recognize me?" said the man in a velvety baritone.

"I'm embarrassed to say I don't. I think that if we've met, it must have been a long time ago… and perhaps in the dark." He eyed the man, a bit of the old mischief bubbling to the surface in a grin.

"I'm your brother Urhi-tesshub. Murshili son of Muwatalli."

Kurunta sprang up from his chair so fast he overturned it; his cup tottered and fell from the edge of the table. Like the cup, his heart exploded—with longing, with joy… with fear. "H-How dare you show up here," he stammered, but his wrath was unconvincing. "There's a price on your head, and I'm the king's viceroy."

"But you're *my* brother, Ulmi-tesshub."

"I can't permit you to use your throne name under my roof. I… I…"

"Relax. No one will know that two proscribed men are your guests unless you yourself choose to make it known." Urhi-tesshub leaned back in his chair, wonderfully at ease, big and expansive, radiating charm. How could anyone ever have put this man from his throne, hounded him into exile, tracked him like a stag from land to land?

Kurunta felt like a little child in his presence. He had been separated from this brother, who was fifteen years his senior, almost at birth. He had never seen Urhi-tesshub except from afar and with the eyes of a small boy; he had never spoken a word to the pretender. No one had ever told him what manner of person his brother was, only that he had offered Uncle Hattushili an affront that an honorable man could not overlook. No one had ever said that Urhi-tesshub was warm, charming, articulate, beautiful, more a father than a brother.

The deposed king rose and held out his arms. Kurunta froze a moment, then he rushed forward and embraced him with all his strength. Bittersweet relief melted in his veins. It was as if a part of his stolen life had been given back to him after all those years of being an outsider, when "brothers" meant someone else's brothers.

"My brother!" he cried, scarcely able to believe the words were true. He leaned his head upon Urhi-tesshub's shoulder and wept in his arms. Behind Urhi-tesshub's back, he was dimly conscious of Alantalli smiling broadly beneath his crooked nose. At length, somewhat embarrassed, Kurunta stood back, sniffing, and the two men sat again. The *walhi* drink had heated his blood. He felt as if he could weep all over again.

Urhi-tesshub watched him benevolently. "They told me you're the handsomest man in Hatti Land, and I see it's true."

"Our mother must have been a beauty, eh?" laughed Kurunta, offering his brother the compliment of including him in this tribute. Tears formed anew in his eyes. *And I never knew her; I haven't so much as a single memory of her.* His shoulders shook with sobs of self-pity he couldn't contain. He realized he was desperate for someone's love now that Tash had abandoned him.

"Our mother?" Urhi-tesshub looked confused. "But we have different mothers." He exchanged a disturbed glance with Alantalli. "They never told you? We're half brothers, Ulmi-tesshub. You're a first-rank son by the *tawananna* Tanuhepa."

Something flipped over in Kurunta's stomach, and it wasn't just *walhi*. "What?"

His brother clapped him on the arm with a compassionate hand. "By the thousand gods, they never told you? You're a first-rank son."

Kurunta fell silent, his jaw dropped, as effectively stunned as if by a blow to the head. He was unable to digest this new reality. Outrage began to bubble in his heart. All those years, and everyone had treated him like some lesser being, a mere appendage to Tash, who was the first-rank golden boy. Even Nerikkaili—why, he was only a second-ranker, and look how he lorded it over his cousin. Kurunta remembered Mashturi's analysis of legitimacy and stammered, "Th-Then why was it you on the throne?"

"Our father had deposed his *tawananna*, and you, her infant son, were to be exiled, too. But Uncle Hattushili didn't want to see that happen. He took you in to raise you as one of his own sons."

"Our father didn't want me?"

"He was afraid, Ulmi." Urhi-tesshub's rich voice throbbed with compassion. "He was going off to do battle against the Great King of Mizri himself, and he feared that partisans of your mother would use you to make trouble while his back was turned. You were only a baby after all. If he died, I at least was old enough to rule, with uncle's advice. And one of the first things I did when I came to the throne was to recall your mother."

Kurunta's head was spinning. "But why did she leave

me with Uncle Hattushili at that point? She could have taken me back…"

Urhi-tesshub dropped his eyes. His hands, upon the table, curled into fists. He said in a low, grim voice, like a storyteller building up to some villainous event, "It was Puduhepa, the wife of our uncle, who would not let you go. Your mother pleaded to have you back at her side, but our aunt wouldn't permit it. She wanted you to be the companion of her son. I guess she feared you would become his rival if you ever found out your real rank."

Kurunta was overwhelmed with so many emotions at once and was so little in control of himself, thanks to the *walhi* drink, that he hardly knew what to think. He felt he should call the guards and have both these dangerous men arrested. He felt he should abandon his viceroyalty and run away and join their cause. His life was overturned. His life was given back to him. Anguish twisted his heart. Joy mounted in him like the Marrasshantiya in flood. All those years he had been used and abused. *First rank!* And they had never told him. Never even told him who his mother was. She had a name…

All those years—unknown to him—he had been loved and longed for.

His heart in tumult, he gazed at his brother, who had the wisdom not to speak and just sprawled there like a lion, looking magnificent, while Alantalli's sharp little kestrel eyes cut back and forth from one face to the other.

"Listen," said Kurunta apologetically after a moment, "Prince Nerikkaili is in the house. If he should see you here, he'd almost certainly report you to Tash."

Urhi-tesshub had a history with Nerikkaili that went

back to the early days of his exile, when he had eluded the prince, who had been sent to escort him back from Mizri.

"Is he so loyal?"

"I think so. Doesn't like Tash much. But he won't push back against the king."

"The king?" said Urhi-tesshub, smiling darkly. "You know, my brother, once a man is consecrated, he can never be unconsecrated, even if he is driven from the throne."

"*You* are the king," murmured Kurunta, transfixed, a small, stupid rodent in the presence of a snake. He felt the power of his brother to persuade, to lead, radiating from him like light. Here was a man who was not afraid of the truth, a man who had given him back his life. Here was a man whom one might address with conviction as "My Sun."

"And my own sons are all of lower rank. You, my brother, are my heir."

His heart burning, Kurunta clutched his brother's hand and pressed it to his lips as if Urhi-tesshub had just given him a gift. He had—the former king had given Kurunta back his identity, his dignity, his life.

Urhi-tesshub smiled his satisfaction and clapped his brother on the shoulder. "So what manner of man is our cousin Tashmi-sharrumma, or should I say Tudhaliya?"

"He's… he's a good man," admitted Kurunta, unable to lie. "Honest. Obsessed with satisfying the gods." *Heartless.* "He finds it very hard to be the ruler, I think, because… because he knows"—he looked up at his brother, wanting to please him more than anything in the world—"that he's not the rightful king."

There was a long moment of silence, during which

Kurunta dimly understood that he had said something imprudent.

Urhi-tesshub leaned toward his brother across the table. "Let me tell you why all this happened, Ulmi," he began in an intimate voice. "Your mother and our father had a falling-out. He accused her of impiety, and he deposed her, sending her—and her son—into exile. As we know, our uncle interceded for you in order to raise you himself. I suppose he was afraid you'd become a rival if your mother filled you with ideas about your right to the throne. I was a mere stripling when our father died, and so, of course, a regent was appointed. This was our Uncle Hattushili, Father's youngest brother—a trusted man, head of his *meshedi* guard, an experienced general. Father had made him a kind of co-king, in fact, during the war in the East—king of Hakpish, in the north, while our father had moved his capital here to Tarhuntassha, the city the god directed him to build. You know all this, of course." He smiled, graciously admitting his brother to the ranks of those who knew.

"And while I remained a child, his guidance was important. He was competent, wise, devoted to my interests—all the things uncles are supposed to be. But as I grew older, I could see how little he was willing for me to become my own man. He wanted the decisions to be his, not mine. He didn't object when I returned the capital to Hattusha, naturally; the need for a divided kingdom had long passed. Still, he was not at all happy when I dissolved the kingdom of Hakpish. But what else could I do, Ulmi-tesshub? Hatti Land is one. And it was I who was its king."

"Of course," murmured Kurunta.

"He never accused me of misrule, only of showing him disrespect." His brother sighed as if his words had revived a painful memory. "We met on the field of battle. Hattushili was in his fifties with a long career as a military man and many friendships among the Lords of Hatti. I was a mere boy in my twenties with few friends of my own and not even the loyalty of my own army. You know the outcome."

"It was wrong," cried Kurunta, his voice choking with emotion. "He wronged you, my brother. He wronged us both."

A noise from the vestibule drew their three pairs of eyes, and Alantalli suggested in an undertone, "Perhaps we should be going, my lord."

Urhi-Tesshub rose, unfolding his powerful height, and the other two men rose, too, in obedience. The king's viceroy was no more in charge in his own household than the littlest slave.

"I hope we can speak again, my dear brother. How wonderful it is to find you again after so long." Urhi-tesshub beamed.

"Yes, wonderful, wonderful. I'm sorry I can't offer you hospitality overnight."

"Not at all. We'll meet again, eh? In the name of our royal father."

They embraced, and then Alantalli and the former king left Kurunta standing alone, his thoughts in turmoil.

The next morning, the viceroy rose with difficulty to find that Nerikkaili and his wagon train had already set out for Hattusha. Kurunta was relieved. His head was splitting, his mouth like tree bark, his eyes swollen from weeping. He remembered crying like a child. *What was that about?*

Then it came back to him—his brother had returned. The infamous Urhi-tesshub, pretender to the throne, archenemy of the line of Hattushili, provoker of civil wars. After thirty-two years of exile, running from Mizri to the Eastern provinces to the Lower Land and back, always a jump ahead of his uncle's men. Now Kurunta realized why Uncle Hattushili had considered the former king so dangerous. If he, Kurunta, had a certain candle-flame reputation for charm, this man was the very sun in the sky. People would follow him anywhere. And he had only been twenty-four when he'd been deposed, at the very peak of his beauty.

But the viceroy in Kurunta was not as delighted by the evening's events as was the brother. Officially, he had offered hospitality to the king's enemies, enough to warrant being deposed, even executed, for treason. *By the thousand gods of Hatti, how could I have been so imprudent?*

And yet he wasn't as sorry as he should have been. He wouldn't have missed this ghost from his own past for anything—for all the military exemptions and salt rights in the Lower Land, he thought bitterly as if addressing himself to Tashmi-sharrumma. *Tash, Tash, what have you done to me? If you don't believe in your own legitimacy, how can I?*

He realized it was only ever Hattushili's version of events he had been fed, and Puduhepa's. Perhaps she was more at fault than anyone. How could she have denied him the knowledge of his own mother's name? How could she have denied his mother's plea for her son to be returned? He had a sudden memory of his aunt begging him to save the king at Nerik. *See? Mothers love their real sons*; naturally, Puduhepa had cared about Tash, her flesh and blood. His own brothers had hated him because he was below them with his ugly face and dim-sighted eyes and his youth and yet above them with his intelligence and prowess and first-rank mother. He had needed a friend. And who better to befriend the outcast than the naughty cousin, acting out his own loneliness? *She manipulated us both. May the lords below the black earth take her.*

But then Kurunta felt the knife twisting in his heart like the iron dagger of Lelwani, driven into the ground at her festival. The *tawananna's* machinations had worked only too well. He had fallen in love with his cousin. Who wouldn't have, who really knew him? He was kind and sensitive under the facade of ice. For all his accomplishments, he was modest, and despite the fact that he was a first-rank prince who might have demanded the first place in everything, he was humble. He never held himself above the abandoned cousin, whom everyone believed to be a second-ranker. If Tash was a little stiff and self-righteous, Kurunta's flamboyance and laughter and sense of daring brought him out. If Kurunta himself lacked prudence, then Tash's serious nature tempered him. Dear gods, they were so good for each other.

But that was just a dream of childhood, he realized. *It's over.* They were grown men now; tastes changed. Tash had moved on. Now Kurunta was just a vassal to his cousin, a vassal whose loyalty could be bought. *Well, maybe it can also be sold,* he thought grimly.

No, Kurunta wasn't that sort of person. He wasn't the stubbornly upright sort like Tash, but he wasn't a turncoat, either. He had sworn an oath to defend the man who sat in the arms of Halmashuit at that moment, and he would do it. Kurunta shouted for his secretary—he had a letter to dictate. And perhaps his cousin would finally be grateful.

The king was closeted with Nerikkaili in the smaller audience hall of the palace. The other Lords of Hatti had been sent away to a recess after the latter's report on the grain shipment from Mizri, and only the king and his brother remained. Nearly two weeks had passed since the Purulli festival. Whether their prayers had succeeded in winning the gods' favor remained to be seen, but Tashmi-sharrumma dared not leave the food supply to chance. He had commended his brother publicly for his service, but now another service was left to be performed.

"How does the viceroy these days?" Tashmi-sharrumma asked quietly. His throat was tight as he spoke; the answer was more important to him than he wanted to admit.

"Oh, the same as ever, My Sun." Nerikkaili shrugged. "He's a frivolous fellow. His kingdom is run competently because he listens to his advisors. In fact, I might say he listens rather too much to other people, although given the absence of serious thoughts in his own head…"

Tashmi-sharrumma longed to defend his cousin, but instead, he forced himself to remain silent.

"He's drinking rather a lot these days," Nerikkaili added, his mouth curling in a deprecating half-smile. He had never cared for the son of Muwatalli. "I tried to feel out his loyalty, as you instructed me. I'd say he stands beside you still. I heard nothing that would shake my belief in that. Although I would watch him, My Sun. He's flighty. One never knows where he might land."

"I see," said the king dully. He sat for a moment, pondering this information, then said,

"What about Hishni's plot?"

"He seemed genuinely flabbergasted at the idea of being involved. I think Lurma-ziti must in fact have died before he was able to approach him."

The king nodded. "Thank you, brother." *Ulmi will be loyal.*

The elder prince took his leave. The king rose and stretched uncomfortably—his back had been aching. No doubt he had twisted some muscle launching himself down the stairs at Nerik. In fact, he wasn't feeling particularly well in general. The fear of plague was always in the back of his mind, but so much time had passed since he was exposed that he assured himself he was just exhausted. He wasn't the sort to make much of the state of his health, which—apart from the usual childhood ailments—had always been solid. *Forget about it, and go on with your business,* he told himself in a matter-of-fact way.

In a few moments, his advisors would return and resume their regular review of affairs. Perhaps that was why he felt unwell: the state of the kingdom was enough to sicken anybody. Flooding in the mountains; absence of spring rains on the highlands. Perhaps the pollution of the Storm God's temple had angered him. The king sensed that he was powerless to make things right, just as he was with Kurunta. *Only tell me what's wrong, what I can do to make it better,* he thought helplessly, either to the god or to his cousin.

The Lords of Hatti filed back in, and the Lady, too. Even before the king had called the meeting to order, his mother demanded angrily, "You countermanded my letter to the queen of Assyria, didn't you?"

"I take it Assyria is the first order of business," the king said dryly. "Yes."

"Have you read the King of Kings' response? He's laughing at us. You've exposed to an enemy our internal disagreements. That's shameful, Tashmi-sharrumma. And it makes painfully clear your lack of experience in these delicate matters."

He wanted to say, *Then don't you contradict the king's policies.* But that would only provoke an argument that he couldn't win. He cocked his head and raised an eyebrow, not knowing what to say that wouldn't leave him rolling in her dust. This pose might make him seem judicious. There were looks of amusement and much sucking of teeth among the advisors, who were both exasperated and diverted by the way he and his mother seemed to tangle over every issue.

"Laughter doesn't hurt as much as swords, my mother. If they observe the peace—"

"If they hold us in contempt, they *won't* observe the peace." Her face was high in color, her big, dark eyes snapping.

"Anything else to discuss?" the king said, cutting her off. He didn't feel he had the energy to endure one of her tirades.

Tattamaru, for all that he was the *tawananna*'s man, unwittingly came to Tashmi-sharrumma's rescue. "My Sun, I have some very bad news. Alantalli of Mira has attacked Arinna."

A babble of horrified cries arose from the men assembled. Even Puduhepa seemed to have known nothing of her nephew's report. Everyone began to offer advice simultaneously. Someone expressed the hope that Alantalli would contract the plague there.

Vertigo suddenly swept over the king; sparkles danced before his eyes. He swallowed with difficulty then took himself in hand. "They're under attack now?"

"Yes, My Sun."

Someone murmured, "The holy city's only a day's march from Hattusha."

This is very grave, the king told himself, but he held on to his concentration with effort. The room was spinning. He clenched his hands more firmly around the arms of his throne.

"My Sun." It was Nerikkaili. "Your secretary just handed me this message for you from the king of Tarhuntassha as I entered. Shall I read it?"

The king's first muddled thought was, *No; it's for my eyes alone.* But clearly, Tarhun-miya would not have given the prince a private letter to deliver. Tashmi-sharrumma nodded, his breath starting to come heavy.

"Urhi-tesshub and the king of Mira are in league," read the prince. "That's all it says, apart from the greeting."

The Lords of Hatti erupted into curses, shouts of anger, threats of extreme bodily harm to the pretender.

But the queen's voice cut suddenly through the chaos, and she sounded frightened, "Son, are you all right?"

Because he wasn't, the king realized. His vision was swimming, and he could feel his breakfast rising in his gullet. He was clammy and shaking. His hands weakened on the arms of the throne, and the last thing he saw before he slid to the floor was his mother's round, terrified eyes.

CHAPTER 11

Puduhepa hovered over her son's bed, murmuring tremulous prayers to Iyarri, Lord of the Bow, sender of plague. *No, lord, no; don't let this be anything serious. Just some passing indisposition such as we all suffer from time to time.* She had sent for the Old Women and all the physicians in Hattusha, even written away for some from Kizzuwatna, for if the healers of her homeland were not as eminent as those of Mizri, still, they were far better than the local ones. She had also charged Mahhuzzi with a message for the Great King of Mizri: "Send us your best doctor."

After the king had collapsed in the council room, she had dismissed the assembled lords, called for servants to carry him to his chamber, and hustled after him. He had vomited in the courtyard and again as soon as they had him in bed. Now he lay there as unmoving and flat as a plank, his face whiter than the linen, his brows crumpled against the pain. *Oh, son,* she thought in an agony of fear. *You never show you are hurting. If you can't control it now, you must be sick indeed, my poor, poor little Tashmi-sharrumma.*

He groaned. The *tawananna* massaged his temples and the bony ridge marked by his eyebrows. She knew he sometimes had headaches, but she didn't know what was wrong now. He wasn't exactly unconscious, but he was clearly dwelling in some remote land of private suffering.

She saw that his hair was already graying at the temples, and her heart constricted with sorrow.

In time, the court doctors arrived, established their altars at his bedside. They offered him water, but he threw it up. The king writhed and shivered until his teeth clattered.

The Old Women came in and began their rituals in the corner of his chamber. Incense began to rise.

The queen came, too, but Puduhepa drove her out. "We don't know what he has. Keep the baby away."

Ellat-gula craned her neck to see her husband, but what she saw seemed to frighten her. She cried out a prayer to Gula, the Babylonian healing goddess. "My poor Sun!" Her voice was mournful, as if he had already become a god. "I will write for good Babylonian doctors; they are the best. I want to see Tashmi-sharrumma."

She never pronounces his name quite right. For some reason, this irritated Puduhepa disproportionately. She barked back, "No, he may have the plague. And no Babylonian doctors, do you hear?"

"They are the best. You're going to kill him with these people who know nothing. I want to see him," Ellat-gula declared angrily, and the *tawananna* remembered her daughter-in-law was far from the meek little foreign bride she had expected.

"He needs to rest. I'm his mother, and I say he is to have no visitors until we know what he has."

"Well, I am his wife, and I want to see him." They confronted each other nose to nose, two diminutive women contending the long body of the prostrate man. Ellat-gula shouldered her way past her mother-in-law, who grabbed at her plump arm, crying, "Guards!"

"My husband!" the queen shrieked as they hustled her away.

Puduhepa was crackling with the cold fire of protective fury. Her eyes followed Ellat-gula to the door. The foreign woman's selfishness at a time like this was simply beyond imagining. No godforsaken Babylonians were going to attend her son.

The day wore on. Doctors, priests, and servants with basins and clean sheets came and went. The king huddled up on his side, shivering, then he flailed around in a fever. His mother bathed his face with a wet towel until he began to twitch with cold, then she tucked the furs up around his neck. His pallor frightened her. He tried again and again to vomit, but there was nothing left. He was limp and moaning, his lips beginning to peel from the fever and dehydration. Her heart ached for him.

She looked up to see Nerikkaili standing at her shoulder, his face somber but carefully schooled. "What, my prince?"

"Do we go ahead and attack Arinna without him?"

"Of course. The whole kingdom can't stop because the king is indisposed. You know how often your father was sick."

He nodded but didn't leave. They watched the patient in silence for the space of a heartbeat.

"The *tuhkanti* is only a baby. There'll be need for a regent."

"Don't talk that way," cried the *tawananna*, incensed. "He isn't going to die." She clung to her son's limp hand as if she could forcibly retain his life.

"Any possibility he's been poisoned?"

She considered this. "The priests are taking oracles. They'll tell us. But none of the tasters has gotten sick."

"Wouldn't hurt to have a substitution ritual just in case."

"Yes. See to it, Nerikkaili." He turned to leave, but she called out after him, "Nerikkaili, what... what do you think of him?"

"What do I think? I think he's sick as a dog."

"No, I mean, as a man. As a king."

He widened his eyes as if to say, *Gods help me if I give the wrong answer,* but he responded seriously. "I think he's a good man. Suspicious. But also naive, which seems like an odd combination. Maybe... *idealistic to a fault* is a better way to put it. Why?"

"Do you think he's intelligent?"

"Yes. Why, don't you?"

"I do," she said, and her voice began to tremble. "Why were you unkind to him as a child?"

Nerikkaili made a noise of dismissal. "Boys are always like that. And he was such a little prig. *Anna*'s favorite and all that." He smiled at her meaningfully, his mouth a bit awry. Her fifty-four-year-old stepson patted her on the shoulder and left.

A week passed. The Egyptian doctor came with his shaven-headed acolytes. Babylonians were camping in the vestibule. The king's bedchamber was unendurably close, with the crowds of priests, physicians, and servants. His condition didn't improve. It not only didn't improve, but it seemed to grow worse. He was delirious, thrashing about, shouting out and weeping, muttering, praying, laughing as if a whole other reality was living itself out behind his closed eyelids. The priests who had seen the plague-stricken in Arinna shook their heads darkly; still, no one dared give the *tawananna* a definitive diagnosis. She stayed at his bedside as often as she could, but she had a kingdom to run—their army was besieging the Luwian rebels at Arinna, for one thing. She was trying to smooth out the Assyrian king's anger over the mixed message Hatti Land was sending him about Karduniash. The crops were growing poorly, and more grain had to be purchased from Mizri.

The priests had ordered that all the clothes the king had worn the day he fell sick had to be burned. Even his jewelry had to be melted down and all the chairs he sat on, the dishes he ate from destroyed. A slave was dressed in royal vestments and set upon the throne. It was he who would carry out the passive ceremonial duties of Tashmi-sharrumma in the hopes that whatever evil spirit was stalking the *king* would be deceived and relent.

The Egyptian doctor had sent even the king's mother away while he performed his anointing and purging. She hovered in the vestibule. Ellat-gula and her mother and cousin huddled nearby. *That Patiya wails and laments as if the loss is hers,* thought the *tawananna* in disgust. Puduhepa had tried to kick them out, even physically, but they kept coming back. Ellat-gula had almost garnered the sympathy of the lords of the kingdom by her persistence.

Well, of course she is concerned, thought the king's mother bitterly. *If he dies, she'll be nobody.*

There was a squeal as the interior door opened, and the Egyptian doctor—a dark, stocky man in a white linen kilt and shirt and a round wig—emerged. Mahhuzzi, her own secretary, was at his side as translator. His chinless face was drawn, his close-set eyes uneasy, as if he wouldn't have chosen to spend time in a sickroom. The doctor beckoned the two women into the chamber with him, and the *tawananna*'s heart sank. This couldn't be good news. She had forgotten what good news looked like.

The doctor was saying something in Egyptian. He pulled back the sheets and showed them the king's chest, which was covered in a flaming rash that went down his arms and up his throat but left his face untouched.

Mahhuzzi translated, and his voice shook a little. "He says it's the plague, my ladies."

Puduhepa's heart plunged like lead, but she stayed strong. Ellat-gula began to wail, her palms to her cheeks. Watching their reaction with his dark, kohl-lined eyes, the doctor appeared to understand what was going through the women's minds and nodded sympathetically. They didn't even hear his words, but Mahhuzzi said loudly, "He says they'll continue to do what they can. Many people recover if they are well cared for."

"Let the Babylonian doctor—"

"Shut up," rasped the *tawananna* at her daughter-in-law. "No Babylonians. Don't think I don't know what your brother is after. Let me find one little piece of evidence of witchcraft here, and your head is coming off, do you hear?"

"Why are you so hateful?" shrilled the queen. "I love my husband; can't you believe that? He may not love me, but I love him. If I have ever used witchcraft, it is white. Just to make him love me."

Puduhepa rolled her eyes and said mordantly, "How touching. And I don't suppose—"

But the Egyptian doctor interposed something in warning, and Mahhuzzi transmitted it: "He says we can't be sure the king doesn't hear. He says not to upset him."

The doctor's acolytes swept the women out. The two queens shrank away from one another to avoid touching as they passed through the doorway, and the *tawananna*'s lips were pressed grimly together with the effort to control her wrath, her apprehension. Fear perched upon her shoulder, sharpening its beak. With all the terrible things going on in the kingdom, they couldn't lose the king, too. His death and the ascension of an infant to the throne might provide just the moment of chaos that Urhi-tesshub was waiting for.

And if he's cultivating the support of the West... With all the venom she could summon, she cursed Alantalli of Mira. She herself had paired Kurunta with his daughter to keep the shifty vassal loyal. But apparently, it hadn't worked. She began to wonder about Kurunta himself. What a disappointment he had turned out to be, now that it really mattered. Yet perhaps it was her son who was at fault there. She had tried so hard to encourage them to cement their friendship by deeper bonds. But that had fallen through, it seemed. The king had turned into a frozen piece of stone who seemed to have no desire for men or women. And Kurunta was not the steady sort. She wasn't sure he'd stay the course of friendship without some reward. She had hoped the heaping of power and wealth would be sufficient, but she had misread him. And now, it might all become moot. *Don't even think that,* she told herself sternly. *Tashmi-sharrumma will survive.*

⸙

Kurunta had been behind the reins of a light Hurrian chariot for days: he had lost track of how many. He had galloped with the speed of a courier, he alone, his bones rattling and his face wind burned, as his team pounded the road from Tarhuntassha to the capital. He arrived in the city with his relays exhausted, and he himself was ready to drop. But despite his haste, he feared he might be too late.

The *tawananna* had written to him to say that plague had struck the king.

Plague! The most terrifying word in their language, surely. Even Kurunta's thoughts trembled, like the muscles of his legs as he plowed up the long, long causeway to the royal citadel. He had left his horses in the care of the royal stable in the Upper City—*the Upper City below,* he thought with a kind of giddy irony—and here he was, dripping with sweat, covered in dust, his clothes white ringed, and his hair tangled into strings. They wouldn't even have let him in the palace gate if everyone hadn't known him.

The climb had completely blown him: impossible to think it, but he wasn't so young anymore. Kurunta was heaving as he crossed the courtyards—public, then interior, then private—and entered the vestibule of the king's chamber, where the guards recognized him and let him pass. The vestibule was full of people, including the queen and her mother and cousin. The women recoiled from him, aghast, but Ellat-gula saw who he was and came forward kindly, taking him by the arm. He noticed she was pregnant again.

"Kurunta. Our Sun is very sick." Her voice was tremulous, her smile unsure. "He is sleeping, and the doctors told us to leave, but you must go in to him."

"Is the *tawananna*...?"

"No, she is with the council. There is no one inside but the doctor's man."

Seeing that the queen had given her blessing, the others made no effort to stop Kurunta. He pushed the heavy door open, his hand shaky with trepidation as much as weariness.

Tash lay asleep, perhaps drugged, his chest rising and falling with the effort of drawing breath. Otherwise, he might have been mistaken for a corpse. He was pitifully gaunt, colorless, his eyes crusted and sunken and his mouth hanging open. Although Kurunta had told himself he would be cheerful, positive in his cousin's presence, a sob of horror and grief broke from him. He fell to his knees at the bedside. In the corner, the Egyptian acolyte keeping watch glanced at him and looked away, carefully expressionless.

Kurunta gestured to him peremptorily. "You, go out. I want to be alone with the king." The young man probably couldn't understand his words, but he knew he was being dismissed. He packed up his papyrus scroll and a mortar full of something he was grinding and let himself through the door. Kurunta fell across the king's body and howled. Exhaustion had eaten up all his self-control, what little he had ever had.

"Tash! Tash!" he wailed. "Don't die."

Had Kurunta thought he had accepted the end of their friendship? The danger of losing his friend in the most permanent way showed him how false that was. He felt he couldn't continue to live himself if Tash died. The king was younger, by all the gods; he should live longer. Kurunta should never have had to see him lying dead. His heart in tatters, the viceroy drew back, sniffing and gasping, then felt for his cousin's hand under the furs and took it in his own. With a finger, he traced the blue veins across the double groove of tendon at Tashmi-sharrumma's wrist. It was as cold as that of a corpse... but there was a pulse. Hope struggled against the pain that racked Kurunta.

"Tash, Tash. If only you could know that I'm here by your side," he murmured, his lips against the back of the king's hand. "There are so many things I want to tell you. Do you really know how much I love you, Tash? I want to think you do. But... but how can I tell if you care? You never show what you feel."

Weeping overcame him—his shoulders shaking, his teeth clenched—for all that he had lost. All the promised flame of their youthful love gone cold. Lost, like everything good in his life. Like everyone who had ever loved him, Tash had drifted away over the years, abandoned him. The king would hardly touch him anymore. Was it something he, Kurunta, had done?

Kurunta fought back the self-pity and struggled to get control of himself again. *What happened, little cousin? Why don't you love me anymore? It was Lurma-ziti, wasn't it? He scared you back into your hole, the rotten dog turd.* Rage sank its teeth into him, but it wasn't against Tash, who was the victim.

"I know you're scared, little cousin, but I don't know why. Are you afraid someone will take away anything you love too much? Or are you just scared of anything that's pleasurable or easy or natural? For some reason, you think that only things you have to force yourself to do are worthwhile." Kurunta gulped down a bitter throatful of tears. "Even as a child, you wanted nothing but to please your parents, and they were like giants, like gods. Only great, big, heavy things pleased them. You'd do anything, no matter how frightened you were, to make them happy. What's wrong with you, man? Duty isn't the only good, you know."

Anger welled up in him again, bitter as bile in his throat, but this time, its object wasn't so clear. He was furious with life, the unfairness of it, and desperate to regain what he had lost. *Tash, come back.* Desolation contorted his face, twisted his viscera. *Nobody thinks any ill of us, damn it. They all think we're still lovers, and nobody cares. Do you think the gods don't want us to have some joy, too? And it's not just that. If we were more than friends, you could count on me forever. I'd know you loved me the way I do you—the way you used to love me. Don't you remember how beautiful it was?*

His words shattered, their shards lacerating his heart. "And I'd be faithful through everything, Tash," he said, weeping. "But as it is, how can I know I'm not just making a fool of myself? I do have some pride, you know."

Kurunta fell to his elbows on the bed, sobs racking his body, his hair hanging in black curtains around his face like a mourning cloak. His insides seemed to be incinerating. His voice came out in shreds.

"You're driving me to something I don't want to do, Tash. Give me a sign, please, please. Just a little word, a touch—anything. Save me, Tash. Don't let me do what I might. Don't abandon me."

But the king lay there, insensible, incapable of giving a sign.

Eventually Kurunta, the viceroy of Tarhuntassha, wiped his nose and, with a heart full of pain, rose to his feet. He feared he would never be a whole man again. He bent over and kissed the king on the lips—plague be damned—and headed to the door, his weary shoulders drooping.

As the fever broke, the rash withdrew, and the plague began to loosen its grip on him, Tashmi-sharrumma returned to the world of the living. But he was far from recovered. He found himself so weak he could scarcely raise his head. It was as if his senses were swaddled in a thick blanket of wool. He could hardly comprehend what people said. Words seemed to be in a foreign language; ordinary items had no meaning. It was a long time before he could even think.

He had no experience of being an invalid, and it was harder to bear than he could have anticipated.

His mother refused at first to bring him up to date on the matters facing the kingdom. "It's enough for you just to regain your strength, my dearest. Eat and rest. Don't push yourself. We're taking care of things for you."

He ate and rested dutifully, but he was impatient. The responsibility before the gods was still his, after all. And yet he found he had very little control over anything, including his own body. He lay in bed, conscious for the first time of his own frailty, and thought of all the duties he was unable to attend to, and he wondered why the gods had struck him down only to let him live in the end.

Was this the punishment for his father's usurpation? If so, things were perhaps coming to a head. Urhi-tesshub was back, in league with Alantalli—the king himself was laid dramatically low. What next?

And that carried his thoughts to Kurunta. Ellat-gula had told Tashmi-sharrumma the viceroy of Tarhuntassha had paid him a visit while the king was sick. Tashmi-sharrumma had had no awareness of Kurunta's presence, although he had dreamed of his cousin often in his delirium. Dreamed they were children again. Oh, happy Kurunta, full of laughter and mischief, always daring him to attempt something—a spring of brightly colored ideas, wild heroics, shooting stars. Or he dreamed they were going into battle together, as they so often had, urging one another to glorious deeds, with the innocence of youth. Or dreamed they consummated their love.

A strangling brew of gloom and longing rose in Tashmi-sharrumma at the thought of his cousin. Reality was so much more complicated than the world of dreams. He would have liked to think that Kurunta's visit means that the viceroy had forgiven him. But forgiven him for what? He could no longer recall the provocation for their falling-out. *The vassal treaty. Kurunta feels bought. And yet he signed it.*

The king grew steadily stronger; youth was on his side. He learned to discipline his impatience. Recovering became a duty he shouldered with resignation but no self-pity. And finally, he was seated again with his advisors in the council room.

It was harder than he remembered to sit upright upon the pitiless lap of Halmashuit—literally harder as well. His long frame was so gaunt, his bones so protruding that he couldn't get comfortable no matter how he positioned himself. His head seemed heavier than a human head could be, and the simplest task—lifting a hand, calling for his secretary—became an exercise in doggedness. He remembered his father in his old age, hunched and immobile upon his throne; even closing his mouth had taken more effort than the old king could muster. But his mind had still been still sharp, his blind eyes seeing every affair of Hatti Land in order of importance, precedence, and proportion. The late king had had to fight his treacherous body for his whole life, never knowing when it might fail him, forcing it to go where duty demanded against this frightening thing that was weakness.

Tashmi-sharrumma realized he had had it easy in many ways and had taken the gods' gift of health for granted. Like so many things.

Like people's love, which he so ill deserved.

His reverie was cut short. Walwa-ziti, the chief scribe, approached to present his report.

"I have summarized the findings of the overseers of the granaries, My Sun. The crops are sown, but, er... so far, the yields don't look promising. There's some kind of worm in the barley in the Lower Land, and a plague of starlings carried off much of the wheat before it could sprout."

"We'll have to buy grain again," the king said.

Nerikkaili sighed. "Alas, we're not infinitely rich."

"We should make a formal annexation of Kuwaliya," the *tawananna* said. "Make them pay their tribute in wheat. And that reminds me, My Sun. Mashturi of Sheha River Land has been assassinated by his own vizier. We sent troops to put down the rebellion, but you need to appoint a successor. Perhaps you could put Kuwaliya under Sheha River Land in some way."

"But even so…" Nerikkaili grumbled.

Alalimmi looked around, his face flushing, and pounded one fist into the other palm. "Why, it's easy enough, all of you. Why is no one saying it? Take out Mira, and make the bastards pay indemnity until they squeal. That Alantalli needs to learn a lesson about where treacherous vassals go."

"It's not so easy as all that, my cousin," the *tawananna* countered primly. "He's been driven out of Arinna, but do you know *where* he is?"

"Strike his kingdom while he's gone. All the better."

The king listened to them argue, his eyes glazing, remembering the good old uncle in Sheha River Land who was now lying under the black earth. Betrayed by those he had relied on. It suddenly occurred to the king that Kurunta was Alantalli's son-in-law and that Urhi-tesshub, Kurunta's brother, was in league with Alantalli. His thoughts began drifting where he'd rather not have gone. *Stop. You must trust someone.*

He realized that Walwa-ziti was now saying something about an earthquake. *Dear Lords of the Air, is there no end? This can only be the wrath of the gods.*

He interrupted the vizier. "Have we offered thanksgiving to Iyarri and Sharrumma for my recovery?"

"Of course, My Sun." The *tawananna's* tone was lightly patronizing. How could he doubt that she had seen to all the details of piety—she, the great religious reformer?

Irritation rippled across the king's calm. He leaned his chin upon one hand, his elbow on the arm of the throne, physically wearied. But he was strong enough to keep his silence. Somehow, minor slights like these seemed much less important to him than before.

He reflected to himself that his mother must have lived some heady days during his illness. She had never been especially patient. For those who were slower than she, like himself—the millstones of whose reflection ground more deliberately—she had never had much tolerance. After this brief regency, perhaps she really thought he couldn't rule without her.

They spoke to him of so many disasters and reverses that he almost laughed out of sheer despair. Except for the reconquest of Arinna, which was no small thing, everything had gone wrong in a month's time. He dared not ask about Assyria; it would degenerate into a rebuke from his mother about undercutting her foreign policy.

What have I done? Have I offended one of the thousand gods?

Or is it my father whose sins I am being punished for?

The advisors were still talking. The king nodded and looked wise and acted as if he was paying attention, but his mind was elsewhere. There was something he had to do. He glanced around under his lids for Tattamaru, the chief shepherd of Arinniti, but the priest wasn't there. They had told Tashmi-sharrumma that Tattamaru was supervising the rebuilding of Arinna after its siege, he remembered. Some other priest would have to do. He himself was one but not a taker of oracles. He needed to ask a question.

CHAPTER 12

THE KING WAS RELUCTANT TO let his mother know he sought the mind of the gods in this matter, although he was almost ashamed of his reason for secrecy. She would take over the project, call in her own men. That seemed like a paltry motive for an action, he thought, embarrassed. But there it was. It was much the same with his plans to enrich the temples of the gods. Nothing could be more important—he wanted it to be the centerpiece of his reign. Yet it was the *tawananna* who had begun the religious reform in Hatti Land. She had ordered all the numerous gods of Hatti and its vassals, explained how they were really the same, made them stronger, built them new cult places. He had to think of a way to separate his works from hers so that those who came after did not see him as one who had simply done what his mother had told him.

But first of all, he needed an honest answer to his question from the oracle. He wanted his own formulation of the question, because while the gods never lied, they answered only the questions they were asked. He supposed he no longer trusted even his own mother. It was just as well that Tattamaru, her kinsman, was occupied.

The next day, he summoned Dulakki, the second priest of Sharrumma, the man to whom Tashmi-sharrumma's own duties were delegated when his kingly tasks impinged upon the demands of priesthood. They met very quietly in the king's private chamber. Only Tarhun-miya was present.

To Dulakki's obvious discomfiture, the king humbly lowered his head for the priest's blessing. "I have a question for the oracle, Dulakki. How private can we make this?"

"As private as My Sun wants it," the priest answered with a shrug. "There is no requirement of high ceremony. Do you want a divination from the flight of birds, or from oil on water?"

"Which is more reliable?"

"It depends on the nature of the questions, My Sun. For the future outcome of actions, the flight of birds is best, or the liver of a sacrificial sheep. For questions about the past and present, perhaps oil is more precise. Not that the gods lie, but it's easy for their servants to misread the signs."

"Can you do it here?" the king asked.

"Not I, but my best practitioners. I send them both because they can correct one another."

Tashmi-sharruma nodded. "Good. Do it today."

The priest bowed to his superior and prepared to back out, but the king stopped him. "To whom would I go for a... a consultation of the dead, Dulakki?" Tashmi-sharrumma was reluctant to speak of this matter. He feared it was somehow a weakness, a childish dependency on his part.

The priest looked up, a faint unease in his eye. They both knew it was no small thing to call up the dead. "To the priestesses of Lelwani, My Sun, the Queen of the Underworld. To the Old Women."

"Send them, too," Tashmi-sharrumma instructed.

The king told the Lords of Hatti he was going to rest for the afternoon and remained cloistered in his chamber, but he didn't lie down. He paced compulsively around his room, preparing to ask a question that might determine the fate of his kingdom. Until weakness overtook him, he walked to and fro, then he sat slid down in his chair, his mind churning like beer in fermentation. Sometime in the afternoon, the diviners arrived, and Zuzu admitted them to the royal chamber. Despite the blindingly blue early-winter day that brightened the court beyond, it was stuffy inside and dark.

The two priests could hardly have been less alike, the one short and stout and the other bone thin and nearly as tall as the king. Tashmi-sharrumma would have found it amusing were this not such a grave moment. Kurunta would have found it amusing in any case.

The men, austerely dressed in the unbleached woolen tunics of shepherds, set up a ceremonial wicker table, as if for offerings, and upon it they set their shallow bronze bowl. With chanting and incense, they poured clean water into the bowl, rinsing it and discarding the water onto the king's floor, until on the third pour they permitted it to remain. It quivered for a moment as the surface stilled, and then it lay there as perfect as a water mirror. The king leaned over it, perceived his cadaverous reflection from beneath the chin, and withdrew quickly.

Now one of the priests poured a fine stream of oil from a narrow-necked ewer while his companion recited prayers in Luwian and Neshite. The oil pooled thinly across the face of the bowl but didn't cover the entire surface. He invoked the Storm God of Nerik, the king's personal patron, and looked up at the king.

"Present your first question, My Sun."

Tashmi-sharrumma gathered his courage. He had written several questions on Tarhun-miya's wax dictation tablet. He took a deep breath and held the tablet close to his eyes. "The first is this: 'Is the king's illness caused by any sin of his father's?'"

The tall priest took a slender bronze rod a little longer than a stylus and slowly stirred the surface of the water in the shape of a Luwian pictogram. The oil swirled richly, curling and doubling upon itself. The three men hung over the bowl, scarcely daring to breathe as the oil continued to undulate, even after the diviner had removed the rod. This seemed to go on interminably, until the king found himself almost sliding into a trance as he watched it. At last it grew still.

The short priest stared at it for a long time and finally pronounced a single word. "No."

A wave of relief passed over Tashmi-sharrumma like a shudder, yet perhaps this wasn't good news. *Is the sin my own, then?*

They poured out the water and repeated the entire process. This time the tall priest read. "No."

They passed to the second question. Weariness was beginning to overtake the king. It wasn't the exile of Hishni. They passed to the third question. It wasn't the king's obduracy toward Kurunta. It wasn't Tashmi-sharrumma's want of respect for his mother. It wasn't his unkindness toward his wife. It wasn't his impatience with his vassals after the battle at Taite.

The king's back was spasming from hanging over the bowl, and he finally had to sit. They came to the last question.

"Was the king's illness caused by the enmity between the *tawananna* and the king's wife?"

"Yes."

Tashmi-sharrumma let out the breath he had been holding. He put an unsteady hand over his eyes for a moment. So. He had not been firm enough with the women, and now he had paid.

But the fault was first of all theirs, he had to admit, and surely his mother's more than Ellat-gula's. No one in the kingdom was as powerful as she, except himself... perhaps. She had the unfair advantage over her adversary, and so her enmity reeked both of injustice and of lack of mercy. *All you thousand gods of our land,* he prayed silently, *forgive her. Forgive me for not stopping her. She's too strong for me.*

He thanked the priests and sent them away with the injunction to speak to no one of what they'd seen.

Now he had to decide what to do about it. It was he who was responsible for justice in this kingdom. If he turned a blind eye, the guilt would be his own. Next time it might not be he personally who paid but the innocent people he stewarded for the Storm God.

Later, the Old Women came. They were three, wrapped in long black cloaks, their veils pinned under the chin to expose nothing but their faces, and only one of them was old. One was a pale-faced girl of an almost ethereal beauty; the other, who appeared to be their leader, was a woman his own age or a little more. She had a hard, austere look about her. He knew she would not spare him, and he welcomed her truth telling.

They didn't bow; they served a power higher than him—Lelwani, the Night Sun, Queen of the Underworld. The Old Women seemed to radiate darkness so that the dimly lit bedchamber appeared to grow blacker at their presence. The king's poor eyes failed him, and he could barely see except for the white disks of their faces; they were like three barn owls. He inclined, because he was a pious man and remembered them with awe from the funeral of his father.

"My mothers," he said in a faint voice. He was like a small, timid child in their presence. "I have a favor to ask of your queen. I… I would consult the dead."

"You would consult the dead, would you? This is a dangerous request and perhaps no favor to you at all." The leader of the three had a voice as low as a man's. Her eyes seemed to bore into his, and he lowered them, uneasy. Although he was so much taller than she, he felt her power hanging over his head, dominating him. "Who is it you would consult?"

"My father."

The Old Woman did not answer immediately. She seemed to be listening to her mistress in the silence. "He is not hostile to you. It may be possible to speak to him without terrible danger. But your father has become a god. Why do you not pray to him in his statue somewhere?"

"I… I want to consult him as a human spirit. I need to

know what to do, how he perceives things now by godsight." *I need to know he watches over me and guides me,* he thought, a knot gathering in his throat, *because I can't do this thing I must alone. I want to see him again.*

She appeared to consider for a long space of time, her face lifted, her eyes remote. The king heard his own breathing, as loud as a bellows in the silence. Did the women's cloaks ripple? There was no wind in his bedroom. He was painfully conscious of his weakness; it required effort to lift his head and speak. Desperate, he said, "Other people consult their ancestors."

"Angry ghosts can be dangerous, hard to control. Sometimes they escape from the summoner. Your father was more powerful than other people's ancestors. We are endangered, too. It is no light thing you ask, shepherd of the people."

It occurred to him that it might well be the goddess herself who spoke to him through this woman.

"Please, great lady," he beseeched, lowering himself to his knees. "Let me talk to my father one last time. I'm willing to take the risk."

The women turned one to another in a circle so that their white faces were momentarily eclipsed, and darkness swallowed up the king. His laborious breathing filled the silence once more.

Then they faced outward again, like a flower unfolding, and a glow pale and cold as starshine illumined the king's strained face. The leader said, "It can only be done when the moon is black. That will be four nights from tonight. Meet us at the east postern gate at the deepest hour of the darkness. If the spring still runs, we can proceed. If it has frozen, we cannot."

They turned and filed from the room without taking their leave. The shadows curled around him. He remained on his knees, wondering if he had made a mistake.

Four nights thence he left the citadel by the side gate, accompanied only by his secretary and the elderly Pirwannu, who carried lamps. Neither was much of a fighting man. It occurred to the king that he would be vulnerable with no guard at all. His mother would have been furious if she had known what he was doing—at the very least, risking contamination through some encounter with a layman. The three men descended the long, snaking back staircase down the cliffside into the Upper City, and the king found he was already tiring, his breathing labored, his legs unsteady. They crossed the corner of the city through the streets of the temple district and the houses of the rich, their footsteps ringing softly on the bedrock. If the night guards at the east postern gate were surprised to see the king afoot at this hour, they showed nothing but, unspeaking, broke the clay seals and rocked back the inner door.

The party passed through the tunnel under the walls, Tashmi-sharrumma's hand brushing the relief of the double-headed eagle that was the symbol of his empire. The outer gate swung open, and they passed outside the city into the gelid winter night.

A still, burning cold enveloped the men, as it always did at night in the highlands. There was no moon, and it was as black as the realm of the Lady Lelwani. Pirwannu gazed up and murmured, "Look how bright the stars are," but to the king, the sky was opaque as black wool.

The air smelled different here than it did within the confines of the citadel: earthy, ancient, dark. The defenses of man had no power against the earth. The Old Women stepped out of the shadows where they had been waiting, invisible in their black cloaks, and without a word, they led away, across a footpath that descended the ravine behind the citadel. Only then did Tashmi-sharrumma perceive that they carried tallow lights.

The king couldn't see it, but he could feel the presence above him of the cliff that loomed overhead, the naked black rock upon which his ancestors had built their aerie. He prayed to the god of the rock. Its damp chill radiated out upon the travelers, who crawled blindly, like a line of ants, into the crack in the earth, their steps sliding and rattling upon the stone. The king heard Tarhun-miya panting nervously behind him. The king, too, was frightened— there were more dangerous things than doing battle against men—but he was accustomed to riding down his fear. More than the usual sense of vulnerability invaded him, however. He knew he couldn't trust his body to summon whatever strength he might need. It could fail him. The thought was humbling.

They stumbled down, down, through the darkness. Undergrowth, crisp and frozen, clawed at their skirts. The tiny lamplights were nearly worse than nothing, occasionally blinding with their glare before the immense night swallowed them up again.

At last, the king felt the ground growing level beneath his feet. He heard gurgling water, an owl's lonely cry. Somewhere the howl of a wolf hinted at a night more populous—and more perilous—than men suspected.

Nearby, a goat bleated out its fear, and mist began to gather, as it so often did before dawn in the mountains.

"The spring is flowing. The goddess is present." The Old Woman's deep voice emerged from the darkness. "We can summon the dead."

They crouched at the edge of the spring and prayed to its god. The whole cliff suppurated with water from the bedrock, and here the liquid forced its way up from beneath the black earth, from the realms of Lelwani, dark and frothing, swelling and rippling. It trickled in a narrow stream down the ravine, cutting its way through the rock eon after eon. Not even the drought had managed to slay it, not even the ice that had begun to constrict its flow.

The dead had to cross running water to come back to the living.

The priestesses had dug a small trench along the edge of the stream. They had tethered a kid nearby. Now the leader of the Old Women drew out her dagger of iron from the sky and slit the goat's throat while her sisters chanted. A cataract of dark blood flowed into the trench, releasing the rich, metallic odor of death, and she pushed the body of the animal in after. They lifted up bowls of groats and curds they had concealed in the brush and offered them to the goddess, dumping them into the trench. The leader plunged her dagger blade into the earth with a violent gesture.

"Great Lady, hear us!" she cried, raising her fists, and her voice echoed against the cliff. "I knock on your door. Hear us, and release to this seeker the soul he desires."

The mist thickened and swirled. The king could feel it on his face, like a cold hand stroking his cheek. His eyes were straining across the stream to see if his father would come, but between the darkness and the fog—and his own poor eyesight—he was nearly blind. They waited. The silence seemed to devour them. The owl was hushed; the burbling of the spring seemed to fade. The mist slithered and writhed among the rocks.

Suddenly, he thought he detected a lighter patch. *Is that a man's face? Those shadows—a man's long hair?* His heart was pounding; his breath shuddered in his throat. No one spoke. Did they see it, too?

"My father?" he whispered. "Is that you?"

He couldn't tell, but he believed he felt the presence of Hattushili, a powerful, benevolent fullness of being, hovering just at the edge of his vision. The young king shivered; tears sprang to his eyes. *Help me, Father.* Surely Hattushili was there, behind the mist. *Speak to me. Tell me what to do.* It had to be he; no one else could be so strong as this Great King who had become a god. Tashmi-sharrumma was paralyzed by the masterful presence, caught up in it as if it were a flood. He couldn't struggle against it; he couldn't breathe. He longed for it; he feared it. The power of its excellence crushed his own mediocrity beneath it. Its love overwhelmed him, commanding him. He shuddered and began to weep openly. *Father! Father! Tell me what to do. Make me stronger.*

Tarhun-miya gave a fearful little whimper behind him. The others had to have seen it, too.

Tashmi-sharrumma strained his ears. Would the presence speak? *Oh, let him speak.* The king felt himself pulled toward the stream and the mist in the darkness and the lighter place that could be a face. His heart seemed to be emerging from his mouth, throbbing and hammering, yearning toward the dead king. He wanted with a sudden all-powerful longing to join his father, to lose himself in Hattushili's immensity, to be no longer the one who carried the weight of a kingdom... but the Old Woman reached out a sudden hand and jerked him back.

"We must leave," she whispered. "The power is too strong. You will die if you stay."

They herded him back. He cried out brokenheartedly, "My father!" but the priestesses were implacable. Around them, the mist swirled and undulated and closed in like an opaque curtain. The king came to himself as if awaking from sleep, the tears freezing on his face, and realized that he had no answer to his question. He had forgotten to ask it.

The Old Women said nothing. They were inscrutable, but Pirwannu and the secretary were clearly shaken. They stared at the king with a mixture of awe and uncertainty. The party moved up the cliffside, feeling their way. Hours had to have passed; the mist was beginning to brighten with the cold, hard silver light of a winter dawn. Behind them, they heard the padding and snarling of animals and the sounds of crunching; something had found the carcass of the kid. Tashmi-sharrumma only hoped it was something of this world.

The priestesses left them at the gate, and the king and his attendants trudged silently to the stairs that led to the back corner of the citadel. They climbed, they climbed, they climbed. His elderly valet and the hollow-chested little secretary were wheezing and groaning, but the king plowed upward by sheer force of will. He stood for a moment at the palace gate, strangely exhilarated, looking down upon the fog that obliterated the city below him, and he realized that his father had indeed spoken. The view up here was very clear. He knew just what had to do.

In the morning, the king sent Tarhun-miya to the chancery to do some research among the tablets of the law. The night's journey had tired Tashmi-sharrumma but left behind a deep comfort. He felt his father's fearless presence at his side. He had to put an end to the contention between Ellat-gula and the *tawananna* before it brought down more disaster upon the kingdom. And, he realized, he had to end his mother's benevolent tyranny over himself. He was far too old to be so subservient, he knew, but he had no stomach for conflict. It had been easier simply to let her have her way than to fight. This, he told himself, was cowardice, and he had no mind to permit it to rule him. He didn't want to lose her love, but he couldn't let her pressure him into injustice.

Justice.

With his father's help, he would act.

Some days later, Tashmi-sharrumma was seated behind the table in his private office when his mother entered. His clasped hands were resting upon the tabletop in seeming tranquility, but his fingers were tense. He stared at his blanched knuckles and willed them to relax. The *tawananna* had been summoned, and that would have put her on her guard. He had pondered for days how to go about this interview, had practiced the conversation in his head. But the reality would be outside his control, as were so very many things. He was still half-sick; he knew his eyes were sunken, his cheeks hollow, and like a wary animal, he feared that this appearance of weakness might embolden his enemies.

He committed himself to Sharrumma and greeted with a tilt of the head the woman who had borne him. "My mother." He spoke Hurrian, the language of her birth, rather than Neshite. He hoped this would disarm her, but part of him resented the need to be so calculating. The king wanted simply that things continue to be as they always had been between them. This, however, he was convinced would not happen.

"My son." She made a kind of half obeisance, sensing the formality in his reserved bearing. He watched her eyes flick up and down over him and wondered what she was thinking. Her face, her beautiful face, the very first thing he had ever seen upon this earth, was carefully fixed in a pleasant but concerned mask. His own mask was in place as well. She couldn't know his thoughts.

She said in a motherly way, "Should you be up so soon? You look tired. Don't forget you've been very sick. Perhaps this should wait—"

"This should not wait, Mother," he interrupted calmly. "I've invited you here to discuss the cause of my illness."

"Yes, perhaps we should have an oracle taken. I can contact one of the Old Women if—"

"It's already been done."

The vertical line between her eyebrows deepened. She was surprised and displeased. He had taken care of things himself and had not relied on her. The new reign would not be like the last one. He found that he was strangely saddened for his mother, whom he loved, after all. He was sure that in her mind, everything she did was for him, and he was not ungrateful. That capacity for gratitude was both a strength and a weakness of his character. Now he had to displease her even further—he, the good son.

He lifted up the wax tablet that lay at his elbow and said as gently as he could, controlling the nervous desire to swallow, "Would you like to read the results, or do you prefer me to read them to you?"

Suspicion was growing in her face, which she turned slightly away from him as if she could see his real intentions more clearly from the corner of her eye. "Why don't you read it to me, my son? Unless it would tire you."

"Not at all. I'll just summarize: we asked a lot of questions." He lowered his eyes a little too close to the tablet and read the text, which he had in fact memorized: "In answer to the question 'Is the king's illness caused by any sin of his father's?' the oracle answered, 'No.' In answer to the question 'Is the king's illness caused by the enmity between the *tawananna* and the king's wife?' the oracle answered…'Yes.'"

He looked up at his mother and waited for her reaction.

The *tawananna's* face was frozen. Was it anger, denial, guilt? Her lips were pursed, her shoulders drawn back as if in retreat from some abomination. Certainly, she couldn't be pleased that the cause of her son's grave illness had been laid at her feet. Tashmi-sharrumma watched her with half-closed eyes, ready to learn from the master of cultivated outrage. It helped him that her reaction was the product of artifice, because he would genuinely have hated to hurt her. That, too, was a weakness of character—he had no doubt that she'd hurt him without a qualm if she needed to. They stared at one another for a long space of time like two old wolves sizing up the competition. One of them would have to drop his gaze first. But neither did. They were well matched, he saw for the first time. He smiled at the thought and cocked his head, inviting her to reply.

After a moment, she said with a little shrug, "The gods have spoken". She was going to play the reasonable person, but the hard crimp in her eyebrows betrayed her displeasure. "I just hope that you have also informed your wife about this. Arguments take two parties, you know."

"Yes. But you're much more powerful than Ellat-gula, Mother. More of the responsibility falls on you. She's at a disadvantage."

The *tawananna* had taken on that sphinxlike arch of the neck. He had offended her, and she would strike back. Perhaps later she'd cover him with kisses and swear she did not mean it, but he knew her—she would draw his blood. He was as tense as a lion hunter closing in on the kill, possessed of a hunter's calm focus. There was no fear, just the cold, clear awareness that any miscalculation might be fatal.

"I would say that your wife and her mother, with their cabal of self-interested plotters, deserve to be *disadvantaged*, my son. They are, frankly, a pack of spies for Karduniash. With a little more experience, you would have observed that for yourself."

Tashmi-sharrumma felt the sting of her rebuke, but it was no more than he expected. He was not a man to let a little pain stop him from what he believed he had to do. He picked his words carefully, wishing he had a larger share of her eloquence. But maneuvering within range of her murderous claws as he was, he knew enough to stay watchful until the *coup de grace* was delivered.

"I'm not the only one who has seen you be hostile to her. I think were your motives as objective as you believe them to be, you would remember the bonds of alliance between Hatti and Karduniash that our marriage represents and not make constant efforts to undermine it."

"*I* undermine your marriage?" the *tawananna* shot back, real anger crackling through her words. "Who do you think arranged your marriage, Tashmi-sharrumma?" She was no longer addressing him as king—he was almost amused by her transparency—but as her little boy. "Who saw to it that you were married to the daughter of a Great King while your elder brother—who was then the *tuhkanti*, if you please—was matched with the child of a paltry vassal?" She advanced on the table where her son sat and leaned above it as if to overshadow him. Her mouth was twisted with contempt. "Who gave your father the idea of bestowing on you all the responsibilities *he* had in his ascent to the throne: the priesthood of Sharrumma, the *meshedi* guards, the, the… everything. It was a message that *I* designed so all the world would know that you were chosen, even before Hattushili announced you as his heir.

"And as for your marriage, it's you who are clearly uninterested in being a husband to her. What's wrong with you, son? You don't like women, but you don't like men either? Why don't you give Kurunta what he wants, before we lose him?"

She had steered the conversation away from his accusation. The king said very quietly and a little dangerously, "Perhaps if you stopped pushing so hard…"

"You're a grown man," she shot back, not hearing the warning in his voice.

He swallowed his anger and drew her back to the affair of the oracle. "I think that you didn't expect Ellat-gula to be quite so intelligent and so unwilling to obey you. She might actually be able to exercise some influence over my opinions, and you wouldn't like that, would you?"

"Are you actually proud to admit that a woman might control your opinions?"

"You mean a woman other than you?" he said, but she talked over him, her voice rising.

"Have you ever asked yourself why her mother came with her to Hattusha, my son? Have you ever heard of such a thing before—a king's wife accompanying her daughter abroad? Ellat-gula is a creature of her brother. Their whole concern is for the interests of Karduniash. That influence you talk about is counter to your own best interests, but somehow, you're so besotted by her that you can't see that. I'm surprised, frankly. I thought you of all people would be proof against her, but no. Like all men, you think with your prick."

"Like my father, for example, when he married that beautiful but ambitious young priestess from Lawazantiya?"

The *tawananna* was almost speechless with indignation, but she fought down her fury and hissed, "Careful, my son, lest your father's ghost demand satisfaction for such disrespect."

Weariness suddenly overwhelmed Tashmi-sharrumma. His father's memory was enough of a problem for him already, casting its gigantic, ambivalent shadow over every corner of his life. Now he had let his own anger herd him into shallows where he'd rather not have waded. He could only extricate himself by a flurry of explanations and excuses that would be his mother's best argument. He slowly set his elbows on the table, clasped his hands, rested his chin upon them, and stared at his mother without a word. He couldn't engage her on the playing field of respective wraths; that was a duel he hadn't the temperament to win. But he was good at not speaking.

There was a long silence. The king's face began cooling down. He lifted an eyebrow in deliberate provocation or invitation.

"Why, I don't think I've ever heard you use so many words at one time, Tashmi-sharrumma," his mother said with a sneer. Then she shrugged, regaining her composure. "Believe whatever you like. My record speaks for itself."

He refrained from pointing out that a record is by definition a thing of the past. "I'm responsible for justice in this kingdom, Mother. I cannot tolerate such behavior. The gods have seen it and punished me already." He drew to him a second tablet that had sat upon the tabletop, and looked up at her from under his lids. "I've dictated a decree, and it has been passed by the chief of the scribes, who's in full agreement." He held it up—although he knew what it said word for word without looking—and began to read a summary:

"I, Tudhaliya, Great King, son of the hero Hattushili, do declare that Lady Puduhepa shall be removed from the office of *tawananna* and that my wife, the queen, Lady Ellat-gula, shall replace her."

As his mother absorbed what the decree was saying, her pupils grew rounder and rounder with incredulity. Her arched brows contracted; her nostrils went white and rigid, her lips thinned with the effort of controlling the outburst that welled up within her. Tashmi-sharrumma observed her over the top of the tablet, his chest tight. He finished reading and set down the wooden tablet frame, awaiting the full blast of her reaction. The tense efficiency of the lion hunter had passed, and he was more conscious than ever of how tired he was, of how his illness had drained him. He smiled placidly but expected the worst.

"How dare you!" she spat, almost stuttering with outrage. Suddenly, she had switched to Neshite. Perhaps it had more satisfying, explosive sounds: slushy sibilants that expressed the viperine hostility he had awakened in her. Perhaps it simply signaled that their history as mother and son was over. "I'm afraid you can't do that. The office of *tawananna* exists independently of the king."

"Ah, but I can," he said, glad he had had the foresight to consult with jurists. "The most recent precedent is my own uncle, who removed his wife from the *tawananna*ship and left the office vacant. There are others."

"Have you gone mad?" Her eyes were goggling with wrath and disbelief. It was she who had the appearance of having gone mad. "What sort of insane enmity have you conceived against your own mother? I've served Hatti Land for forty years. I've given my very best effort to put you on the throne—you can't even imagine all the things I've done to get you there. Dear gods! I nursed you back from the grave for months. I was at your bedside, risking the plague, to help you heal. What lack can you pretend to find in me—you, a green boy? Are you so besotted with your Babylonian that none of my lifetime of service means anything to you any longer?"

Not long ago, she had accused him of being uninterested in women. If the situation had not been so serious, it might have been funny. "You've served well. But at the moment, the best interests of the kingdom demand that you step down. It's the oracle that says so. Since you're so devoted to my interests, no doubt you'll comply without objection."

"So Ellat-gula can become your unchallenged puppet master? I don't think so."

"I, on the other hand, do think so," he said, standing up. She had to back away from the table or let him tower over her. "I believe the word of the gods when they say your enmity for the queen has brought sickness upon the king and the threat of disaster to the kingdom. For the moment, it's just me, but who knows what catastrophe may be next." He lowered his voice and spoke with gentleness. "The decree has been signed. You will vacate your office immediately."

There was a long space of stunned silence, during which Puduhepa stared at him expressionlessly, as if his words were finding it difficult to bore into her ear, as if he was speaking some foreign language that she couldn't understand. At last, comprehension dawned in her eyes. She saw what this sentence would mean: the utter end of her ambitions.

"You ungrateful hound!" she hissed, her words so venomous that Tashmi-sharrumma suspected her spittle would burn his skin. He was glad he had risen and was no longer sitting beneath her, within reach of her fingernails. "You pitiful, besotted, ungrateful... from the moment

you were born, I have schemed and worked and, and...
sweated, and... broken rules. But no, you push me aside for
that Babylonian harlot. Do you think you can even govern
without me? You have no idea how much of the weight of
your government I actually take off your shoulders."

She swallowed the spittle that was all but flying from
her lips. "Do you know how many webs of friendship and
interdependence I've woven with the other great kingdoms,
how many personal relationships I've been building for
thirty years with the Great Kings and their wives? Do you
think that fat Babylonian cunt is going to be able to help
you make diplomacy like I have? She'll drag Hatti into
vassalage to Karduniash; it's the only thing she cares about.
It's the reason she's here. Do you really think she loves you,
Tashmi-sharrumma? Are you so fatuous? Have you ever
looked in a mirror, my son?"

Tashmi-sharrumma thought of himself as a man
uncommonly devoid of self-pity. But then, if he was at
peace with his shortcomings, it was partly thanks to the
unconditional love his mother had shown him throughout
his life. He realized that, in her anger, she had passed
beyond the borders of her own personality. She had become
someone else, some*thing* else: a dragon, an Illuyanka-
serpent, a fire-breathing monster that would incinerate her
own brood rather than accept humiliation. The sorrow that
had nibbled at him already, seeing her on the defensive,
gnawed a painful wound in his soul. This woman had been
a kind of goddess, and not just to him; others, too, had
referred to her as the Goddess Queen. But now he saw her
under a new light. All these years, she had told him, "The
gods have chosen you; it is you they want upon the throne

of Hatti," and he had believed her. Had it only been her personal ambition speaking? And did that mean that in fact he was *not* the man the gods wanted upon the throne—that he was an illegitimate king? Unease rose in his gorge like a wave of nausea. He wanted to be quit of her presence.

Yet he couldn't resist saying—in a level voice but one that carried a warning edge—"I believe there are penalties for insulting the king. You should be more prudent, now that the chancery won't be so eager to curry your favor."

The *tawananna* was ashen with fury. She realized, no doubt, that her advantage had fled with the loss of her control. She struggled to keep her mouth shut until her lips were a trembling line. Finally, she spat, "I am a priestess. I am consecrated to the Lady Shaushga." Her voice was raw, a slithering on gravel.

"No one is taking your personal priesthoods from you, mother, only the ones that are *ex officio*. No more am I taking your income or your property. The decree deals only with your formal political position."

She looked her age all at once, now that she had transformed from a warmly beautiful woman into something reptilian. Those soft cheeks her son had felt pressed against his since his earliest years seem to glitter now with scales. He seated himself and picked up a tablet, as if to read it. The interview was over. "You're dismissed," he added, looking up from under his lids, in case she had not understood.

She bowed with sarcastic formality, her earrings clacking like claws on rock. "I will be at my estate when you decide you want me back. Good luck to you. Good luck to us all. This is an act of stupidity you will live to regret, son."

Against all protocol, she turned her back on the Great King of Hatti Land and strode from the room, slamming the door behind her. A drift of attar of roses trailed after her.

He watched his mother go, sensed the wake of unassuageable anger eddying invisibly behind her, and said goodbye to the security of his childhood. He was Tashmi-sharrumma, Puduhepa's child, no longer. Now he had put on his throne name at last. He was Tudhaliya, the Great King. But there was no joy in the new identity.

He tried not to feel anger, not to feel wounded by his mother's harsh words. He concentrated on pitying her. But he was so weary that he wanted only to lie down and allow sleep to wash all emotion from him altogether. He let loose an enormous, shaky breath, as if he had forgotten to respire during the interview, and laid his forehead on the table. This ordeal was behind him. But he wasn't sure he could ever trust his mother again.

Puduhepa managed to draw herself up and unclench her jaw as she passed through the antechamber. The king's eunuchs bowed, noses to the ground. Had they heard the raised voices or witnessed her shame through the cracks of the door? She sailed past them, down the corridor, across the courtyard that separated the royal apartments from the women's quarters. The cold hit her like an open palm, a slap from the hand of the Storm God that snapped her out of her self-pity. The wind had swept the snow into the corners of the buildings, leaving the paved court scoured down to its wet black stone. She stood for a moment at the door of her apartments, her skirts whipping, letting the icy air lave her and chill the perspiration on her back. She was still poleaxed by the monumental ingratitude of Tashmi-sharrumma. He had always been a serious, docile boy who seemed to understand and appreciate what she had done for him. And affectionate, in his shy way. Respectful. An ideal son. Where had this stupid rebellion come from? Well, from Ellat-gula, of course. But that he should have believed her rather than his own mother...

If he wasn't interested in the Babylonian sexually, what was her hold over him? Yet Puduhepa knew very well that women had other wiles. She knew how uncomfortable Tashmi-sharrumma became around feminine weeping and emotional excess and that he would do almost anything to be relieved of them. He was weak in that way. She had made use of this weakness against him herself.

She ground her teeth against the indignity and pain. There were actually tears in her eyes. She dashed them away with the back of her hand.

You're not the first mother whose heart has been broken by an ungrateful child.

The former *tawananna*—a change in title she contemplated bitterly—eyeballed the guard at her door. He stood to attention in his sheepskin cloak, motionless as if the biting cold were nothing. His nose and cheeks were scarlet, but his back was erect, his gaze was focused on the air above his queen's head. At her unspoken command, he pushed the panel of the door inward for her and bowed as she passed him. This had happened for nearly forty years. She tried to imagine life as a provincial priestess of Shaushga again. Anger flushed through her veins once more, and she wanted to scream at someone, but she realized that it was precisely this loss of self-control that had cost her the battle. She had raised her voice in shrill fury, like the woman in the throes of change of life that she was. Her damned son had had only to stay calm and wait till she made a fool of herself to carry off the prize. She steamed with anger at herself—she had acted like a raw novice. But the provocation had been too much to endure. The shock. She had had no inkling of what had been coming. How was it that none of her supporters had gotten word to her so she could have prepared her defense?

Puduhepa passed by her handmaidens without a word, bristling with recrimination and shattered pride, as brittle and wounding as the sheets of ice that glazed the edges of the palace roof and hung in crystalline swords from the downspouts. She carried the smell of snow with her into the room, which was dark and almost too hot from the braziers that heated the air to a shimmer. The servants surged forward in a wave but dared not approach any closer, sensing her anger.

"Does my lady wish to put on fresh clothes?" one of the slave girls asked in her breathless little voice. A sideways glance revealed the girl's round eyes; she shrank at the expectation of her mistress's temper. And her fear made Puduhepa's wrath flare up again. She saw in her mind the long, calm face of her son, smug in his male superiority. If he had not been behind the table, she might have struck him.

But he had looked terrible, she had to admit with a pang. His eyes had been hollow and bloodshot. She recollected calling him ugly. *Dear gods, why did I do such a thing?* It had been so cruel. And he had almost died only a few weeks ago. *Perhaps the fever has turned his brain, and he isn't responsible for his actions.*

She finally remembered to answer the handmaid. "No. But take my veil and cap." The girl unpinned Puduhepa's headdress and lifted it, veil and all, from her head.

Tashmi-sharrumma—"Tudhaliya" thanks to her, only thanks to her—had crossed some kind of bridge into another country. He was no longer her protégé, perhaps no longer her child. He had aligned himself with her enemies, ripped out her fangs, humiliated her. There would be international repercussions from this decision; he'd find out soon enough. He had no doubt underestimated the power of her contacts here and abroad. Her followers would not accept this quietly.

Then she realized she was thinking of him as an enemy to be outmaneuvered, defeated. *But he's my son, my baby boy,* she reminded herself, momentarily unmanned. She remembered his childish arms around her waist, his little brown head against her bosom, so happy to have her love. Her little prince. *Everything I've fought for was for him.*

Have we come to this? Sweet Lady Hepat, what now?

Yet to submit quietly was not in her. She was the provincial priestess who had conquered the heart of a third royal son and helped him to attain the greatest throne upon the black earth.

She had clenched her hands without even noticing, and now she forcibly relaxed them. Perhaps there was even some law against what her son had done; perhaps the *panku,* the council of the Lords of Hatti, had to pass upon the act. The gods would not accept it lying down. She wondered what Kurunta would think—he had his own history with deposed *tawanannas*, although he didn't know it.

Puduhepa pounded her clenched fists down upon her clothes chest, and the tears jetted from her eyes as if under pressure. She began to howl.

CHAPTER 13

THE COURT WAS CELEBRATING THE birth of their king's fifth first-rank child, a daughter whom he had named Gasshulawiya, after his sister and their grandmother. Puduhepa no longer chose to midwife the royal births. She had retreated to one of her estates and, despite her son's request, claimed that the snow made it impossible to travel to the capital.

Perhaps it's true. Tudhaliya sighed. But it was also clear that his mother no longer cared to cooperate with him on anything in the slightest degree. He would not have chosen to excise her so completely from his life, but it seemed she had to have all his loyalty or none, all his love or none. Part of him felt he was well rid of her, whose affection he now saw as calculating.

But her departure left him friendless, because Ellat-gula had changed with the acquisition of power. *Well, don't we all,* he said to himself, trying to defend his wife. She enjoyed the role of *tawananna*, enjoyed the deference it had earned her in the eyes of the Lords of Hatti. She was very forward with her advice in council, even on matters of which she knew nothing—clever but not wise. And she was no longer quite the restful, affectionate-but-not-too-affectionate partner he had become accustomed to.

He glanced down at her now. She was still in bed after her lying-in, beautiful with her apple cheeks aglow and her glossy blue-black hair artfully visible under her veil. The birthing chamber had become a veritable throne room. She received the wishes and gifts of foreign dignitaries with the gracious languor of a great lady. Her husband, who was in fact the Great King of a mighty empire, stood quietly and uncomfortably in the shadows, his hands clasped behind his back, smiling and nodding at the congratulatory exclamations of his diplomatic corps.

This was the sort of semiceremony he hated. He couldn't make pleasant small talk. He felt isolated and gauche, superfluous among all the women in their bright clothes. Patiya saw him and scurried over, bubbling her praise of the beautiful children Tudhaliya had given her daughter. In fact, they weren't beautiful; they resembled him. The whole gaggle of Babylonians surrounded him, smiling and petting him. Their perfume, mixed with perspiration from the overheated room, rose up to his nose and made him a little nauseated. He still wasn't quite himself.

"You now give oldest little girl to Shagarakti-shuriash, no? Karduniash big friend to Hatti Land. Together we make Asshuriya go 'boom,' eh?" The *tawananna*'s mother laughed hilariously and rocked against him, hanging onto his arm, pressing her palm against his chest in a too-familiar gesture. Tudhaliya grew rigid with discomfort but forced himself not to pull away. He looked into the woman's rouged mouth, which was so wide open he could see down her throat, and

261

thought he might have nightmares about this. For once, he was grateful for being nearsighted.

"Yes, I…" He feared he must get out or risk fainting. "If you'll excuse me, please?"

He wanted to edge out of the room inconspicuously, but everyone fell to their knees and murmured "My Sun" as he sidled past. He felt Ellat-gula's eyes on him; perhaps she wasn't sorry to see him go, as he was far from an ornament at such an occasion.

The door fell shut behind him, and the noise ceased. He tipped back his head and gulped down the cooler air of the vestibule with relief. Pirwannu popped up from wherever he had waited and threw the king's cloak over his shoulders, and Tudhaliya emerged into the snowy courtyard with a profound sigh. The sky was white; more snow was coming. He breathed the clean, frosty air in deep drafts and pulled his furs about him. He longed to go up onto the roof, where he would be alone, but the doctors had told him not to— the wind was too cold. There was nowhere else within the citadel where he was unlikely to encounter others dropping to their knees, kissing his hand, and forcing tablets upon him—business that needed tending to, treaties he had to sign.

He was never alone, and yet he was painfully alone. He had always been a solitary child and man, but never had the weight of solitude hung upon him so crushingly as since his mother had withdrawn from his life. And yet it was not she he longed for…

Kurunta. He had not come to pay his respects on the birth of the king's daughter. But Tarhuntassha was far away, and the capital was almost inaccessible in the snow. Perhaps he would come. Winter had not hit yet with all its rigor, and there might be a thaw. Everyone spoke of Kurunta as if he were neither serious nor intelligent, but in fact, he had depths of feeling, a kind of delicacy of soul. For all his jokes and flamboyance, he was restful. He would have understood the burdens his cousin carried and would have applied just the right mixture of tenderness and humor. *Kurunta's touch would be soothing*, the king thought longingly—not like his crass, overfamiliar Babylonian mother-in-law's, which made his skin crawl. He felt he carried her perfume upon his tunic still, clinging to him like a miasma.

The thought of Kurunta brought almost physical pain. Because, of course, they were no longer even speaking.

Tudhaliya drifted around the courtyard, pretending to look at the sky so he didn't have to see people dropping to their knees as he passed. Eventually, feeling he owed it to the continuing functioning of the palace staff, he made his way back to his chambers and reluctantly went inside, into the stuffy heat. He had a bit of time before the council meeting in the afternoon and the formal reception of credentials of some diplomats.

The king sat dispiritedly upon his lonely bed. He saw his harp in the corner and realized that he had scarcely picked it up since his father had named him coregent six years ago. He leaned over and drew it to himself. Once, he had been an excellent player, really uncommonly good for an amateur. Perhaps if he had not been born a king's son, he would have been a musician. But now his calluses had all gone soft. The instrument was completely out of tune.

Tudhaliya strummed a chord or two, tightening the pegs. It gave him some comfort, but his fingertips were already getting sore. He so rarely had any time for something like this now. And yet, he had to admit, he did have idle moments here and there, especially in the winter, when military campaigns ceased. He could have played again if he had wanted, but something in him rejected the idea. He felt that perhaps it was weak, frivolous, to want distraction. He owed the gods a keener discipline. He stretched out on the bed, and almost before he had time to heave a sigh, he had fallen asleep, the harp at his side.

At the council meeting, Nerikkaili had some bad news. *Is there any other kind,* the king wondered, disheartened.

"Plague has broken out again, My Sun, this time in the Lower Land and also in the East, in Nuhasshe and Ashtata. Ini-tesshub just sent word about the latter."

His words were met with groans.

"Whenever people are pent up in the winter, or in a camp, you can bet on it," someone muttered.

"If we lose too many people in the Lower Land, we won't have enough men to sow or bring in the harvest next year." Huzziya had joined them now. He was only five years younger than Tudhaliya, who had appointed him as chief of the *meshedi* after the exile of Hishni, and it was certainly time the king's brother took his place among the Lords of Hatti Land. He was proving to be an intelligent councilor, although there was always a touch of antagonism in his manner. He was the handsomest of the brothers, resembling their mother with his oval face, dark eyes, and fine, straight nose. The king now perceived how angry all those years of being in the shadow of his elder brother had made him.

And yet Tudhaliya had never wished Huzziya any harm. He had hardly known him at all. He had spent no time with his brothers, because he had always been with Kurunta.

That reminded him that Tarhuntassha was contiguous to the plague-stricken Lower Land—it was, in a way, a part of it. His concerned appreciation of his brother's comments faded to a grim dismay. The conversation had continued without him.

"We hardly have enough men to make an army as it is." Alalimmi sounded gloomy.

"Move some of the deportees from Mira in," said Tattamaru.

"We don't have any yet," the king said. "We've yet to attack the rebel Luwians."

Nerikkaili finished for him. "There won't be any till spring. And no point in putting them in the region before the plague burns out, or we'll lose them, too."

"Has My Sun made a decision about the replacement for Mashturi?" Alalimmi asked.

"Yes. His young kinsman Tarkashnawa. If we take Mira, I think we can combine the two kingdoms and Hallapa and make him a kind of viceroy in the West with a level of power over his neighbors." The king was aware that this new viceroyalty had been his mother's idea.

But Huzziya spoke up sharply, his eyes narrowed in suspicion. "Tarkashnawa? Doesn't Alantalli have a son by that name?"

The king looked at him with his blandest expression. "Yes."

This revelation was greeted with silence. The others exchanged stares ranging from confounded to disbelieving.

Nerikkaili finally put their confusion into words. "And… is this he, My Sun?"

"Yes. He's Mashturi's great-nephew on the maternal side."

Again silence. Alalimmi tried to put the best face on the information. "I take it he doesn't agree with his father, eh?"

"No," said the king, feeling their disapproval chill the air around him. "He can legitimately unite Mira and Sheha River Land."

"Well," Nerikkaili heaved a sigh that indicated he was yielding but not convinced. "It isn't the first time a son has remained loyal despite his father's rebellion. That's how Mashturi himself was put on the throne. Perhaps you can marry this Tarkashnawa off to one of our lower-rank sisters." Then he added, "Oh, speaking of viceroys, the chancery reports a communiqué from our cousin Kurunta stating that Hishni has been seen in the company of Alantalli."

The men all cried out in dismay and disgust.

Why was this sent to the chancery and not to me directly? Kurunta is deliberately snubbing me. The king was not offended but saddened. Kurunta did have a little streak of petty vengefulness. The man was so much more sensitive than people gave him credit for being.

Alalimmi sputtered in his high-pitched voice, "What in the name of all that's holy is he hitching up with that Luwian for? I'm surprised they even talk to a man of Hatti."

"Half Luwian," Nerikkaili reminded him dryly. "I'm half Luwian, too. It's never been a divisive issue before now. Ours is a cosmopolitan kingdom. Our Sun is half Hurrian, after all." He gave the king one of his impenetrable smiles that could have been mocking or not. "But what they want from Hishni, I don't know. Perhaps he's said he'll give the West its independence if they make him king."

Tattamaru protested, "Then what's Urhi-tesshub there for?"

"He's half-Luwian, too, my dear." Nerikkaili grinned.

The men laughed, although it was troubling to think of all those pretenders making common cause, pooling their supporters. Tudhaliya thought again about the fact that Kurunta's father-in-law and brother were chiefs of the rebels. And the king's own brother... Hishni didn't want to be king; he just didn't want Tudhaliya to be. He had seemed to remember the king's relationship with Kurunta from the time of their youth. Perhaps he thought Tudhaliya was morally unworthy of the throne. That idea had Lurma-ziti's dirty fingerprints all over it, and it might actually carry weight with some people who were looking for an excuse to rebel. Those priests, for example, who had already been of families that supported Urhi-tesshub. The king pondered how best to obliterate this messy legacy. He recalled his mother's insinuations about his clemency toward his brother, but he wasn't sure killing Hishni would have solved anything. Exile could be undone; it was true. But the gods surely had to know the dangers of mercy— and yet they still demanded it.

The king realized he had said nothing for a long time. "I suppose the *tawananna* will be back soon."

Alalimmi looked surprised and delighted, then his expression changed to one of disappointment. He had undoubtedly perceived that the king had been referring to Ellat-gula.

Nerikkaili smirked. He turned to the king, his head cocked and an eyebrow raised. "My Sun, will you entrust us with the reason for the former *tawananna's* deposition? It was a rather unusual step, barring real legal cause, as was the case with our uncle's wife. In former times, it would have required a trial before the *panku*."

"An oracle said the reason for my illness was the hard feelings between her and my queen. It was... it was our divine father, whom I consulted, who told me how to deal with it." The king's cheeks were burning like coals. He could have defended himself. *There's precedent. I'm fully within the law. She has undercut my foreign policy.* But what he could never have said aloud was, *She's been trying to make me commit taboo with Kurunta.* So he said nothing further and met his half brother with a calm, chill stare. Behind Nerikkaili, Huzziya's hostile face watched him. Tudhaliya had certainly alienated his younger brothers by deposing Puduhepa.

Before long, he concluded the meeting. As the men dispersed, he heard someone, probably Huzziya, mutter in an undertone, "... trusts no one except his enemies..."

The king thought that he should have explained about Tarkashnawa, how he knew the man would be loyal. He should have enumerated the charges against his mother. But he had missed his chance, failed once more by his lack of eloquence.

After the others had drifted out, Tattamaru approached him. Tudhaliya was braced for some attack from his mother's kinsman, but in fact, the priest told him quietly, "You did right, My Sun. It wasn't good, how she was opposing you behind your back."

"Ah," the king said, surprised.

Tattamaru looked around him as if he feared to be overheard. "I know you think I am your mother's creature, My Sun, but since my wife—your mother's niece—died, I've had time to think about things. A man doesn't want to be ungrateful to someone who has helped him rise, but right is right. What I mean is, I felt obliged to support her, but I didn't always agree with her. I'm freer now. You'll find me to be your man, My Sun. Count on me."

Tattamaru's statement touched the king. He couldn't help but admire anyone who stood up for what was right. This spontaneous expression of loyalty was more valuable than the formal oath everyone swore every year, whether they meant it or not. He only hoped it was real.

"Thank you, Tattamaru. That takes courage. She's not dead, after all." He favored the priest with a wry smile. *So it's so clear that one's loyalty need belong either to the king or to the* tawananna, *is it?*

Tattamaru accompanied the king from the council room, the two of them silent, lost in their own thoughts. Walwa-ziti had abandoned Puduhepa, too, but for less admirable reasons—he would crawl before anyone who was on the ascendant; now he was Ellat-gula's man.

And why not the king's? Was it too much to look to his councilors—his own relatives—for unforced loyalty? He considered the likelihood that there was something in him that did not inspire people's confidence or affection. He hadn't even displayed a very solid military record since he had taken the throne. Or perhaps it was because he had only been king for a year; perhaps such fidelity needed to be built up over time. There was only one man ever who had offered unconditional loyalty, even when Tudhaliya had had no power and had seemed unlikely ever to have it.

The king left Tattamaru at the edge of the public court and made his way through the lion-guarded gate into the residential precinct. People drifted out of the court of women. The *tawananna's* audience had to be ending. There was tubby old Walwa-ziti, with his hair like a snowfall, his rocking gait. He saw the king and hustled in his direction. Tudhaliya ignored him and turned back to the public court. He decided he would go up onto the roof despite the advice of the doctors.

The Lady Puduhepa found herself approaching the royal citadel for the first time since her humiliation. Her son had only banned her from the palace precinct, but she had chosen not even to come so far as the gates of the city. The thought of begging at the door sent her into a cold rage. She had had to cut herself off from her eldest son completely, or her bitterness would have poisoned their relationship forever. As it was, she needed to guard her tongue carefully to avoid displaying the depths of her hurt and anger to her other sons, who had come to see her frequently until the snow had set in. They couldn't understand what had happened. They sided with her.

Only a matter of importance could now bring her back to the king's presence at all. And—she hardly dared admit it to herself—the need to see him in pain, like the pain he had inflicted on her.

Puduhepa emerged from her litter and ordered the bearers to withdraw out of earshot. She sent her secretary

Mahhuzzi into the palace to call her son. Before long, he returned.

"Our Sun is on his way, my lady."

She ordered Mahhuzzi down the causeway far enough not to overhear and waited for her son in the tunnel of the gate, blessing the cold that made it empty of the usual gossip and assignations. She had no desire to be accosted by her former colleagues or servants. The queen saw the silhouette of her son's tall, fur-clad figure enter the gateway from the other side, his hair whipping across his face. He did not see her at all; his head was down, his face preoccupied.

She called out and stepped forward, and he stopped, looking blankly up at her through the dark tunnel. Perhaps he didn't recognize her with the light at her back.

But he said, "My mother," and joined her in the sunlight. His nose was red with cold, his cheeks still gaunt, his lips chapped.

Ask me why I'm here, damn it, she thought. *That would be the normal thing to do.* "My Sun, I have some news for you, and it won't make you happy. I didn't just want to send a messenger."

The king's eyebrows rose in question. She could see he was uneasy, but he wouldn't ask *what.* Perhaps he was still actively angry with her, although she had never known him to hold on to a grudge. It was she who had gnawed on their rupture with bile in her heart. She gave him the news with savage bluntness. "There's plague in Tarhuntassha. Our dear Kurunta has been struck down."

Puduhepa saw a look of pure anguish writhe across her son's face before he controlled it, and despite a moment of satisfaction, her heart was rent for him. Poor boy. She knew he wasn't nearly as unfeeling as he pretended to be—quite the contrary. She took him in her arms, her head only coming up to his chest, and rocked him like a little child. In a moment, his arms encircled her as well. She felt him jerking with suppressed sobs.

After a long, agonizing silence, he said unsteadily, "Is he dead, then?"

"Not when the messenger left Tarhuntassha, son—but gravely ill. His court is decimated. His two sons have succumbed."

"Dear gods."

She hated to say what she felt she must say next. "Perhaps, perhaps... it's for the best if he dies, Tashmi-sharrumma. He seems to have ties with the Luwian rebels."

The king pulled away from her, his storm-gray eyes churning. "How can you say that? That means he deserves to die?"

"No, my son, but... it may save you some real heartache later."

"Let me deal with the present heartache, all right?" He turned away from her so that his hair obscured his face except for the angular line of his cheekbone. The muscles in his jaw were jumping. His teeth were clenched with the effort to control himself. Pity filled her.

"I know it's hard, my dearest. It's like a part of your childhood gone."

She knew because she, too, was sad that his childhood was gone. She was no longer that seventeen-year-old mother who had presented the king with their first boy child. Her son's hair was grayer than hers.

"We'll send the Egyptian doctor," said the king in a choking voice. "He seems to work miracles."

"Of course, my dearest."

"He saved me. He'll save Ulmi."

"Yes, of course." She could no longer add *I'll see to it*. He was on his own. She said instead, "I'll be going now if you don't need me. It's starting to snow again, and I won't be able to get home if it piles up."

But as she turned to depart, he called out after her, "Why did they send the message to you and not me?"

She did not want to say *He isn't speaking to you, remember?* but she said it anyway.

He nodded, his face shuttered, and murmured, "Godspeed, Mother."

She emerged from the shelter of the gateway and felt the snowflakes strike her cheeks. Below, her secretary and the litter bearers looked up and began the ascent to fetch her. She was already wondering who should be the next viceroy of Tarhuntassha.

Nerikkaili was adamant. "No. Flatly no. You survived the plague once. To head right into it again is tempting the Lords of the Underworld, My Sun. You will not have my vote." The other Lords of Hatti were equally opposed to the idea that the king travel to Tarhuntassha. Tudhaliya wasn't sure whether the demotion of the *tawananna* hadn't cost him whatever goodwill his brothers might grudgingly have conceded him before. They spoke to him as if he had lost his mind, as if he were a stupid and willful child.

Ellat-gula berated him shrilly. "My Sun will endanger his *tuhkanti* if he comes back polluted."

The king suspected that since he had been spared once, he was not meant to die of the plague, but he hadn't the will or the eloquence to batter down the arguments of his advisors—especially since the snow had continued to fall, and it was altogether possible that the roads would no longer be passable for a populous caravan such as a royal progress. He had sent a fast messenger with the Egyptian doctor in tow. *If anyone can get through, they will.*

And his queen was no doubt right. He would have been foolish to risk the health of little Arnuwanda, because as yet, he had no other first-rank son. The *king* reluctantly submerged his personal desires beneath the collective wisdom of the Lords of Hatti. He feared in his heart that his love for Kurunta was just another luxury—like the harp—that the shepherd of his people couldn't indulge. His cousin would understand.

CHAPTER 14

THE SUMMER OF THE KING'S fifth regnal year was upon them. Tudhaliya had only just returned from campaigning in the West, and he had paid his *tawananna* a visit. She, too, was preparing for a battle: the birth of her eighth child. The pressure to produce another first-rank son was growing for them both. Little Arnuwanda, who was five, showed signs of having his grandfather's precarious health. The king thought hopelessly that if something should happen to his eldest, one of his second-rank sons would become the *tuhkanti*. Then the lad would be back in the old position of having vassals refuse to accept him. And perhaps one of Tudhaliya's own first-rank brothers—would it be Huzziya or Shanda-kurunta or even Hannutti, who was now seventeen?—would decide to take over... much as their father had done. It never seemed to end.

Tudhaliya was sprawled in a chair in his wife's chamber. This appeared to be the only way he could visit his heir.

Ellat-gula had perfected the art of leverage. "If you want to see him, My Sun, you must come to me. He is only a little boy, and it was you who wanted him to stay by my side." She was a zealous gatekeeper, although he hadn't envisioned her using this protectiveness against him. At the moment, she was very pregnant: a great, round, maternal mountain. He held the cup of beer she had offered him, drinking little, and eventually set it down. He was still dirty, malodorous, and unshaven from the journey back from Puranda, in the West, and his arm was in a sling from an accident with his chariot horses, who had backed into him and pinned him against the wall of the stable.

Arnuwanda was a pale, overweight child with his mother's dark hair and small features. So far, it was hard to tell whether his nose and face would lengthen like those of his father's family. There was something lethargic about him at even the best of times. Tudhaliya watched him sitting against Ellat-gula's knee. The boy's eyes were dull and resigned as she pushed bits of sweetmeat into his mouth, cooing at him as if he were a baby.

"Stop feeding him all the time. You're making him fat," the king protested mildly. He thought the same injunction might apply to her, but he wasn't about to say it.

"You make the children, My Sun, and let me raise them." She dimpled.

The king suspected this was more about entertaining herself than doing right by the child. Sadness for his son melted him—for the prince's lonely, pampered life and for the burdens that lay in store for him… if he lived. Tudhaliya held out his good arm to the boy and smiled encouragement, but the child shrank back and looked up at his mother for support. She addressed him soothingly in Akkadian, the language of Karduniash. Somehow, this chafed the king like a burr in his shoe, although he and his mother had always spoken Hurrian together. Ellat-gula had total control of the child and he, the father, was cut out completely. He couldn't remember whether he had ever been afraid of Hattushili before he had worshiped him.

"Send him over here, my dear. I want him to get to know me," he said.

She chattered at the child in her tongue. Arnuwanda looked dubious, his feathery brows wrinkled with anxiety, but obediently he picked himself up and approached the king's knee. The prince stared timidly at his father's face as he might have at a large, dangerous-looking dog. The king drew his son toward him in an awkward one-armed embrace.

Arnuwanda was a soft little armful, as pudgy as a baby. Tudhaliya felt the boy's wheezing breath in his small chest, and thoughts of gloom overwhelmed the king. Ellat-gula kept giving him daughters.

"Are you happy, my son?" he asked the child, trying to make his expression gentle. The boy looked back at his mother.

"He doesn't speak Neshite," she said.

"What? The languages of this kingdom are Neshite and Luwian. Not Akkadian. You've got to teach him his own subjects' tongues, by all the gods." He had let his irritation show more than he had intended to. In a calmer voice, he added, "He needs to be around the other children so he'll learn."

"You were the one who wanted me to raise him myself, My Sun—"

"No, you were the one. I just went along with you."

Stop arguing. You're not someone who can win a war of words. Exhaustion and hopelessness pressed him down into his chair. His arm throbbed, and it was difficult to guard his tongue.

Perhaps he couldn't win any kind of war. His campaign had gone successfully enough, but the Luwian lands were a hemorrhaging wound. There would never be a clear victory in the West. He and his descendants would do battle there forever. He neither needed nor wanted an argument with his wife.

"Before you get mad at me again, My Sun"—*again?* he thought helplessly—"it will not be long before I give you another child. I have had contractions. I will go to the birthing room very soon. I just wanted to see you when you came home."

"Ah," he responded with less enthusiasm than he would once have felt.

"Yes, and I am sure this one is a boy."

"Are you?" Hope fluttered feebly in his heart. There had been many such announcements and many disappointments. Not that he didn't love his daughters, but he felt more and more desperate for a back-up heir. The omens didn't promise Arnuwanda a long life. "Why, that's wonderful, my dear." He heaved himself from his chair—frightening the child, who craned his head back to watch him rise to his full height—and kissed his wife upon the forehead. "May it be so."

She accepted the kiss as her due but made no move to reciprocate. They were frankly tired of one another. The king was so weary of his duties to the endless wives and concubines that he felt like a barnyard animal. He wanted to flee at the sight of a woman, but he had a horror of being unkind to the poor things. They did their duty uncomplainingly.

Ellat-gula found her satisfaction with the children and the running of her share of the kingdom. She had become a very engaged *tawananna*, lavishing gifts on those who supported her, filling the domestic quarters with Babylonians. He feared she was on her way to becoming more dangerous than his mother.

The Great King stretched his back and headed toward the door, cradling his injured arm. A vague yearning for someone to pet him and feed *him* sweetmeats, for a change, overcame him. He turned at the last minute. "Goodbye, son. How do you say that in Akkadian?"

"*Ina shulmi alik*," Ellat-gula told him. He attempted it, and she and the child had a good laugh at his accent.

Their mockery rankled, more so than the occasion warranted, and he said sourly, "You should be nicer to me. I can break you as easily as I made you." But they both knew it was an empty threat. He would never have dared repeat his extraordinary maneuver; the Lords of Hatti would never have had it. The queen smiled with the smug satisfaction of a cat, and the king headed off to his own chambers, feeling ashamed of himself.

Tudhaliya was in a deep, exhausted sleep when the pressure of someone shaking his shoulder broke into his dreams.

"My Sun! My Sun! Wake up."

He forced his eyes open a crack and saw a blurred white moon that his mind told him was Zuzu's face leaning over him. It had to be the middle of the night, which was short enough at this time of year.

"Hmm?"

The eunuch murmured urgently, "The *tawananna*, My Sun. She's in labor, and it isn't going well. Lady Patiya sent for you to come quickly."

"What do they want me to do? I'm not a midwife," the king said, but he swung his feet to the floor and began to pull on his military boots, which were still lying by the side of the bed.

"I think... I think they don't expect her to live, My Sun."

Tudhaliya's heart sank, leaving a fluttering hollow of foreboding in his chest. "Dear Hutellurra, have mercy," he cried. Still in his linen night tunic, he bolted out the door. In the vestibule, Pirwannu rose from his pallet, gaping with alarm, and rubbed his eyes. The king gestured to him to stay put, and he pushed out into the courtyard. Amatalla awaited him there, her face twisted with fear.

"Come, My Sun. Come quick. Our Ellat-gula in danger." She rushed ahead of him, her plump body jiggling beneath its shift.

It was chilly at night in the mountains, even though it was summer, and the crickets were pulsing. The moon was a vast white smear in the night sky that illumined the courtyard like day. The king loped after his wife's cousin across the silvery pavement, his purple shadow strung out like a flapping scarecrow before him. The gate to the women's court was open, and they dived through. He bumped his injured arm against the doorframe in his haste and smothered a yelp. Inside, they had to push their way through the company of handmaids and priests, who clustered and wept or raised their fists in prayer. The smoke of offerings swirled upward from somewhere, and divinatory rods clinked. The birth stools lay overturned and forgotten.

The king pushed aside a Gula priest in the doorway and forced a path to his wife's bedside. The stench of blood appalled him; surely, there was too much of it. His heart started to pound. Of Ellat-gula, who was surrounded by midwives and doctors, he could see only the legs, but he heard her low, growling moan punctuated by howls of suffering. The hair rose on his neck.

Patiya swayed at Ellat-Gula's feet, her teeth clenched in anguish, her hands raised in prayer, a wail brewing somewhere inside her. A midwife's head appeared between the queen's thighs. Her arm was inserted to the elbow; her face was bloody and sweat drenched. She saw the king and cried, as if to excuse herself, "It's in the breech position."

They all glanced at the king, but no one had time to pay him mind. He forced the expressionless mask onto his face because he was very much afraid, picking up on the fear of the women around him. His wife was tossing, her face gray and wet, her hair in sweaty strings. There was nothing he could do, and his helplessness overwhelmed him. He withdrew to the outside and leaned against the wall, breathing hard. Inside, he heard someone yell, "Save the baby!"

All at once, he remembered that his mother was an experienced midwife who had delivered hundreds of royal children. He turned and jogged out into the outer courtyard, where he nearly collided with Zuzu, who had followed him.

"Get the Lady Puduhepa, quick. She may be able to save the queen." The eunuch took off toward the public areas on his stork legs. The king stood unsteadily and put his good hand over his face. He prayed to the Hutellurra, to Anzili and Zukki, goddesses of childbirth. He prayed to the Great Mother Hannahannah. The screams inside were weakening, and his hair stood on end. He prayed to the Gulshesh, who cut the thread of life. He prayed. He prayed.

He was still praying, his own breath ragged with dread, when Amatalla came to tell him the queen had gone beneath the black earth. He heard Patiya's wail rise within, loud enough to shatter stone. *A mother's grief,* he thought, shuddering. He remembered how Ellat-gula had wailed when their first son had died. He waited for tears to come to his own eyes, but he felt a calmer sorrow. It had been a long time since he had cared about her enough that her loss was one that would move him deeply. As his friend, she had been dead a long time.

He reflected sadly on the mystery of death, which left a young, healthy woman a piece of carrion in a moment. Would she wander the dark halls of the *Tenawa,* the underworld, or rejoice in the flowery meadows of *Liliahni,* where royals were said to take their ease after this life? He wondered if the child had been extracted safely. He wondered how Arnuwanda would manage, poor little lad. He wondered what he should now do with all the Babylonians that had thronged his court in the last few years.

The three Hurrian midwives came bustling out with their Babylonian colleagues in their wake. They were filthy as butchers, exhausted, and terribly afraid that he would punish them. The leader, still in her bloody smock, fell on her knees, grabbing at his legs, and cried, "My Sun, there was nothing we could do. We couldn't get the baby out; he was crosswise in the opening. She just became exhausted; she lost too much blood. We had to cut her open afterward to save the child."

The thought revolted him, but he said dully, "You did what you could." He stared expressionlessly at the pavement, which seemed to swim a little, and after a moment, remembered to detach the woman's fingers from his skirts. "Is... is the child alive?"

"Oh, yes, My Sun." The midwife brightened—here was her pardon. "A fine boy."

Thank you, all you gods of Hatti Land. He breathed in silent relief. Ellat-gula had done her job until the end.

Amatalla emerged tearfully from the doorway. "My Sun," she cried. "You want to say goodbye to her?"

He felt he should, so he reentered the room. It had cleared out to some extent—the midwives and the doctors were gone, at least. They had covered Ellat-gula to the neck, for which he was very grateful. He couldn't imagine what it meant to cut a woman open; he wasn't even sure what women had inside. Did they possess intestines, which he had seen spilling out of men many times on the battlefield? His wife's waxen face was frozen in a look of anguish, and pity clutched at him. He stroked her hair, knowing that he'd polluted himself.

"Goodbye, my dear," he murmured and turned to go, unnerved, but Patiya blocked his way. In her arms was a small bundle, mewling and protesting. She held it out to the king, who took it awkwardly in the crook of his good arm.

"Is little son," she said, her face deformed with weeping.

The king's sorrow, too, began to fog his eyes at last.

The hours passed. The women did what women always did for the dead. Ellat-gula had wanted to be buried, not burned, but that was a choice the *king* couldn't honor. *Tawananna*s had to ascend in smoke, and their bones be laid in the bosom of the rock with all the pomp accorded kings.

The king mounted the ladder to the roof of the palace. It was still night, but far away across the mountains, dawn was gathering. Below in the courtyards, torches and lamps appeared as the palace servants began their work. Tudhaliya stood with his back to the breeze and watched Lord Kashkuh, the moon, set. He wished he himself could go to bed as well, but his day had only begun. Alas, no dreams would come soon to soften the clear edges of loss with their forgiving mist. Tudhaliya tipped his face up and gazed at the milky darkness of the sky, trying to still his breathing. His thoughts were far away, and when he heard a voice behind him, he started.

Puduhepa had received the desperate midnight call to come to the palace and save her daughter-in-law, and—despite her lack of goodwill toward the woman who had supplanted her—for her son's sake, she came. This would be something for which he owed her a favor. But her estates were leagues from the city. By the time the messenger had arrived and she had accompanied him back to the capital, half the night had passed. The *tawananna* was dead.

The ineptitude of the midwives filled the king's mother with disgust and fury. They had clawed and pierced Ellat-gula inside so appallingly in their attempt to get the baby turned that she had bled to death. The palace was filled with incompetents, who surfaced like chaff on water if you so much as cast aside your eyes. The king was not the man to keep track of such things.

She knew where to find her son. He would have crawled away to be by himself, unable to face the suffering of real people. And there he was, in fact—on his favorite desert roof. She saw his tall silhouette against the rising dawn, a little hunched, skirts flapping, one arm pressed to his chest, the other hanging. Simmering with rage, she hitched up her skirts and climbed the shaky ladder.

"Tashmi-sharrumma."

The king turned abruptly. "Who's there?"

"Your mother. Why didn't you call me sooner? I could have saved her." She emerged from the trap, and her son took her arm and helped her to her feet.

"I didn't know what was happening until they told me she was in trouble." His eyes were red but dry, and his face looked long and drawn—an expression she had seen often on him as a child; he knew he had disappointed her. There was blood on his lip where he had to have bitten it. Her heart thawed, and she put her arms around him. He winced in pain.

"What is it? Are you hurt?" she asked, drawing back.

"My arm. I don't think it's broken, though."

She stroked his cheek and said gently, "I'm sorry for your loss, my dear. But it was so unnecessary."

He nodded, lowering his head. After a moment, he said, "Good to see you again."

She declined to answer right away, allowing his guilt to soften him up. "It's been a while, yes, my dear. But it was always in your power to reverse my banishment, you know."

"The last time I saw you was when Kurunta was sick."

"Yes. You'll start to associate my presence with tragedies, won't you?" She spoke in Hurrian and smiled at him—a warm, all-healing smile, intimate, meant to remind him of all the smiles they had exchanged in his childhood.

"But he's all right after all. It wasn't a tragedy."

Puduhepa had corresponded with Kurunta in the intervening years, and she knew that in fact, it *was* something of a tragedy. But her fatuous son continued to deceive himself.

The sun was warming the plain below them now, although the palace courtyards were still in their own shadow. She saw that the king's hair had gone as gray as a goose; he looked every moment of his forty years. With the ruddy tan of the fair skinned growing lined and weather-beaten, the likeness to his father's face was more striking than ever. Although, in fact, they were nothing alike inside. Tashmi-sharrumma was not a fearless man of action like Hattushili. He thought too much, and it confused him sometimes. Yet because he was stubborn, he plunged on, even without knowing where he was going. This was her diagnosis of her own deposition. He had to have regretted it many times, she thought with some satisfaction. He was certainly regretting it now.

The king stood there, gazing out at the plains, as the shadows shrank away before the rays of Arinniti. He looked surprisingly calm despite his grief—less lost than she remembered him. He seemed to be acclimating to the embrace of Halmashuit. With some help, he could become a great ruler.

"I suppose your next wife will be the new *tawananna*…" she said to bait him.

His eyes widened, and he licked his lips uncomfortably. "My next wife? I have eight first-rank children already. A second son, just this night."

"Congratulations, my love. That must sweeten the loss. What will you name him?"

"I thought Shuppiluliuma, after my great-grandfather."

She made no effort to conceal her disappointment. "Not Hattushili?"

"It's still a bad name to some people. We have to end these civil wars."

She drew her heavy, pleated skirts up and took a seat on the roof. The king lowered himself, awkward with one arm, to her side. She saw, to her amusement, that he was clad in a nightgown with bloody handprints on the skirts, and low military boots with curly toes.

"Sleeping in your armor these days?" She grinned at him.

"We just got back from Puranda yesterday evening. Then no sooner had we entered than I hurt my arm. I'm still polluted from battle."

"And I'll bet you touched a corpse, too," said his mother

dryly. She paused, and her voice became grave. "You need to be very careful in the West, son. They're serious about pulling loose from our claws." The symbol of their empire inserted itself into her mind—the two-headed eagle clutching a pair of rabbits in its talons, its eyes ever looking in all directions, fighting to keep the vassals subdued as it soared over the mountains.

Her son nodded. After a moment, he said, "Will you be the *tawananna* again if I apologize humbly?"

She smiled into her lap—a satisfied smile but gracious in victory. "I will, My Sun. And you don't even have to apologize." She looked up at him from the corner of her eye with that intelligent coquetry that had made her such a formidable diplomat. "Everyone knows you behaved stupidly."

They both laughed, and she gave his booted ankle an affectionate shake. But her merriment faded as she added, "And one of the first pieces of advice I want to give you is this, Tashmi-sharrumma. Pay some attention to Kurunta. I mean it."

"What kind of attention?" he asked uneasily.

"He thinks you have abandoned him. Just like his own parents. He may or may not remain faithful."

"Abandoned him?" There he was, acting half-witted again.

"He waited and waited for you to come to him when he was in danger of death—"

"My advisors wouldn't let me come," her son reminded her.

"That's not what he thinks. He's shown up at the capital

for every festival, every royal birthday, every oath-swearing ceremony, and he says you've avoided him."

"*Me*, avoided *him*? I'm the king; I can't just chase after people. If he wants to talk to me, he should find me out. The gods know how I've longed for it."

Puduhepa sighed. "You aren't very good at reading him, Tashmi-sharrumma, after all these years."

The king fell silent, his jaw twisted. He was clenching his teeth. After a moment he said, "How do you know what he's thinking?"

"I've talked to him. That, my son, is how you know what people are thinking. You should try it."

He looked up at her with his blank gray gaze, and she realized she might have gotten through to him.

CHAPTER 15

SUMMER WAS ENDING. NOT A drop of water had fallen for three months. The wheat crop was blighted. The fruit trees were barren, dying in their orchards. Prayers went up day and night to the Storm God of Nerik, the Storm God of Hatti, the Storm God of Lightning, and to all the thousand gods of Hatti in the hope that whoever had been missed and was angry would relent. There had been five straight years of drought, and the granaries were emptied out. Famine was here.

In desperation, the king bought ship after ship of wheat from Mizri, all the while dreading an attack on the sea. And now he feared more than anything that Kurunta would close the port of Ura. Hatti was a landlocked country; it depended upon its vassals for harbors, as for so many things.

Famine was the main topic of discussion at every council meeting, but it was one of those problems that no amount of talk could solve.

"How long can we keep feeding the entire population on Egyptian grain?" grumbled Nerikkaili. "How are we going to keep paying for it? And the Ugarites don't ship for free either, for all they are our vassals."

"Copper, silver, and gold is how we pay," said Tattamaru. "At least as long as Assyria keeps its paws off our mines."

The *tawananna* added darkly, "Not to be alarmist, but they're stirring around in Shubari again. Apparently, some of the tribes there have rebelled, and that's given Tukulti-ninurta the excuse he needs to invade. The next move could well be into Nairi Land."

"And then Ishuwa, and our mines. Gods protect us." Alalimmi sighed. "The fall of our buffer, Hanigalbat, was the biggest disaster of the generation… begging your pardon, My Sun."

Tudhaliya nodded his pardon but said nothing. What could be a response appropriate to the magnitude of this dreadful situation? Dispirited, he continued to lean his cheek on his hand and listen to his advisors. Perhaps they would eventually think of some ideas, and then it would be his responsibility to choose one and put it into effect.

Puduhepa looked around at the Lords of Hatti. "We've said this before, but it's truer than ever now—Ehli-sharrumma is wavering. He says if we don't intervene before Assyria reaches Nairi Land, he may defect in the hopes of saving Ishuwa intact. You know how those beasts come down on anyone who resists."

"His attitude is understandable," said Nerikkaili, pursing his lips.

The king finally spoke. "Send Tukulti-ninurta a letter." He sat up and gestured to his secretary. "Tell him that if he goes any farther than Shubari, he deals with us."

"Well done, My Sun." The *tawananna* smiled. "A show of strength is all they understand."

"But then let's be ready if they call our bluff," Huzziya said with a flush of ferocity. He had already become the voice of belligerence. He was thirty-five but still seemed much more of a youth. Even as a child, he was always trying to provoke his older brother, who fortunately had been almost impossible to arouse. Huzziya wanted to distinguish himself in some way, to attract someone's attention. "You should call up our vassal levies, my brother. Let Ini-tesshub start right now. If the Assyrians see us massing, they'll know we mean business."

The older men smiled indulgently at the hot-blooded prince, but in fact, the king was relieved his brother was still willing to participate in the discussion. Huzziya was hostile to him—even after their mother's reinstatement—but at least he wasn't drawing away.

"Write the viceroy," the king told Tarhun-miya. "Have Ini-tesshub take a count of the troops from the East we can rely on. But don't bring them together yet. It might become an excuse to move on us."

"Speaking of the East, My Sun," said his mother grimly, "we've received word that Benteshina of Amurru has just died."

There were murmurs of sorrow from the brothers and cousins. This relic had been Gasshulawiya's husband.

"He must have been nearly as old as our father," said Nerikkaili with his habitual smirk. "He was in trouble when Uncle Muwatalli was still on the throne. But he came around with age... and our sister's good influence."

The *tawananna* continued as if she had not been

interrupted. "You should make clear to his successor the situation with Assyria, my son, and be sure he understands just how important his cooperation is. Make him swear his fealty immediately, before they get to him. This is my grandson, Shaushga-muwa, you know—your nephew."

"Benteshina had no children by his first wife, my lady?" Walwa-ziti spoke with hands clasped and snowy head tilted in rapt attention. He was avidly currying the *tawananna*'s favor now that Puduhepa was back in power.

"None living," she replied coldly, avoiding the chief scribe's eyes, "except for Nerikkaili's wife. Only Gasshulawiya's. That's good for our cause."

"Perhaps I'll betroth Ehli-nikkal to him," the king said. "She's eighteen; I've been waiting for some special need."

"Excellent, my brother," said Nerikkaili. "A Great Lady is a rare catch for a vassal. He should be impressed with your generosity."

And maybe disappointed with the modest beauty of the girl, her father thought, calling to mind the tall, flat-chested young woman with his own equine face. *But she's smart and gentle. She'll be a good helpmeet. I hope he'll be kind to her.*

After the meeting, he dictated to Tarhun-miya the various letters that needed to go out. He was just rising to leave the emptied council room when his mother came stalking back in a flurry of skirts.

"Well, troubles never come singly," she began without preamble. She shook a tablet at him. "Here is a message from Ini-tesshub that just arrived, saying that the king of Ugarit is divorcing his Amurrite bride."

What else is missing, thought the king, heaving a sigh. His coastal vassals, on whom he was so pitifully dependent to keep his Egyptian grain coming, were going to blow up in his face over a woman. "Shaushga-muwa's sister? Sad welcome to the throne for the lad."

"Yes, well, his sorrows are the least of it. Apparently she not only adultered on the king of Ugarit, but she joined his brothers' conspiracy to overthrow him."

"I thought that was years ago."

"They did try it years ago, and Ini-tesshub exiled them, under your instructions. Now they're back—as exiles so often are."

He was mindful of her jab but said nothing, only pursed his lips into a crooked, pensive twist.

Puduhepa forged on. "According to Ini-tesshub, they first sent her home to Amurru. But now Ammishtamru wants to execute the girl, and her brother refuses to give her up."

"War, then." The king expelled a heavy breath through his nose.

"That's what he says. He's trying to get the Ugarites to relent, because, well… you know what will happen if the two of them come to blows. They'll be using the ships we need for our grain convoys."

"So," said the king, scrubbing his face wearily with a hand, "I need to adjudicate between them."

"Not unless they approach you directly, My Sun. Let Ini-tesshub sort it out otherwise. He's their immediate superior."

"And if we levy troops against Assyria, will either of them come?"

She raised her eyebrows in an eloquent gesture of ignorance.

"We can't let them fight," he murmured, mostly to himself. But even if he gave them an order, they might or might not obey. It had come to that in his empire. Perhaps that was why his mother seemed to want him to stay out of it—with all the issues confronting Hatti Land, a loss of face would be catastrophic.

"Well, I thought you should know immediately. Oh, and I recommend replacing Walwa-ziti as chief scribe. He's getting too old to be effective."

He voted to put you out of office and defected from your camp when you were in eclipse, didn't he, Mother? You want to punish him, he thought acerbically, but aloud he said only, "Replace with whom?"

"Mahhuzzi. He's been faithful for years."

The little weasel was to have his reward, then. Tudhaliya sighed. "So be it."

Only a few weeks later, as soon as the king returned from celebrating the fall equinox at his father's Stone House, another letter arrived from Ugarit. It was a direct request from King Ammishtamru that he be allowed to seize and execute his unfaithful, conniving wife.

"This goes against my better judgment." The king set down the tablet.

"But you have to do it, My Sun. He has gone over the viceroy's head and appealed directly to you. And he has every right to put to death an adulterous wife, quite apart from her sedition. The brother they caught has already been beheaded." His mother and his new vizier, Mahhuzzi, were huddled around him, hanging over him as he sat. He found such proximity unpleasant. They were pushing, even physically, the choice he had to make.

"It'll alienate Amurru. And it'll undercut Ini-tesshub."

"But My Sun, it's perfectly legal. A show of force is what these vassals need." Mahhuzzi had been well coached. The man's close-set eyes sparkled with the enjoyment of his new prestige. He was the only man on the council who wasn't a member of the royal family.

"Hmm," the king grunted. He skewed his jaw skeptically.

"Come on, my dear. Don't be so idealistic. The lowliest man in the kingdom can have his wife executed if she betrays him," said his mother.

The betrayal of wives. Not for the first time, it crossed the king's mind to wonder what the nature of the relationship between his mother and Nerikkaili was. They were of an age, and Hattushili, her much-older husband, had been bedridden for four years before his death. The thought disgusted him profoundly, and he pushed it from his mind.

"Very well. Tell Ammishtamru yes." *And the matter of Ugarit is ended, I hope.*

But not so. Less than a week later, Ini-tesshub sent a messenger to report that King Ammishtamru had been assassinated. He wasn't much older than Tudhaliya himself.

The Lords of Hatti received the message with dropped jaws.

"I can't believe it," cried Alalimmi, his voice rising to a squeal. "I thought the viceroy nipped the coup in the bud."

"It had nothing to do with that, my lord," the messenger said, panting. "Some disgruntled palace functionary—"

"Who may have changed the course of the world," growled Nerikkaili bitterly. "Will they send soldiers to the levy now, or are they having to put down some insurrection at home?"

The king ran a hand over his face as if to brush away cobwebs. He felt trammeled, trapped, tripped up by the thread of the Gulshesh, who were spinning out the fate of his kingdom. Did the gods expect him to control things like disgruntled servants in Ugarit? Was he a bad king if such things befall his people? He refrained from letting out a deep, discouraged sigh. "Who succeeds him?"

"His firstborn, My Sun. A prince named Ibi-ranu."

"Better have him swear the oath, eh?" the king said, looking at his mother under his lids.

"Indeed, My Sun." She was playing the modest servant of the ruler. "Rumor has it that he inclines toward an alliance with Assyria. Perhaps you should give *him* Ehli-nikkal—or give her to his son, since Ibi-ranu is already married."

And it was true, Tudhaliya thought to himself a day later—the Eastern vassals needed to swear their oaths and mean it. Assyria had started to move. The temptation to push into Nairi Land—where forty independent kinglets who couldn't stay allied for half a morning held tenuously onto their scattered tribal population—was too powerful. Because beyond the marches of Nairi Land lay Ishuwa with its copper mines—the raw material of armies. Ishuwa was, as it happened, a vassal of Hatti Land, its king a nephew of the Great King. And that vassal king was prepared to break away to save his own skin.

"You threatened Tukulti-ninurta, My Sun. Now you have to put some muscle behind your words," growled Nerikkaili.

"Teeth, as it were," said the king, not too proud to make fun of himself. He hoped his wry grin made it clear that this was meant as humor. They were all so convinced that he was slow that he wondered if it would penetrate. He had reached the point where hopelessness had turned to giddiness. Once, he and Kurunta would have laughed until they cried over a remark like that.

Nerikkaili did smile, but the *tawananna* snapped, "Can you please be serious, son? This is very, very grave business. It means war with Assyria. They're clearly spoiling for a fight."

"They'll have one," he said. "But first, extend the usual offers of amnesty if they'll agree to negotiate."

"With all respect, My Sun, the chances of them negotiating when they hold the upper hand is remote," Tattamaru said.

"The choice is theirs." The king shrugged. "We prepare for the other possibility."

"Very well, My Sun. The viceroys will be notified to mass their troops," said the eager new vizier. And the Lords of Hatti dispersed to round up their own men for war.

Fall had set in, and in the mountains of the East, it was already growing cold. The nights were downright frigid, and there was ice on the horses' water buckets in the morning. The king hoped that the cold would control dysentery and plague because it was a great army he had gathered, huddled into a space small for so many men and horses and asses and oxen. The terrain didn't permit of a more relaxed arrangement.

He loved the sound of an encampment—even the smell of it, rank as it was—and the purposeful busyness of it, the sense of waiting. He loved the rising tension that clutched a man's heart and stopped his breath and only released in the thick of battle in a kind of ecstasy of relief.

And yet a weight of dread sat upon his chest these days. If there was a war, the consequences might be graver than those of Uncle Muwatalli's famous confrontation with Mizri. At Taite, they had attempted to draw a line against the Assyrians with Hanigalbat as the stakes. Now, if they failed to hold back the men of Asshur, the survival of their very homeland might be at issue. Anyone invading from the east had a direct line of march across the Red Mountains, through Shubari, Nairi Land, Ishuwa... into the Upper Land of Hatti itself.

But war there would certainly be. The men of Hatti had sat in Nairi Land for a week, shoring up their allies against the threat of the Assyrians in Shubari. And now Assyria had warned them that it was going to invade Nairi. Tukulti-ninurta said, *Get your troops out, or get drawn into our wrath.* The Great King could hardly step back under such a provocation. So there he was.

The wind was parched and chill, and it breathed a scent of dust and dried herbs. Tudhaliya squinted against the sun, with a hand shading his eyes, and gazed around him at the generalities of the topography. They were encamped on a high, uneven plateau in the foothills of the mountains, which rose in arid ochre tiers behind them. Before, maquis-covered high plains undulated steeply. Hills guarded them on all sides but also blocked their direct vision of the distance. It would be impossible to use a chariot charge

299

here, he saw. He would have to send in foot soldiers, then, and even their progress would be laborious—up and down, over rocks and brush and shallow dry runnels. Many of his men were civilian levies with little experience. He had beefed up his standing troops with some mercenaries, but most of all, he counted upon his vassals.

The king heard footsteps crunching and turned around. Ini-tesshub and Nerikkaili were trudging toward him, their cloaks wrapped around themselves.

"So here we are," announced the king's brother in his booming voice. At nearly sixty, he was portly and losing his hair in front, which gave him something of the air of a charioteer with a shaven forehead. But he was still a fine, impressive figure of a man in armor, with his martial jaw and thick arms. Ini-tesshub looked unchanged—dry and lugubrious.

"I've brought troops from as many vassals as would answer the call, My Sun," the latter said with reluctance, "and that means no one from Ugarit. They're having their own troubles. No great loss; they wouldn't have brought many anyway. They're chiefly a maritime power." Ini-tesshub shrugged fatalistically. "But the lands I control directly are here. Karkemish, of course, Nuhasshe, Mukesh, and the rest. Our cousin Halpa-ziti in Halep has brought his contingent."

"I see the men from Tarhuntassha are here," murmured the king, and his generals exchanged a glance. "How many?"

"Only five thousand, My Sun," Nerikkaili said, watching Tudhaliya's face with trepidation. "Kurunta says he can't release his farmers, who are desperately trying to tend their crops."

"Why, that's good news, then, if they have crops to tend." The king couldn't prevent a note of sarcasm from creeping into his voice. Anyway, his cousin was technically exempt from the levy. What really drove a dagger into his heart was the fact that Kurunta had made no effort to speak to him, even though his tent was pitched only *iku*s away. The viceroy had spoken to his fellow generals but not to the man who loved him more than anything in the world.

Ini-tesshub looked down, as if embarrassed, then continued. "As for Ishuwa…"

"They didn't come. I know." Tudhaliya forced down a sigh.

Nerikkaili cursed. Ishuwa was a big contingent. But no one was surprised. Ehli-sharrumma didn't want to be found on the wrong side, no matter who won.

From afar, Alalimmi and Tattamaru waved and trotted toward the gathering of their king and his generals, away from the rows of tents and picket lines.

Tattamaru hailed them. "My Sun, my lords." The two men saluted their sovereign and clapped their confreres on the back. "Taruisha didn't come," the priest said grimly. "The king has been deposed, and the usurper is friendly to Alantalli. Young Tarkashnawa has just arrived from Sheha River Land. He doesn't have as many men as we had hoped, though. He says he's still having to fight the pretender to his throne and feared to leave the city unguarded."

Is that what I have done? wondered the king uneasily. Somewhere out there, Urhi-tesshub and Alantalli were stirring behind his back. He had to trust his mother to keep the capital safe, but he had not left her enough troops. "So where do we stand, with all counted?"

Alalimmi tallied briefly on his fingers with an expression of concentration upon his face. At last he looked up. "Maybe twenty thousand, My Sun."

The king nodded silently, but his heart clenched. *That's not enough to give us a clear victory. It will be touch and go. Runda, the god of luck, must run before us into battle, or all may be lost.* If only Ishuwa had come. Even little Ugarit. If only Kurunta had brought more men, and Sheha River Land. If only Mira had not been in rebellion.

"We'll have to fight like sons of Wurukatte," he said, realizing it was usually Kurunta who said things like that.

"We've sent scouts out, My Sun," said Tattamaru. "The Assyrians are moving slowly up from the south. I don't know whether they've seen us yet or not."

Nerikkaili laughed darkly. "I think we can be sure they have."

"How many are they?" asked the king.

Tattamaru looked grim. "Lots. Not many chariots—"

"Which will be of no use anyway." Nerikkaili snorted.

"—But a lot of infantry. Maybe thirty thousand, maybe more."

"They're much closer to their supply lines than we are," grumbled Alalimmi. "There's no water around here, and wagons can hardly get over the Red Mountains."

The king was eager to end the pessimistic talk. "Get some rest, my brothers. We'll meet in council in the morning."

Tudhaliya himself found rest eluded him. A sense of doom sat like a rock in his stomach. Without a full levy, he didn't have enough troops to overpower the Assyrians, who were notoriously fierce and well-trained fighters. He found himself praying as often as debating tactics with himself. After some hours, he slid from his camp bed to his knees and began to pray systematically to every god he knew of, his fists upraised. The next morning, when Tiwatipara came to rouse him, the king awakened to find himself curled up under his cloak on the carpet-strewn ground.

He crawled to his feet, stiff and cold, rubbing sleep from his eyes. Today was the day his army would meet the Assyrians. His undermanned army. He or any one of his brothers or cousins or nephews might be dead by nightfall. He wanted his conscience clean before he went beneath the black earth, and there was a task he had to carry out before that could happen.

He had to talk to Kurunta.

Who knew? Perhaps this excruciating exchange would be the sacrifice that won the favor of the gods.

If the king dreaded the interview ahead, he knew it was only his cowardice that had made him postpone it all these years. He couldn't indulge himself any longer, even if it meant the permanent end of their friendship—or the ineluctable knowledge that their friendship had ended long ago.

The guard on duty at the flap of the viceroy's tent recognized the king in his golden armor and plumed helmet. He stepped aside. Within, Kurunta stood, his back to the entrance. His valet had buckled silver bracelets around his wrists and was setting his helmet upon his head when the servant raised his eyes and realized the Great King was standing before him. Tudhaliya gestured to him to leave, and the man rushed away, bobbing an apologetic bow. Kurunta turned around and froze. In the helmet, he

303

seemed to have gained a cubit in height. He was Wurukatte in the flesh, and his hard, bitter face was what a war god's face had to resemble. Even the nearsighted king saw the deepening grooves in his cousin's cheeks that pulled the corners of his mouth down like carven rock, sooty with poorly shaved stubble.

"My dearest cousin," the king murmured, overcome with longing to the point that he could no longer remember what he wanted to say.

But Kurunta eyed him with something colder than snow in his eyes. "Oh, you're still alive," he replied sarcastically. "I thought I must have missed the death notice."

Tudhaliya dropped his eyes, ashamed of his cowardice. "It's been too long, I know. I... I'm sorry."

"I was sick there a few years ago. I thought you might have come to see me, but no."

"I couldn't. They wouldn't let me." The king writhed inside with helplessness. He feared he was trying to excuse himself, but he longed desperately for Kurunta not to be angry with him.

"They wouldn't let me," the viceroy mimicked with a sneer. "How hard did you try?"

"I sent a doctor," Tudhaliya stammered.

"Oh, did you? Ah. Then I suppose I should fall on my knees with gratitude. Let me point out, however, that when *you* were sick, I got to your side—through five *wakshur* of snow, burning out two teams of horses. But I got there. That's the difference between caring and not caring."

"I did care, Ulmi; I do care. I thought..." The words choked in his throat. His cousin was angered, and Tudhaliya didn't know how to make him relent. *Don't be angry at me.*

Kurunta snorted in disbelief and advanced on his cousin. They stood face-to-face like two street dogs contending for supremacy.

Look at us: armed and armored, thought the king miserably, *ready for battle. And yet this man is dearer to me than my own soul.* The sense of impotence was eating him alive. He didn't know how to make everything all right. He wanted to fall to the ground and sob. But he wasn't a man who could do that.

"I don't believe it for a minute," growled Kurunta. "And yet here I still am. Because I, unlike some people, do believe in fidelity, in standing by the ones I love. Faithfully."

"Ever faithful," agreed the king, lowering his eyes.

"Or maybe not for*ever* faithful. After all, even the court jester has some pride. I can't predict how long I'll be content to stand at your heel without so much as a pat on the head." Kurunta's face had grown hard and sharp as granite. He was simmering with something deeper than fury.

"But I've given you every reward I could think of…"

"What a poor imagination you have, Tash. But it's always been true, and I should have remembered that. Don't dare to cite me the cities and the fucking salt rights, all right? Why am I always begging for your crumbs? I'm a first-rank son of a Great King, too." His voice was rising. "Oh, they wouldn't let you come to me, would they? You're the fucking *king*, Tash. You can do anything you want."

"I can do *nothing* I want." The king was growing numb with pain; he couldn't endure the anger another minute.

"And what exactly do you want to do? Flagellate yourself with thorns? Stick your hand in the fire? Something sweet and beautiful like friendship doesn't even figure in your poor, warped dreams, does it? You dried-up stick! You piece of fucking stone!"

Kurunta was yelling now, spittle flying. Tudhaliya could almost feel the waves of his voice striking him in the face, blowing back his hair. He suspected the entire camp could hear the viceroy of Tarhuntassha hurling insults at the king.

"I thought you didn't want to talk to me." The king's voice was barely audible, but he tried to keep it neutral.

"Maybe I was just tired of throwing myself at you and hitting a damned stone wall. Maybe I thought, 'Well, he's the Great King of Hatti Land now; I guess he doesn't have time for his childhood friend anymore—who's just a shitty vassal anyway. I guess he never really loved me as well as I loved him.'"

Kurunta's nostrils were pinched and white. His voice, which was rising higher and louder with every word, was starting to crack. "You know what? Without intimacy, there's no friendship, Tash. Just waving at ceremonies doesn't count. But even as a child, it was agony for you to talk to anyone for fear they'd actually see you. I guess now that we're older and you have so many more sources of guilt, you just can't make it over that wall, can you? Fucking *coward*!" Kurunta shouted. The viceroy's face was crimson, the veins of his neck distended.

"Ulmi, we…" The king felt he must try to explain, but he wasn't sure he understood his own reasoning. He spread his hands helplessly. "We can't be like we were. It's an abomination. It's—

Kurunta's eyes bugged with rage. "Are you calling our love for each other an abomination, Tash? Is that what being a fucking priest has done to you?" He thrust his face up in Tudhaliya's. "We're kings, man. Who's going to call us to court? We make our purification, and that's it—no different than sex with our wives. This is just another of your excuses. If one doesn't work, you pull out another one. *Abomination* indeed. Your fucking hypocrisy is the only abomination. Just be man enough to say you don't want me anymore."

The king bore his cousin's tirade in abject silence, almost unable to breathe. He wanted to say, *There used to be a death penalty,* but that just proved the charge of cowardice. He wanted to say, *The king has to judge cases of taboo. How could I do that, knowing I, too, was an offender?* But this whole argument was nothing but an excuse, and Kurunta had seen through him. Inside, the king was a crumpled heap of shame. His mother had said repeatedly that he loved neither men nor women, and that was true. There was only one man he loved: this idol of fury incarnate who stood before him now, almost nose to nose.

He realized for the first time what a burden of pain his cousin was carrying—and how truly guilty he himself was. He, in his weakness, had hurt this being he so valued and driven him away forever. Tudhaliya's worst apprehensions were more than fulfilled. He could make himself do things he didn't want to, but he couldn't change his fundamental nature any more than Kurunta could. Tudhaliya longed to take his cousin in his arms, to succumb to the vulnerability of love, taboo be damned. But he wasn't fundamentally a man who could risk that.

And having been abandoned in childhood, Kurunta felt he had again been abandoned.

The king faced his viceroy with a stone-blank expression,

too lacerated by this terrible vision of himself to dredge up words. His chest was heaving under its golden scales.

"So, My Sun." Kurunta was calmer now, deathly calm, almost lighthearted. He strolled away a few paces, pushed up his sleeves a little, put his hands on his hips. "You've lost a friend and gained another self-serving vassal. That's the way you've always treated me; perhaps you can't imagine any other relationship. So I'll play your game. It's all over between us as men—it could have been sweet, Tash; don't you remember, or have you just put it all out of your mind?—and I'll learn to be content with trade concessions. And you'll have to make do with my army showing up when the levy is raised, *for now*—I may or may not be with them, but you won't miss me."

The king was suffocating. He couldn't trust himself to speak. After a moment he stammered, "Is that a threat? You mean you might not respond to the levy?"

"I'm not an oracle, My Sun. I can't foretell the future. Now, if you'll pardon me, I have troops to lead. Enjoy your safe little chariot up on the hill."

Kurunta turned away and feigned busyness. The king lingered for a moment, enthralled by the waves of long black hair falling down his cousin's back. He reached out as if to touch it, but his hand dropped, and he let himself out through the tent flap, drained and empty. He passed officers and servants on all sides, and they sank to their knees, murmuring "Hail, My Sun." He wondered numbly how much of that scene they'd heard.

He did his best to walk erect and not like a man who had been flayed, crushed, stabbed through the heart. No wonder the gods had punished Hatti Land. Its king was neither just nor merciful.

He had said nothing of what he had intended to say; words, as usual, had betrayed him. *Did Kurunta say he was a first-rank son? What's that about?* Tudhaliya hadn't even had the presence of mind to ask. He felt nothing but revulsion for himself, got up in his golden armor.

CHAPTER 16

B Y NOW IT WAS MIDMORNING. The camp had
emptied out, and the troops were gathering by unit
on the deeply sloping terrain near the village of
Alatarma. They were prepared to march south to meet the
Assyrians, who approached unseen behind the surrounding
hills. All the king's brothers and cousins and nephews had
dispersed among their men. Hannutti was serving as the
king's aide de camp and eyes. He was a tall, slim, athletic
stripling, plain of face but somehow attractive just by
virtue of his youth, full of bright-eyed eagerness for all the
trappings of war.

Dressed in purple and red and gold, Tudhaliya felt
keenly his solitude here on the hillside above his army. How
gladly he would have traded places with the meanest foot
soldier with no greater responsibility than his own survival.
How gladly...

The white-clad host seemed to undulate over the broken
terrain. *There appear to be too few of them*, he thought,
vaguely alarmed.

"Is that all the units?" he murmured almost without realizing he spoke aloud.

Hannutti craned his neck to see then turned abruptly to his brother, his eyes wide with horror. "Tarhuntassha isn't there, My Sun!"

Dread uncoiled like a dragon in the pit of the king's stomach. His worst suspicion had come to life. He had meant to appease Kurunta, to win him back by talking to him at last... but it had been too late. It had been too little. He hadn't been an eloquent enough defender of his good intentions; he had been insufficiently able to charm his mercurial cousin—and he had only made things worse. Feeling himself abandoned, Kurunta had abandoned him.

Words failed the king. He forced a painful swallow down his throat, clutched the chariot rail as if he could wring the desperation out of his life.

"The double-dyed bastard! He's run away!" Hannutti's young voice broke with tears of rage. "Should we go after him, my brother?"

Tudhaliya shook his head slowly. Fight his own men? To what end? The Gulshesh, with their spindle, were spinning out the fate of kings: for some, they would apportion victory; for others, defeat. Perhaps he was the one who was destined for defeat. He offered himself up to the will of the gods. *Sharrumma, punish me if you must. Just don't let my people be wiped out.*

"Do you think the sheep fucker has gone over to Assyria, brother?" asked Hannutti, his face deformed with fury.

"No." It was enough that he would not fight with his king; Kurunta had cost them the battle, Tudhaliya feared. He knew he needed to comfort his brother, whose sense of gallantry had just been shattered, but he had no words. He laid a hand upon the shoulder of the youth who stood beside him in the chariot, but the king said nothing, his heart dead. The viceroy had to have marched his men out as the pipers summoned the units to mass and simply kept going into the hills. Had no one seen them? Were there other traitors among the army who had turned a blind eye?

"Go tell Ini-tesshub and Nerikkaili what's happened," he said at last. "They need to adjust their spacing."

Hannutti hopped down and raced into the white-smeared maquis.

Around noon, they heard the approach of the enemy troops—drums and pipes, the thunder of thousands of feet, a rhythmic chanting of soldiers on the march. His own men had drawn up on the down slopes just to the north of his vantage point. Other units waited in wings to either side. But there were not enough to carry out anything resembling an offense. It would be Taite all over again, only worse.

Tukulti-ninurta would see for himself that Hatti Land was as fragile as unbaked clay and that it had fallen to pieces even before it was struck.

The Assyrians appeared on the crest of the southern hill. Hannutti described for him what the king saw only vaguely as blurred silhouettes: the royal chariot with its gold-fringed parasol; banners, and the vehicles of officers. Behind this ceremonial front row, infantrymen began to rise with the glint of helmets in the cold morning sun. The king heard the pipes that marked their cadence.

"Send a herald to offer them a last chance at peace," Tudhaliya instructed his charioteer. Tiwatipara obediently stepped down, but the face he turned to his king as he passed was blanched with hopelessness.

Hannutti described the herald, staff in hand, walking up the hill to the Assyrian line. There was a confabulation, and some long moments later, the herald jogged back down the hill and returned with Tiwatipara.

"My Sun, he has declined your offer."

"Then we fight. Signal the generals, Hannutti."

The flagmen passed their signals. The armies of the Great King began to move forward slowly. *Slower, slower,* he willed them. *Don't lose your downhill position.*

The Assyrian king had withdrawn from the crest. The front ranks of Assyrians were poised against the sky. They were better disciplined than Tudhaliya's own troops, the king thought numbly. They would be running downhill, while the troops of Hatti would have passed the valley and found themselves fighting upward by the time they collided. The thunder of jogging footsteps gathered speed from both directions. Tudhaliya's heart was pounding, and cold dread sat in the pit of his stomach. The god's hand was against them, he feared. But they had to fight as if they believed in victory.

He saw the wings fall in behind his advance guard. A vast white tide of soldiers flowed down and then up, toward the descending hosts of Assyria. The king clutched at calm and drew it into himself. But it was a wild fox that would escape as soon as it could.

"Signal the bowmen," he ordered. Suddenly, the sound of whistling wind marked the flight of hundreds of arrows. Hannutti stared into the sky, although the king could see nothing of the delicate rods of death that arced across the valley like a flock of sinister birds. The foremost ranks of the red-and-brown wave flickered as men dropped, but it refilled itself instantly. *It won't be easy to decimate this vast army.* And they were beginning to shoot their own volleys into the ranks of Hatti Land—downward into an undermanned force.

The whiteness rippled as shields were held overhead and lowered. Now the two waves mingled. The crash of colliding wood and leather echoed up to the king's hilltop along with the war cries. The grunts and screams. The screeching of metal on metal. The king was quivering like a hunting dog that smelled its prey, longing to throw himself into the melee, where survival was all that mattered and thought ceased. Even without his notice, his hand closed over the haft of his battle-ax. He heard Hannutti yelling at his side. Both of them were unable to stand still. Tudhaliya willed his men up the hill. *Up, up.* He felt their bursting lungs as they tried to hold their ground against the falling weight of red-brown. He saw the two armies slide into the valley, still struggling and pushing, shield against shield. Bows were useless now. It was hand-to-hand fighting. This was the combat in which the king excelled, with his long arms and patient, methodical style. But he was pent up here, out of the danger of regicide, his breath rasping with frustration, his nerves twanging like bowstring.

The morning crept on, the sun swinging across the meridian. The Assyrians kept coming. Tudhaliya's own forces were all engaged, fighting valiantly but profoundly outmanned. He saw their position shifting gradually backward, backing up their own hillside. They were exhausted but forced to fight on—those few thousand men were all that stood between an invader and the open door to their own land. And the king watched numbly as the sheer force of numbers pushed his diminishing army back and back. Finally, the men broke rank and started to flee northward. His generals couldn't stem the flight.

Hannutti screamed, "Wurukatte, no! No! I don't believe it!"

"My Sun," murmured Tiwatipara uneasily, "I think we should move from here."

The king gave him a nod, and the charioteer clucked the two stallions into movement.

"Signal a retreat," Tudhaliya said levelly. "Try to keep it orderly."

But it was a rout. They had taken the precaution to leave their wagons and supplies and unused chariots deeper into the mountains to the north so the materiel could be collected as they fled. Still, the train would never be able to keep up if the Assyrians chose to pursue them far. They might lose their food and water as well as their dignity.

The royal chariot rocked and jolted through the maquis. Tudhaliya's fingers on the rail were so tense they were as white as if the bones were exposed. He tried to control his breathing so as not to frighten Hannutti any worse. He knew he should say something reassuring but couldn't think of what that might be. He heard the boy's sobs of frustration and fury, heard him shouting, "May the gods blast that Kurunta, the treacherous bastard!"

As for the king, his anger at the vassals who had cost him victory was swallowed up in a more gut-twisting rage. He himself had caused this debacle. He had alienated his most important viceroy. He felt his sinfulness upon him, like a polluted garment that he longed to shrug off, with revulsion in his heart. He was unjust. He had had no mercy. He had failed his people, his parents, his gods.

He ground his teeth, but there was nothing he could do, or he would have done it before. The worst, the unimaginable worst, had happened because of his unworthiness. His empire had splintered before his eyes, like a bad walking stick one leans on that breaks the moment one needs it most. With bile in his heart, he pictured Ehli-sharrumma groveling before Tukulti-ninurta, offering him the copper mines in exchange for protection.

They finally halted at Alatarma, where there was at least water for the animals. It seemed the Assyrians were not going to pursue them at the moment. The evening shadows, in fact, were beginning to grow long. The king investigated the grain supply of the village then assigned his survivors a double ration and as much beer as could be found, although Tudhaliya had no appetite. He longed to walk among the men, who sat around listlessly or stared southward in fear. He longed to praise their courage, tell them they had had no choice but to run. However, his council no longer permitted him to do such a thing, after the attempt on his life at Nerik. The soldiers wept in shame, cursed the defectors. But their king couldn't comfort them.

Tudhaliya realized his army would need to move back within its own borders as expeditiously as possible. They were in Nairi Land, the territory of the Forty Kings, who had sent no levies to their ally as he had tried to defend their kingdoms from invasion. The Assyrians would assuredly not stop where they were. Nothing stood between them and Ishuwa and the Upper Land of Hatti itself. He dictated as Tarhun-miya wrote out a letter for the *tawananna* and a sarcastic rebuke to Ehli-sharrumma. As he concluded, his generals filtered back to his side.

Ini-tesshub looked gloomier than ever. "Tattamaru is wounded, My Sun, although not gravely, I think."

"Alalimmi?"

"Captured. You'll need to ransom him."

Huzziya was there unharmed but steaming with humiliation. Ini-tesshub's brothers and sons had survived. No one had seen Shanda-kurunta, and the king feared the worst for his younger brother. Surely, the Assyrians would permit them to search the battlefield and burn their dead.

That evening, as Pirwannu undressed his master, Nerikkaili entered the tent with a pot of beer for the king.

"Since you didn't eat, you might want this," he said, offering it to Tudhaliya.

"Thank you," the king said expressionlessly. He was seated on the edge of his camp bed, surrendering his boots. Tudhaliya lowered his eyes and stared into space. Exhaustion so profound that he could hardly lift his arm to drink had settled over him. Nerikkaili watched him for a moment, said nothing, clapped him on the shoulder, then left.

Pirwannu extinguished the lamp and bowed himself out, but the king did not lie down. He sat there as the sounds of the camp grew silent around him, and the noises of night in the mountains began. Sharp, melancholy cries of some animal, perhaps a fox, echoed from hill to hill. After a while, an owl hooted softly overhead and disappeared. Tudhaliya threw his cloak about his shoulders and pushed back the flap of the tent.

The camp was mostly dark. The men slept the dead sleep of the defeated. Here and there, a watch fire burned, sparks swirling up into the cold black sky. A horse nickered and blew out its lips with a ruffle of air. The Great King padded out barefoot and stood unseen in the darkness, his arms wrapped around himself. The twenty-four guards who stood in a circle around his tent made themselves known by an occasional sigh or rustle of brush under their feet.

He was almost past thought and feeling, stunned, like a sacrificial animal, by this blow of the gods. He was not shocked by the defeat itself or by the truancy of his defecting vassals so much as by the betrayal of Kurunta. *And yet,* he said to himself when the pain had receded enough to think, *I should have seen it coming, at least from this morning. And in fact, he's been sending me signals for years. I could perhaps have forestalled this had I been more aware of what I was doing to him, how broken he was.*

And then his sense of guilt gave way to a brief flash of anger. Kurunta, the two-faced bastard, had been saying with one side of his mouth that he would be faithful, while with the other he had made it clear that he was getting ready to abandon Tudhaliya. *To abandon me. Before I, like everyone else, abandoned him.* And imagining the agonies it must have cost his cousin to be untrue to his faithful nature, the king's anger settled like dew. It left his heart wet with sorrow so heavy that he feared it would drive him to the ground. He could barely drag himself back inside the tent.

But his chagrin as a man was as nothing to the sense of dread and guilt that haunted him as sovereign. Would the Assyrians pursue them straight back into the Upper Land?

This could easily become the spearhead of an invasion of Hatti Land's highland core. Would they peel off the rest of the eastern vassals, beginning with Karkemish? Force their way through the mountains into Kizzuwatna? This broken remnant of an army was certainly in no position to stop them.

He thought about the famine. Every man taken from the fields to put into the army was one less pair of hands at the harvest, one more mouth to feed on campaign. Now that Ishuwa and its mines were almost certainly going to be lost, he didn't know how he would continue to pay Mizri for grain.

The king couldn't sleep. His mind was so twitchy he couldn't even make himself lie in bed. Instead, he paced back and forth in the chilly darkness, massaging the aching ridges of his eyebrows. At one point, he stumbled on and kicked over the pot of beer he had set upon the ground. He heard the silver drinking straw clink, pictured the liquid spreading out and sinking into the earth. Just so did a man's soul sink beneath the black earth into oblivion. *If only we could be sure death was the end of pain,* he thought longingly. He realized he wanted not to be responsible for all this. But there was no one above him except the gods. His thoughts turned to his dead father.

You are wiser and greater than I, Father. Help me to be strong. Help me.

⁑

Kurunta had returned to the capital of Tarhuntassha—the city built by his father—with his five thousand men. They had come by the southern route and followed the coast then turned up from Kizzuwatna. It had been cold, but there'd been no snow, and his men were fresh and unwounded. They had made much better time than the king's units.

Kurunta found himself in a state of frenzied anger that he feared might never dissipate; he suspected he might have become a little deranged by the bitterness of his falling-out with Tash. He couldn't relax, couldn't stop thinking about how he had been wronged, couldn't enjoy anything anymore. He had become just as obsessed as he had accused Tash of being. He longed to have some kind of revenge, and yet the memory of their friendship and all the sweet moments of intimacy they had shared and even the image of his cousin's homely face, so prematurely aged, with his gray hair at only forty, threatened constantly to unman him. Torment boiled within him. He yelled at his servants, mistreated his queen, snarled at his advisors, wept in private, drank.

The viceroy's only consolation was the presence in his life of Urhi-tesshub. Kurunta thanked the gods that his half brother had come back to him. Indeed, the elder son of Muwatalli was living quietly at the viceroyal palace along with Kurunta's proscribed father-in-law. Urhi-tesshub was billing himself as a merchant from the southern coast who had come to discuss harborage. It had seemed to them both that there was less risk of a search under the very roof of the Great King's representative than in some safe house in the country. Besides, it would be Kurunta who carried out any such search.

Alantalli came and went, feeling out the loyalties of the Luwian vassals that ringed the western and southern coasts of the empire, while Urhi-tesshub stayed out of sight.

"Can I interest you in some more *walhi* beverage, brother?" Kurunta asked his sibling one evening as they lingered over dinner.

The pretender held up a hand to decline. "You treat me too well, my brother." He smiled with his warm, affectionate smile. "I don't want to dull my powers of reflection."

Kurunta had no such scruples, and he upended the ewer into his own cup. He leaned on his forearms, the cup cradled between his hands, and looked up at his brother with bleary, worshipful eyes.

"So tell me what happened in Nairi Land," said Urhi-tesshub.

"The king and I argued, and I picked up my troops and left before the battle. Found out later it was a huge rout. The Assyrians swallowed us alive. It was a terrible humiliation for Tash." Kurunta couldn't hide the ghost of a smile.

"Five thousand men made that much difference?"

"I'm important." The viceroy grinned wryly—an expression with no humor in it—but added, "Also, a lot of other vassals didn't show up at all. Ishuwa, for one. Taruisha. Ugarit. Hatti Land is falling apart."

Urhi-tesshub sighed, his brow crumpled with sorrow. "I'm afraid that's what happens without the blessing of the gods. The empire of our forefathers is shaken to its very core since Hattushili grabbed my throne. Famine, civil war, now the Assyrians. Does our cousin think he can reverse any of this as long as he is an illegitimate ruler?" He shook his head as though it was all too heavy to digest.

"Once I could have told you what he thinks, but not anymore." Kurunta snorted. "I can assure you, though, that he's not having any fun. He looks as if he hasn't slept in a month."

"I guess he has a conscience, eh?" Urhi-tesshub chuckled. "Perhaps if we wait long enough, he'll voluntarily return the throne to me, eh?"

But Kurunta's face buckled into a bitter scowl as he considered his cup. "Not a chance. The man is stubborn as an ass. And the more miserable it makes him, the better he likes it."

His brother shrugged expansively. "Well, he's really as much a victim as we are, Ulmi-tesshub. He was only a child when all this got started. And to be honest, I blame Puduhepa even more than Uncle Hattushili. The minute she entered the scene—and I remember that; I was fourteen when they married—it became all about how to get Muwatalli's children out of the way and put her own in there. Even when our father was still on the throne and I was the *tuhkanti.* Our mothers didn't stand a chance against her. Who knows why our father really expelled his *tawananna,* eh?"

Kurunta tried to picture the mother he had never known, but she always had Puduhepa's face. "She was good to me," he murmured reluctantly.

"Of course. She had plans for you. She wanted to keep you sweet. But don't think she wasn't watching out for her own. Why do you think she never told you who your mother really was? Why do you think she picked Tashmi-sharrumma, of all charmless people, for Uncle's heir? She knew you'd never betray *him,* even if his kingship were unjust, whereas for any other candidate, it would be an issue of justice alone."

Kurunta felt a pang of guilt. He *had* betrayed Tash— left him on the field of battle to what could have been his death. But he remembered that Tash himself had said the same thing to him long ago—*You're the reason it's me on the throne*—perhaps without really knowing how true it was. And Kurunta had laughed about it and said, *I didn't know I was so important.*

His thoughts were simmering, hampered by a grogginess engendered by *walhi* drink. "I've been used…"

Urhi-tesshub nodded solemnly. "But that doesn't mean you have to stay a victim, Ulmi-tesshub. You see the difference your troops made at Alatarma. You're crucial in our battle, too, brother. Bring those men to the fight, and victory is ours. The king is crawling home with a defeated, dispirited army. They're tired and frozen and underfed. Maybe half of them are morally on our side already. Think of Sheha River Land. Tarkashnawa is Alantalli's son. Did you know that? He's as Luwian as his father. Why should he side with Tashmi-sharrumma against his own people?"

"Of course I know Tarkashnawa. He's my brother-in-law. And he hates his father. He's Tash's hand-picked lapdog."

"But why is he even on the throne of Sheha River Land? Because there was already a movement to overthrow old Mashturi and his antiquated loyalties, right? The rebellion is already coming to a boil out there. I can't help but think a lot of the king's soldiers will refuse to fight for him, brother. I mean, he's been completely discredited before the eyes of the world. This may be the moment."

Some ember of conscience was still glowing in Kurunta under the deepening ash. "Hold on, I didn't say I was part of your political group, Urhi-tesshub. I'm still the Great King's viceroy."

Urhi-tesshub locked eyes with him and grinned a knowing grin. "But who is the Great King? If you say Tashmi-sharrumma, I'm not so sure. I think that ended at Alatarma, brother, and you just haven't noticed yet. I think you're *my* viceroy."

Kurunta pushed himself up from the table and paced back and forth, a little unsteady on his feet, a great deal unsteady in his mind. Urhi-tesshub didn't know how many of the rebels' plans the viceroy had revealed to the *tawananna*. He didn't know that Kurunta still loved her, even knowing that she had used him. He could unburden himself to her about Tash, trusting she understood how infuriating the king could be but how kind and honest under it all. Even when he had spoken angrily to Puduhepa, it had been because of his anger against her son, never her.

"Look, I'll help to the extent of lodging you and Alantalli secretly, but I... I need more time to decide about lending you troops. That's a big step."

"That's what Ehli-sharrumma said before the battle at Alatarma, brother." Urhi-tesshub rose, stretched, and clapped Kurunta on the shoulder. "Sometimes you have to commit, or victory eludes you. You've got to decide what you really want."

Kurunta sank back into his seat, watching with bloodshot eyes as Urhi-tesshub pushed in his chair. The pretender retreated to his chambers, smiling. His departure left his brother conflicted and depressed.

As if the *tawananna* had somehow heard the previous evening's conversation, a letter arrived in the morning from her, begging the viceroy to let bygones be bygones and to lend her his troops for the defense of Hattusha. She begged this by the love he bore for her son.

When Kurunta had his secretary read it aloud to Urhi-tesshub, the latter just smiled benevolently and said, "Looks like you have a decision to make, brother. The old master, who is going down, or the new master, who can protect you. Think of Ehli-sharrumma."

But in fact, Kurunta didn't think much of Ehli-sharrumma or any vassal who betrayed his oath of fealty. His own grievance was a personal one with the king as a man. He had tried hard not to let private rancor interfere with his duties. Admittedly, that had broken down at Alatarma, but he had been provoked. He wasn't sure he wouldn't still respond to the next levy as faithfully as before. It was his habit, to be sure—in fact, the habit of deferring to Tash went back deep into their childhood, for all that Tash was younger—but loyalty was also his firmly held principle.

However, now that he was forsworn, he found it hard to think straight about principles. He perceived that the first infidelity might have been difficult but that the second one would be easier... if he wanted there to be a second one.

In short, he was far from proud of his action, no matter how satisfying a gesture it had seemed at the time. He desired very much to please and support this splendid brother of his who had returned from the dead, but he wasn't quite resolved to do further violence to his honor. Such anguishes were new to him, and he didn't like them. They were Tash-like.

Eventually, he dictated a reply to the *tawananna*: "I will send the troops."

CHAPTER 17

"YOU DID WHAT?" CRIED ALANTALLI, aghast. His sharp little kestrel eyes bugged. He had returned from his scouting to find that Kurunta's troops not only would not be swelling the ranks of the rebels but would oppose them when Urhi-tesshub's army besieged the capital.

"I only did what a viceroy is expected to do," muttered Kurunta. He couldn't endure consciousness anymore and avidly threw back a cup of wine.

Laying a brotherly hand on the viceroy's arm, Urhi-tesshub defended him. "He hasn't abandoned us, my friend. He just hasn't fully made up his mind yet. His love for the king has deep roots; we can't expect him to pull them up all at once."

But Kurunta exploded bitterly, spraying his guests with wine. "Love for the king, my ass. I hate his black soul. It's just… I can't get used to the thought of being a renegade. I swore an oath."

"So did Tashmi-sharrumma," Urhi-tesshub said. "It

didn't seem to stop him from dropping you like a hot rock in the Shalashu ritual."

Alantalli shook his head and made a hissing noise of dismissal. "Too much conscience and not enough courage, if you ask me. When I married Anitti to a son of Muwatalli, I thought that meant he'd be part of the royal family, not some remote vassal no better than me, afraid to use his own head for fear the grown-ups will smack him down."

Kurunta shot his father-in-law a snarl. "Enough, you jumped-up bandit."

"Gentlemen," Urhi-tesshub interposed peaceably, "let's save our rancor for the usurper's family, shall we? We each have our own goals: Alantalli here wants to see his people restored to independence. You and I want to see the rightful lineage of Muwatalli's sons back on the throne. But of course, the one is linked to the other. As king, I will recognize the Luwian kingdoms as free allies, not vassals. And Alantalli knows that Tashmi-sharrumma will never give him his freedom, so supporting me is in his own best interest. We must stay friends, gentlemen, or we all lose."

The little man of the West subsided reluctantly, still muttering suspicious warnings in Luwian. "And then there's this Hishni. Where does he come in?"

"Prince Hishni is willing to support me at the moment." The pretender spread his hands as if to say, *This is all I can expect.* "I don't doubt that he hopes eventually to supplant me, but I'll deal with that when the time comes. Mostly he just wants revenge on a half brother he's been convinced he resents. For now, he's useful. He can't bring us troops, except for a few *meshedi* guards, but he's a skilled general. He can lead some of our units effectively.

"Now, let's get down to practicalities, brother," said Urhi-tesshub, turning to Kurunta. "When do you have to have the troops to Hattusha?"

Kurunta shrugged. "I'm sure the *tawananna* would like them as soon as possible. She thinks you people are going to pounce on her before Tash gets back. Or the Kashkans."

"Let's see," his brother mused. "I should expect the army to be back in the capital within four weeks or so, unless they hit heavy snow in the mountains, wouldn't you think, Ulmi-tesshub?"

Kurunta nodded, with an uncertain gesture of his shoulders.

"How long will it take to move your troops up there?"

"Two weeks maybe, once they actually get ready to march. It's the supply wagons that are so slow."

"So let's see. If you wait a week and a half and then push them, they would arrive before the usurper's army does, right? That means we need to attack before that. Within the week."

"What in the name of the Marwainzi Gods? We can't get there that fast," squawked Alantalli. "Why so soon?"

"Because otherwise we'll be facing five thousand more men. The capital can't be that heavily defended at the moment. We need to take it out before the Tarhuntassha levy or the returning army gets there." Urhi-tesshub pounded a fist on the table and nodded.

Kurunta stared at him, his thoughts teetering. The viceroy had a certain reputation for daring, but this was lunacy. This was the kind of lunacy that afflicted truly great generals. A glow of admiration flushed his face.

"Brilliant," he said, marveling. "And I will have obeyed

the summons. They can't fault me for anything. Who could know you'd be there so soon? But you'll have to leave almost immediately."

"It's impossible." Alantalli crossed his arms stubbornly. "I'll have to raise troops piecemeal from all the kingdoms that are joining us, and it'll take time."

"Ah, but if this is a siege, it will last for a while. We invest the capital with the troops we know are all ready and loyal, and then additional soldiers join us as they can. Ulmi-tesshub withholds his men as long as possible, and by the time they get there... damn, it's all over!" Urhi-tesshub grinned with the infectious enthusiasm of a boy.

Kurunta laughed for the first time in a long while. What a man this brother of his had turned out to be!

"Anyway," Kurunta reminded his father-in-law, "you've got to beat the snow or wait until next spring. This is probably your best chance."

Alantalli held up his fists in supplication to the gods to deliver him from these madmen. "All right, I'm off. Let's see who will respond on a moment's notice. Where do we mass our troops?"

"I suggest the hills just south of the salt lake," said Kurunta, warming to the idea. "Near the border of Pitassha, north of Ikkuwaniya. It's technically in the Lower Land, but it's wild and uninhabited, and the governor relies on me to patrol the area. That will put you as near to Hattusha as you dare to be. Once you cross the river, they'll see you for sure."

"You still say 'you,' my brother. Sure you won't join us?"

"I... I don't know. I won't fight against you, though.

329

Even when I send my troops, I don't have to lead them personally."

"That makes a pretty good rallying point for the troops from the West, too, now that my son, the viceroy, is absent—Lords of the Underworld take that boot-licking bastard," Alantalli said, nodding slowly. "And I've been told some of the tribes in the Lower Land itself may be ours for the asking. Oh, and did I tell you Millawanda is willing to help nudge the kingdoms of the West? But we need to get couriers headed out immediately."

"My vizier can see to it. We don't have to tell him what the message will be." Enthusiasm was crackling in Kurunta's breast like a cheerful fire. He loved a good adventure, was always full of romantic schemes of glory.

His brother laughed in honest delight and clapped him on the back. "What an ally the gods have given back to me, eh? Brothers shoulder to shoulder. Who can stop us?"

Alantalli rolled his eyes, but even he was grinning as the two guests made their way back to their chambers for the night. Kurunta watched them go, his heart full of joy for the first time in years. He imagined Tash coming back and finding the capital held by Urhi-tesshub, the rightful king in the arms of Halmashuit after thirty-five years. How appalled Tash would feel, how sad, how helpless, how frightened. How abandoned. Vengeance distilled its liquor into the viceroy's veins, sweeter and more powerful than *walhi* beverage. And he grew really and truly drunk with it.

❖

The next morning, Alantalli presented himself for an early breaking of the fast, and then he headed off to solicit troops. Kurunta was awake to see him depart. He really wanted to talk to his brother again and recapture some of that heady lunacy of the night before, but Urhi-tesshub was still asleep. Kurunta would have been sleeping, too, if his life were yet rolling along in its usual fashion. But oh, how his routine had changed! How he relished the intrusion of this mad daring. He felt as if he had awakened after the long nightmare of responsible adulthood.

He dawdled over breakfast, expecting his brother to surface. Then he drifted into his chancery to take care of some business with his secretaries. When he returned, he still saw no sign of Urhi-tesshub. He wondered if he should send a servant to wake his guest, but he preferred not to advertise the proscribed man's presence, even to his own household. Finally, wondering if his brother had left before dawn, Kurunta made his way to the guest chamber and knocked on the door.

No answer.

"Urhi-tesshub?"

Only the devouring silence of a stone building wherein no one makes a move greeted him.

"Brother? Can I come in?" A faint sense of unease began to niggle at the viceroy's stomach. He pushed the door open. The shutters were still drawn, and the room was dark, chilly, sour. The coals in the brazier had burned to ash; it seemed too quiet. He pushed the wooden panels back, and late-autumn sunlight flooded in, but the shadows still clung to the corners. The cold smell of snow drove out the fug of an inhabited room. He saw his brother's bed, the covers in disarray.

"Have you left, brother?"

He wondered if Urhi-tesshub had gone to the latrines. Kurunta approached the bed, began to walk around it, and stopped, frozen. Stretched out on the floor on the far side of the bed lay Urhi-tesshub. His limbs were twisted strangely, his face was down, hidden by his grizzled hair, which trailed in a pool of vomit.

"By the thousand gods!" Kurunta cried, his voice rising shrilly. Stark horror overwhelmed him. He sank to his knees, lifted his brother's shoulders, turned him on his back. The man's face was set in a rictus of shock and pain, his wide-open eyes protruding.

Kurunta let a strangled cry escape and dropped Urhi-tesshub back to the floor with a thud. He was dead. Cold and hard, as human flesh should never have been. The very touch made Kurunta's skin crawl with a ghastly awareness of how he had polluted himself. He wiped his hands on his skirts in horror. For the first time, he understood why death should carry pollution. He had seen plenty of dead men on the field of battle, but they were only puppets with lots of red paint. No one dear to him had ever lain dead before his eyes. It was an obscene violation of the right order of the world. It was impossible.

"Urhi, no! All you gods, no! No!" *After this endless lifetime, to have you for only a few years? Such cruelty can't exist.* Perhaps he was mistaken; perhaps the man was not dead—he saw no blood, no wound... But he knew. The gods had taken Urhi-tesshub from him.

Kurunta sat on the floor and wept. He felt like a small child, abandoned all over again. His life was just a repetition of the same event, over and over again. This was clearly a message from the gods, but what did it say? Perhaps he was doomed never to take more than a sip of happiness before the cup was jerked away. Perhaps the plot to seize back the throne for its rightful occupant was displeasing to them.

Kurunta no longer cared about the grand and daring plot. He just wanted his brother back, this big, splendid, brilliant, loving father of his own. Not Uncle Hattushili and his wife, who were Tash's parents; not all the brothers, who were Tash's brothers—but this one, who was his own. Who *had been* his own.

Now he had no one again. Not even Tash loved him. Kurunta was a beautiful, talented, funny, warmhearted forty-five-year-old son of a Great King whom nobody loved. Bitter tears coursed down his cheeks, but he made no move to wipe them. Why bother? He was completely alone.

The sun had moved across the wall by the time the viceroy climbed to his feet. He would have to see to it that his brother was cremated as befit a king, but somehow without making the pretender's identity known. Kurunta would have to break the news to his father-in-law, who might well call off the attack on the capital. After all, there was no longer any rightful king to enthrone. There was Hishni, of course, but he wasn't very bright. He made a good second-in-command, but Kurunta was hard-pressed to imagine the Luwians excitedly pledging their fealty to him. Tash probably hadn't risked much in pardoning Hishni. *He just made himself feel virtuous, the hypocrite.*

Kurunta waited in his throne room, seated dully on the viceroyal throne until Alantalli's return. A cup of strong *walhi* cradled in his hand, he hardly had a thought all day, preferring to let someone else make sense of the blow that had been dealt him. He had instructed the servants to

333

direct his father-in-law in to see him as soon as the little man came back. It was almost dark when he heard the big doors creak open and the brisk footsteps of the king of Mira. Kurunta saw a flicker of torchlight on a bald head before the door slammed shut behind Alantalli.

"Hello? Are you sitting in the dark, son?" Alantalli called. He was dirty and wind whipped, but his voice was bright, full of energy. It had been a good day for him.

Kurunta rose and went to him, stood in front of him, looming over the small man. His ravaged face was no doubt invisible in the twilight, but Alantalli would smell the *walhi* drink on his breath. Kurunta said, "He's dead, Alantalli."

The older man sounded nonplussed. "Who's dead? Tudhaliya?"

"Urhi-tesshub." Kurunta's voice began to come apart until he was sobbing. He covered his face with his hands and turned away.

His father-in-law neither spoke nor moved for the space of several heartbeats, trying to digest something so unimaginable, so clearly the hand of the gods. Alantalli tried to say something—"Wha...? How...?"—but he was manifestly caught off guard. At length, he cried, "By all the gods of our ancestors. I don't believe it. What happened?"

Kurunta could only shake his head until he was able to regain control of himself. He murmured at last, "I don't know. I just found him. There's no wound or blood or anything."

"Some kind of seizure, then? Your family seems to have those."

The viceroy shrugged. His family medical history was

not what concerned him. Urhi-tesshub had left him; that was what mattered.

Alantalli fingered his ill-shaven chin. "What do we do now? The kings I've spoken to are all sending troops, and they'll meet us in the lake country in four days' time. I'm not sure I could stop this even if I wanted to. But who will lead us?"

"Hishni," said Kurunta in utter indifference. It was someone else's rebellion now.

"Nobody owes him any allegiance. And I don't know what his attitude toward the West is. He's been the Great King's military man for thirty years."

"This is no longer any business of mine, Alantalli. Get out from under my roof, and go do your seditious work. In two weeks, my troops are heading up to the capital. Better have finished your job by then, or they'll fight you."

"Not so fast, son." Alantalli held up a warning hand. "Urhi-tesshub didn't have first-rank children, but he had a first-rank heir. You." He poked his son-in-law in the chest. "You're the rightful king now."

Kurunta glared down at him with baleful eyes. *What a moment for a tasteless joke.*

"No, I mean it. Brothers inherit the throne from brothers all the time. You're experienced in ruling, you're good in the field, you're popular enough among your vassals… why not?" The little Luwian's dark eyes had taken on their predatory gleam again. "Maybe the gods are telling us that *you're* the king they want, son. Think about it!"

Kurunta laughed at the sheer absurdity of it. He knew himself to be a follower, not a leader.

But Alantalli grabbed Kurunta by the arm and forced

the viceroy to look at him. The Miran's intensity was almost frightening. "No, listen to me, son. You don't know everything. Your father took a Luwian throne name, right? When was the last time a Hittite king called himself Muwatalli? 'The Valiant'—it's an epithet of Tarhunta. Muwatalli wasn't just another Great King of Hatti; he had a mission. He moved his capital to the Luwian-speaking southwest. He took a Luwian god for his personal patron. He was consecrated to Tarhunta Pihasshasshi, the Storm God of Lightning. *Our* god, man. He was *ours*, ours. He wanted the Luwian lands to be independent, ruled from Tarhuntassha. Don't you see what this means?"

Kurunta eyed him uncertainly. "Why, no. What? How am I part of this picture?"

"What kind of throne name did you pick, son? Eh? Eh? Luwian!"

"Lots of people have Luwian names," Kurunta protested, but he was beginning to get caught up in Alantalli's mystic fervor.

"The gods have chosen you to rule us, a Luwian kingdom. We will impose ourselves on those smug northern bastards, just as they've imposed themselves on us for five hundred years!"

"I happen to be one of those smug northern bastards, Alantalli," said Kurunta with a sarcastic smile.

"And so was your father. But he listened to the voice of the gods."

Kurunta fell silent, not sure how seriously to take all this. He was far from sober and felt as if someone had spun him in circles and pushed him. He stammered a little, trying to find objections. "And who exactly will be willing to consecrate me?"

"Any priest. The West is full of them. I mean, you're a legitimate king's son, aren't you? You've lived so long among Hattushili's brood they've convinced you you're nothing but a cipher. You're more legitimate than this dogface on the throne now."

"I'm as good as he is," Kurunta muttered, beginning to wonder why Tash should always have had all the advantages.

"But you weren't one of their own. And as some second-ranker, you were less of a threat to their own. Still, even second-rank sons can inherit."

"Except in Uncle Hattushili's world."

"Uncle is dead, son. This is the son of Muwatalli's world."

It took Kurunta a moment to realize that this son of Muwatalli was himself and that it might well suddenly have become his world. Urhi-tesshub had taken a traditional Hittite name on the throne—Murshili—a name that had harked back to a generation before all this splitting up, before all this rivalry among brothers' lineages. But their father had *wanted* to split the empire. He had wanted to set the South and West free.

"I… I don't know, Alantalli. What is it—you just want to see your daughter as a queen of Hatti Land?"

"Your children are half-Luwian. Think about what that will mean to your… *allies* in the West. My Sun. Look, this Tudhaliya is a weak man. He lets his enemies get off; he can't protect his vassals; he lets the Assyrians run all over him. The gods have abandoned him. We need someone strong and blessed by the gods, right? You, son. You!"

Kurunta spun away so his father-in-law couldn't see his face. He felt like a vise had closed on his head, crushing his skull. Alantalli had to be crazy.

And yet, the laws of succession were clear enough. He was the legitimate heir of Urhi-tesshub. What, in fact, was so absurd about the idea of Kurunta in the lap of Halmashuit? His father-in-law had this much correct: only the enmity of the household in which he had been raised had robbed him of his sense of birthright. He had been reduced to an inferior appendage of Tash. No one had ever spoken of his mother, of his rank, ever. Maybe Tash hadn't even known the real identity of his childhood companion. Maybe his brothers hadn't. But Puduhepa surely had.

"Perhaps. I need to think about it."

"Well, think fast, son. In four days, we march on the capital." Alantalli shot him a significant look and headed for the door.

Kurunta was thinking as fast as he could. He was thinking that the reason Tash was on the throne at all—and not Nerikkaili, who was nearly twenty years his senior—was because his, Kurunta's, support was that important. Uncle's heir had had to be *the man Kurunta supported*. And why was that? Because Kurunta himself was before Hattushili's children in the legitimate line for the throne.

Kurunta was the rightful king.

"I'll do it," he called out after his father-in-law. He couldn't wait to see Tash's face.

The *tawananna* received her son's terse message from the front with a sinking stomach. Defeated. And why, if you please? Because the vassals had not responded to the levy. Because Kurunta, who had been there, had turned back before the battle. She emitted a howl of rage and hurled the wooden tablet to the ground with a clatter, sorry only that it did not smash into pieces. *Damn them all. Are they completely given over to self-interest? Have they no sense of honor? They're all bound by the most solemn oaths before the thousand gods of Hatti Land to defend Hatti and obey its king.*

The Assyrians couldn't be trusted to follow the protocols of civilized nations. Anyone else would simply laugh at her son and wait for the vassals of a humiliated Hatti Land to come flocking to them. But the Assyrians—oh, no. They might just invade Hatti and try to take it over, the way they had obliterated Hanigalbat. She cursed them, cursed their duplicitous young king, cursed their gods, and cursed their beards and their big bellies and their thick arms and their oiled black curls. She would die rather than see them marching into Hattusha, the city of her husband's ancestors.

She called out to Mahhuzzi, forgetting that he was no longer her personal secretary. He was happy enough to receive her confidences, however, and drew near, his close-set little eyes bright with enjoyment of the royal intimacy.

"Yes, my lady? Can I serve you?"

"Mahhuzzi, we must prepare for a siege, should it come to that. The king and his troops are on their way back from Nairi Land as fast as possible, but it will take weeks at the least, and we can't know if some turncoat in the West may decide to take advantage of the defeat to attack us. It could be the Kashkans; it could be Alantalli and Urhi-tesshub. It could be Hishni; I'd forgotten all about him. How many troops have we left?"

"Not many regular troops, my lady. The *meshedi* and the Golden Spears, except for those on duty with the king; the royal heavy-armed guard; the garrison at the palace; those at the city gates... It is in the hundreds, not the thousands, I fear. The citizens could be armed to provide perhaps a few thousand more."

"Gods grant it not be necessary." She exhaled grimly through the nose. "It's my understanding that Kurunta marched five thousand men to Alatarma—which are few enough, given the population of Tarhuntassha—but if he would consent to put that number at the disposal of the defenders of the city, we might be all right."

Yet she no longer had any idea of what Kurunta would and would not do. Despite their communications over the years, in which her nephew had inveighed against her son and pleaded for her intercession, his defection had taken her completely off guard. She hoped that it was only intended as a personal message of contempt aimed at Tashmi-sharrumma but that the viceroy had not really and truly abandoned his vassal duties. After all these years of cultivating their friendship, grooming them from childhood, to see her investment thrown away... *Oh, son, couldn't you have helped me just a bit?* she thought, weary. *You know yourself so little.*

A stab of grief pierced her for her poor eldest boy, who had to be crushed by this betrayal and the subsequent defeat. He was so alone now—no wife, no friend, his kingdom falling to pieces in his hands. *What dreadful times we live in.* It had never been easy for any king, but somehow, poor Tashmi-sharrumma had the worst of everything to deal with. *May Shaushga and all the gods look out for him.*

Mashamuwa, their ambassador, who had been pulled out of Asshur when the Assyrians had rejected Tashmi-sharrumma's peace overtures, was now assigned to the court in Karduniash. He had recently brought her evidence that Urhi-tesshub and the Babylonian king had been in communication again, after all these years—in spite of the treaty. The pretender had sought arms and aid from Shagarakti-shuriash so that he could recover his "lawful throne." Righteous vindication surged in Puduhepa's veins. Her suspicions about the Babylonians had been correct all along, but she was not sure how Ellat-gula and her henchmen figured into this arrangement. Had the late queen been aware of her brother's maneuvering? It was difficult to imagine how she might have intended to profit by the replacement of her husband on the throne, which would have cut her sons out of the line of descent. Had she been planning to marry Urhi-tesshub? But perhaps Ellat-gula's loyalty to her homeland had run that deep. Puduhepa was more than willing to assume the worst of her—with all due respect for the dead. Maybe it had been the king's coldness toward his wife that had alienated her, as well, just like Kurunta.

Puduhepa counted the weeks that passed, trying to picture what point the returning army would have reached each day. Winter was setting in early, and if the snow overtook the men, their journey would become doubly miserable. Many, especially the wounded, might die before they ever reached home. Puduhepa prayed that her third son Shanda-kurunta was not among these unfortunates. Tashmi-sharrumma had told her that he had been found injured on the field, but he seemed to be coming around. *If only I were there with him*, she thought, her heart softening. *Nothing helps a wounded man to heal like the ministrations of his mother.* The *tawananna* wondered if she hadn't neglected her younger sons somewhat over the years, while she and her husband had been grooming Tashmi-sharrumma so carefully for his succession. The way they had rallied round her during the dark episode of her deposition had been a welcome revelation. But perhaps resentment of their elder had played its part in that.

She instructed priests at every temple to send up prayers for the king and his men.

Not long before she calculated the likely arrival of the army, the *tawananna* received a message from the governor of the Lower Land with some good news—the first good news in a very long time, she thought exultantly. It would certainly please the king.

Urhi-tesshub had died. He had no first-rank sons.

Kurunta was his heir.

CHAPTER 18

A FLOOD OF RELIEF WASHED OVER the *tawananna* as she perused the tablet Kurunta had dispatched to her. He had agreed to send her the levy from Tarhuntassha, and she chose to see in this his declaration of loyalty. Now that he was the last high-ranked son left of Muwatalli's line, things could only look up. Kurunta had no personal ax to grind like Urhi-tesshub, who had admittedly been removed from the throne by force. Kurunta had spent his entire life in the bosom of Hattushili's household. He considered it his home. His fidelity was to Tashmi-sharrumma, whom her nephew loved with all his heart, despite this unfortunate recent conflict. And he was loyal to her. Kurunta had unburdened himself by letter to her, his foster mother, and she felt sure she had his measure. Her nephew wasn't very stable perhaps—which hadn't been so apparent to her in his childhood—but he was full of heart. Once his angry emotions died down, he would become his old self again. *He would never betray my son.* Or so she hoped.

Tashmi-sharrumma had also sent her a letter, saying

the returning troops were passing through Malitiya. That should put them back in the capital in another week or so if the weather held. It couldn't be soon enough. The *tawananna* had scarcely slept a whole night through since word of the army's defeat. The expectation of an attack upon the undefended city had hung over her like a black cloud. Only let the Kashkans find out that there were almost no troops on watch, and they'd be knocking on the gate. Or that ridiculous Alantalli and his disgruntled Westerners. And of course, all the loyal ones, like Tarkashnawa, were with the king, leaving their homelands vulnerable. She wouldn't even take the king of Mira seriously except that he had managed to capture Arinna with so much ease.

Hishni? Puduhepa couldn't imagine that he was a real threat. What supporters had he? Only the king's own brothers stood to gain anything from his attempted coup, and she knew Nerikkaili was no danger. Perhaps her son hadn't risked much in sparing Hishni after all.

How she wished Nerikkaili were here with her, as in the days when he was *tuhkanti*. His experience was so valuable, both in the field and in the halls of diplomacy. She thought of all the years she had spent trying to win his support for her son. Dear Hattushili had been a remarkable man to countenance his wife's flirtation with his own first-born. It hadn't been easy to navigate. The least public whiff of scandal could have undone everything. But Nerikkaili's continued loyalty had been that important. He had been the chief rival of her own son, upon whom all their hopes had been pinned.

Like many a daring gamble, it had paid off, and indeed it had become its own reward. She wondered what Tashmi-sharrumma would think of that if he knew. He was so innocent in some ways, even at his age—especially sexually. Puduhepa felt she didn't understand him at all in that regard. But she knew he was idealistic. She was certain it would shock him to the core to realize the extent to which his parents had schemed for him and what they had been prepared to do.

She stood now on the parapet of the citadel wall, looking out over the rocky plain that fell away from the capital city. The sky was cold and white—not exactly cloudy so much as veiled. The pastures and orchards were dusted with snow until everything had a silvery shimmer under the sunless glare. Even the rugged gray outcroppings of naked rock that thrust up and up at the feet of the city walls were softened with a fine film of powder. Behind them, the mountains were shaggy with leafless oak and sycamore. This was a harsh land into which she had married but not without its beauty.

Any day now, the *tawananna* expected to see the troops from Tarhuntassha, and until then, she couldn't rest easy.

Cold had begun to radiate from the packed-clay paving up through the soles of her shoes. She wrapped her furs about her and descended the ladder with care, drifting through the nearly empty courtyards of the palace to her room. *Might as well wait where it's warm.* Someone would certainly report when Kurunta's men arrived. She found herself anxiously counting the days until her sons' return as well. Perhaps the snow had already reached the mountains.

In the vestibule, her ladies clustered about her, ready to do her will. Puduhepa told them she wanted to spend some time alone, and they subsided into their spinning once more. They reminded her of the divine Gulshesh. How did the passage about them in the coronation liturgy go? "One holds a spindle; they both hold filled mirrors. And they are spinning the king's years…"

The pulsing coals of three braziers overheated her chamber but lit it poorly. The *tawananna* dropped her cloak on the floor for one of her handmaids to collect. On the table lay the dark bronze dish of her mirror. Almost with trepidation, she filled it with water and waited until the ripples subsided. Her white visage stared up at her in reflection, emerging crisply from the darkness of her veil. *Not too bad for a fifty-seven-year-old woman,* she thought with some satisfaction. Although the years had dulled her creamy, fresh complexion and blurred the perfect oval of her jaw, she was still a handsome specimen.

Sad, she thought with a bitter little laugh. Who would have dreamed at the age of fifteen that someday she would count herself lucky to be *handsome*, grateful to have a fairly trim waist and breasts that hadn't sagged too badly? Unfortunately, none of her daughters and only one of her sons had inherited her beauty, and the elder ones seem to have fared the worst. Poor Tashmi-sharrumma was the homeliest of them all, but he had the intelligence and solidity he needed to be a good ruler. He had really been the best choice, even without the support of Kurunta, although he was as opaque as anyone she had ever met.

She glanced again at the mirror with its still, untroubled surface. If only she had had some oil, she would have tried to scry the outcome of this dreadful moment in the life of her country. *Will Hatti Land prevail over the Assyrians: yes or no? Will the civil war finally end with victory for my son: yes or no? Will… will he find someone who really loves him?* But she realized that might be a mother's fond and unattainable hope. How many monarchs had that luxury? She and Hattushili, an unlikely pair if ever there was one, had been favored by the gods above the common run of kings. It was simply a lonely calling.

Puduhepa looked up at the sound of voices in the vestibule. A moment later, her eunuch chamberlain entered in a flurry.

"My lady, an officer of the Golden Spears to speak urgently with you."

"Send him in." She stood in front of the mirror and folded her arms against the cold air that had invaded the room with him. It seemed all the chillier after the heat of the braziers. She shivered in spite of herself.

The young officer knelt before her and blurted out his message: "An army's approaching the capital from the south, my lady. Thousands of men. They're still too far away to identify."

"It's the viceroy! Thank the gods!" Puduhepa plucked her cloak from the floor and rushed out with the saffron-clad officer in her wake. They retraced her steps across the court to the watchtower and mounted the ladder up to the parapets. She had forgotten how strong and frigid the wind could be up here. Who but her son would really enjoy these heights? She drew her furs about her neck and shaded her eyes, straining to see the distant horizon in the milky glare. Sure enough, line after line of tiny crawling figures, like an army of white ants, approached, accompanied by flashes of bronze armor, flickers of colored standards. *They're still some hours away—at least several leagues.* "If you haven't already, send a scout to identify them before we open the gates. It could always be Alantalli's Luwians."

"We've done that, my lady. We should know as soon as the scouts get back."

She dismissed the man to gather those who were left of their military leaders. Old Nuwanza was too far gone, alas. She would rather have had his wise insights than fifty of these boys', but the most experienced officers were all with the king. They would have to make do with what remained to them. Mahhuzzi appeared above the trap and pushed against the wind toward her, his skirts flying, to expose his skinny shanks in their woolen leggings. "Is it the viceroy at last, my lady?" he called.

"One can only hope. I won't rest until he's here. I suppose I shouldn't worry too much about an attack from Kashka this late in the year, but no one seems to behave normally anymore." They faced the crenellations, the better to see the approaching troops.

Someone hailed her from behind. The *tawananna* turned and greeted the young soldier, who plowed upwind to fall on his knee at her feet.

"The scouts have returned, my lady. It's my lord Kurunta and his troops. We saw him leading them in person."

"Gods be praised!" Puduhepa cried in relief, raising her fists to the white sky. "Open the Lion Gate for them."

Dear Kurunta himself has come, she thought gratefully. *I knew he wouldn't fail me. This will give us some time to talk together, too. Maybe I can figure out what it is between him and Tashmi-sharrumma that has him so upset. Perhaps we can put things right, and the two of them will be together again in a week or so.* She might just be able to save their friendship after all. She might just be able to save the kingdom.

The *tawananna* remained on the wall, despite the cold. She fancied she could see the messenger running through the twisting streets of the Upper City toward the Lion Gate, bearing the joyful orders: *Open for the viceroy!* The wind made her eyes water, whipped her veil across her face. In the distant east, dark clouds were clotting the smooth, gauzy sky—the Storm God rode over the Red Mountains. *May he spare his priest, Tudhaliya,* she prayed.

Below the city's southwestern walls, which were themselves distant from her post above the citadel, Puduhepa watched the approach of Kurunta's army. They were recognizably men now. When the wind shifted, she could hear snatches of their marching feet, the rumble of chariot wheels, the trill of their pipers. Battle flags fluttered overhead, marking the units. There seemed to be a surprising number of them. *Has he brought reinforcements?* A little thrill of uneasiness tickled her stomach.

She wanted to see at closer range and began to walk quickly down the stepped parapet that joined the citadel enceinte to the wall that separated the Lower from the Upper City. *It must be a half a league in distance just to reach the gate from here,* she thought, breathing hard. Although not densely settled—it included many zones of bare rock and steep drop-offs—Hattusha was an enormous city.

Mahhuzzi trailed after her, sniffing rhythmically as the cold made his nose run. Ahead, below the walls, she saw the army drawing nearer and nearer, slowing and pooling at the base of the ascent up to the gate. She thought she could even recognize Kurunta, glittering in his armor under the viceroyal banners.

There was a sudden rocking movement among some of the troops. She realized, as if through a confused haze, that they were archers, drawing back their bowstrings.

"What? What are they doing?" she and Mahhuzzi cried out almost simultaneously. And then a volley of tiny arrows launched through the sky toward the city wall. She saw soldiers falling up on the parapets.

"Sweet Shaushga! He's attacking!" the *tawananna* shrieked in disbelief. "Close the gate! Close the gate!" She ran down the wall, waving her arms, knowing how ineffectual this was. She could never get to the gate in time. Please the gods, the men posted there had recognized the act of treachery for what it was and would shut the gaping mouth of the city. All those troops out there were Luwians, she realized in consternation.

Puduhepa was breathless and almost whimpering with exertion by the time she reached the parapet over the gate and had left Mahhuzzi far behind. The men had sealed it just in time; she heard the deep boom below her feet as each pair of doors crashed shut. Messengers passed her at a run as they transmitted the same order to the keepers of every other of the city's numerous gates.

What has happened, by the thousand gods of Hatti? Was this, in fact, not Kurunta but someone raising his banners? She stared down wild eyed and disbelieving at the army spreading out below the secondary wall. *Only the gate is vulnerable*, she thought feverishly. There were flanking towers, from which bowmen could defend the entry, and a bastion with its tight wall that crowded the approaching soldiers into bowshot range but no doubling of defenses across the doors themselves. If, despite the slope, the attackers could position a battering ram and protect their men long enough to take out the wooden gates...

Risking an arrow in her shoulder, she peered around the crenellations and down at the troops below her, swarming the steep rock, starting to grapple themselves over the outer wall. In the road, some scant few *ikus* away—just out of range of the city bowmen—stood the royal chariot with the viceroy, resplendent in his bronze scales and plumed helmet. She could see his blue-jawed face, his floating black hair; it was surely Kurunta. In a second chariot at his side stood a small man and a large, thickset one with a bull neck. Was that Alantalli? Was it—could it be—Hishni? Above Kurunta, a banner rippled and opened in the wind: the double-headed eagle. Not the lightning bolt, symbol of Tarhuntassha, but the eagle of Hatti Land. *Dear gods...*

As understanding dawned, she emitted a little moan of horror. It was blown away on the wind. Mahhuzzi had caught up to her and panted at her side, his close-set eyes fixed in disbelief upon the banner. He saw it, too.

"Rebellion?" He could hardly speak and not only because he was winded. This, of all the twists of fate possible in a land of numerous and capricious gods, no one had seen coming.

The *tawananna* stood frozen for a moment, her thoughts galloping. *If he has turned against us,* she asked herself in confusion, *why did he attack before he entered and not just reveal himself after he'd breached the gate?* Kurunta wasn't subtle, but neither was he a fool. She could only conclude, with a pang of tenderness, that he still loved her and wanted to leave her time to escape. *Let me not waste this gift.*

She turned to her vizier. "Go quickly. Tell the mayor of the city to evacuate through the God's Gate. We'll leave only enough soldiers to delay an entry, but when Kurunta gets in—and he will get in—there must be no one left. You!" She hailed a soldier. "Go tell the king's chamberlain and the chancery scribes to pack up all the archives and the treasury and the statues of the gods and everything that can be carried by tonight. And empty the stables. We evacuate the capital."

Puduhepa hadn't been part of her husband's life when the Kashkans had last taken the city in his youth, but she had been with him when he himself had displaced Urhi-tesshub and seized Hattusha for his own. For all its awe-engendering double walls, which spanned ravines and mountaintops, the capital was a feeble giant. It was easily stormed.

She began the long walk, quick marching back to the citadel, hustling at a trot as often as she could. But it was steep, and every breath was so cold it seared the lungs. Her mind was surging like the Inland Sea. Here she had been, congratulating herself upon the death of Urhi-tesshub, thinking that once Kurunta had found himself as the last scion of Muwatalli, he would put an end to the schism between rival lineages. *How naive, dear gods. How have I missed the signs of the poor boy's utter disaffection?*

Now the most pressing thing was to get the archives and the treasury out and move the government. Where to go, exactly? She would like to think Lawazantiya, her hometown in Kizzuwatna, but it was far too close to the

Lower Land and the tribes loyal to Tarhuntassha. Holy Tapikka? Nesha? Sharissha? Only days away from the capital. Shamuha? Malitiya? She could join the king in Malitiya... but the Assyrians might be on his heels, and it wasn't distant enough from Ishuwa.

She shook her head as if to clear it. That was the trouble with having to react to someone else's first move: there might be no good choice. How she wished her son were here. At least he could have led the army. And he was calm. She needed someone calm. Nerikkaili with all his experience. Or her dear, calm son.

As soon as she returned to the royal citadel, she sent a message to Tashmi-sharrumma to warn him what had happened: "We'll meet you at Sharissha and take the records wherever you want us to from there."

Maybe Tegarama or Kummatini. Maybe Karkemish, although that would take a very long time. But they must not be caught between the hammer and the anvil, between the usurper and the Assyrians.

The forty thousand inhabitants of the city began their exodus almost as soon as the word was given, departing by the eastern gates, which were unguarded—a detail that confirmed Puduhepa's suspicions about the attacker's chivalrous intentions. But then, the average citizen had few possessions to tie him down. Moving the government of a mighty empire was another tale. Oxcarts would be too slow. Every horse was taken from the renowned royal stables, and all those with the strength for it were harnessed to war chariots that could roll like the wind. The chariots were loaded up with the gilded statues of the gods, the temple treasures, the stacks of clay and wooden tablets that made up the royal archives, the personal wealth of the royal family. Next came the endless servants and scribes and hereditary officials and craftsmen. Her son's women followed, and all the children who inhabited the royal nursery, especially the little *tuhkanti* and his brother. Anything that might be of use to the attackers or attract their vengeful wrath had to go. The meager contents of the granaries were dumped down the cliffside; the cisterns were drained. Soldiers heaved carcasses into the spring-fed fountains, until only the sacred pools remained as water sources.

At sundown, the caravan began to move out through the God's Gate. The chariots proceeded cautiously down the sloping, snow-slick rock of the road. But as soon as they dared, the charioteers whipped up the horses, and they clattered off into the twilight, heading east toward the mountains. They would stop in some villages overnight and reach Sharissha within the week. Puduhepa rode with her little grandsons, Arnuwanda and Shuppiluliuma, who had to be protected at all costs. The latter, a babe in arms, was held close, wrapped in furs, by his wet-nurse. The *tuhkanti* was sick, his puffy little face dull and miserable, now with the added fear and discomfort of flight by night. The *tawananna* cradled him in her lap as she sat on the floor of the chariot box. He huddled against her, unspeaking, his small hands clinging to her fur cloak, bouncing back and forth against her as the chariot swayed. She petted him and told him—in a language he barely understood—not to be afraid. His father would protect them all. But she wondered what he even remembered of the tall stranger with frightening teeth, whom he had seen so rarely. *Poor motherless mite.*

Winter darkness fell early, and they had made less distance than Puduhepa had hoped before they had to stop for the night. They found shelter at Alalimmi's estate.

Anxiety written plain on her wide face, his wife welcomed them. "It's true then, what we've heard, my lady? The capital is under siege?"

"It's true," the *tawananna* confirmed grimly. "The viceroy Kurunta has gone over to his late brother's cause, it seems. We don't have enough men to hold out against him, so we've abandoned the empty capital to him. I'm hoping to reach Our Sun's troops in a few days. Then we'll take it back."

"They say my husband has been captured by the Assyrians," their hostess said, forcing a brave smile. "I know Our Sun will ransom him; Alalimmi is his kinsman, after all."

"And a valuable man, my dear. You need have no fear. He'll be ransomed and brought back to you soon."

The woman thanked her with trembling hands clasped and hurried to do her duty as hostess. She offered the *tawananna* and the two princes her own bedroom. The rest of the numerous royal children were put up in the other rooms of the family quarters. Scribes and servants and soldiers slept so thickly on the floors throughout the rest of the villa that one could hardly walk to the latrines. In the barn, the priceless royal horses were fed and rested. The gods kept their silent watch in the vestibule, while *meshedi* and Golden Spears made their rounds under a powder of falling snow.

Puduhepa found herself unable to fall asleep. The responsibility for all this menage—the entire government of the empire—was upon her shoulders. She couldn't bear to think of what a disaster it would be for the treasury or the royal princes to fall into Kurunta's hands. As it was, Nuwanza had refused to go. She hoped Kurunta would respect his white hairs and sickness.

She heard the wind moaning around the house and dreaded that snow might cover the road in the morning, make it impassable. Alalimmi's storehouse couldn't sustain this number of guests for long, and they weren't far enough away from Hattusha to feel safe yet. She sat up, undid the braid that confined her hair, and replaited it mechanically. She wanted to leave the room and wander a bit but feared to wake the children, who were bundled up next to the wet nurse. Arnuwanda coughed from time to time in his sleep.

Dear Lady Shaushga, she prayed, *give your servant light.* She had weathered many tense situations since she had married her husband forty-three years ago, but this was the most nerve-wracking. Enemies beset them from both directions. This could really be the end of them all.

She thought of her son, how weary he had to be.

Dear Lady Shaushga, give me light.

CHAPTER 19

THE KING'S DEFEATED ARMY HAD made its way westward for nearly a month through the Red Mountains. By the time they entered the Upper Lands, snow had begun to fall on and off. It wouldn't be long before it closed the roads and locked his hungry and staggering men into its murderous embrace. He had to get back to the capital soon.

Before he had left Nairi Land, though, Tudhaliya had taken time to negotiate the return of Alalimmi and the other aristocratic hostages. And with what had he been supposed to pay their ransom? He had been ready to send the Assyrians all his personal jewelry and armor, but his councilors advised him against it: "We'll be entering towns seeking lodging. You'll want to look like the Great King you are." So he had borrowed the amount from Ini-tesshub... from a vassal. *Luckily,* the king thought with something resembling black humor, *I've never been too proud to crawl. I owe my brothers that skill.*

They had fled the region of Alatarma in fear, starting at every noise, certain the Assyrians would be on their heels.

But so far there had been no sign of a pursuit. Perhaps the impending winter would keep them safe for a while. It was a brutal retreat. The supply train fell farther and farther behind as the weather worsened and the mountains grew more impassable. Rations were austere, supplemented by hunting. Ishuwa was a bleak, rocky land of mines without much to eat.

They stopped at the capital of Ehli-sharrumma, who truckled abjectly and offered them whatever he had. Fortunately, Tashmi-sharrumma could appear in his purple-and-gold magnificence. He had seared his vassal with contempt in his letter; now the Great King showed mercy and forgave the king of Ishuwa. For once, not one of the royal councilors objected. They couldn't afford to alienate the man who held the copper mines.

Then on through the middle route, because they could no longer risk the northern part of the Upper Land in the gathering winter. At Malitiya they stopped for a necessary rest, and the governor, one of the king's lower-rank brothers, did what he could to replenish their supplies, repair the chariots, and care for their abused horses. The supply train finally caught them up, and the king got his first decent night of sleep in a very long time.

There his mother's messages reached him in dizzying sequence. First, that Kurunta's defecting host would consent to defend Hattusha. A great weight lifted from Tudhaliya's shoulders. *I knew he wouldn't stay angry,* he thought gratefully. The pain of his interview with his cousin began not to ache so unendurably. The king told himself that Kurunta had not abandoned him after all.

But then, a few days later, his mother informed him

that the viceroy had gone over to the rebels. Urhi-tesshub was dead, and Kurunta was claiming the throne for himself. The king's men had abandoned the capital and were heading to Sharissha to intercept him, awaiting further orders about where to send the government and the royal heirs.

Tudhaliya, who was standing when he read the dispatch, had to sit down. A wave of something like vertigo overcame him, compounded with dread and shame. The king lowered his hand with the tablet to his lap none too steadily. He stared into space, his throat constricting, for so long that the Lords of Hatti, who were clustered around him in the governor's council room, exchanged looks of concern.

"My Sun?" said Nerikkaili finally, his brows knit with trepidation. "Is it bad news? Is the *tawananna* all right?"

"Yes and yes," the king answered. A hard lump had formed in his chest, preventing him from breathing or swallowing. His cousin's words—that Kurunta was a first-rank son—rose from his memory like a spiral of smoke. *So this is where he was leading.*

Tudhaliya wasn't sure exactly how literate his brothers were, so he handed the tablet to Tarhun-miya to read aloud. The poor secretary's voice broke with tears before he had finished. The other men looked stricken. They gaped at one another.

"Shit," hissed Huzziya, stamping a foot in helpless rage. Tattamaru, who was seated because of his wound, raised his fists in a mute appeal to the gods, while Nerikkaili and Alalimmi stared at one another with grim resignation. Everyone was reluctant to look at the king, who had gone so pale beneath his windburn that they were uneasy for him.

Tudhaliya had washed his face of expression, but he couldn't so easily subdue his fear and anger. He was now a hunted beast, driven from his own capital, tracked from the East by the Assyrians and from the West by upstart vassals, his own brother, and the man he loved more than any other creature upon the black earth. He had failed to protect his children and his mother, his people, and the ancestral seat of his empire. He wanted to dissolve into the earth in a slime of shame.

But self-pity was not a place where the king was accustomed to sojourn. He recalled sternly to himself that he was the shepherd chosen by the gods to watch over their people in Hatti Land. He had never had many illusions about his personal attributes, and the gods had to know him better than he himself. Therefore he had to do his poor best, which was all they could demand. If he died in the attempt, so be it.

He drew a deep breath of submission to the Lord Sharrumma and looked up at his councilors. "How many of us are left?"

Alalimmi reflected for a moment. "Perhaps ten, twelve thousand, My Sun. Not in the best of shape."

"Kurunta has at least five thousand," the king said. "I can't imagine that Alantalli has many more than that rounded up—maybe even that's a high figure. We may outnumber them."

"It won't be easy to bring in reinforcements from the West, now that the winter is closing in. Whatever they have now is what they'll fight with." Nerikkaili looked a little more optimistic.

"They have the advantage of being inside the city,

though," Alalimmi said. "We'll have to besiege them in the snow. Who ever heard of such a thing?"

"My mother emptied out the grain stores and the cisterns." The king gave a carnivorous grin. Suddenly, the impossible looked a little less so. "They won't hold out long, no matter how many men they have. In fact, the more they have, the worse it is for them."

The priest Tattamaru laughed and slapped his thighs. "The gods are with us! And that, my brothers, is an official pronouncement!"

A flutter of hope settled with white wings over the weary Lords of Hatti. They were, after all, rough military men who were accustomed to making their own luck without much introspection. It was the king who overthought things. If he could see his way to optimism, why shouldn't they? A babble of eager talk, insults, and threats of aggression erupted. The king listened to his officers laugh and excoriate Hishni and rip apart the viceroy of Tarhuntassha. Alantalli, the sheep fucker, would be thrown from the cliffs when they were victorious.

Tashmi-sharrumma tried not to let his mind roam. *We must take back the city,* he thought calmly. *To accomplish that, we must do this and this.* But in the back of his mind, he could see a face dearer to him than life, laughing and merry or grave and sympathetic, melting with tenderness… or a flame of wrath. *There is nothing upon the black earth I'll ever be called on to do that's more difficult than this.*

Their progress became less laborious the farther west they went, the farther behind they left the highest mountains. Sharissha, on the east bank of the River Marrasshantiya, was perhaps two thirds of the way from

Malitiya to Hattusha, but the remaining distance was high plains, and the chariots would travel swiftly—it was two or three days' journey, no more. The infantrymen would proceed at the quick march, and the supply train, now replenished, could follow at its own pace. Mercifully, Kurunta had neglected to destroy the bridge across the river. Tudhaliya made a note of this because it confirmed what he knew of his cousin's generalship. He was brave and blunt, not thorough.

At Sharissha, the king found his mother and his government in exile. He had no sooner entered the bedchamber assigned to him, Pirwannu at his heels, than she pushed in behind. Brushing off the protestations of the guard, Puduhepa gestured the valet out with a snap of her fingers.

"My son! At last!" She flew to the king and threw herself into his arms, clinging to him fiercely.

It touched him to see how tiny she was; he always forgot that she was not bodily the giant she seemed to him. She brought with her, as ever, the scent of roses into this dismal winter.

"You're so thin," she said, touching his face. "It must have been awful in the mountains in this weather."

"My mother," he murmured. A smile of relief parted his cold-chapped lips. He peeled her off and held her away to look at her. "Thank the gods you got out all right."

"Yes, and we brought the horses and the treasure and archives and the children, of course. There was no point in trying to withstand a siege, son. You didn't leave us nearly enough men."

He tried not to feel corrected, and he nodded

understanding. Lack of manpower had come to be the demon that haunted his empire.

She continued to cling to his hands, gazing at his face with a mixture of pride and tenderness that he hadn't seen for many years. There was none of that brisk, almost antagonistic sufficiency he had become accustomed to. He realized that in fact she loved him still, even after what he had done to her. And then he thought, *Kurunta has never known his mother's love.* His nose prickled, and he lowered his eyes. But she had seen and embraced him again.

"My sweet boy, you're really very sentimental, aren't you?" she said, misunderstanding. He made an ambiguous little noise, saying nothing. She drew him to the bed and seated herself, patting the fur coverlet beside her. He sat obediently.

The *tawananna* shook her head. "I never thought I'd see the day when we waged war in the snow. The whole world seems to have turned upside down."

"It's still not really winter," the king said.

"Then perhaps there'll be a thaw. Will you attack directly, or wait for reinforcements? Did Ini-tesshub come with you? The viceroy of Halep? Or did they go straight home?" she pressed.

"They went home. I'll wait for them, but only briefly."

"What about siege equipment?"

"Mother, leave all this to the generals." He knew, as she had perhaps forgotten, that Sharissha was one of the royal depots. Everything they would need, including timber for siege machines, was stocked at their fingertips.

She bristled a little, made a tight smile at him. He could sense her holding back some comment about how "the generals" had managed to lose the confrontation with the Assyrians pretty dramatically. How *he* had lost. It occurred to him that both her real love and her impossible goals of perfection for him had shaped him from his earliest years.

"We outnumber him," he said in order to reassure her. Then he added what he should have asked earlier. "How are my sons?"

"Arnuwanda is a little ill, but I think it's just a cold."

"I'll go see them." The king thought, pained, about his small children fleeing the city in the freezing night. He had not asked about his wives and the concubines. He assumed that no tragedy had befallen them, or his mother would have told him. He certainly hadn't missed them, but he wished the poor creatures no harm. He could imagine a jealous Kurunta descending to cruelty. Then he corrected himself, ashamed. *No, Kurunta is better than that.* By letting the *tawananna* evacuate the court, he had already shown he wouldn't wage war against women and children. *One can say many things about Kurunta, but he doesn't have an ungallant bone in his body.* Tudhaliya's heart constricted with a tender anguish.

"Of course, my son," the *tawananna* said as Tudhaliya pulled himself back to the present. "But let me ask you first where you want us to set up the archives and the treasury. Someplace safely distant from the capital but not too close to the eastern frontier."

The king twisted his jaw in somber thought for a moment. Everything hinged on the result of his eventual confrontation with the pretender. With Kurunta. "Stay here for the time being. Let's see how the siege goes."

He rose. She followed reluctantly to the door, where he ushered her out.

"Aren't you coming to see the children?"

"Tomorrow, when they're awake," he said.

The *tawananna* took her son's hand, its knuckles red and cracked with cold. She held it against her breast for a moment and stared up at him with something resembling pity. "This is going to be hard, isn't it? I mean, you do care for him, don't you?"

He smiled enigmatically then said in a carefully level voice, "Is Kurunta a first-rank son of Muwatalli?"

She froze. "Why do you ask?"

"He seems to think he is."

Puduhepa chewed her lip and hesitated as if she was wrestling with herself. Then she sighed and looked up at her son a little defiantly. "He's right. He's the son of the *tawananna* Tanuhepa, the impious traitor whom Muwatalli deposed." She glared obliquely at her son, daring him to remind her of her own temporary deposition. "I suppose Urhi-tesshub told him."

The king's jaw skewed with the intensity of his suppressed fury. "Why didn't *you* tell him who he was? He thought he was the son of some lesser wife."

Puduhepa expelled a heavy breath as if this should not need explaining. "Two reasons, Tashmi-sharrumma. One is that we wanted him to feel like part of our family, like a real brother to you, and not be preoccupied with thinking about his role in Muwatalli's family. And second, if he was a potential rival to you as a second-rank son of a king, how much more as a first-ranker. Don't you see that? We didn't want him to get ideas. And look—as soon as he finds out, there he is, marching against you."

Tudhaliya nodded slowly, disgust simmering in his soul. He saw very well. Kurunta had been kept in darkness, lied to, deprived of his identity for the sake of the *tawananna's* favorite son. *No wonder the poor man is bitter against me.* "How did you keep her from taking him back?"

The *tawananna* remained silent for a beat, her nostrils taut, then said, "We promised her to let him inherit after your father."

The king was so stunned he could hardly react. Anger was rising within him like a flood in spring. His voice was jagged with the effort to control it as he said, "But you didn't keep that promise, did you?"

Puduhepa said nothing, just stared him incredulously in the eye with an expression that implied he had to be mad to suggest it.

Tudhaliya was reeling. *Dear gods, the perfidy of it.* He tried to think of something cutting to say, but all he managed was, "How unjust." He glared at his mother accusingly. The taste of bile was in his mouth. "How horribly unjust."

She bridled, her cheeks growing red, her chin drawn in. "My dear, you have no idea how dynastic politics works. How many times have I told you that we need to do everything humanly possible to keep Kurunta in our camp, but you made light of me."

He turned away, unable to look at her. He felt filthy with shame at having been dragged into this injustice. How many lies upheld his throne?

The *tawananna* rose and left with a vexed sigh. Over

her shoulder, she said, "Don't lick your lips in this cold weather, my son. They're all chapped."

After his mother had departed, the king kicked off his boots and stretched out, still dressed, upon his host's bed. The room had a low, beamed ceiling, darkened from the smoke of the brazier. He listened to the popping of the wood for a while, gazing blankly into the shadows, and considered her penultimate words. He saw clearly that she had manipulated him and Kurunta from the beginning. Spied on them. Judged the temperature of their friendship. Fanned the flames when politics demanded, raked apart the coals when it suited her. It plunged him into a cold gloom to think about it. She had set the corrupting stamp of political expediency upon the one beautiful thing in his life.

Tudhaliya had enough trouble envisioning a relationship with his cousin in the midst of all his adult responsibilities, quite apart from the *tawananna*'s pressure. He cradled his head in his clasped hands and forced himself to stay calm, to think clearly.

What is it Kurunta wants? It seemed he wanted the throne. Oh, poor, poor Kurunta. All those years, told he was a second-ranker, only to find he was his father's highest-born son. No wonder he wanted his due. The whole injustice of usurpation seemed uglier and more insoluble than ever.

What did Kurunta want of him personally? Two grown men, rulers of countries, no longer had the luxury of long days spent in one another's company, dreaming, their arms around one another, sharing childish secrets. It would be such manifest partiality to one of his councilors, such self-indulgence, to spend time with him this way. The king would be taking time away from his duties.

What was it his mother wanted him to give Kurunta—sex? That was the most sordid of subjects, because the king associated the act with the loveless service he owed his childbearing women. It had no meaning by itself and would somehow cheapen his friendship with Kurunta, which was deeper than the body—turn it into an affair. And two men—it was taboo, abominable. No one had ever corrected them because they were kings' sons. But still. The gods might be disgusted, and he dared not offend them.

And yet, when they were young… he remembered with such vividness the sweetness, the power, the ecstasy. They had just been boys experimenting and exploring. They had gone hunting together in the hills, and someone, no doubt Kurunta, had suggested, *What if?* It was so overwhelming and addictive it had scared him. But he couldn't stay away. He had felt he no longer had any control over himself. He had lost his stoic indifference altogether. It became the golden object of all his waking dreams. He, who seemed like such a dry, dutiful boy, was secretly counting the moments until he and Kurunta could enjoy one another again.

This sweet interlude had come crashing down when he'd been twenty or so. How could Tudhaliya ever forget Lurma-ziti and Nerikkaili walking in on them? He could still hear his brothers' prurient laughter and sense their unspoken contempt as they stared down at him and Kurunta. Lurma-ziti had never let him forget it. The bastard had poisoned his life with it, turned the most beautiful part of his youth into a weapon against him. The king had never again been able to give himself to his cousin. He had found all sorts of excuses to put him off, longing for him all the while. They had married foreign brides. Kurunta had gone away to rule Tarhuntassha. Tudhaliya had become the *tuhkanti*... there was always some reason.

Such a relationship was much less harshly treated than had been in ancient times; the gods had grown tolerant. But worse fear had Tudhaliya by the throat. *Can it be right to desire any mortal thing so much?* It would be taken away from him, used against him. He wondered again if it had figured in Lurma-ziti and Hishni's rationale for rebellion.

His heart was pounding even now at the memory of what he had rejected, and he had to work hard to calm himself.

What is it I myself want?

But that was the question he dared not ask. The answer was too clear. And there were too many reasons why it couldn't be. He shoved his mind away from it, beating down the pain and longing. *What I want is irrelevant,* he told himself doggedly. Tudhaliya was the Great King. It wasn't what he wanted that mattered; it was what he *should do*. And the desire for love had nothing to do with his duty.

Then he thought about something Kurunta had once said to him in anger: that he, Tudhaliya, was afraid of pleasure—that he felt he had to do great things, make great sacrifices, always overcoming his own desires no matter how harmless, or else he wouldn't be... what? Pleasing to the gods? A serious king? His father's worthy son?

He thought dismally of the harp lying untouched in his room for years. He thought of Kurunta's long, beautiful body. He said to himself in contempt, *I have so many reasons for acting. If this explanation doesn't work, I pull up another.*

Kurunta had seen that long ago. And the king realized with a disgusted pang that he didn't know himself at all; he had no idea why he behaved the way he did. He had hidden himself so successfully from others that he had disappeared even to himself.

But all this was in the past anyway, he reminded himself with a gloomy sigh. Now his only relationship with Kurunta was to kill or be killed.

Tudhaliya heaved himself wearily to his feet and drifted over to the brazier. It pulsed with a cozy red glow, the air around it rippling. He squatted beside it, holding out his chilled hands to the warmth.

And who, really, is in the right in this contest? he asked himself reluctantly. *If the gods judge between us in this combat that awaits us, whom will the Gulshesh favor? Can I pretend I think I'm the legitimate king—I, the son of a usurper?*

Yet he knew that there had been so many usurpations in the millennial history of his family that no living man could claim true legitimacy. After all, how far back could one push the guilty deed for which one paid? At some point, the gods had to say, "Well, all right; there you are. Be king." He had sons now. The throne would be theirs. He needed to defend it on their behalf.

Tudhaliya rose to his feet and heaved a deep breath with the lassitude of one who had found no answer to his questions. The sight of his mind was no keener than the sight of his eyes. He simply had to push on, doing his mediocre best. *Sharrumma, run before me into this fight,* he prayed.

❖

Tudhaliya and his army were camped on the plateau at the foot of Hattusha. Two and a half days had passed since they crossed the Marrasshantiya, a quicksilver ribbon of glass with mist dancing on the surface in ornate tendrils. The weather had held, had even begun to thaw, and the dusting of snow that had argented the plain had disappeared. The king heard the distant honking of wild geese, although he couldn't see their rippling wedge trailing southward high over the plain. The white sky was darker and wetter; it wouldn't snow again soon.

The chariots had made good time across the undulating pasturelands. Relay horses had galloped along unburdened at their side, and more would catch up to them with the infantry. They had just enough supplies on board to feed and house the men that evening, and the supply wagons, with their siege towers and rams packed up, would join them in the morning. Everything was working to perfection so far. The gods were with them.

The Lords of Hatti were in grim high spirits, the king realized. After their humiliation in Nairi Land, they had prayed for a fight they could win, and here it was. Kurunta had long been the object of bitter envy, and no one was sorry to be able to teach him a lesson.

Just outside the perimeters of the camp which their men were setting up, they stood around their sovereign, the wind whipping their skirts. Under his heavy cloak, the king was clad in the uniform of a common soldier: fringed white tunic, leather leggings, and simple conical helmet. *Meshedi* and Golden Spearmen ringed them at a distance. Nerikkaili, who was looking quite svelte after their hard trek across the mountains, shaded his eyes and stared at the capital on its formidable rock, at the massive double enceinte. At the remote, cloud-scraping aerie that was the royal citadel. And he smiled, the king saw. Nerikkaili knew the secret flaws of these defenses, which he had helped their father design.

"I hope Cousin Kurunta sleeps well tonight," he said, grimly sardonic. "It will be his last night snoring in the arms of Halmashuit."

Alalimmi laughed his high-pitched, hooting laugh. "I bet he hasn't even had time to be consecrated. Barely had time to have seals cut, the bastard. Everything's a game to him. Always has been." His rugged face was wreathed with smiles because his wife had ridden out to meet him briefly from their country estate as they had passed.

The king heard his words of disparagement of Kurunta and felt a pang but kept his expression unreadable. He knew his brothers and cousins had never respected Kurunta, whom they perceived to be shallow and unpredictable. He wanted to tell them they were wrong, but perhaps events had proved *him* the wrong one.

Huzziya, who hated Kurunta more than any of the others, was breathing fire. "Do we have to wait for Initesshub, my brother? He may not get here for a week yet."

"Not for a siege." The king did not say that what he hoped for was a sally on the part of the defenders, which would pit the two armies—and their kings—hand to hand. For that he would like a clear numerical superiority.

Tarkashnawa, the young king of Sheha River Land, was among them. The Great King had given him old Arzawa and his father's kingdom of Mira, with Kuwaliya added in, and he was now equal to a viceroy in rank. He was a wiry little fellow, no older than Huzziya, with a crooked nose and thinning, curly hair and a big gap where his two front teeth had once reigned. He had the air of a mischievous seven-year-old, but Tudhaliya thought he would be a solid ally against his fellow Luwian speakers—although he talked with an unintelligible lisp in any language.

Tarkashnawa reported, "My spies in the West say this, My Sun." Nerikkaili pretended to recoil from a spray of saliva. "That while many Luwian kings have promised my father reinforcements, none of them plan to send anyone this late in the fall. They're afraid the winter will come upon them. They think of Hatti Land as a place of perpetual snow and ice!" The Luwian laughed at their folly, although the last few abnormal weeks might have borne this misconception out.

"They should be here in the summer," said Tattamaru dryly. He was given the privilege of remaining seated in his king's presence since he was still recovering from his wounds. Shanda-kurunta had stayed behind at Sharissha in the *tawananna*'s care.

The officers continued to discuss the siege, the turn events had taken, and the fact that they had always suspected Kurunta of something underhanded. The king gazed in abstraction at the distant city and said nothing. He had sunk into the calm of the battlefield and was laying his plans for the fight. He hardly responded when a clatter and shouts attracted the attention of the men around him. Finally, he turned to follow their faces, only to see Ini-tesshub and the *tawananna* approaching at a quick pace. His mother's short legs managed to keep her a stride or two in front of the viceroy, despite his long ones, so that it appeared to be he who was struggling to catch up.

"My lady! Cousin!" Nerikkaili greeted them first because the king didn't open his mouth.

Tashmi-sharrumma lifted his eyebrows in surprise, but his thoughts were still elsewhere. "My mother," he murmured finally.

"We've come, son. The viceroy of Karkemish thought you were still at Malitiya and was heading there to rendezvous with you, but they told him you had moved on. At Sharissha, he found me, and I decided to leave everyone under Shanda-kurunta's authority and join you, too."

"I don't know," muttered a frowning Nerikkaili, looking to the king for support. "This is no place for a woman."

"I'm not just any woman, my prince; I'm the *tawananna*," Puduhepa said with a dangerous edge of truculence in her voice. Nerikkaili put up his hands in quick surrender, and the men all laughed.

"May our queen disarm the pretender just as easily." Tattamaru chuckled. The king smiled but without humor. He wanted his mother safely away. If anything should happen to him, she had to be the regent for Arnuwanda.

"You made good time, cousin," Tudhaliya said to his viceroy.

"We never reached Karkemish, My Sun. When the *tawananna* informed me of the turn of events, I realized that there might not be time to go home and back, so we doubled on our tracks and cut straight through the mountains. I left the chariots on the wagons, thinking they would slow us down. They'll follow, thanks to this warmer weather."

The king clapped him gratefully on the shoulder. "How many troops have you brought?"

"Nine thousand foot soldiers, My Sun—all that were left from Alatarma."

There was a joyous outcry on the part of the officers. Huzziya laughed aloud and made a triumphant fist. "This is like a tale of the heroes. Who ever heard of moving troops like this in the winter? The gods are surely on our side!"

"This changes our strategy, then." The king scratched his stubbled cheek thoughtfully. "We must provoke the pretender to emerge from the city. I want a pitched battle, not a siege."

"You're right, My Sun," said Alalimmi. "We need to finish this up before the weather sours on us again. And if I know Kurunta, he'll lead his troops in person."

"And so will I."

"No, My Sun! You mustn't!" Nerikkaili's big voice cut through the clamor of objections. "If you're killed or captured, you'll have handed him the kingdom."

"Don't do this, My Sun," begged Tattamaru, horrified.

But the king turned off all expression until he was as blank as a rock and as unyielding—he would not be moved. "Nothing else will draw him out."

"They've been pent up there for over a week without much food or water. They'll come out in no time," Tattamaru objected.

"I lead. That's my will."

His mother gaped at him, round eyed, her lip caught between her teeth, but she said nothing. She knew how stubborn he could be. He shot her an icy look that defied her to interfere, but she seemed for once to be speechless.

"Dismissed. Tomorrow at dawn, we attack—as provocatively as possible." He turned away, leaving the protests of his councilors to sputter out.

Nerikkaili hurried after him and grabbed at his arm. "Please, brother. Don't do this. Think of what you will put the country through if—"

"I have no intention of dying," said the king grimly, still walking.

"It only takes one arrow."

"Ask of the oracles who is going to win."

"We can win and you still die, you know," the king's brother shouted. He was red faced, his teeth bared in frustration.

But the Great King had spoken. No one could force him to back down. And after all, they knew he was right. Kurunta would come out if he saw Tash standing before him. The king was the perfect bait.

CHAPTER 20

P UDUHEPA WAS BESIDE HERSELF WITH fear for her
firstborn. He had that look she knew so well; he
would listen to no one now. He had in his mule's
head some act of heroic duty. She fully suspected he
intended to engage Kurunta in hand-to-hand combat, and
she did not know what he would do if confronted by his
cousin. Would Tashmi-sharrumma even defend himself
against the pretender?

She couldn't settle down in her tent, and finally, the
tawananna emerged and walked quickly to the pavilion of
her son. In conscience, she had to try to stop him, whether
or not her efforts succeeded. Surely, he was not so far gone
in stubbornness that a mother's authority couldn't move
him.

She elbowed through the line of *meshedi* and Golden
Spearmen, who knew her well and let her pass. They would
surround Tashmi-sharrumma in battle, even if he insisted
on entering the melee, but that was no guarantee of safety.
Kings had been killed in battle before. That was why the
tuhkanti never fought alongside his father.

She pushed through the tent flap without ceremony and found her son sharpening his own sword. He was bent patiently over the blade which lay across his knees, massaging it with oil and sand. She looked down at the part in the top of his gray hair, the thin, bony bridge of his sunburned nose. The thought of him swinging that blade at people no farther away from him than the end of his arm made her heart curl up in anxiety. He was a good swordsman, but his poor eyesight worried her. What if he didn't see a sudden movement? What if he misread a feint?

He didn't seem to notice her entrance—or chose not to react.

"My son," she cried out, unable to contain herself. "You can't do this. You absolutely cannot do this."

"I can, and I will," he said blandly, never looking up. He continued to make circular movements along the edge of the curved blade.

She was growing frantic with vexation. "Listen to your advisors, Tashmi-sharrumma. This is insane."

He shrugged and kept working.

"Why are you doing this? Do you even know? Do you want vengeance? Do you think he'll just forget his grievance when he sees you, and everything will be all right? Are you trying to commit suicide?"

"I'm a better swordsman than he is."

"You're evenly matched, son. It could go either way. In fact, there's always that chance, even if you were enormously better than he. Look at me, damn it." Her voice grew shrill. "Stop that, and look at me."

He looked up at her from under his hooded lids with an opaque, expressionless gray gaze.

She saw that, as she had feared, she had no chance of shifting him, and anger blazed out in cruelty. "You idiot! Will you ever just think about the good of your kingdom? If you had even once listened to me, you wouldn't be in this bind. I begged you to be good to Kurunta, but no. 'I'm the king; let him come to me.' Well, now you see what following your own counsel gets you, Tashmi-sharrumma. Do it again, why don't you, because it worked so well before."

He stared at her imperturbably, and frustrated rage consumed her in its flames.

She slapped him across the face.

All at once, her anger flooded away, and she realized what a horrible breach of protocol she had committed. She sank to her knees and cradled her son's face in her hands.

"Oh, my dearest, I'm so sorry. It just slipped out of me; I didn't mean to do that to you. Oh, forgive me, son. I love you so. I'm just upset because of the danger to you…" She began to weep. "Oh, my poor son. What have I done to you?" She threw her arms around his shoulders—awkwardly because of his knees and the blade balanced upon them— petted his cheek, kissed his hands, and murmured, "Please, please don't do this."

He sat unmoving, hunched over his lap. She couldn't tell if he was angry or hurt or indifferent, and it was that she couldn't endure about him. There was something wrong with him, she was sure. No one could be that unfeeling with a mother in tears before him. She climbed laboriously to her feet, shaking her head, almost dizzy with effort and emotion.

"The gods are my witnesses—I've done everything I can

to stop you. Upon you be the consequences." She turned away, breathing heavily.

"Thank you for caring, Mother."

She spun to face him, thinking he was mocking her. But his eyes were gentle; there was an expression almost of sweetness on his ugly face. He was sincere.

She stifled a sob and fled.

The *tawananna* was not a woman to give up easily. If her son wouldn't listen to reason, she'd go to Kurunta. She persuaded Nerikkaili to lend her a chariot and driver, although she wouldn't tell him her destination. She lifted a herald's staff from her son Huzziya's tent, without his noticing. As soon as night had fallen, she told her driver to take her to the Gate of the God, and there she dismounted and trudged up to the sealed doors.

"Show me to your king," she cried up to the sentries. "I am a herald of the Great King Tudhaliya son of Hattushili."

She heard ribald laughter and remarks about lady heralds, but she stood firm and as tall as her small stature permitted. After a moment, the great doors opened a crack, and several arms reached out and drew her inside. A knot of soldiers examined her, eyed her long skirts, her veil and cap, her diminutive size, her bosom—yes, she was a real woman. They spoke Luwian, not knowing she could understand them.

"I'm an official delegate to your king, protected by the conventions that render heralds sacrosanct." Her voice was firm, but she heard how high-pitched and defenseless the warning rang, and fear fluttered in her stomach. Her position was dangerous. Not only was she a woman alone with these ruffians, but she was a potentially priceless hostage. It occurred to her all at once what a terrible liability she would be to her son if Kurunta decided to hold her for ransom or against a promise of withdrawal.

The men sent one of their number away with a message to the pretender. He returned after a bit with a torch in his hand, and the man marched her inside the city.

How strange it was to walk through her own capital, occupied by a usurper, in the dark of a winter night, under these stars like flowers of flame across a pitchy meadow. The Upper City was silent, dark. No watch fires burned; the temples were unlit, the aristocratic houses were unoccupied, their inhabitants fled. She followed the torch through the black streets to the long, steep causeway that rose up to the royal citadel. It was a formidable climb, which she realized she had never made on foot before. She was heaving by the time they reached the gate at the top. Her guide called out to his counterpart on the wall, and the gate swung back. They passed down the tunnel to the second set of doors, and the arched opening revealed itself in a spangled sky.

Kurunta was standing inside, a tall silhouette against the stars. Even in the darkness, she could see his white teeth flash a grin. She started to cry out and fall at his feet, but he shushed her with a finger to his lips and drew her after him. They passed through the gate court and then the public court, lit only by starlight, their footsteps barely breaking the cold hush of the night. Cracks of yellow brightness at the shutters of the banquet hall revealed that Kurunta's men were at supper. They continued through the administrative area and the lion-guarded inner gate into the private court.

Kurunta led her to her son's bedchamber, where a

soldier stood guard. They entered, and her nephew shut the door carefully behind them.

"I knew it must be you," he said, still smiling. "No one else would have such nerve." He opened his arms to her, and she embraced him, her shoulders shuddering with the suppressed fear and hope that stormed through her. He stroked her back for a moment with real tenderness then drew away from her. She saw that he looked changed, aged. His face was swollen, lined, red veined, his mouth hard and downturned. He had once been the most beautiful specimen of manhood she had ever seen, but no longer. His black hair was salted with gray, his belly slack. Pity for him melted her, but the hopeful thought that he could no longer outfight her son also passed through her mind.

"See this bed?" He gestured to the king's bed with a bitter smile. "I always wanted to sleep here. But not alone."

Puduhepa spoke low and urgent, as if the moments allotted her to change his mind were melting like an icicle in spring. "Kurunta, I've come to beg something of you. My son wants to fight you in the open field, but you mustn't do it. You must not do it, do you hear me? Don't come out."

He listened, but that little defiant sneer of sarcasm she remembered from his naughty childhood was upon his face. "Oh, I mustn't, must I? And why is that, Tash's mother?"

She flinched at his tone, at the name. He had always loved her as his own mother. She was counting on that to persuade him.

"Because he wants to fight you hand to hand, Kurunta. I don't know why. But you mustn't, you mustn't."

He turned away and seemed to consider something

invisible upon the table at his side. "I thought you would say 'Give up your pretentions to the throne.'"

She wrung her hands. "That, too. Think of what you are doing to your country, to your family."

He snorted. "To quote Tash, 'I can't help being king. The gods have chosen me.' I *am* the first-rank son of a king, you know. And I'll bet you *do* know only too well, eh, Auntie?" He gave her a penetrating glare that contained a world of acrimony, then laughed.

She hung her head, hopeless. *He's not even sober. This will go nowhere.* She had risked her life for nothing. "What has happened between the two of you?" she murmured, more to herself than to him. "I just don't understand."

"Don't you, now? Your son is fickle, my lady. He is now too good for me. Or else he's not good enough. I think I deserve someone better than that sanctimonious jar of buttermilk, don't you? What kind of king is he, who trusts his enemies but not his friends? Everything is falling apart under him." His face was growing crimson with grievances remembered. She saw that there were bags beneath his eyes, and his dark irises glittered with rancor. She wondered if he would attack her.

"I've never met a more self-righteous bastard, if you'll pardon the term. No merely happy human relationships for him. Everything has to be hard and unpleasant. No more time for poor old Ulmi-tesshub. That was my name, remember? Before you made me vassal king of Tarhuntassha to get me out of the way."

"Out of the way? Kurunta, dearest, we wanted to honor you, reward you for your fidelity…"

"You didn't need to buy me, my lady. I would have loved him anyway."

Tears began to run down his lined cheeks, and she thought, *Oh, the poor, poor man. He's completely ruined by his own bitterness.*

"Why, just consider my return to my family's rightful inheritance as the greatest of your bribes. Thank you for this throne, Auntie. You and Uncle kept it warm for me. How kind."

He's making no sense, she thought dismally. *Drunk? Crazy? I don't know, but he won't understand a thing I say.*

"Kurunta, you know I love you, don't you? I raised you like my own son. Won't you do this one little thing for me? Just stay inside, and don't come out."

"Oh, but I have my honor, too, Auntie. I'm not a coward. It's your son who's the coward. He's afraid of everything that doesn't hurt. He's desperately afraid he might enjoy something, and then you and Uncle won't be proud of him. Maybe he'll enjoy losing the battle. Maybe being a king in exile will suit him—he can be a paragon of abused virtue."

"Just don't fight him hand to hand, Kurunta."

"But isn't that what honorable men do? It will be judicial combat, a fair fight between two first-rank sons."

She feared she'd burst unless she could make him understand. Her voice was shrill as she cried, "But it *won't* be a fair fight. I'm afraid he won't strike you, Kurunta. He'll let you kill him first." And that was really what she was afraid of.

The pretender's tear-streaked face grew hard again. "Then more the fool's he, my lady. Because I'll strike *him.*

I'll strike to kill. And enjoy every minute of it. I'm not ashamed to take my pleasure where I can."

The *tawananna* clutched the herald's staff to her breast, fighting back her own tears. *Dear Lady Shaushga, this is going all wrong.* She felt as tongue-tied as her son. "Kurunta, my dear boy…"

"I'm not your boy. The woman who could have called me her boy was never permitted to have me back."

"What?"

"You kept me from going back when she wanted me to return to her."

"I… I don't know what you're talking about, Kurunta. Do you mean your mother?"

"Of course I mean my mother," he bellowed. "Tanuhepa, the *tawananna*. Who else?"

"But she—"

"No more lies, all right? Urhi-tesshub told me the truth."

Puduhepa understood that this interview had escaped her control. Kurunta was raving. She had no idea what Urhi-tesshub had told him, but nothing she could say would do anything but inflame him. She realized that her position was by no means safe. Her heart was pounding. She tried to keep a pleasant, calming smile on her face.

"Whatever you say, dear. I have nothing else to ask you, so I'll just be going." She began to back up toward the door. *Dear gods, what a fool I was to come here with no one knowing where I've gone.*

Kurunta had sunk into a chair and buried his face in his hands. His shoulders were shaking. *That beautiful, funny man, always so cheerful, has turned into this pitiful wreck.*

They'd all lived too long, seen things they shouldn't have seen—done things they shouldn't have done to one another.

As she slipped through the door, she heard him weeping, "Of course you love Tash better; he's your son..."

The *tawananna* knew her palace well. She made her way with trembling haste through the courtyards, past the throne room, the dining hall, back to the causeway, where her guide awaited her. She couldn't get out fast enough. The poisoned memory of her once-beloved foster son followed her like a miasma. *Does Tashmi-sharrumma really have the power to destroy a man like this?*

She practically ran through the streets of the Upper City, straining for the gate and freedom like a drowning woman gasping for air. Not until she was back in her chariot, streaking for the camp with the clean, chilly air of night blowing in her face, did she dare to draw a breath.

The dawn sky was clear, white as silver before the rays of the Lady of Arinna flooded the high plain with winter sunshine. It was cold. The breath of men and horses rose in clouds of vapor. Water buckets were covered in thin ice. The pastures and bare orchards that surrounded the city of the king's ancestors climbed in rolling, stony swells up to the cliffs and forests where the dun walls of Hattusha reared. Inside those walls were the king's cousin and a handful of rebellious Luwian vassals—and, it seemed, his brother Hishni as well.

Why are they against me? Tudhaliya asked himself. *Am I a bad king? Is that why everything is coming apart?* Or was it simply that Hatti Land, like many another kingdom—like

Hanigalbat—had reached the end of its god-allotted days and was shattering, scattering like the woolly seeds of a dandelion?

Behind him, the noises of an awakening encampment began to make themselves heard—the clip-clop of chariot horses being led to their feed; the quiet, purposeful jangle of men arming; an occasional shout. He turned and saw a small city of leather tents—a misleadingly small city, since his men had slept as close together as possible with half the usual baggage. Scale-clad officers passed between the rows of tents. White-tunicked infantry emerged, stretching their arms, while charioteers, with long robes and shaven foreheads, led their horses to the troughs. Tudhaliya's *meshedi* and Spearmen guard approached. The king's propensity to wander off before they rose disturbed them, it seemed. He sighed, regretting his lost solitude. War had once been a place he could hide himself, but even here, that was no longer true.

He had given his generals their instructions. If he died, it would be Nerikkaili who commanded the army. But he wouldn't die. Perhaps something worse would happen to him, but he wouldn't die.

"My Sun, we didn't know where you'd gone," said the captain of the guard, his voice laden with veiled reproach. The king used to know and enjoy the respect of his father's *meshedi* as their commander, but many of these guardsmen were new, and Huzziya had perhaps taught them to dislike him. Tudhaliya chuckled but without humor. When the gods had set their faces against one, the way became heavy, like an uphill climb with a knapsack on one's back. A whole people on one's back.

"Twenty-five more years," he murmured, just barely aloud.

"My Sun?"

"Nothing." In twenty-five more years, he would have reigned for thirty years like his father. He thought he could just endure that. By comparison to today, everything would seem easier.

He returned to his tent with the guards in tow. There he called a brief meeting of the Lords of Hatti since all the other needs of the kingdom wouldn't stop just because he had to face Kurunta this morning. His mother forced her way, with busy efficiency, into the tent. She had obviously been weeping, but her manner was brisk and unsentimental as any man's.

"Any word from the Eastern border?" the king began.

Ini-tesshub shook his head slowly. "None, My Sun. The Assyrians will no doubt wait until spring to invade, if they do at all. Our ambassador has heard no concrete rumors in Karduniash, but they seem to fear that *they* will be Tukulti-ninurta's target."

Nerikkaili said, "Give the Assyrians a nudge in that direction, My Sun. Now that we know Karduniash is in league with your enemies—"

"We know only that Karduniash was approached by my enemies, not that it helped them," said the king.

But his mother countered him. "What's the difference? They talked. No more of this treaty-with-Shagarakti-shuriash business, son; they've broken the treaty themselves."

"I prefer to wait and see."

Her face grew red with exasperation. "How can you

trust them, Tashmi-sharrumma? They're all out for their own good—as we should be."

"I *don't* trust them," he said frostily. "Treating them honorably has nothing to do with trust. Anyway, if I die, you'll be the regent, Mother, and then you can do whatever you want."

She looked distressed by the thought but also angry that he had cut her off. Her nostrils were white. Nerikkaili lowered his eyes and pursed his lips as if unwilling to get caught in the crossfire.

"The grain situation? Now that Ura is lost to us?" the king said.

"Well, if we win, My Sun, perhaps we'll get it back," said Alalimmi.

"Let's assume the worst. Other options?"

"Lashti? Kutupa?" Nerikkaili proposed. "But they're in Tarhuntassha, too. Kizzuwatna? They have no deep-water ports, but perhaps the wheat could be off-loaded onto barges as far as Adana then carried overland."

"Through the worst sort of mountains," said the *tawananna* with distaste. "This will cost a lot more. And we may or may not have our mines."

"Then we have to win," said the king with a calm smile. The men echoed this with resolve, if not conviction. Huzziya punched the palm of his left hand as if spoiling for a fight. This gesture touched Tudhaliya, even though he knew that his brother's hostility toward Kurunta had nothing to do with protecting the king's honor. He looked around at his officers with gratitude, but as they dispersed, his mother rushed up to him and put her hands on his chest as if to block him.

"Don't do it, please. Please," she said, her voice shaking with intensity.

"We've already had this conversation, Mother."

"Don't fight him face-to-face, Tashmi-sharrumma. I have a bad feeling about this." Her face was buckled with distress, her eyes starting to leak.

The king spoke gently. "This is a personal issue Kurunta's fighting over. I want as few people as possible to pay my personal debts for me."

"Kings have no—"

"Kings have no personal life," he finished for her, lowering his eyes with a sigh. "Yes, I know." There lay the precise problem, the thing Kurunta couldn't understand.

His mother stood before him, her head bowed, her hands still upon him. She seemed so defeated he felt his heart melting within him. He was willing to pay the price of kingship, but it grieved him to see it carved from the flesh of others, too. Not that this woman hadn't known what she'd been doing all those years she had connived to get her son on the throne. Perhaps, in fact, it was he who was paying the price of her unworthy desires. But still, her smallness moved him. Her hands were no longer the fresh hands of a young woman. She was nearing old age. He should protect her and his little sons. Yet if he should die...?

"I won't die, Mother," he said. "The gods are on my side."

She held up her hands and pursed her lips, and he lowered his face to hers. She kissed him on the cheek, caressed his hair, and smoothed it back from his temple.

"Be careful, my dearest. He hates you. He wants to kill you."

The king nodded. The *tawananna* spun on her heel and headed to the door. Before she left, she turned back and said in a voice scarcely louder than a whisper, "He's drinking, Tashmi-sharrumma. He's let himself become dissipated. You can wear him down."

The first rays of the sun had cracked open the southeastern sky. It would be the defenders of the capital who looked into its brightness. The omens had been taken; the troops had sung the old song, commending themselves to the gods and praying to be buried with their mothers. The king's army stood ready, a glittering host of nearly twenty thousand men. There were chariots, but the terrain did not permit of a real charge. They would merely ferry the officers into the battle. It was the white-clad foot soldiers of Hatti Land, Karkemish, Halep, Sheha River Land, Nuhasshe, Amurru, and the other Eastern vassal states who were the millstone that would grind up the false claims of Kurunta to the throne. The wind held its breath. The banners hung, barely moving, including the banner of the double eagle that was held aloft at the side of the Great King's chariot. The orchard-covered plain stretched upward to the walls of the capital, inflamed to molten gold by the light of first morning as they loomed against the indigo northern sky. The city of his ancestors was like a city of the gods.

Tashmi-sharrumma himself stood in his vehicle side by side with Tiwatipara and a shield bearer, resplendent in golden scales and plumed helmet with gold and silver jewelry at his ears, wrists, and throat. If anyone sought him, they would find him easily. He held a spear; his sword and battle-ax hung at his hip—it would not be a cordial meeting. Although he himself couldn't see that far, he knew that Kurunta was watching him from somewhere on the battlements,.

The king gave the signal to advance, and the lines began to move slowly forward. No one said a word; there was only the heavy percussion of a slowly advancing army—the heavy, booted steps on wet earth, the clopping of hooves, the jangle of harnesses, and the chink of armor. They passed between the rows of apple trees and stopped just out of range of arrows from the parapets. The king sent a staff-bearing herald into the empty no-man's-land between his own chariot and the outer wall.

"The Great King of Hatti Land, Tudhaliya son of Hattushili, calls upon his cousin and viceroy, Kurunta son of Muwatalli, to surrender the city like a good and loyal vassal. If he surrenders, he will be received with clemency, and an amnesty will be granted to him and all his followers. If he declines to surrender, let him be prepared to do battle for it."

The man's booming voice seemed to echo against the walls. *Kurunta must be listening,* thought the king, his stomach tight. *Let him surrender, all you thousand gods of Hatti.*

There was an endless space of silence.

"Perhaps he has no herald inside," Nerikkaili said dryly from some distance behind the king.

But at that moment, there came to them the voice of Alantalli of Mira from up on the parapet of the Lion Gate. It seemed he spoke Neshite perfectly well after all. He was no trained herald, but his voice had a sharp, high-pitched quality that carried well.

"The Great King of Hatti Land, Kurunta son of Muwatalli, to his cousin the usurper Tudhaliya son of Hattushili and all the Luwian soldiers in his army—"

"The sheep-fucking bastard!" barked Huzziya from somewhere.

"We decline to surrender, and we will fight for this city and this land and for the freedom of the Luwian states, who confront you here not as vassals but as allies of the Great King. And we offer our amnesty to any of you who chooses to join us and turn on your old master."

There was a rumble of anger from Tudhaliya's officers behind him. An uneasy flutter in his stomach, the king realized he had no idea how this would be received by his infantry—many of whom were in fact from the West, quite apart from the loyal sons of Sheha River Land. Fractious Luwians had been transplanted all over the country for generations and now served in the levies of many provinces.

Tudhaliya compressed his lips sadly. There was no help for it, then. He was preparing to give the order to commence the siege when the great arched gates with the carven images of lions at either side begin to grind open. He saw the glitter of armor and the brief flashes of banners as Kurunta's troops passed the bastion and its restraining wall. Out of the ramped entry poured a stream of chariots and lines of foot soldiers at the run. They careened down the slope fast. In the lead chariot was a figure in gold scale armor and plumed helmet—the king's very double. At his side rippled the standard of the two-headed eagle. It was a disconcerting sight, like a mirror image. But Kurunta had always been the king's other self.

Down the steep roadway they galloped, the horses flying ahead of the massive vehicles. Tudhaliya ordered his charioteer to whip up his own animals. His lines began to flow forward at a trot, but he passed them by as his two stallions gathered speed. He knew he was leaving the *meshedi* and the Golden Spears behind. Some officers' chariots were keeping pace with him, he could hear, but his attention was fixed ahead.

Tiwatipara's whip cracked. The horses thundered across the plain, between the rows of leafless apple trees. The king's left hand gripped the rail as the calm exhilaration of battle settled into his bones. He handed his spear off to the shield bearer and drew his sword, which slid from its scabbard with a savage hiss. He saw Kurunta's chariot galloping directly at his own—one of them would have to swerve. The thunder of hooves grew louder and louder. Now he perceived the round, excited nostrils of his cousin's chariot horses bobbing before him and the clouds of steam they puffed out as they pounded closer and closer. He and Kurunta knew one another so well, had sparred so many times, that their crossing was like a piece of choreography— Tudhaliya skidded to his left, Kurunta to the king's right.

The king slashed down with his blade as the other chariot passed and severed its reins. He yelled at Tiwatipara to turn around. With much jolting and jouncing and whinnying of frustration, the overstimulated animals were curbed. They backed and whickered but turned to confront the disabled vehicle. Kurunta's horses reared, fidgeted. His charioteer was helpless, could only pull his team in circles.

All around them, the foot soldiers had begun to hack and slash. They were intent upon their own battle, oblivious to the confrontation of their rulers. The king grabbed the waisted leather shield from his bearer's hands and jumped from the platform. His breath was fast and shallow now, his every movement controlled. This, he thought, was his advantage over Kurunta—Tudhaliya fought patiently. Kurunta fought in a frenzy.

The king saw his cousin spring from his chariot as well. The pretender approached him in an expectant crouch, his shield on his left arm. Tudhaliya couldn't see Kurunta's eyes, only the long black hair and a grim mouth curled back from the teeth. His sword was drawn.

"Surrender, cousin," Kurunta cried in a voice splintered with hatred. "Or I'll chop you to pieces for the crows."

The king said nothing, just continued to circle his opponent. Every so often, Tudhaliya pushed his shield at his cousin a little to make him take a defensive slash. At last, Kurunta rushed at him, snarling, laying about him with wild, powerful arcs of the blade. Tudhaliya parried with the slightest possible effort, although he could feel the shock of the blade as it struck his own. He knew that he mustn't let down his guard, or those same blows would sever his arm.

An eternity seemed to pass, measured by the hammering of the king's heart, the clang of his parries on Kurunta's blade. Tudhaliya had rationed his own strength out, conserving as much as he could. The long, weighty scale coats would protect them but were designed for chariot warfare—they would wear the men down as they battled on foot. The king's breath was beginning to rasp through his mouth. Sweat ran down his forehead and into his eyes.

But Kurunta was exerting himself much more. His face was a crimson mask of fury and exhaustion. He wanted to kill his cousin. The king could hear the loud grunts and squeals of effort, and his opponent's increasingly ragged panting.

"Fight, damn you!" Kurunta shouted at one point. But the king would not break out of his methodical defense. He had fenced with Kurunta since he was seven years old. They were like the two arms of one body. Even without seeing his opponent's eyes, he knew where the next strike would fall.

And then suddenly, Kurunta's sword flew from his hand and clanked to the ground. Was his grip sweaty? Was he tiring so much? Tudhaliya realized he could maim or decapitate his cousin with a blow, could beat him to the ground under his shield as Lurma-ziti had once done to him. But he threw down his own sword and pulled the ax from his belt. Kurunta froze for a heartbeat of confusion then dragged his ax out, too. Now they had to fight within arm's length of one another. They closed as if for a wrestling match. Their faces were only a matter of cubits apart. Tudhaliya could feel sprays of Kurunta's sweat flung at his cheeks. Warily, they circled, crouching behind their shields, panting, eyes locked, hefting their axes. The ax was a fearsome weapon, with a hooked hatchet on one side and a claw like a heavy bronze flame on the other. It could crush bones, pull off armor, rip out flesh...

Kurunta smashed his blade through his cousin's leather shield. It snagged there for a moment, then Tudhaliya pulled the shield loose and pushed the viceroy backward with the flat of his own ax, knocking him almost off his feet. Kurunta stumbled, regained his footing. They struggled hand to hand, blocking one another's blows with the short hafts of their weapons as often as with their shields.

The king heard his cousin's sawing breath and could finally see his scarlet face, stretched in an agony of exhaustion. It was clear now that Kurunta was the older man; he was wearing down fast. Only his hatred kept him upright. Tudhaliya was gasping for breath, too, but he wasn't angry. He saw Kurunta, but he didn't think, *That's Kurunta before me.* He just said over and over to himself, *breathe, parry, breathe, parry.* All around him, the thousands of men fighting at his elbows, the screams, the blood, and the clang of weapons disappeared outside his concentration, which surrounded him like a body shield. Like a city wall.

But at some point, he felt rather than saw that many men were bearing down on him, dressed in white and in saffron. They were closing in on the private world of his battle. Kurunta was distracted and glanced around. The king ignored them and swung a short, punishing blow at Kurunta. The pretender let out a wail. The blade had struck his arm, audibly shattering the bone. He dropped the ax, sank to his knees, and clutched his forearm, moaning and cursing. Tudhaliya came to himself. Chest heaving, he stood, unsteady on his feet, over Kurunta, while the *meshedi* and the Golden Spears seized the viceroy.

"Shall we finish him off, My Sun?" one of them asked. Tudhaliya shook his head, too winded to speak. Finally he gasped, "Tie him up, and get him a bonesetter."

He stared around him, heaving, the sweat running down his face. His men were all about, sweeping the pretender's troops from the field. He saw soldiers yielding their arms. White-tunicked troops led chariot teams at a trot back toward his own lines. Did he dare to think they had won? He began to trudge up the hill toward his capital city, tottering with exhaustion.

Now, finally, Tudhaliya let his thoughts free. *I broke his arm,* he thought in shame. But the king might have killed his cousin and had not. *I struck that body I love. But he would have killed me.* Their friendship was over now, over forever. Tears were gathering in his eyes, washing over the edges of his salt-burned lids. *It's just the letdown of nerves,* he told himself. But he knew that he had driven from his life the only truly beautiful thing he had ever had.

The city was freed. The Lords of Hatti chortled with malicious glee over the downfall of their presumptuous cousin. *But why? Kurunta was such a funny, charming, goodhearted boy.* Tudhaliya supposed they were jealous of Kurunta's influence with him, the favored son, and of all the honors and exemptions and rights and honors showered on the scapegrace cousin over the years, unworthy though he had seemed to Hattushili's brood. They were perhaps even envious of his good looks and resentful of the innocent arrogance of the beautiful. *But they didn't know him,* Tudhaliya thought. *They didn't know him.*

Delirious with relief that her son had survived unharmed, the *tawananna* followed the army into the capital as soon as it was secured and tracked Tashmi-sharrumma into the council room, where he was dictating the terms of the surrender. She saw him hunched wearily in his chair, streaked with dirt and Kurunta's blood, his hair and tunic wet with sweat, embossed with the weight of his helmet and armor. There was about him the look of a water skin that had been emptied and then wrung out—emptier than empty. The very flesh of his cheeks seemed to have sunk into itself until he had the visage of a skull.

Tarhun-miya stood before him, scratching away on his wax tablet, his woodpecker face fixed downward in concentration. In their accustomed chairs sat the more important of the king's brothers, cousins, and nephews.

The king looked up, his eyes red and haggard.

The *tawananna* longed to embrace her son, but she wouldn't embarrass him in the presence of his councilors. Instead she cried triumphantly, "The gods have judged, My Sun, and found you worthy of the throne."

The king grunted as if too depleted to shape words. His hands on the arms of the chair were hanging limp. *The poor dear is exhausted.* And not just physically. If only he had been kinder to Kurunta—or held onto the Egyptian doctor and let Kurunta die of the plague.

"So," she asked briskly, "what disposition are we making of the rebels?"

Nerikkaili answered in a carefully neutral tone. "We've just been arguing with Our Sun that he should execute Alantalli, but he inclines toward exile."

"Exile," the king confirmed. "Tarhun-miya has written it down."

Puduhepa caught Nerikkaili's eye, and he lifted his brows as if to say, *There's no reasoning with him.* Initesshub—gloomy and noncommittal as ever—looked at the floor, and Alalimmi made a little shrug at the *tawananna*. Huzziya eyed his brother with frank disgust.

"But why, my son? You know he'll just reorganize and come back. He's a zealot."

"We have to give him a chance to prove himself," said the king wearily as if he had said this over and over. "If he backslides, we can execute him."

"He's proved himself, Tashmi-sharrumma, and he's a turncoat. Just kill him now, for the sake of all the gods." Her voice rose shrilly. *Do we have to go through this every time he conquers someone?* "If you're going to have to face Assyria in the spring, you don't want a turncoat at your back."

"Our Sun has reminded us that clemency is a cardinal virtue, my lady," said Nerikkaili, on the edge of sarcasm. There was just enough diplomatic smoothness left in his tone to avoid sheer rudeness.

The king eyed his brother from under his drooping lids, but his expression was unreadable.

"Exile," he said again. "He won't be at our back. He'll be in Amka."

Amka was between the uninhabited Southern Desert and the border with Mizri. If Alantalli could, in fact, be kept there, perhaps it wasn't a bad plan. There were certainly no Luwians down there for him to rouse, she admitted to herself.

"Why don't you send him to his friends in Karduniash?" suggested Huzziya sourly.

Ini-tesshub spoke up. "And what about… the pretender, My Sun?"

"You must put him to death, My Sun," the *tawananna*

urged fiercely. "He hates you now as much as he loved you before. You'll never be able to trust him again. He's become a mad dog."

"You're speaking of the son of a king, my mother." There was something tight about the king's jaw that could be anger, but his expression revealed nothing.

"Well, I think we all understand that the sons of kings can do bad things like anyone else, son—"

"And people don't always step in to prevent them."

She stopped, her mouth agape. It occurred to her that he was referring to the torment his brothers had inflicted on him in childhood. He had never said a word about that, neither at the time nor through all these years. Was he really bitter about the fact that she had never intervened? She said in a very quiet, motherly voice, full of intimacy, as if the others were no longer present, "Tashmi-sharrumma, my dear, I wanted you to learn to deal with problems on your own. I didn't interfere because I didn't want you to be weak."

"And so I am dealing with this problem on my own, and I expect no one to interfere. Kurunta will be exiled."

The *tawananna's* face grew hot with anger and astonishment at this rhetorical trap her slow-tongued son seemed to have caught her in. She fixed him with an outraged stare, and he stared back at her with his tired, expressionless eyes. She had no idea what he was thinking. She looked to Nerikkaili for support, but he seemed to find something fascinating that held his gaze near the ceiling.

She threw her hands up, her lips tight with exasperation. "You'll regret this."

"It will be nothing alongside my present regrets."

There was a momentary wobble in her son's voice, and she realized that something of the real Tashmi-sharrumma had just escaped him in spite of himself. She remembered how Lurma-ziti used to collect such little flashes of people's weaknesses for later use against them, and she wondered for the first time if that was why the king had grown so extremely closed, even in childhood.

There was a long, uncomfortable silence, broken only by the soft popping of Tarhun-miya's stylus in and out of the wax.

"Is there anything else, My Sun?" asked Nerikkaili after a moment.

"No. Go and relax."

As for the king, he bathed, underwent the appropriate purifications for one who had shed blood, and let Pirwannu dress him in clean clothes—a warm woolen tunic and soft red shoes. He told Zuzu he would dine alone in his chamber. Tudhaliya wanted very much to talk to Kurunta, but he didn't feel he had the strength that evening, nor was he sure Kurunta, with his smashed arm, would be in any condition for an interview. *I didn't mean to do it,* he thought dully. *I didn't want to strike you.* He had intended to fight a purely defensive battle, let his cousin exhaust himself, and then accept his surrender. But somehow Kurunta had allowed the fray around him to distract him, and the king's parry had become an unparried blow. Or so it seemed to the king now. Tudhaliya hadn't been in sufficient control of his weapon; he hadn't been in sufficient control of himself to avoid hurting someone. As usual.

He felt the exhaustion of the day dragging him down, turning his limbs to trembling, rickety, boneless stalks that couldn't hold him up. He fell backward across his bed and sank like a stone into the soft silver fur of the coverlet. *Only twenty-five more years.*

He prayed to Sharrumma, his special patron: *Don't let my weaknesses cause harm to my people, lord.* He prayed to his father, who was now a god: *Make me a good shepherd of our people, Father. Help me to be merciful and just.*

The king's weary mind just wouldn't lie down and rest. He thought: *Hishni came back after his sentence of exile and took part in today's rebellion. No one knows where he is at the moment. Perhaps tomorrow's search of the battlefield will discover him; perhaps he has fled, to sink into obscurity. Perhaps he'll try again to dislodge me from the throne. But how much danger is he, really? He's no leader. Who will follow him?*

He thought: *Alantalli will be sent to Amka. If he stays there, no harm will be done. He'll be far from his people. But what if he goes over to the Assyrians, who are not that far away? Has he any information he can give them? What if he dodges his monitors and runs back to the West and stirs up trouble again, as Urhi-tesshub once did?*

He thought: *What will Kurunta do if I turn him free into exile? Perhaps I can convince the Great King of Mizri to keep him down there, although that didn't work out well with Urhi-tesshub. Who will gather around him if he tries again to take the throne? The Luwians, even without Alantalli?*

The long-ago words of the odious Lurma-ziti echoed in his mind: *What happens when it's unjust to be merciful?* He wondered if there was ever such a moment. Was now such a moment? He didn't know if in being merciful he had been just. He did not even know if exiling his cousin *was* mercy. The thought of Kurunta, aged and bitter in a foreign land, was too painful.

After a while, Tashmi-sharrumma decided that his reluctance to meet with Kurunta was cowardice. He hauled himself to his feet, aching in every muscle, and made his way with the slow pace of an old man to the apartment where he had imprisoned his cousin. The guards at the door stood to attention and unbolted for him. It was dark inside and very warm, and the close air reeked of sweat and blood. He could only dimly see Kurunta stretched out on the bed under the luxurious wolf-skins the king had provided for him, his thickly wrapped arm lying across his chest, his hair spread over the pillow around his face.

Tashmi-sharrumma said nothing but stepped quietly to his cousin's side. The pretender's visage was flushed and strangely blurred. The king saw the telltale little bulbous jug of poppy juice from Alashiya on the table at his side and realized that the Egyptian doctor had administered the potent painkiller. Kurunta's eyes were closed, his breathing heavy. The king stood gazing at him for a moment, his heart wrenched between tenderness and shame, then said softly, "My cousin."

The pretender's eyes flew open. He exerted a feeble effort to raise his shoulders and draw back, but the king shook his head and seated himself with care at the edge of the bed. Kurunta glared at him through the drugged fog. He made as if to say something, but the king interrupted.

"I'm sorry. This didn't have to happen."

"Oh, yes, it did. Some day, I was bound to realize what a spell you and your mother and father and everybody had put on me." Kurunta spoke thickly and with effort. "The throne was my brother's all along, and then mine. Your spell kept me from seeing that."

Tudhaliya wondered if he meant a real spell, but it didn't matter. The spell was love. It was broken now.

"I didn't mean to hurt you, Ulmi. Not today, not ever. You know how inept I am."

"You are. You're cruelly inept. I wish you had killed me outright."

"I couldn't."

"Well, you should have. But that's your weakness. You have to try to be virtuous. I spit on your virtue, Tash. You're not pleasing to the gods; you're just weak, that's all. Everybody thinks I'm weak, but it's really you."

The king nodded sadly, saying nothing. He sat there, hunched over, his hands cupped around his knees, absorbing the truth with resignation.

"I curse you, Tash. You'll try and try to be good, but no one will ever love you. No one will ever love you again… not like I have." Kurunta began to cry, his eyes slitted with pain and bitterness.

After a moment, the king leaned over him and wiped his cousin's cheeks with his own sleeve. Kurunta's words wounded him, but he knew he couldn't fight the will of the gods, and it was their voice he heard. "Will you try to rebel again?"

"Yes, until the day I die. You should kill me now."

"No." How could he put Kurunta to death for seeking to inherit his father's throne? He was, in fact, perfectly legitimate. And Tudhaliya, who had no intention of relinquishing that throne—because now he had sons—was not legitimate. He knew that. But he didn't know what to do about it and probably never would.

"I don't care about the damned capital," Kurunta sobbed weakly. "Only you could love a frigid place like this. But Tarhuntassha—*my* father founded that city. I fought the Lukka men for twenty years to make it safe. I'll never give you peace, Tash. Never. I'll get it back..."

Tudhaliya sat there for a long moment while Kurunta, drugged and in pain, wept. All at once, the king felt he was being split in two like a tree struck by lightning. He could feel the terrible burning down his middle as the purifying flame of the Storm God consumed his organs, one after the other. At last, unable to bear any more, he got to his feet, trying to breathe.

He stood there for a long time while Kurunta wept then sank into silence. The king's thoughts were bouncing around like an empty chariot drawn over rough ground. It occurred to him that the Storm God of Lightning, Tarhunta himself, might just have told him what to do.

"Kurunta," Tudhaliya said at last.

His cousin opened a swollen eye. His mouth was a downward crescent of pain and bitterness.

The king asked him gently, "What do you want?"

"So is Our Sun taking orders for dinner?" the pretender murmured in a blurred voice.

The king had to smile. Even in this extremity, Kurunta was Kurunta. "Why have you risen against me? You want Tarhuntassha?"

"I want... to be my own man for a change, damn it. Once we were equals, but now you give orders, and I obey. You're a Great King, and I'm a fucking vassal. I was only king of Tarhuntassha, my father's own city, because you let me be... and I'm as much a first-rank prince as you, usurper's son. You know what I did with that fancy bronze treaty you had made up? I buried it under your gate so every time anybody entered the city, they'd trample it underfoot."

The king chewed his lip, thinking hard.

"What if we were peers, Ulmi? What if you were a Great King? You *are* a Great King in the gods' sight. This is no gift from me."

His cousin was staring at him with narrowed eyes, suspicious or uncomprehending. "Then what are *you*?" he sniffed.

"I'm... the son of a usurper. But I have sons. I can't just go away."

"Oh, can't you? Oh, right—that's what that battle we just fought was all about." Kurunta snorted sarcastically. "I'm not wholly stupid, you know."

"What if you were king in Tarhuntassha, and I was king in Hattusha? Great Kings, both of us, independent allies. That's what your father wanted, and mine, too, really. My father was legitimate king of the north, remember—no usurpation needed."

Kurunta lay with his eyes closed, his mouth sullen, making no motion. Tudhaliya sat carefully on the bed beside him once more. After a moment, he laid his hand upon the good hand of his cousin, which rested on the fur coverlet.

Kurunta opened his eyes and looked up blearily at the king. "You're... dividing the empire?" His anger had ebbed away; he was only surprised.

Tudhaliya nodded.

Kurunta's fingers closed upon his own. "What... what does that mean?"

"Justice."

There descended a silence so thick that it lay almost visible between them in the room. At last, the king heaved himself to his feet and walked slowly and wearily to the door. He knew he'd probably never see Kurunta again. There would be no more shared battles, vassal visits, council meetings. They'd be rulers of two different kingdoms, immured in their two separate capitals.

At the last minute he turned and cleared his throat with effort.

"Cousin," he murmured, forcing himself to open the gate, "I love you."

And he left.

⟡

Outside, the day was drawing to a close. The conflagration of a winter sunset lit the western sky, against which the battlements of the citadel rose in silhouette. The king drew his furs around his neck. He had promised last night—had it only been last night?—to look in on his children, so he made his way to the court of women, and from thence to the royal nursery.

How familiar these rooms were from his own childhood. The very walls were impregnated with memories. Kurunta was everywhere, a laughing, black-maned ghost.

Tudhaliya saw the night nurse walking back and forth, singing softly to little Shuppiluliuma in her arms as he fell asleep. Two other women, clad in smocks, were feeding a group of toddlers at a long, low table. He wasn't even sure which were his own. He saw his heir sitting on the floor, playing with a toy horse all by himself, and the king's heart went out to him.

The two women on duty caught a glimpse of their sovereign and fell to their knees, embarrassed. He gestured to them to go on about their work, but the children all stared at him, and to the king's discomfiture, the women made them stand up.

"Hello," he said, his face reddening.

"Good evening, Our Sun," the older ones answered in a ragged chorus. He tried to make a pleasant smile and, followed by the children's eyes, headed over to the corner where Arnuwanda stood alone, swaying back and forth on his fat little legs, swinging his horse.

"Hello, son."

The boy looked up at him, craning his head back so far his mouth fell open. Tudhaliya remembered he did not speak Neshite. Although the king was so tired he was not sure his legs would hold him, he squatted at the child's side and drew him to him.

"I'm your father," he said, pointing at himself. "*Atta*, father."

The *tuhkanti* mumbled, "*Atta*," in a shy voice.

Arnuwanda was pale and too fat, but his features were pretty, noticed the king, his heart swelling. The child was Ellat-gula to the last detail with large, heavily lashed black eyes and small, scrolled pink lips. There was a scared look on his face.

Tudhaliya remembered the bitter words of Kurunta—*No one will ever love you again*—and thought sadly, *I frighten my son*. He took the child in his arms, and at first, the boy pushed away from him, stiff. At last, the king found a stool near the wall and lowered himself to it. It was sized for the children, and his knees stuck up at a ridiculous angle, but he settled his first-born son upon his lap and held him against his chest, wrapping his arms around the boy. There was comfort in the sweet, slightly salty smell of a little child and in the warmth of his small body. A bit at a time, the boy relaxed and melted toward his father. The king thought to himself that he would have died of joy if his own father had embraced him like this. Yet perhaps he had, and Tudhaliya's memories simply didn't extend so far into his youth, which seemed unimaginably distant.

After a while, the child went limp, and the king realized he had fallen asleep. Before long, he, too, leaned his head against the wall and sank into dreams.

The *tawananna* entered the nursery in a bustle.

She called out, "Girls, it's time for the children to go to bed. I know it's been an extraordinary day, but we're all home now, so let's get back to normal."

In an embarrassed dumb show, the nurses indicated the king, asleep on the stool, his long legs doubled up, his head back, his jaw sagging, and the child asleep against his chest. Puduhepa tiptoed over to observe, her heart molten with affection. Her son and her grandson, two generations of kings—the future of Hatti Land. She thought how Hattushili would have loved to see this son of his son, who had been born only months after the old king became a god.

How unlike the two of them were in appearance. Her

own children were the spat-out image of their father, except for Huzziya, who resembled her. She couldn't see Tashmi-sharrumma, especially, without seeing her late husband. She knew exactly how he would look in his old age: thin, tall, raw boned, stooped. She remembered Hattushili's pride upon the birth of their first son, coming after two girls. A good boy, he had been, their little prince. She had hardly ever had to raise her voice to him. *He seems to be making up for his past docility since he's become king,* she thought, but not unkindly. She reached out and stroked his gray hair very lightly. *Somehow his face looks younger in sleep, my good, dutiful son.*

Well, he can't sleep there all night, poor boy. What a day he's had. She patted his cheek until he awakened with a jerk. He looked up at her from under his heavy lids, momentarily confused. Then he smiled, indicating the sleeping Arnuwanda with a nod of the chin. The king rose, gingerly, and laid the child in his little bed with great care. Together he and his mother walked to the door of the nursery.

"You made good on your promise, I see," she murmured softly so as not to wake the children.

"The gods let me live," he agreed. He was very tall at her side, his shoulders sagging with weariness, his hands behind his back.

They emerged from the vestibule into the biting cold of an early winter evening. The western sky was still a luminous green, but to the east, indigo darkness had conquered the vault of heaven.

"There's Pirinkir, the first star," she said, gazing upward. The stars were alive, divine… but not kindly.

"Can't see her," said the king. After a moment he added, "I went to talk to Kurunta."

"Stop torturing yourself over that man, Tashmi-sharrumma. He's turned out to be a huge disappointment."

"He cursed me," he said with surprising calm. "He said I would try and try to be good, but no one would ever love me again."

"How awful. What a cruel thing to say. He's just bitter and hateful. You see what I mean? Who would say a thing like that to someone he has loved all his life? And after you spared him." But she realized she had said more than her share of cruel things to Tashmi-sharrumma. "Yet I love you," she added, although in a sense she was speaking to herself. She slid her arm around his waist. No one love him, indeed—her kind, quiet boy.

"Do you think Arnuwanda does?"

"He doesn't know you yet, my dear. He will. You loved *your* father, didn't you?"

The king nodded. After a long interval of silence, he said, "I'm going to exile Kurunta to Tarhuntassha, Mother."

"What!" She turned on him, her eyes wide with astonishment. At first, she doubted that she had heard him right. "But that's no exile."

"No. He'll be Great King there. That's really all he wants."

The *tawananna* was momentarily speechless. "You're dividing the kingdom again?"

He nodded.

She felt she should be outraged, but somehow, this decision didn't strike her as so outrageous after all. It had been done before… and her husband had profited from it. Perhaps that was what the gods had wanted all along.

Out of the habit of countering him, she said, "But that will seem to encourage rebellion. And I'm not sure the Lords of Hatti are going to go along with this."

The king shook his head. "*He's* the legitimate king, Mother. I'm here on his sufferance."

"Don't talk that way, son. You have sons of your own to think about."

"I don't want them to face war to the south when they go against Assyria or the West. This way, the heirs of Muwatalli will no longer be a threat. Just as my father would have been no threat to Urhi-tesshub if he had left the kingdom divided."

Puduhepa revolved the idea in her mind as if it were a smooth pebble in her mouth. It would look at first like a loss of face perhaps. She wished Nerikkaili were here to consult. But the biggest obstacle was the grain, which could only be shipped through Tarhuntassha…

"What about the ports?" she asked.

"He'll let us use Ura."

"That might be a naive assumption, Tashmi-sharrumma. If he hates you so much, what better way to thwart you?"

"He doesn't hate me. He won't. He hates… he hates having been made a nobody, having to beg for everything."

She stared at him in the gloaming for a long moment, trying to read his face, but her son was a master of concealment. He looked calm and blank.

After a while she murmured, almost in awe, "You really do love him, don't you?"

"It's not for Kurunta, Mother. It's not because this is him."

"Then why?" But she knew the answer: *justice*. He smiled as if he had heard her thought. Then he turned away.

She glanced at his face, which was no longer easily visible in the impending darkness, just the bony profile of his nose and cheek against the green sky. From this angle, he wasn't ugly at all. He seemed at peace, she saw with relief. Tired, but at peace finally.

"Twenty-five more years," her son said cryptically.

"You're very alone, aren't you, my son?" she murmured.

The king said nothing.

They walked on with daylight burning out around them. Night was coming soon, but not yet.

THE END

ACKNOWLEDGMENT

T HE AUTHOR GRATEFULLY ACKNOWLEDGES ALL those who have helped her in the production of this book. To the wonderful women of my writers' group, for their critique and encouragement, my thanks. To Lynn McNamee and her editorial team at Red Adept—Jessica, Sarah and Irene—profound gratitude (and Lynn, for so many other forms of help). To the flexible and talented gang at Streetlight Graphics for the cover and map. To my cousin and her husband, my technology guru: thanks, guys. To Enid, who urged me forward by her support, I can't thank you sufficiently. And most of all to my husband, Ippokratis, who put up with the months of fixation it takes to write a novel, many, many thanks.

ABOUT THE AUTHOR

N.L. Holmes is the pen name of a professional archaeologist who received her doctorate from Bryn Mawr College. She has excavated in Greece and in Israel, and taught ancient history and humanities at the university level for many years. She has always had a passion for books, and in childhood, she and her cousin (also a writer today) used to write stories for fun.

Today, since their son is grown, she lives with her husband and three cats. They split their time between Florida and northern France, where she gardens, weaves, plays the violin, dances, and occasionally drives a jog-cart. And reads, of course.